D1016734

INTERNATIONAL

THE
ARK
SAKURA

KOBO ABE

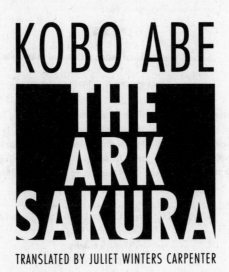

THE ARK SAKURA

TRANSLATED BY JULIET WINTERS CARPENTER

VINTAGE INTERNATIONAL

VINTAGE BOOKS   NEW YORK

A DIVISION OF RANDOM HOUSE, INC.

First Vintage International Edition, March 1989

Library of Congress Cataloging-in-Publication Data
Abe, Kōbō, 1924–
The ark Sakura.
(Vintage international)
Translation of: Hakobune Sakura Maru.
I. Title.
[PL845.B4H2713 1989] 895.6'35 88-40377
ISBN 0-679-72161-4 (pbk.)

Manufactured in the United States of America
10 9 8 7 6 5 4 3 2 1

1

O N C E a month I go shopping downtown, near the prefectural offices. It takes me the better part of an hour to drive there, but since my purchases include a lot of specialized items—faucet packing, spare blades for power tools, large laminated dry cells, that sort of thing— the local shops won't do. Besides, I'd rather not run into anyone I know. My nickname trails after me like a shadow.

My nickname is Pig—or Mole. I stand five feet eight inches tall, weigh two hundred fifteen pounds, and have round shoulders and stumpy arms and legs. Once, hoping to make myself more inconspicuous, I took to wearing a long black raincoat—but any hope I might have had was swept away when I walked by the new city hall complex on the broad avenue leading up to the station. The city hall building is a black steel frame covered with black glass, like a great black mirror; you have to pass it to get to the train station. With that raincoat on, I looked like a whale calf that had lost its way, or a discarded football, blackened from lying in the trash. Although the distorted reflection of my surroundings was amusing, my own twisted image seemed merely pitiful. Besides, in hot weather the crease in my double chin perspires so much that I break out in a rash; I can't very well cool the underside of my chin against a stone wall the way I can my forehead or the soles of my feet. I even have trouble sleeping. A raincoat is simply out of the question. My reclusion deepens.

If I must have a nickname, let it be Mole, not Pig. Mole is not only the less unappealing of the two but also more fitting: for the last three years or so I've been living underground. Not in a cylindrical cave like a mole's burrow but in a former quarry for architectural stone, with vertical walls and level ceilings and floors. The place is a vast underground complex where thousands of people could live, with over seventy stone rooms piled up every which way, all interconnected by stone stairways and tunnels. In size the rooms range from great halls like indoor stadiums to tiny cubbyholes where they used to take test samples. Of course there are no amenities like piped water or drainage, or power lines. No shops, no police station, no post office. The sole inhabitant is me. And so Mole will do for a name, at least until something better suggests itself.

When I go out I always take along a supply of two items: a key to the quarry entrance and a small card with a map on the back and the words "Boarding Pass—Ticket to Survival" on the front. Late last year I picked up thirty-five leather cases, and put one key and one card in each. I keep three in the pocket of my good pants. If I happen to come across any suitable candidates for my crew, I can invite them aboard on the spot. I've been ready for the last six months now, but the right sort of person has yet to appear.

Preparations for sailing are virtually complete; in fact, all I lack now is the crew. Despite the urgency of the situation, however, I have no intention of conducting any recruiting campaigns. Why should I? In payment for their labors, crew members will receive a gift of incalculable value—the gift of life itself. Were this known, I would be swamped with applicants. Just keeping order would be a problem. Call it an excuse for my retiring ways if you like, but I've always felt that eventually the right people will gravitate to me without my having to go search them out. So you see that whether I have any shopping to do or not, it is essential that I go out once a month or so to mingle with the crowds, come in contact with people, and make my observations.

Ordinarily I use the outdoor parking lot next to the prefectural offices, because the rates are low and it always has plenty of parking space. But today I decided to park underground, beneath the department store across from the station. The notice on a banner hanging from the roof caught my eye:

WONDERS AND CURIOSITIES NEVER SEEN BEFORE!
EXHIBITION AND SPOT SALE OF FAMILY
HEIRLOOMS AND TREASURES

This was obvious hype, but it succeeded in arousing my interest. Also, I wanted a look at the customers. When I entered the store, an announcement was being made to the effect that members of the general public were offering rarities and curios from their private collections for sale at the rooftop bazaar. Evidently I wasn't the only one attracted; almost everyone in the elevator was headed for the roof.

I discovered that the entire rooftop was covered with a maze of some hundred or more stalls. It was like a festival or a fairground; a great tangle of people filled the aisles, some hurrying along, others hesitating in apparent bewilderment. Among the items available were these:

Key chains made of owl talons.
A "bear's ass-scratcher," looking something like dried

seaweed. This was apparently a kind of parasitic plant; the seller himself had no idea what to do with it.

A cardboard box filled with assorted springs and cogwheels.

Three sets of horses' teeth.

An old-fashioned inhalator, heated by using an alcohol lamp.

A sharpener for bamboo gramophone needles.

Two whale turds, each a foot in diameter.

Glass nails.

Ointment to rub on the trunk of an elephant with a cold; made in Singapore.

A bloodstained signal flag claimed by its owner to have been used in the Battle of the Japan Sea.

An adjustable ring with plastic ballpoint pen attached.

A sleep-inducing device to plug into your home computer; worn around the ankle, it applied rhythmic stimulation timed to the user's heartbeat.

A jar of sixty-five-year-old *shochu*, low-class distilled spirits ("Drink at your own risk").

An aluminum-can compressor, utilizing water pressure in accordance with the lever principle.

A privately printed telephone directory purporting to contain "all you need to know" (for residents of Nerima Ward, Tokyo).

3.3 pounds of powdered banana peel (a marijuana substitute?).

A stuffed sewer rat, nineteen inches long.

A baby doll that could suck on a bottle.

And then—the eupcaccia.

Camped somewhere in the heart of the maze was a stall with a display of insect specimens. The stallkeeper must have had in mind schoolchildren with vacation bug-collecting assignments to complete, but his display was devoid of popular items like butterflies and giant beetles. Several dozen little containers about the size of a pack of cigarettes lay heaped in the center of the counter, and that was all. Each was made of transparent acrylic plastic, and each appeared empty. Aluminum foil labels bore the name "Eupcaccia," neatly typed, with the Japanese name in parentheses beneath: *tokeimushi*—clockbug.

The containers appeared empty only because their contents were so unimposing: what was inside looked like a relative of one of those nameless bugs that crawl through garbage, unnoticed and unloved. The salesman himself cut no great figure. His glasses had lenses like the bottoms of two Coke bottles, and the crown of his head bulged. All in all, a dour-looking fellow. Somewhat to my relief, he had customers to occupy him: a man and a young woman, both sensible-looking types, were turning containers over in their hands and studying them as they listened to the salesman's pitch. I couldn't help pausing to listen in, attracted as much by the authentic ring of "eupcaccia" as by the intriguing nickname, "clockbug."

I learned that in Epichamaic, the language spoken on Epicham Island (the insect's native habitat), *eupcaccia* is the word for "clock." Half an inch long, the insect is of the order Coleoptera, and has a stubby black body lined with vertical brown stripes. Its only other distinguishing feature is its lack of legs, those appendages having atrophied because the insect has no need to crawl about in search of food. It thrives on a peculiar diet—its own feces. The idea of ingesting one's own waste products for nourishment sounds about as ill-advised as trying to start a fire from ashes; the explanation lies, it seems, in the insect's extremely slow rate of consumption, which allows plenty of time for the replenishment of nutrients by bacterial action. Using its round abdomen as a fulcrum, the eupcaccia pushes itself around counterclockwise with its long, sturdy antennae, eating as it eliminates. As a result, the excrement always lies in a perfect half-circle. It begins ingesting at dawn and ceases at sunset, then sleeps till morning. Since its head always points in the direction of the sun, it also functions as a timepiece.

For a long time, islanders resisted mechanical clocks, deterred by the clockwise rotation, and by what appeared to them the suspiciously simple movements of hands measuring off the passage of time in equal units, without regard for the position of the sun. Even now it seems they refer to mechanical clocks as *eupcanu*, to distinguish them from "real" clocks—*eupcaccia*.

There was a charm to the unassuming eupcaccia that went beyond mere practical concerns. Perhaps its almost perfectly closed ecosystem was somehow soothing to troubled hearts. Guests at the Hotel Eupcaccia, the only such facility on Epicham, would come across the insects lying on flagstones (thoughtfully provided by the management) and become riveted to the spot. There were reports of a certain businessman who had sat day after day in the same place, magnifying glass in hand, and finally died raving mad, cheeks bulging with his own excrement. (He seems to have been either a Japanese watch salesman or a Swiss clock manufacturer.) All of this was doubtless more sales talk, but I chose to take it at face value.

The native population, in contrast, showed no such obsession with the insect. Around the start of the rainy season, when tourists went away, the bacterial action so crucial to the well-being of the eupcaccia would fall off, effectively slowing the progress of time. Next came the annual mating season, when time died, as the eupcaccia flew off like clock hands leaving their dials. Then impregnated females crisscrossed clumsily over the ground, fluttering wings as thin as the film on a soap bubble, as they searched for semicircles of dung on which to lay their eggs. The cycle was suspended, time invisible. The clocks shorn of hands were like claw marks on the surface of the ground, lifeless and sinister.

For all this, the islanders have never rejected time itself. The signs of regeneration are always the same.

I couldn't help marveling at the uncanny resemblance that the eupcaccia bore to me. It was as if someone were deliberately making fun of me, yet this insect dealer had no possible way of knowing who I was.

The male customer spoke, after clucking his tongue like someone sucking on a sour plum. "Funny kind of bug," he said. "Looks to me like it's sulking in there." His speech was unpleasantly moist, as if his salivary glands were working overtime. The girl looked up at him and said—her voice dry, the voice of someone sucking on a sugar candy—"Oh, let's get one. They're so cute."

She smiled prettily, dimpling the corners of her naturally red lips. The man stuck out his jaw and produced his wallet with an exaggerated flourish. All at once I decided to buy one too. I felt a strong sense of intimacy with the bug—the sort of feeling aroused by the smell of your own sweat. Fastened with a pin, I would doubtless make just as novel a specimen. Whether the price of twenty thousand yen was high or low I couldn't say, but I had a strange conviction that I had found exactly what I'd been looking for.

The eupcaccia was suspended inside its transparent acrylic container on two fine nylon threads hung at right angles, to make it visible from below as well as above. Without the clear vestiges of atrophied legs, it could have been a dung beetle with the legs torn off.

I paid my money after the couple paid theirs, and watched as the salesman inserted tablets of a drying agent into the top and bottom of the container. Then, slipping it in my pocket, I felt a great easing of tension, like stepping into a pair of comfortable old shoes. "How many does this make?" I asked. "That you've sold today, I mean."

As if the question somehow offended him, the salesman kept his mouth clamped shut. His gaze was refracted in the thick lenses, making his expression hard to read. Was he just ignoring me, or had he not heard? Cheerful background music rose and fell with a passing breeze.

"As soon as I get home I'm going to get out my atlas and see if there really is such a place as Epicham Island," I said, and then laughed. "Just kidding." Still no reaction. Maybe I had gone too far. I hesitated to say anything more.

2

SOMEDAY I'D LIKE TO DESIGN

A LOGO BASED ON THE EUPCACCIA,

AND USE IT FOR A GROUP FLAG

S T R A I G H T back from the entrance was a canvas-roofed rest area that probably doubled as a stage for outdoor concerts. Next to stands selling iced coffee and hamburgers was one selling shaved ice; I ordered a bowlful, flavored with syrupy adzuki beans. Seen through the protective wire-mesh fence, the dusty streets below looked like old torn fishnet. It seemed about to rain: mountains in the distance were swathed in clouds. The noise of thousands of car engines bounced off the sky and merged, interfering with the department-store Muzak in spurts like the gasps of a winded bullfrog.

The bowl of shaved ice and sweet purplish beans chilled my palms. People in the unroofed area were starting to head for the exits, but here nearly every seat was filled. I shared a table with a student (so I judged him to be from the long hair that fell to the nape of his slender neck, and his bloodshot eyes) wearing a dark blue T-shirt with white lettering that read PO PO PO. His face was bent over a bowl of chilled noodles. I crushed the beans in my ice with the back of my spoon, then scooped them up and ate them. The student looked up with a sound of joints cracking in his neck. Evidently he was offended by the critical gaze I had turned on him. It's a bad habit I've developed ever since I started carrying the boarding passes with me. As I go out only once a month, I have to make the most of my time.

"Did you find anything?" I asked.

"Nah." A noodle hung down on his chin; he pushed it into his mouth with a finger and added in a tone of disgust, "What a bunch of junk."

"Even the eupcaccia?"

"The what?"

"Eupcaccia." I pulled the plastic case out of my pocket and showed it to him. "It's the name of an insect. Didn't you see it? Second aisle from the back, around the middle, on the left."

"What's so great about it?"

"It's a beetle, a kind of Coleopteron. The legs have atrophied, and it goes around and around in the same place like the hour hand of a clock, feeding on its own excrement."

"So?"

"So isn't that interesting?"

"Not especially."

So much for him. Disqualified.

At the risk of sounding pretentious, let me say I believe the eupcaccia is symbolic of a certain philosophy or way of life: However much you may move around, as long as the motion is circular you haven't really gone anywhere; the important thing is to maintain a tranquil inner core.

Someday, I thought, I'd like to design a logo based on the eupcaccia, for a group flag. It would have to be based on the back, not the belly. The segmented belly has too many lines, like the underside of a dried shrimp, but the back could be represented easily enough by two adjacent ovals. Sort of like the radiator grille on a BMW—the car with the world's top driving performance. That settled it: I knew now where I was going to keep the eupcaccia. There could be no better place than the shelf over the toilet in my work area. That was where I kept all the luggage and other travel equipment. Suddenly I grinned, my humor restored at the notion of the eupcaccia as a travel accessory.

The student went off with a look of uneasiness. I had no intention of stopping him. Even apart from his boorish way of slurping his noodles, his approach to life was obviously wanting in gravity. The eupcaccia promised to become a useful litmus test, I thought, one that gave me an objective standard for deciding among potential crewmen. Anyone who showed no curiosity about such an insect—the fulcrum of a compass with which to draw the circumference of the very earth—was simply too insensitive to merit serious consideration.

I felt far greater interest in the young couple who had bought a eupcaccia before me. Where could they have gone? *They* were the ones I should have sounded out. Why did I never make the most of my opportunities? On second thought, however, the man anyway was no loss. He had been too restless, as if there were a Ping-Pong game going on inside his head. Hardly the type to adapt well to the life of a mole. The girl was another matter; she certainly would bear careful investigation. It had been *her* idea to buy the eupcaccia; besides, it was only logical that my first crew member should be a woman. Savoring the coldness of the ice in my mouth, I turned regretful thoughts of her over in my mind. Why hadn't I spoken up right then? By now we might have been fast friends, based on our mutual interest in the eupcaccia. The only problem was the nature of her relationship with that man. If they were married, or anything like it, my hopes were wasted. Of course the eupcaccia itself belonged to the realm of soliloquy. It was hardly the sort of thing you'd expect a married couple to purchase together. On the other hand, I had to admit that unmarried couples who behave like man and wife are rare—far rarer than married couples who behave like mutual strangers.

Time to go. I had already had the amazing good fortune to stumble on the eupcaccia; it wouldn't do to be greedy for more. And on a windy day like this I couldn't drive after dark along that rocky ledge by the coast: salt spray would rust out the body of the jeep.

A shadow fell on the seat just vacated by the student. Conspicuously large cranium, heavy glasses for nearsightedness, dingy skin—it was the insect salesman. He unwrapped a sandwich and dragged a chair up, scraping it loudly against the floor. He still hadn't seen me. It wasn't an amazing coincidence that we should end up face to face, considering there were only a few seats vacant. He peeled off the top slice of bread from his sandwich, rolled it up into a cylinder, and began to take careful bites, sipping now and then from a can of coffee.

"Taking a break?" I said.

The insect dealer stopped chewing and looked up slowly. "You talking to me?"

"Don't you remember me? You just sold me a eupcaccia a few minutes ago."

For several seconds he continued to stare at me silently, through lenses so thick they seemed bulletproof. He seemed wary. Was it my weight? People tend to equate obesity with imbecility. Members of the opposite sex are distant, those of one's own sex derisive. Fat is even an obstacle to finding employment. The ratio of body size to brain size suggests unflattering analogies to whales and dinosaurs. I don't even like fat people myself—despite the obvious irony—and I generally avoid getting into conversations with them if I can help it.

"What's the matter? You want your money back, is that it?"

In the back of my mind I still had reservations about the eupcaccia, but I didn't want them forced into the open. I was in no mood to hear a confession.

"Not at all. I'm very happy with my eupcaccia. It's given me a lot to think about. Did you collect all those specimens yourself? They say environmental pollution is getting so bad that insects are disappearing all over the place. Some dealers have to raise their own, I've heard."

"Yes, and some go even further—they conjure up non-existent specimens with tweezers and glue, *I've* heard."

"How many have you sold altogether?" I asked, deeming it safest to change the subject.

"One."

"No, really."

"Look, if you want your money back, I don't mind."

"Why do you say that?"

"To avoid a hassle."

"There were some other people who bought one before me."

"No, there weren't."

"Yes, there were. Don't you remember? A man and a young woman."

"You haven't been around much, have you? I hired them as *sakura*—decoys, shills, to lure customers."

"They looked on the level to me."

"Well, they have a standing contract with the department store, so they're in a little better class than your average confidence man. Besides, the girl is terrific. She makes great cover."

"She had me fooled."

"She's a looker, all right. She's got real class. That son of a gun . . ."

"There's a new system for classifying women into types," I said. "I saw it in the paper. The 'quintuple approach,' I think it was called. According to that, women fall into five main types—Mother, Housewife, Wife, Woman, and Human Being. Which one would you say she is?"

"That sort of thing doesn't interest me."

"It's all been carefully researched by a top ad agency. It's some new tool they've worked out for market analysis, so it should be fairly reliable."

"You believe that stuff?"

A flock of sparrows flew low overhead. Then came a rain-cloud that brushed the department store rooftop as it sped by in pursuit. Canvas flaps over the stalls fluttered and snapped in the wind; shoppers paused uncertainly. Here and there some stallkeepers were already closing up. They would be the ones whose goods were sold out, or who had given up on selling any more that day.

"Shouldn't you be getting back to your stall? Looks like rain."

"I've quit." He laid thin slices of ham and tomato on top of each other, speared them with a fork, and grinned. His boyish grin went surprisingly well with his bald head.

"Don't give up so soon," I said. "The eupcaccia gives people something to dream about; I'm sure you can sell at least a couple more if you try."

"You're weird, you know that? What do you do for a living, anyway?" He stroked his head with hairy fingers until the smokelike wisps of hair lay flat against his scalp, making the top of his head look even bigger.

A customer wandered up to the stall next to the rest area where we were sitting. The item for sale there was an all-purpose vibrator, oval in shape, featuring a metal fitting for an electric drill on the end, in which a variety of tools could be inserted: back scratcher, toothbrush, facial sponge, wire brush, shoulder massager, small hammer . . . you name it. It certainly was ingenious, yet it failed to fire the imagination. Besides, there at the counter they had only samples. To make a purchase you had to go through some fishy rigmarole, leaving a ten percent deposit and filling out an order blank with your name and address; the device would supposedly be delivered to your doorstep (for a slight charge) within a week. I found it hard to see why anyone would want to buy such a thing.

"There you have the opposite of a dream," I said. "Sheer practicality."

"There you have a lesson in how to fleece people," said the insect dealer. "Nothing wild or fantastic, you see. Plain, everyday items are best—kitchen stuff, especially. If you're clever, you can even fool people in the same line. But it doesn't bear repeating. You can never work the same place, or the same item, more than once. And until you've mapped out your next strategy, you've got to keep jumping from town to town. Not an easy life."

"Does the eupcaccia bear repeating?" I asked.

"Ah—so now you've made up your mind it's a fake."

"Just eat your sandwich, please. What did you have for breakfast?"

"What does it matter?"

"I always have sweet potatoes, or pancakes, with coffee. I make my own pancakes."

"I can't make a good pancake."

"Neither can I."

"Haven't eaten breakfast in a good ten years."

"Was that thunder?"

"Who cares?"

He bit off a piece of his sandwich as if tearing into the world's betrayal. I couldn't blame him. If I were the discoverer of the eupcaccia, with sales so slow I'd undoubtedly feel the same way. A pillar of sand, understood only by dreamers. But even a pillar of sand, if it stands inside the earth, can hold up a skyscraper.

"If you like, I'll take the rest of the eupcaccias off your hands. Another four or five wouldn't hurt, anyway."

"Why should you do that?" the insect dealer said, stuffing his mouth with the last of his sandwich. "Don't talk like an idiot. I don't know what little scheme you may have in mind . . ."

"All right. Just because I'm fat, you don't have to snap at me that way."

"Obesity has no correlation to character." He stuck the wad of bread he was chewing over on one side of his mouth, and added in a muffled voice, "It's caused by the proliferation of melanoid fat cells; only involves an inch or two of subcutaneous tissue."

"You know a lot about it."

"Just something I read in the paper."

"Do you plan to sell the rest of the eupcaccias somewhere else?"

"Frankly, I've had a bellyful of them."

"Surely you wouldn't just throw them away?"

"They're not even worth grinding up for medicine. I'll save the containers, though; I paid enough for them."

"Then why not let me have the lot? I'll trade you that for a boat ticket. If you're going to throw them away anyway, why not? You've got nothing to lose."

Whoops—too soon to bring up the boat ticket. After this slip, I felt as unnerved as if someone had just goosed me with an ice cube. I'd been too anxious to keep him from belittling my purchase, feeling that any criticism of the eupcaccia was a reflection on my judgment as well. The clockbug contained, I felt, a revelation that could save humanity much rancor and anxiety.

Take the anthropoids, who are thought to share a common ancestor with the human race. They exhibit two distinct tendencies: one is to make groups and build societies—the aggrandizing tendency—and the other is for each animal to huddle in its own territory and build its own castle—the settling tendency. For whatever reason, both these contradictory impulses survive in the human psyche. On the one hand, humans have acquired the ability to spread across the earth, thanks to an adaptability superior even to that of rats and cockroaches; on the other, they have acquired a demonic capability for intense mutual hatred and destruction. For the human race, now on a level equal with nature, this two-edged sword is too heavy. We end up with government policies that make about as much sense as using a giant electric saw to cut open the belly of a tiny fish. If only we could be more like the eupcaccias . . .

"Trade it for what, did you say?"

"A boat ticket."

"Ah, the old survey con." He drank the rest of his canned coffee, and looked at me intently through his thick lenses. "If you're trying to pull off one of those on me, better wait till you're a little more experienced."

"Huh?"

"You never heard of it? I guess not, from the look on your face. You know, you see them everywhere, those people standing on street corners with a pad of paper and a ballpoint pen in their hands."

"I've seen them. What are they there for?"

" 'Tell me, madam, have you settled on your summer vacation plans?' They start out like that, and they wind up extorting an entrance fee for some super-duper travel club."

"You've got me wrong." After some hesitation, I decided I had no choice but to bring out one of the leather cases. "See? A key and a boat ticket. It's a ticket to survival."

A tap on the shoulder from behind. A pungent whiff of pomade.

"No soliciting without a permit, buddy. Pay the fee and open your own stall, just like everybody else." A boxlike man, hair parted on one side, stood looming behind me. His eyes, moist with intensity, were round and deep-set. His erect posture and the badge on his chest immediately identified him as a member of the store's security detail.

"I'm not soliciting."

"You'll have to come with me. You can file your complaints over at the office."

Eyes converged on us. A wall of curiosity, anticipating a show. Then Goggle Eyes grabbed my arm, his fingers digging into the flesh until my wrist began to tingle—a form of punishment he was evidently used to meting out. With my eyes I signaled to the insect dealer for help, expecting him to be able to say something in my defense. But he kept his head lowered, and did nothing but fumble in his pocket. The man was all talk, not to be trusted. Let that be a lesson to me. It wouldn't do to start passing out tickets recklessly.

Resigned, I began to get up. All at once, Goggle Eyes softened his grip. The insect dealer's right arm was extended toward us, displaying in two fingers a tan card.

"Permit number E-eighteen."

"That won't work. This guy is the one who was soliciting."

"He's my partner. Since when is use restricted to the bearer?"

"Oh. Well, in that case . . ."

"I'll go along with you," offered the insect dealer genially. "It's the least I can do."

"No, that's okay, as long as I know the score."

"Not so fast. You've embarrassed us publicly. Now there has to be a proper settling up."

"I am sorry this happened, sir. But we do ask in principle that you restrict business activities to the place stipulated."

"Yes, certainly. Sorry to have troubled you."

Palms facing us in a gesture of apology, Goggle Eyes backed speedily off and disappeared. I was filled with remorse, abashed that for those few seconds I had doubted the insect dealer.

"Thanks. You saved me."

"A lot of those guys are former cops. Out to fill their quotas."

"Anyway, please take this," I said, pressing the case on him. "It may not be as fancy as the one for the eupcaccias, but it's pretty nice, don't you think? Real leather, hand-tooled."

"So the case is imposing and the contents are worthless, eh? At least you're honest."

"No, no—this is a ticket to survival. Open it up and see for yourself."

"Survival? Of what?"

"The disaster, of course."

"What disaster?"

"Well, don't you think we're teetering on the brink of disaster right now—nature, mankind, the earth, the whole world?"

"As a matter of fact, I do. But my thinking so isn't going to make any difference."

"Come on. I'll show you."

I stood up and motioned for him to follow, but the insect dealer remained where he was, making no move either to touch the ticket case or to get up from his chair.

"It's just not my line. Social protest, that sort of thing. I'm the type who believes in letting things take their course."

"Nobody's asking you to worry about anyone else. This is strictly for you yourself."

"Thanks, anyway. I think I'll pass it up. Who am I to survive when other people don't? Isn't it a sin to ask for too much?"

There was something to what he said. He had found my vulnerable spot.

"Don't you see, I want to trade you this for the rest of the eupcaccias."

"Some other time. What's the rush?"

"That just shows how little you know. The disaster is on its way. Don't you read the papers?"

"Oh, yeah? When is it coming?"

"It could very well be tomorrow."

"Not today? Tomorrow?"

"I'm just talking possibilities. It could come this very instant, for all I know. All I'm saying is, it won't be long."

"Want to bet?"

"On what?"

"On whether it comes in the next ten seconds." He prepared to start the stopwatch attachment on his wristwatch. "Ten thousand yen says this disaster you're talking about doesn't happen."

"I *said* I'm only talking possibilities."

"I'll make it the next twenty seconds."

"Either way, it's a toss-up."

"And in twenty minutes, or two hours, or two days, or two months, or two years, it'll still be a toss-up, right?"

"You mean the whole thing doesn't interest you unless you can *bet* on it?"

"Don't be so touchy. I know what you're thinking: Even if it *did* come in twenty seconds, winning wouldn't do you much good because you'd be too dead to collect. There could be no payoff unless it didn't come. Not much of a gamble any way you look at it."

"Then why not go ahead and take the ticket?"

"What a depressing creature you are."

"Why?"

"I just can't relate to someone who goes around hawking the end of the world."

All right then, smart-ass, go ahead and drop dead if that's what you want. That head of yours looks terrific from the outside, but inside it must be stuffed with bean curd. Probably I overestimated the eupcaccia too.

"When you're sorry, it'll be too late," I said.

"I'm going to take a leak."

"You're positive you don't want it?"

The insect dealer began to get up. It wouldn't do to leave the precious ticket lying there any longer. My hand started for it, but before I could reach it, he had slid his hand under mine and snatched it up, smiling broadly then as he adjusted his glasses. He might equally have been seeking reconciliation or merely teasing.

"Wait back by the stall. I'll be right there."

"Don't walk out on me, now."

"All my stuff is still there."

"You mean the eupcaccias? You were going to throw them away, anyway. What kind of a guarantee is that?"

He took off his watch and set it where the ticket case had been. "It's a Seiko Chronograph, brand-new. Don't *you* make off with *it*."

3

E V E R Y T H I N G in the insect dealer's stall was packed up, backing his assertion that he had decided to quit. The left-hand stall across the way— I've forgotten what it was selling—had likewise ceased business. The sky threatened rain any minute, and the hour was six-twenty—almost closing time. I entered the stall from the side, ducking under the canvas, and found in place of a chair a large suitcase, which doubtless contained the rest of the eupcaccias. Overly conscious, as always, of the eyes of others, I lowered myself onto the suitcase, shoulders hunched to avoid looking conspicuous. I needn't have worried. The few remaining shoppers went scurrying past like young crabs racing to catch the tide.

I transferred the insect dealer's watch from my back pocket to my shirt pocket. My spirits were low—not, I thought, solely because of the weather. Was I sorry already that I had let him have the ticket? With what eagerness I had waited for and dreamed of this event—the finding of a companion—yet now that one had made his appearance, I began shrinking back. A bad habit. Must take a more positive view. He wasn't a bad fellow in the least. A bit plain-

spoken, but that was better than a lot of high-sounding talk.
Not just anyone could have discovered the eupcaccia. He
was probably a lot more quick-witted than he let on. The
first crew member, above all, had to be far more than a mere
cabin boy.

To erase any doubts, as soon as he came back from the
men's room I could inform him that I was the captain, and
have him sign a form stating that once aboard, he agreed
unconditionally to obey any orders to disembark. The ship
was mine. I discovered her, designed her, and built her. It
was only proper for the crew to fall in line with my policies.
Of course if he had a mind to disobey, no mere signature
was going to stop him. In which case I'd have no choice but
to put my punitive system into action. Basically a defense
against invaders from outside, the apparatus was capable of
inflicting fatal injury; but for communal living to succeed,
minimum standards of order had to be preserved. Certainly
I had no plan or desire to throw my weight around as
captain, but then again, it wouldn't do to turn the ark into a
great coffin.

I couldn't keep putting off the decision. Unless I com-
promised somewhere, plainly I would find myself battling
windmills forever. One or two people could never run a
ship that size; my plans called ultimately for a crew of 385.
Unless I wanted to see the ship superannuated before ever
weighing anchor, I had better make up my mind to take the
insect dealer on board.

The lady directly across the way (whose stall boasted a
collection of thousands of different matchbooks and match-
boxes, candy wrappers and whatnot) had begun packing in
a hurry. Apparently annoyed by the failure of her goods to
sell, she was ripping off the tarpaulin and stuffing it into her
valise without even taking time to remove the thumbtacks.
It was no wonder her sales were poor; the eupcaccia was

eccentric in its way, but her merchandise was just too idiosyncratic. She herself, though past middle age, wore yellow sunglasses with a smart-looking kimono, for an effect somehow out of keeping with the surroundings. To make matters worse, at the bottom of her sign were the pathetic words "Mementoes of My Departed Husband," which could only serve to put off potential customers. Perhaps the insect dealer had been right: expecting too much was indeed a sin.

The man selling a water cannon (*not* water pistol) at the stall on my immediate right was seated chin in hands by a peculiar machine placed directly on the floor. A tape recording recited his spiel for him while he looked resentfully up at the sky. The clouds were higher than before; now a wisp swirled fitfully by at about the speed of a helicopter. It looked as if the rain would hold off awhile longer, but no one was likely to buy a water cannon in any case. Besides, the price was too high. No sane person would part with ten million yen unless either there was solid reason to believe the price would rise further or the item was of enormous practical value. From listening to the tape, I deduced that he had based the figure solely on the number of days it had taken him to make the thing. A former employee of the Japan National Railways, he had utilized the principle of the steam locomotive. He had evidently applied for a patent, but to my layman's way of thinking it seemed hardly likely that steam pressure could have an explosive force comparable to gunpowder. If it was a low-noise, nonpolluting, short-distance projectile he wanted, elastic could easily do the job. I didn't think much of the design, either: an unsightly bulging coal stove, and rising out of it, a stubby cannon. It looked exactly like the male genitalia. Good for a laugh maybe, but certainly nothing I'd pay even one hundred yen for.

These people were obviously genuine amateurs, just as

advertised. Their offerings roused one's curiosity, but ultimately left one disappointed. All I could discern around me
was out-and-out greed, and total lack of concern for psychology. Personally, I didn't mind a little wool over my eyes
as long as the result was sufficiently entertaining. That was
where the eupcaccia shone: now *there* was the unmistakable
touch of the professional.

A man appeared in the corner of the aisle and stopped
lightly, birdlike. In the heat, as sultry as a noodle-shop
kitchen, he cut a conspicuous figure in his suit coat. Even
without seeing the badge on his lapel, I knew instantly that
this was the same security guard who had falsely accused
me over at the rest area. Had he come to stir up some new
storm? I didn't want to be hassled. With the stall cleared of
merchandise, he might well stop to ask questions. I took out
the remaining two tickets and placed them side by side on
the counter. The plain wood surface of the counter, not one
meter long, looked immeasurably vast. No reason to quail, I
told myself; those cases held something of far more value
than ten thousand stalls. The guard walked by without a
flicker of expression. The edge of his glance swept over the
counter in front of me. Sweat was dripping from the point
of his chin, I noticed; I too poured rivers of sweat.

What was keeping the insect dealer? This was taking too
long. Did the man have kidney stones?

A young couple stopped at the counter. The man had a
crew cut, and he wore black trousers with a white, open-
collared shirt. Fastened around his fat, sausagelike neck was
a gold necklace. The woman's hair was mussed, as if she'd
just gone through it with her fingers; she had on purplish
lipstick and a T-shirt printed with a loud Hawaiian beach
scene. They had come to the wrong place. I was only putting
on an act; I had nothing to sell. I started to say so, when it
hit me—this was *her*. There could be no doubt about it: she

was one of the two other people who had bought, or pretended to buy, a eupcaccia. The hair and makeup and clothes were all different, but there was no mistaking who she was. Even the insect dealer had mentioned what "class" she had, and indeed she had a striking way about her that no disguise could conceal for long.

About the man I was less sure. Was he or was he not the same person? That long hair before could have been a wig—if she wears disguises, then so does he, I told myself—but still, something didn't connect. Perhaps offensive people leave a more superficial impression. Unfortunately, he looked ten years younger than the one before, which made him a good match for her.

"Where's the bug man?" The man slid his fingers over the counter as if testing for dust. Uncertain how to respond, I stammered, "Uh, probably the men's room."

"Is he closing up, or just switching merchandise?" His fingers drummed as if hitting a telegraph key. His voice was raspy and monotonous. I knew I was under no obligation to answer, yet I did.

"Closing up. He's given up on selling the things."

"Why?" Wonderingly, the girl tilted her head on its slender neck. She reached casually for a ticket. "They were such cute little bugs."

Had it been the man, I would have reacted differently. But the girl's fingers were transparent, as if she had no bones. There seemed little enough chance that the ticket was in any danger.

"Great," said the man. "We're here to collect some money. Can *you* pay us?"

"I'm afraid business was pretty bad."

"Oh, no, it wasn't." He raised his voice, as if his professional pride had been wounded. "I saw it with my own eyes. They were selling, all right."

The girl nodded her head rapidly in agreement. Her look was intense. It seemed possible to interpret her reaction as a sincere defense of the eupcaccia—but that was ridiculous. She was a *sakura,* a shill; she couldn't be serious. It had to be an act, I knew, and yet I couldn't suppress a rush of affection. Rather like a cat-hater who finds a kitten purring and rubbing his legs. Without thinking, I indulged in a bit of small talk, thus inadvertently handing them a pretext to stay.

"Don't you remember me?" I said, burying my chin in the folds of my neck, prickly with heat rash, to emphasize my bulk. "I remember you."

"I remember you too," said the girl, bringing her hands together. Her eyes sparkled. "You're the one who bought the eupcaccia right after us, aren't you?"

"That's right. That was it; that was the only one he sold."

"What do you mean?" said the man. "We bought one too, didn't we? That makes at least two."

"You can stop pretending. I know everything."

"Like what?"

"Like what you two do for a living."

They looked at each other and laughed nonchalantly. Consternation was apparent beneath the laughter.

"What's *your* relationship to him?" the man asked.

"None. I just took a fancy to the eupcaccia, that's all."

"Funny. Why would he go and leave the store with a total stranger?"

"Nature called."

The girl held the ticket case to her ear and shook it. "Say, what do you suppose this is?" Her voice was clear and a bit high, with a suggestion of strain. Was she flustered at having been found out?

"Any bug that thin and flat could only be made out of paper." His voice was raspy and heavily ironic. He rotated his right shoulder and cracked his knuckles. "These days they have to have horns, or the kids won't buy them."

"Eupcaccias don't have horns," I said.

"That's the whole trouble with them."

"It's something hard," she said. "Metallic."

Swiftly the man reached out for the remaining case. Over my dead body. I snatched it up and pocketed it.

"Is that nice?" he demanded.

"It's not for sale."

"You don't mind if I look inside, do you?" The girl glanced up at me inquiringly.

"Go on and open it if you want. It's a free country." The man's tone was brusque.

She shook the contents out onto the counter. The ornamental brass key fell out with a clatter, while the thin plastic card started to fly away, caught in a puff of wind. The man slammed it down in the nick of time, as if swatting a fly; he shook off my arm, which had shot out simultaneously, and backed off with a mischievous smile. He seemed bent on playing games.

"Well, well, what do we have here? A boat ticket. A 'Ticket to Survival,' no less. What do you know. Looking for people to sign on?"

Bouncing the key on her palm, the girl peered at the card in her companion's hand. "There's a map on the back."

Where was the insect dealer? No matter how crowded the lavatory might have been, he was taking his sweet time. It had been a good five minutes now. Wasn't he ever coming back? Had he taken such a dislike to me that he was willing to sacrifice both his suitcase and his wristwatch for the chance to escape? The irony was that these two seemed more interested than he had been. Maybe it was all for the best. It wasn't sour grapes; there was just no reason it had to be the insect dealer and no one else. I studied the girl, first by herself, then comparing her with her companion. Had she been alone, I would have welcomed this turn of events unconditionally.

"Pardon me for asking, but what exactly are you two to each other?" I said. "Are you business partners, or what?" It was indeed a strange question. Hearing myself ask it, I wanted to stop up my ears. The man's smile faded, and he wiped the corner of his mouth with the back of his hand.

"I know. We're a funny pair, aren't we? People are always asking us that. Every time they do, I think of the saying 'Catch big fish with little ones.'"

"People are always asking you that? What do you mean?"

"This person," he said, indicating her with a jerk of his head, "seems to radiate loneliness. As if she were a pitiful waif forced against her will to do nasty men's bidding. She stirs up men's combativeness. It's a kind of fishing by lure, if you follow me."

"This person," he had said. How much more impersonal could you be? Perhaps there was hope. Or perhaps he was only glorying in his fishing skills. The sight of him became even more irritating.

"Sorry—I don't go in much for fishing," I said.

Slowly the girl's smile faded. She did have an air of loneliness about her, despite her way of glancing up at you, and the lines at either corner of her mouth, and her fairly heavy makeup. It might well be a look that was carefully contrived and calculated, I thought.

"Well, what about this merchandise? Don't we at least get an explanation?" He flicked the card with a fingernail and spoke with rising insistency. "You can't choose your customers; it's not fair. Once the goods are on the counter, that's it. You have to play fair. The bug man may have told you— half of these stalls are here only because I put in a good word for the owners with the management. That gives me a certain stake in what goes on here. I can't have you picking and choosing among customers."

"You don't understand. These aren't for sale. That's what I've been telling you all along."

"Tsk tsk. The rule is that anything displayed on the counter has to be for sale."

"In that case, I apologize. I'm sorry. Now will you please hand it back?"

"The bug man must have told you some ridiculous story about us. That we're a couple of *sakura* or something."

"Well, aren't you?"

"Officially, a *sakura* is a shill, a sidewalk vendor's assistant —somebody who makes a purchase or lays down a bet to encourage onlookers to do the same. Only nobody calls us that anymore. The job's no different, but we have a respect-able-sounding title: sales promoters, we're called. The department stores treat us like proper agents, with our own accounts and everything."

The girl grasped the man's wrist to hold it still, as the excited swaying of his body interfered with her attempts to focus on the map on the back of the card. Now was my chance. I reached out for the ticket, my fingers moving to the precise spot, at the precise speed, that I had intended. In fat people, the bottom half of the body may be weighted down, but from the waist up, heaviness is no bar to agility.

Yet I failed. The ticket was gone from between his fingers. Sleight of hand. He waved his other arm with a flourish, and the ticket reappeared, ensconced between two fingers; he blew on it, and it spun like a windmill.

"I give up. Please let me have it back," I said. "Then we'll talk."

"Say, this must be pretty valuable, from the way you're carrying on about it."

"Didn't use the right psychology." The girl laughed, glancing from the card to me. "You're just encouraging him."

"It *is* valuable," I said, in a voice so feeble that I made myself sick. "It's worth more than anybody here could begin to afford."

"Don't underestimate me."

"That's not what I mean." That crazy insect dealer, I thought—how long could he go on peeing? "If you don't know how to use it, it won't do you any good." Nothing to do but relax and wait to be rescued. "It would be a total waste." Still, no telling how effective his reinforcement would prove until the time came. "It's not like ordinary merchandise, where you pay the money and it's yours." In terms of sheer physical strength, the insect dealer might have an edge, but in actual combat the shill would probably prove the more adept. It was a good match. If the shill had the sharpness of wire, the insect dealer had the toughness. And I myself counted for something. Weight can be a valuable weapon, provided you use it correctly.

The girl spoke up. "A boat ticket can only mean some kind of boat. What kind, is the question."

"The real question is the key," said the man. "What does it unlock?"

"Finding the answer to that may be easier than you think. . . ." Her voice was brightly animated, as if she were leafing through a travel brochure. Then she dangled the key roguishly near the tip of her nose. The ticket might be gone, but I at least wanted the key back. Capturing sitting flies in my bare hands is one of my hobbies. I fixed my eyes on her hand. The man had put one over on me, but with the girl I had more confidence. Still, something made me hesitate. Perhaps it was self-reproach, a warning that I was getting too emotional. The insect dealer had been utterly uninterested, yet I had gone out of my way to press a ticket on him. Now, when the shills grabbed eagerly at the bait, I found myself trying desperately to retrieve it. Mustn't be prey to impulse. The thing to do was play for time, and wait till I could join forces with the insect dealer. Above all, I had to see that tickets to survival did not start getting scattered around out of all control.

A furious rain came lashing down, bombarding us with great pellets of water. Spray obscured visibility. The concrete floor hummed in resonance. Shoppers ran en masse for the exits, while stallkeepers raced to take in their wares.

In the confusion, the pair ran off and disappeared. There was no time even to call to them to stop. I started to chase after them, squeezing out through the side opening of the stall, when the weight of accumulated rainwater on the canvas roof caused the supports to lean. My foot got caught in the crosspiece, and I fell forward, flat on my face. A sharp pain flashed through my knee like incandescent light. Weak knees are the bane of the very fat.

Someone helped me up from behind, so near I could smell the sweat in his armpits. It was the insect dealer.

"Where in hell have *you* been?"

"Sorry. I didn't think it would take so long, but it turned out I had to take a crap too. I've had loose bowels off and on for a while. Maybe it's the weather; who knows?"

"Go after them. Hurry!"

"After who?"

"The shills, of course." I stood and started to run off ahead of him, but my left leg was rubbery and lacking totally in sensation. I clung to his shoulder, barely managing to keep upright.

"That woman is a looker, isn't she?" he enthused. "That face makes me want to take her in my arms. That ass makes me want—"

"Never mind that. They ran off with my stuff."

"What stuff?"

"The tickets. They swiped them and ran off."

"Now why would they want to do a thing like that?" He pulled me back under the canvas, out of the rain. I would have resisted, but my leg wasn't obeying orders.

"You wouldn't take it so lightly if you knew how much those tickets are worth."

"How should I know? I'm sure *they* don't, either."

"Their instincts were better than yours, though."

The scanty hair on his big round head looked as if someone had scribbled it on with a ballpoint pen. Water dripped from his earlobes and the point of his chin, as if someone had left the faucet running.

"Relax," he said. "I think I know where they went. If you can walk, I'll let you lean on my shoulder."

There was pain like a scattering of broken needles, but normal sensation was beginning to return. I gripped the shoulder of the insect dealer, who carried the suitcase, and we headed toward the exit, getting wet to the skin. The store loudspeakers were announcing closing time to the accompaniment of "Auld Lang Syne." The man evidently in charge of dismantling stalls came dashing up the emergency stairway, pulled out a crowbar from the toolbag slung around his hips, and set to work, starting in a corner.

In front of the elevators there was a roofed area some fifteen feet square, filled with a jostling crowd seeking escape from the rain. The overload bell was ringing, and the elevator doors were wide open. No one moved to get out. No one could have—the elevator was packed too tight. Angry shouts . . . crying children . . . women's screams . . . and the bell, ringing and ringing . . .

"Hopeless. Damn!"

"We've got to hurry and find them! The man had a crew

cut, and the woman had curly hair. She was wearing a T-shirt printed with some kind of scenery on the front—"

"Forget it. Take a look at that. No way."

"Why not take the stairs?"

"We're on the ninth floor, you know."

"So? I don't care."

We circled around in back of the elevators till we came to a white steel door. On it was a wooden sign marked EMERGENCY EXIT. AUTHORIZED PERSONNEL ONLY.

4

MY BIOLOGICAL FATHER

IS CALLED INOTOTSU

THE door swung open to a noise like the buzzing of ten thousand horseflies—the hum of motors reverberating down the pit of the stairwell. It was a steep, strictly-business stairway, a world away from the gaudy bustle of the store interior. The walls were of plain concrete, adorned only with large numbers on each landing to mark off the successive floors. The air smelled of raw pelts hanging up to dry.

The railing was on the left, which made it easier for me to favor my injured left knee. On the sixth-floor landing we stopped for breath; I tried straightening my leg and putting weight on it. There was a watery sensation, but the pain remained local. The insect dealer's glasses were starting to steam over.

"Are you sure you know where they went?" I asked.

"They have an office. A rented one, with just a phone, but an office."

" 'Shills for hire,' is that it?"

"It's a referral agency for sidewalk vendors. They keep a percentage of the space rental fee."

"Then they *are* racketeers. I knew it. He tried to gloss it over—called himself a 'sales promoter' or some damn thing."

"They don't seem to have any direct connections to organized crime, though. If they did, they could never deal with the department store here so openly. Who knows, maybe they pay their dues on the sly."

"It wouldn't surprise me. There was something slimy about them."

"Her too?"

The question was impossible for me to answer in an off-hand way. I stopped, pretending my knee hurt. The insect dealer shifted the suitcase to his other hand and looked back at me, a faint smile on his face.

"Doesn't she get to you?" he said. "She does to me. She's too good for him."

"He called her his fishing lure."

"Did he, now." He licked his upper lip, then his lower. The suitcase bumped down the stairs in time to his footsteps. "The man's no fool. You have to give him credit for that."

"Do you really think they headed straight for the office at this hour? Maybe we should phone first, to make sure."

We passed the fifth floor, then the fourth-floor landing, brushing past a pair of uniformed security guards in an evident hurry—probably on their way up to straighten out the crowd and get the elevators going again. Rain washed against the skylight.

"If I were you, I wouldn't even bother doing that," said the insect dealer. "I'd make straight for the harbor."

"Harbor?"

"Sure. That ticket gets you on board a ship, right? A ship means a harbor."

"But my ship isn't in the water. It's sort of . . ." I groped for a way to express it. "It's in dry dock, you could say."

"Well, it's only a question of time till they find it and get on board."

"What makes you say that?"

"There's a map on the back of that ticket, isn't there?"

"You mean you've already looked at it? That was quick."

"It's a habit of mine," he said. "While I'm in the john, I have to have something to read."

"Do you think they could find it with just that map to go on?"

"A fisherman could. I like deep-sea fishing myself, so I knew where it was the minute I saw it."

"Oh . . . What about him? Does he fish? He did make that crack about fishing by lure. . . ."

"That area is full of great fishing spots," said the insect dealer, giving his hip pocket a slap where the ticket apparently was. "I know my way around there pretty well. Wasn't there an old fishermen's inn somewhere near there?"

I felt a sick embarrassment, as if he'd told me my fly was open. I didn't want to hear any more. To have the past dragged aboard my ship was the last thing I wanted. When we set sail, I wanted my slate as clean as a newborn baby's.

"Oh, sorry, I forgot to give you back your watch."

On the second-floor landing, we took a final rest. My knee was almost entirely free of pain now and felt merely a bit stiff—though to keep my companion off his guard it seemed wiser to pretend otherwise. The insect dealer strapped his watch on his wrist, sat down on the eupcaccia suitcase, and stuck a cigarette in his mouth.

"No smoking."

"I'm not going to light it. I only smoke five a day."

"See there? You *do* want to survive."

"No, just to enjoy my last moments. Lung cancer isn't my idea of fun."

We looked at each other, and shared a laugh for no reason.

"Maybe you're right," I said. "I guess it would be smarter to go straight to the ship than to waste time stopping by their office on a hunch. Are you coming with me?"

"Sure—as far as the first-aid room. It's right on this floor, somewhere in back. You've got to attend to a sprain or it'll get worse."

"Hold on just a minute. That's not what you said before. You promised you'd help me find them."

"I did?"

"Besides, first aid isn't going to help me drive my jeep. It's parked down in the underground parking lot. The clutch weighs a ton."

"You want *me* to drive it?"

"What's the matter, can't you drive?"

"Are you kidding? You're looking at a former truckdriver. I'm just wondering why I should go that far out of my way for you."

"Well, I gave you back your watch, but I notice you haven't given me back my ticket."

"If you want it back, just say so. I thought you'd traded me this for the rest of the eupcaccias." He started to get up, fumbling in his hip pocket. Alarm took possession of me, as if I were watching an egg roll toward a table edge.

"Nobody's asking for it back!"

"Lower your voice, will you?" he said. "I can't stand loud voices. Dogs barking, hogs squealing, people yelling—it all drives me nuts."

Hogs. Did someone say *hogs*? My ears buzzed as if filled with crawling insects. I wasn't always a porker. When I was a boy, I was as skinny as a shish kebab skewer. Not all hogs are fat, either, as far as that goes. "Hog" became synonymous with "Fatso" back when ninety percent of all hogs raised were Yorkshires. The Yorkshire is a lard breed, and before synthetic oils and fats came into wide use, it was an important source of fat. Not just cooking fat: lard from Yorkshire hogs was used for a variety of things, from all-purpose salve and tallow to ointment for rectal suppositories—even a mustache pomade said to have been popular with the French aristocracy. Then, as demand for pork grew, the Yorkshire breed gave way increasingly to the bacon-type Landrace breed and the loin-and-ham-type Berkshire breed, both of which have a thin fat layer and a high proportion of excellent lean meat. With four extra ribs, the newer breeds were considerably longer and sturdier than their ancestors.

My biological father (a pariah in his own hometown) goes by the nickname Inototsu—literally "charging boar," which is certainly an accurate description of his personality. Not only is he as reckless and dangerous as a wild boar, but he used to run a fishermen's inn out on a rocky cove called Inokuchi, or Boar's Mouth (who would have thought the insect dealer would know anything about it!). The cove, where Mount Boar trails into the sea, is so called because it looks like the snout of a boar.

That there should be *some* physical resemblance between my biological father and myself probably couldn't be helped. Both of us weigh nearly two hundred twenty pounds, but Inototsu is well over six feet tall and has a neck so short that he can't wear ready-made shirts. He really seems less a hog than a giant boar, with all the domineering brute force of one. As a matter of fact, he is clumsy and timorous, but people always defer to him and are awed by his appearance. To hide a peculiarly wavy hairline, he used to wear a loud green hunting cap, which only increased people's apprehension.

He always liked to stand out. He used to hang around the city hall when he had nothing better to do, and even had namecards printed up with some official-sounding bureaucratic title or other. Eventually he got more ambitious, and started hankering after a real councilman's badge. His wife (my stepmother) was a practical woman; instead of protesting, she had him turn the deed to the fishing inn over to her for safekeeping. The inn was large, with a great many rooms, each provided with its own kitchen; it had a sizable clientele, including a number of cooks who liked to catch their own fish. Inototsu's only other assets consisted of two twenty-five-ton fishing vessels. As his wife had feared, when he ran for office he sold these off to raise funds. But not even changing his hunting cap for a felt hat did any good; he always lost miserably. When his money was gone, he became a terrible alcoholic and never bathed. Eventually he smelled so bad that dogs would run away from him. In the end they even threw him out of the city hall.

One day he tripped over his wife and fell on her as she lay sleeping. He escaped with a nose out of joint, but she died from internal rupture. The rumor was that he had deliberately trampled her to death, but they let him go, for lack of evidence. Even so, his entire staff quit in fear. It was after that that Inototsu took in me and my mother.

My mother had run a little cigarette stand on Mount Boar, just across the town road. She had me after Inototsu raped her. Then the year after we went to the inn to live, the summer I was twelve, it was my turn to be accused of rape. The victim was a waitress thirty years older than me. The one who raped her wasn't me—I just happened to be spying on the scene of the crime. But with Inototsu's blood in my veins, I found it impossible to clear myself. Inototsu suddenly became a self-appointed emissary of justice; he caught me and shut me up in an abandoned underground quarry in the mountain (the present ship), where he kept me chained for an entire week, until Mother finally sneaked in and set me free.

It was then that I started putting on weight. I wish to make it absolutely clear that I was not born this way. My excess weight is compensation for this unreasonable violence inflicted on me in childhood. My left ankle still bears scars from the chain. At fourteen, I ran away from home, but I continued to gain weight, my hatred of Inototsu proliferating along with the scar tissue on my leg. Rumor has it that he still hasn't abandoned his old dream of becoming a councilman. But who can take seriously a thug with a record of four (possibly seven) convictions, who is also an alcoholic and gives off a foul odor for thirty feet in all directions? Even I, his biological son, while living in the same city, have seen him face to face only once in the last few years.

So please, *please* don't talk to me about pigs. Just the sound of that word makes me feel as if my entire personality had been stuffed in a meat grinder. Local people look on me as an overgrown hog, so I eliminated them from consideration as crew members from the start. I eliminated almost everyone I ever knew, however casually. Each person who seemed likely to call me a pig I changed mentally into a louse. And then crushed between my nails.

"Don't hit the ceiling. No harm intended. As long as they don't howl and make a lot of noise, I've got nothing against dogs. I have one myself—a mutt, nothing fancy."

"So do I. What does that prove?"

"A spitz, I bet."

"Flake off."

"Well, if you don't want to go have your knee looked at, I can't make you." He shifted the unlit cigarette in his mouth, and looked up at a nonexistent window. What did he see through it? "At this time of day, the first-aid room will be jammed anyway, with victims of department store fever. They say it's endemic among housewives who go home to an empty house."

"Then you'll come with me to the ship?"

"I didn't say that. I'll hang on to the ticket, though. There's always next time. When the sun starts to go down, I have to have a drink. That's mainly what keeps me going, day in and day out. I'll carry the eupcaccias out to your jeep for you."

"You underestimate the gravity of the situation."

"You overestimate it." Briskly he clapped his hands—fleshy hands that made me think of heavy-duty gloves—and sprang to his feet. "I don't brood over things the way you do. It's not my style."

"Oh, crap—say you'll come with me. I've got booze on the ship, if that's what you want. If we take the bypass, we can get there in less than an hour, and I know a shortcut that only a jeep can manage."

"I can't figure it out—why you're counting so much on me."

"Blame it on the eupcaccia. That's what brought us together."

"Look, as far as I'm concerned, the eupcaccia was a dud. I only sold one, so that proves it. I misread the people's mind. What's-his-name, the German psychologist, has a theory that this is the age of simulation games. Eventually reality gets confused with symbol. There's a desire for enclosed spaces, like pillboxes—or with a little more aggression thrown in, tanks. If you can't follow it, don't worry. It was all in the paper. Anyway, the end result is a boom in electronic monsters, model guns, and computer war games. He could be on to something, don't you think?"

"The shill said the reason the eupcaccias don't sell is because they don't have horns."

"That could very well be. You sure you wouldn't be better off teaming up with him instead of me?"

"Personally, I don't give a shit about horns. One of these

days I'm going to design a ship's flag, and I have in mind a logo based on the eupcaccia."

"In the end, what do you think you'll do with your ship—subdivide or lease?"

"How could I put a price tag on life?"

The stairs came to an end in front of the basement door. The insect dealer put his hand on the knob and paused.

"They station a guard here to keep employees from carrying off merchandise," he explained. "We don't have anything to hide, but still you don't want to undergo a body search, do you?"

He opened the door. Out poured that uniform concentration of noise that characterizes basement grocery sections of a large department store. A standing screen was placed before the door, but there was no sign of anyone around.

"Here we go." Holding up the suitcase like the figurehead on a ship's prow, he plunged into the crowd, shouting, "One side, please, sick man coming through, one side, please. Everybody out of the way, there's a sick man coming through. . . ."

I obliged by walking hunched over and breathing with exaggerated difficulty. In the parking lot, a line of cars had begun to form.

"Hey, this jeep is huge," exclaimed the insect dealer.

"It's 2600 cc; the torque is terrific."

But he apparently felt no temptation to drive. He went around to the passenger's side, pushed the seat forward, and heaved the contents of the suitcase on the floor in the back. "I'll throw in the plastic containers for nothing."

He didn't even ask how my knee was. All right, the hell with him. I'd had enough. The knee was good enough to drive with now. It was *his* loss. I'd given him his chance, but I couldn't look out for him forever. If it came to that, I could drive off the shills single-handed. To prepare for such an eventuality, I had set up a number of traps behind stair-cases and at junctures in the tunnels. They were of all kinds: spring-powered mechanical ones, electronic ones, and devices using chemical sprays. I was confident they would stop any unwanted intruders.

"Take care of yourself, all right?" he said. "When the bomb falls in Lebanon or wherever, I'll drop by your shelter."

"It's not a shelter; it's a ship." I turned the key and started the engine, taking a deep breath to relax. "A shelter is only temporary, but on a ship, life goes on. It's a place to live, day after day."

"But when you put into port, everyone goes ashore, right? A ship is like any other vehicle—a means of going from point A to point B."

"There are people who live entirely on the water."

"So who wants to live like a goddamn turtle? I couldn't stand being stuck in some hole in the ground nose to nose with you every day."

"It's hardly a hole in the ground," I protested. "It's a disused underground quarry—a small mountain of rock has been dug out of it. If you felt like it, you could easily go three or four days without seeing any signs of me, never mind my nose."

The insect dealer spat out his cigarette, which had broken in two from the moisture of his saliva. "A small mountain, eh? Sounds pretty impressive. How many people do you figure it can hold?"

"You could visit every underground station and shopping center across Japan and not find anything to compare with it. The entire population of a small town would fit in comfortably."

"How is it administered? Is there any residents' organization? Are you in charge of promotion?"

"As of now, I'm the sole resident."

"That couldn't be. There must be other people with tickets, anyway, even if they're not living there yet."

"Nobody but you—not counting the shills."

"I can't believe it."

"Then don't."

I stepped on the clutch and put the engine in gear. A faint spasm, weaker than pain, ran through my knee.

"Wait—it's not that easy to believe. Why should you be the only one there?" His fingers tightened their grip on the hood. The tables had turned. I disengaged the gears and gave an exaggerated sigh.

"The former owners want to forget all about it. Four different enterprises got together, swarmed over the mountain, and dug it all out. Then there was a series of cave-ins, and in the end—just eight years ago—they relinquished their mining rights. The tunnel entrances are all sealed, and housing developers are selling off plots of residential land on the surface. I'm certain nobody wants to be reminded of what's belowground."

"Even if operations have been shut down, the place must still be registered in somebody's name."

"Officially, it doesn't even exist. I checked it out at the city hall. There's no street number, no address of any kind."

"But it is Japanese territory, isn't it?"

In place of an answer, I put my foot back on the clutch.

"Sorry." He stuck his big head in the window and grabbed my arm, which was holding the wheel. "Wait, let me do the driving," he said, adding sheepishly, "I suppose you knew all along I'd wind up coming in the end."

"Then you admit the disaster is at hand?"

"Sure. The world is lousy with disasters, everybody knows that. But this is really amazing. I can't get over it. You're like—what should I say?—an emperor, or a dictator, or something."

"Yes, of a ghost country. But I don't like dictators."

He swung into the driver's seat, shaking his top-heavy head. "Funniest darned feeling. I am grateful for one thing, though. When I was a kid at school, no one ever picked me for anything. I guess I do owe this to the eupcaccia, when you think about it."

5

TRAVELS WHILE SQUATTING
ON THE TOILET

H I S experience as a truckdriver had apparently stood him in good stead; soon after we left the parking lot, he was handling the jeep with assurance. It was rush hour, and near the expressway entrance ramp we got caught in a traffic jam. As long as we stayed moving, wind entering through the numerous crevices in the canvas top kept the interior of the jeep tolerably cool, but as we crawled through the rain it became unbearably steamy. Not only was there no air-conditioning, but the ventilation was poor, and we alternated between mopping our perspiration and clearing fog off the windows.

"Is there gas in the tank?"

"Yes. That gauge is off."

"If they took the same route as us, we'll never make it in time, anyway; what say we stop somewhere for a plate of curried rice?"

"It hasn't even been half an hour," I protested. "Besides, I know a shortcut that's made for a jeep. It's too soon to call it quits."

"Aye, aye, sir. It's too soon to give up." Either he was trying too hard to fake it, or else a genuine show of submission came off clumsily from lack of experience. In any case, something in his voice did not ring true. "Then how about if I go out afterwards and pick up something for dinner?" he said. "There must be a grocery store in the neighborhood."

"I've got all kinds of provisions laid in. It's an oceangoing cruise vessel, you've got to realize."

"Right. And I suppose you're a hearty eater. All right, I'll wait. Just in case we get there first," he went on, "have you got some sort of plan? Those two are stubborn. Besides, they've got a key."

"I'll bolt the door from the inside. Steel door, steel bolt."

"They might decide to lay siege."

"I said I was well stocked up, didn't I? If they want a war of endurance they'll get one. I can outlast anyone."

The insect dealer chuckled, apparently satisfied; his voice and eyes alike conveyed genuine mirth. I did not join in. What if the shill—the man—thought of using the girl as bait? Would I be able to stay inside even then? The bolt might be steel, but not my heart.

"And what if *they* get there first? Then what?" asked the insect dealer.

"Then we're in trouble."

"When he talks he sprays saliva, did you notice? I've heard people with overactive salivary glands tend to have a violent streak."

At the tollbooth, they were apparently limiting highway access; we progressed barely three or four car lengths at a time, in spurts. The underside of my chin felt prickly. My skin was so moist with sweat that it seemed in danger of peeling off. Put a penguin in hot water and they say it goes bananas.

"You suppose they went by car too?" I asked.

"Probably, but what make? That I can't tell you."

Knowing wouldn't have done much good, for the wind-shield wipers were having little effect. All I could make out was the hazy outline of the car ahead. I wanted to take off my shirt and wring it out.

"Oh, for a breeze," I sighed.

"Why the jeep?" he asked. "Do you get around much?"

"Did once. I used to be a photographer's assistant."

"Used to be?"

"Yup. Sometimes I think I'll take a shot of something, and I get my camera all set up, and then before I know it I lose interest in the whole idea. I guess I'm just lazy."

"So am I. The human being is basically a very lazy animal, you know. That's how we evolved from monkeys: by using our brains to get out of doing things. . . . But photography's a good line of work, it seems to me."

"Not as good as it seems. Besides, I was only an assistant."

"Still, it's nothing to be ashamed of. You wouldn't have to worry if a policeman stopped you on the street and started asking questions."

We passed the tollbooth. Suddenly the scenery took on a transparent clarity. Traffic still wasn't moving much, but since we were on an elevation, at least there was a breeze. I thought with renewed gratitude of my life in the quarry, where the air was naturally cool and there was no need to worry about asthma or allergies, as with artificial air-cooling systems. I couldn't wait to get back to my ship.

Just to set the record straight, I'm not a stay-at-home by nature. As a matter of fact, I'm very fond of travel—but not in a jeep: I roam all over Japan while squatting on the toilet. The eupcaccia dines as he evacuates, the insect dealer does a little light reading or looking around, *I* travel.

My favorites are the color aerial photographs from the

National Land Board: detailed photographs taken with a special Swiss camera, each one ten inches square. Depending on the area covered, they range in scale from 8000:1 to 15,000:1. Yet each has unbelievable resolving power, so great that with a magnifying glass you can make out not only individual houses but cars and people as well. Fields are distinguishable from rice paddies. You can even tell more or less how the streets are paved.

It's still more interesting when you look at such photos through a special device called a stereoscope. Since aerial photographs are taken at fixed intervals—one every ten seconds from a survey plane—approximately three-fourths of the geographical features in successive photographs are redundant. By aligning two photographs in sequence, therefore, and taking advantage of the resulting parallax, you can make the scene stand out in three dimensions.

The stereoscope consists of a rectangular metal plate fitted with two adjacent convex lenses, and a hollow for the nose like that on a fancy-dress mask; it has a six-inch support at either end. First you locate the same point on both photographs, then you arrange them side by side so that the two points are directly across from each other. The photos should be slightly closer together than the width of the lenses. The important thing is to maintain a fixed bearing. Then place the stereoscope directly over the photos and peer through the lenses from a slight distance. Concentrate your gaze in the center, ignoring the periphery. There is no correction for visual problems, so if you're shortsighted, keep your glasses on. Continue to focus intently, making fine adjustments in the distance between the photos as needed, and at some point you will hit on just the right arrangement: then magically the low-elevation places will drop away, and the high-elevation ones come thrusting up at you. It goes beyond perspective; you would swear you were looking not at a photograph but at an exact replica of the scene. The impression of depth is in fact intensified so that in an urban area, the high-rise buildings and TV towers seem to jump up and threaten to stab you; in a mountainous area it's the crags and treetops on the peaks. In the beginning, I would always find myself ducking or closing my eyes.

It gets to be an obsession. An addiction. I spend about five hours a day roaming around the photo maps, stopping every half hour to cool my eyes with a damp towel and apply one or two kinds of eyedrops. Since the only thing that keeps me home is a desire to spare my knees, it is ideal for me to move about freely this way, using my eyeballs as wheels. Traveling with three-dimensional maps is like learning to walk on air.

You can cross the ocean in a flash, if you've a mind to, island-hopping till you reach the mainland, then perhaps going on to still other islands beyond. I prefer not to get greedy, but to stick patiently to one area, looking at everything until I have familiarized myself with it completely: old mazelike neighborhoods in hilly areas without a single straight road or right-angled intersection; hopeless tangles of winding streets through which not even the local shopkeepers can direct you. The reason residents themselves cannot draw an accurate map is that they see their surroundings from eye level only. I, however, am privileged to have the entire scene spread out before me at once. If there is a branch road that joins the main road ahead, I can divide myself in two and enjoy both at the same time. If I come to a dead end—say, a road blocked off by a cliff wall—I need only pull away from the stereoscope and view the photo as a flat surface again. With no fear of what others may think, I can walk anywhere I want and peer freely into any building. As long as you plan out an escape route beforehand, even fairly bold actions are safe, like cutting across lawns or marching straight through rooms.

And so I explore it all: sluices running the length of a stone staircase; a two-story building whose upper story is a lighter color, obviously a recent addition; a garden with pond, surrounded by tiled rooftops; a cottage buried in a thicket; a house with a vast flat roof, no garden; a farmhouse, under its eaves a glimpse of the hood of a fire engine, converted from a small pickup truck; a Shinto shrine with twenty-four storage drums lined up in the back; the storehouse of an agricultural cooperative, with a hole in the roof; a lumber mill jutting out into the river; a lone dwelling buried deep in the mountains, where it seems no sunlight could possibly penetrate at any hour of the day. . . .

And connecting them all, roads that are not roads. Information accumulating in direct proportion to the passing of time. When I grow tired, it is pleasant to sit on a bench in the park overlooking the harbor, and drink in great drafts of sunshine. Strolling along a riverbank, taking in the view, is also enjoyable. Wheat fields are deep, lush, and even in hue; fields of vegetables, rough-looking and rather mottled. Along the river, it's even possible to distinguish pampas grass from hogweed (disgusting name). I also enjoy flying over mountain paths hidden beneath rows of flowering cherries, finding my way by trial and error. I can lurk in a clump of tall grass and see how it feels to be a peeping Tom, or make believe I'm a detective on a stakeout. If anyone gives me a funny look, I can simply leap over to the radio relay station atop a distant mountain.

It has long been a source of dissatisfaction to me that the real world doesn't operate the same way. Come to think of it, the world of my aerial relief photographs bears a great similarity to eupcaccia droppings.

"Are you sure this clutch doesn't need tuning?" said the insect dealer. "There's not enough give."

"That makes it safer shifting gears on uphill curves," I said.

"Damn, I hate getting stuck behind a truck in the rain. The spray hits you straight on."

We turned off the interchange at the prefectural border and entered the oceanside bypass. Partly because there were no more houses along the way, the wind blew more fiercely, and the rain snapped with a thousand fingers against flapping sails. We had to yell to hear each other, so we said very little.

After a while we came to a long, straight descent, not far from our destination. The line of hills between us and the sea dropped away, and far ahead we saw water. The foam on the boiling waves looked like dirty soap bubbles. A green sign announced: EXIT FOR KABUTO, 1 MILE.

"Take the next exit."

"How do you read that place name?" he asked. It was written in an unusual combination of Chinese characters.

"Ka-bu-to, like the helmet worn with an old suit of armor."

Peach-colored (ham-colored?) rifts appeared in the scudding clouds, and the night scene took on the brightness of late afternoon. A bolt of lightning flashed horizontally across the sky. We pulled up at the service area past the tollbooth and unzipped the windows. Then, raising my shirt to my chin to let in the air, I mopped up my perspiration. Suddenly my eyes took in a familiar sight: *fukujin-zuke*, the red condiment served with curried rice. The picture on the restaurant billboard made me realize I was starving.

"Riding in a jeep gives you an appetite, doesn't it?" The insect dealer seemed to share my reflexes. "That place over there looks empty."

"Forget it. There isn't time." It wouldn't do to betray

weakness. A ship's captain has to maintain the proper dignity. Rather than announce myself to him as captain, I resolved to carry on resolutely until he addressed me as "Captain" of his own accord.

"We don't have to go inside and sit down—let's just get a takeout dinner. We can eat in the car on the way. How about some charcoal-grilled eels and a couple of cans of coffee?"

"If you intend to eat and drive at the same time, it had better be *kamaboko*,"* I said firmly, determined to let him know who was in charge.

"Okay, *kamaboko* it is." He ran off through the rain. Having expected more of an argument, I felt somewhat deflated.

Soon he came dashing back, a handkerchief over his head, his face all smiles. Between the thumb and middle finger of his left hand he was carrying something on skewers, and with his little finger he gripped a paper bag. In his right hand he held two paper cups.

"Jumbo franks and coffee. Also, I got four packages of *kamaboko*, five to a package. We can have them now in the car, or save them for later over a beer."

"Jumbo what?"

"Frankfurters. They're loaded with mustard, so be sure you don't get any on your pants. With that color, it could be embarrassing."

I took a bite—and wondered how I had endured the hunger for so long.

"What's your name again?" I asked.

"Son of a gun. I guess we never did introduce ourselves. Komono here. Manta Komono. Sorry, I'm all out of name-cards."

* Boiled fish paste.

"Unusual name."

"It comes from a word for a kind of reed, the kind used to make mats. My ancestors were probably roadside beggars who sat on reed mats all day. What's *your* name?"

"Never mind."

He tossed the empty frankfurter stick out the window, licked the mustard and ketchup off his fingers, and put the jeep back in gear. "Got something to hide?"

"No, it's not that. It's just that for the last few years, about the only time I've used my name is when I renewed my driver's license."

"That's a good one. But we're going to be buddies now; I've got to call you something."

Now that he brought it to my attention, I realized it was true: unconsciously I had been avoiding having people call me by my name. There were times when the sound of my name called out unexpectedly had gone through me like an electric shock. Even when I was an assistant in the photography studio, it hadn't been long before everybody was calling me Mole. That was so vastly preferable to Pig that I would deliberately introduce myself to people that way. And now I'd become a mole in reality.

". . . Actually, if I've got to call you something, it might as well be 'Captain.' "

His laughter was like the sound of paper being crumpled deep in my ears. I felt the sharp whiff of loneliness. A chance stranger had just volunteered to call me Captain. Perhaps this was all for the best. Brothers end up mutual strangers, they say, and even in marriage, the more distant the relationship the better. As a principle for choosing my crew, the system of random selection fell right in line with the laws of heredity.

"That shortcut you were talking about . . . you mean crossing the river and then going over the mountain?"

"How did you know? You shouldn't be able to figure *that* much out from a map like that."

"A deliveryman develops a sixth sense." He wiped the top of his head with the handkerchief, then blew his nose into it. "Look at those diesel exhaust fumes. That's what I hate most about expressways. Somebody really ought to get figures on the incidence of lung cancer among truckdrivers."

Seen from Kabuto City across the river, Mount Boar was a steep cliff with vertical pleats, somewhat like the *kabuto* of a medieval samurai. In fact, people in the city have always called it Mount Kabuto, using the character for "helmet" to write the mountain's name. On the other side, it's known as Mount Boar. Neither name is on the maps, though; nowadays the area is known officially as Skylark Heights.

Heading north, we crossed Kabuto Bridge and came out on Mount Boar. Tangerine orchards stretched along the skirt of the mountain, to our left. At the first bus stop, we turned off the national highway, took a narrow road that cut through an orchard (it looks at first glance like a private road), and headed straight for the top. This was the short-cut. If you don't know about it, you lose ten or fifteen minutes going out to the railway station and through the underpass, and then skirting back around the foot of the mountain. I'd been counting on this advantage when I'd assured the insect dealer that we could still beat our quarry to the ship.

The road quickly changed to a steep and winding dirt path. Roadside grasses were heavy with rainwater, and the going was slippery. He locked the hubs and went into four-wheel drive. The road finally leveled out near the summit. Here it was less a road than a clearing in a dense woods. The rain had completely stopped, and overhead, ragged clouds flew by like torn shreds of threadbare cloth. Their silhouettes were highlighted by the light of the early moon, or perhaps by lingering rays of the just-set sun.

"What's that over there? Looks like some sort of monument."

Now that he said so, it did in a way. On the left of the woods, the crouching black shadow of a rock suggested some structure of no practical use.

"An outcropping of the rock base," I said. "Apparently a shaft into the original quarry. The land here belongs to whoever owns these orchards, and they must have left it as it was. Everywhere else the land was leveled off."

"That wouldn't be the gangway to your ship, would it?"

"You're way off. You saw the map; it's farther down the mountain, on the coastal side."

"I *thought* it was strange. But the tunnels interconnect underground, don't they?"

"I've done some exploring, but this is much farther than I've been able to go. As the crow flies, it must be a good three-quarters of a mile or more."

At the end of the woods was a fence topped with barbed wire. Along the fence was a light steel-frame building that appeared to be some sort of communal facility (actually it was the office of the Broom Brigade, but at this hour no one would be in yet). In front of it, the barbed wire had been cut, and tire marks were visible on the ground. Then we entered an asphalt road, and the scenery underwent an abrupt change. This was Skylark Heights. The slope, curving gently down to the ocean, was covered with roofs of house after house, all shining in the pale coppery light that leaked from between the clouds until the scene seemed more suggestive of an armadillo than a wild boar.

"We're almost there. Put it back into two-wheel drive and pick up a little speed."

Until eight years before, Mount Boar had been densely wooded, in better keeping with its name. Quarry motors vied in emitting murderous screeches, while big dump trucks fought for space on the narrow roads, flinging gravel and spraying muddy water as they went. Indeed, there had been an atmosphere of sufficient danger to frighten children away without any need for "Keep Out" signs. Now there were orange-colored streetlights at regular intervals, curbs painted in yellow wavy lines, glass-walled telephone booths, quiet cherry-tree-lined streets used solely by local residents, and row upon row of houses, each with its own modest, fenced-in garden, each running its own air conditioner.

Suddenly the insect dealer broke into a nasal falsetto, singing a children's tune: " 'The gold bug is a rich old bug—' " Equally suddenly he broke off into an embarrassed cough. "Sorry—I can't help it. Before the eupcaccia, I used to sell stag beetles."

"I heard about it from the shill. They have horns, don't they?"

"Here's my old pitch." He held up his left index finger in the air, and said in a loud voice, full throttle: "Can you see it? Look, right there, the tiny insect on the end of my finger. Stag beetles bring luck, ladies and gentlemen, just as we Japanese have been singing for centuries in that old song. But did you know that ours is not the only country in the world to value the stag beetle so highly? The ancient Egyptians called it the scarab beetle, and worshipped it as a manifestation of the sun god. And as any encyclopedia will tell you, the famous French entomologist Doctor Fabre devoted his life to its study. Buy one today and let it bring *you* luck. The one I have here is especially rare. This, ladies and gentlemen, is the world's smallest beetle, found only in tropical jungles. Can you make it out? It may be too small to see with the naked eye. They say the magnifying glass was invented just to aid in observing stag beetles. That led in turn to developments in astronomy, so you see you can hardly underestimate their importance."

"Did they sell?"

"You bet they did—more than the eupcaccias, anyway. The best customers are mothers with their children in tow. All the kids have to do is give me a sidelong glance, with just a hint of a smile, and the mothers are caught off balance. They always end up loosening their purse strings."

"You have a smooth delivery."

"That's right, smooth as butter." He stuck out his tongue, wiggled the tip, and said, "Well, that's a mother for you, isn't it."

The downhill road ends by the city hall complex, with its covering of black glass and black imitation marble; from there a four-lane prefectural road carries you due south to the harbor. The area went into a decline after stone hauling came to an end and the bypass opened up, but even so, we encountered a fair amount of traffic as we proceeded—mostly pickup trucks, two or three lined up at every red light. This harbor still has the largest freezing facilities of any fishing harbor in the prefecture.

"The race is as good as over. Whichever way you come, you end up here. I hope we get there before they do."

"I don't know. That wasn't much of a shortcut. All we did was cross one little hill."

I knew that without being told. Did he have to squash my last fragile hope? *He* was the one who made us lose time at the start.

"The national road swings way around, north of the tracks. If we left at the same time they did, we should have picked up a good fifteen minutes on them."

"Aye, aye, Captain. Straight on to the sea it is."

The sensation of being called Captain, now that I could finally taste it, brought nothing like the satisfaction I had so long anticipated. On the contrary, I rather felt he was laughing at me.

"See that row of orange streetlights up ahead? That's the bypass. Take a left just before you reach there."

6

THE DOOR OF THE

ABANDONED CAR

W E crossed over a narrow stream, and the asphalt began to buckle and roll. We were on a dilapidated town road whose surface was rough with gravel. Soon the elevated bypass loomed overhead, supported by thick ferro-concrete piers. At first the town road runs parallel with the bypass, but at the second pier it pulls away, swinging around sharply until the two roads cross by the bay. The crescent of land this formed is private property owned by Inototsu, my biological father, who let slide his chance to sell it to the highway department.

The old fishermen's inn was located on a rocky ledge directly under the present bypass. No trace of it survives, neither grounds nor building nor wharf. All that's left to show for it is that steep crescent of land sandwiched between the bypass and the town road, hardly big enough for a dog-house. It's of so little value that not even Inototsu pays it any attention, so I had no difficulty in appropriating it for my own use. At the center of the crescent is the entrance to the quarry—the place where I was taken in and chained twenty years ago, when I was accused of rape. The vein had been exhausted and abandoned even then. A number of artisans were using the site to make stone lanterns, as I recall; they used to sneak me tidbits from their lunches. Just what connection there was between the quarry and the grounds of the inn, I have never understood. Inototsu probably could tell me, but rather than face him, I prefer to remain in the dark.

The town road was made by open-cut excavation in that steep slope which falls away to the rocky shelf in the cove, like a hard-boiled egg sliced at an angle. From the highest point, the center of the curve, the drop is nearly twenty-five feet, and so rough and precipitous that descent is impossible without a rope.

"Hang a right in front of the first concrete pier," I directed him.

"There's no road."

"You're forgetting this is a jeep."

Tall weeds covered what was once the entrance to the fishermen's inn. To get back to the rocky promontory, you have to go under the bypass and skirt the beach.

"They'll never figure this out," said the insect dealer.

"Now pull over and cut the engine." I took a flashlight from the toolbox behind my seat, and stepped outside.

"Your knee seems okay now, doesn't it?"

"Yes, now that you mention it."

I had too much on my mind to go on pretending otherwise. I crouched down, peered around, and pricked up my ears. If the shill and his companion had indeed read the map correctly and beaten us here, they would have had to abandon their car in this vicinity. There were no fresh tire tracks. The only sounds that I could make out were the vibrations from cars whizzing by overhead and the whistle of wind on the waves. I detected no whir of an engine trying to pull out of

the sand, nor any foreign object interrupting the horizon's
faint glow. We were in time.

"Isn't that a footprint over there?"

The insect dealer, Komono (it will take me a while to
start calling him by his name), leaned out from the driver's
seat and pointed to a section of sand near the pier. I turned
my flashlight on it. In a mound of sand between the pier and
the ledge were two small indentations that did bear a certain
resemblance to footprints. Absorbed in tracing the probable
route of the other car, I had somehow overlooked them.

"Probably a dog."

"Too distinct for that. Or are they?"

"Let's get a move on." Motioning to him to slide over, I
climbed into the driver's seat, put the gears in four-wheel
drive, and started up in second, heading for the sands,
gradually picking up speed as we circled around and went
up from the beach onto the ledge.

"Easy! Don't push your luck." Clutching the dashboard,
he put a cautionary hand on the steering wheel.

"Leggo—you'll break a finger!" I yelled.

Flying to the right, careening to the left, we dashed
furiously along. A shadow crossed the headlight beams. I
slammed on the brakes and broke into a sweat as a stray dog,
one hind leg missing from the knee down, slunk off deliberately into the grass with its head down. A white beard
and a sagging back gave the animal a decrepit appearance,
but he was a wily old rascal, boss of the seven or eight strays
whose territory this was.

"So it *was* a dog's footprints." The insect dealer stiffened,
and added grimly, "Bloodthirsty-looking creature."

I turned off the engine. Low growls crawled over the
ground, and a panting sound like the chafing of pieces of
wood.

"Hear it?" I said.

"Are there more of them?"

"Seven or eight, as far as I can tell. The one you just saw is their leader."

"Dogs seldom attack, I've heard," he said hopefully. "They say if they're not expressly trained to kill, they won't."

"These would. They don't trust people."

"They know you, though, don't they, Captain?"

"Well, yes . . ."

This time I caught a touch of sycophancy in his use of the word. Still, it was better than being laughed at. I switched the ignition back on, drove straight under the bypass, and pulled up as close as I could to the cliff ahead. Insects attracted by the headlights crashed into the windshield.

A mountain of garbage and trash reached nearly halfway up the cliff: besides the usual assortment of kitchen refuse, there were nylon stockings wound around a bicycle seat; homemade pickles, complete with pickling crock; a fish head, its mouth the socket for a broken light bulb; an old refrigerator, now a dog coffin; an empty Coke bottle crowned with an old shoe that had melted into gum; and a TV tube stuffed with an insect's nest that looked exactly like cotton candy.

"Great—a garbage dump. Just great."

"Camouflage," I explained. "I'll bet you can't tell where the entrance is."

"I'll bet I can. Inside the body of that old junk heap on top of the pile."

His powers of observation were impressive. I had to admit that if you looked carefully you could see a rope hanging down inside the rusty, abandoned car. But I had hardly expected my camouflage to be seen through so quickly. Even inside the car, it would have taken someone of enormous experience and insight to find anything suspicious in the smell of fresh machine oil on the door handle and hinges.

"You have good instincts."

"Not bad. How the heck did you collect all this junk?"

"Easy. I just posted a sign on the road overhead reading 'Private Property, No Littering.'"

"Ingenious. But doesn't it make a huge racket when you climb up to grab onto the rope?"

"It's all fastened down."

"Let's go." The insect dealer slapped his hands on his knees and bounded out of the jeep. He spread his legs apart, placed his clasped hands behind his head, and began to do warming-up exercises, twisting right and left. He was more agile than I'd expected, and his oversize head was not terribly conspicuous. There probably were athletes of his build, I thought. "I'm ready for an adventure," he said.

"Look in back under the canvas and you'll find a box with rubber boots and cotton gloves inside."

"I can see where you'd need the boots. Just the thought of worms and centipedes crawling in my socks gives me the creeps."

As if they'd been waiting for him to go around in back of the jeep, several of the dogs began howling. They were apparently roving around in the shadows. Stray dogs are like volleyball players in the split-second timing with which they switch from defense to attack. Forcing open the canvas top with his whole body, the insect dealer dived inside.

"I told you once I don't like barking dogs. And ones that bite are worse."

"Don't worry—they're used to me."

The flashlight beam served to increase the dogs' frenzy: some jumped up and clawed the jeep, others started to dig in the ground for no reason, still others began to mate. After letting the insect dealer get a little scared, I decided to do my howling imitation. For some reason, that always dispirits them and leaves them docile. I leaned partway out the half-open window and let loose three long howls into the night sky. One dog nearby howled an accompaniment in a shrill, nasal voice, while another gave a plangent shriek. The insect dealer burst out laughing, his body rocking with mirth. I could certainly understand why he was laughing, and yet for someone who'd just been rescued, he seemed remarkably indiscreet.

"I had a dream like this once, when was it . . . ?" He changed into a pair of rubber boots, bit off the string joining a brand-new pair of work gloves, and climbed over the backrest into the front seat. "Shall I go first? Two at a time probably wouldn't work."

"You're probably right, although I've never tried it."

"Then let me go first. I can't think of anything worse than hanging from a rope, with a pack of hounds snapping at my rear end. It's true, you know—round objects activate a dog's hunting instincts. Must be the resemblance to animals seen from behind." One foot on the running board, eyes casting about in the dark, he said, "Howl again to distract them, will you?"

I felt a sudden, inexplicable hesitation. Acquiring crew members was a matter of the deepest urgency, I knew all too well. But I had grown used to living in solitude. Logically I was prepared to welcome the insect dealer aboard, but emotionally I was terrified. I suspected that everything to-day had happened too fast. Certainly there had been times, after coming back from an outing, when the moment I inserted the key in the padlock I was assailed by an unbearable loneliness. But that never amounted to more than a fleeting spell of dizziness. As soon as I was settled in the hold, I would return to a mood of such utter tranquillity that the

concept of loneliness lost all meaning. In the words of the
insect dealer—or rather of something he had parroted out
of the newspaper—I had perhaps fallen prey to the confusion of symbol and reality, to the longing for a safe place
to hide.

"Hurry up and do your howl again," the insect dealer
urged. "I'm hungry."

"First don't you think we'd better work out a strategy?"

"What do you mean?"

"Just in case they did beat us here, what are we going
to do?"

"You're worrying about nothing. That's impossible, isn't
it?"

"Maybe."

I wasn't in fact seriously expecting to find them there, but
there were one or two signs that *could* have indicated an
invasion during my absence. For example, that arrangement
of chair legs and storage drums which I always inspected
when I came back from my outings was noticeably out of
order. Probably it meant nothing, considering the heavy
downpour we had just had. Some caving in of the ground
was only to be expected. It was equally possible that a cat
had knocked the storage drum aside, using it as footing to
escape the dogs.

A series of large trailer trucks went by overhead. When
they were gone, the insect dealer said in a fed-up tone of
voice, "All right, then, you want to bet? I say they're not
here. Are you willing to bet me they are?"

"How much?"

"The key to the jeep."

Ignoring this, I said, "Actually I was talking about something different—a more general question of frame of mind.
Having you here is naturally going to change the way I deal
with unlawful occupation, compared to before. . . ."

"If it's general frames of mind you're talking about, how about cleaning up your front doorstep for starters?" He gave a laugh edged in irony. "Between your garbage dump and your pack of wild dogs, I'd say you don't have too much to worry about. Nobody's going to break in here. This place stinks to high heaven. Just trying to breathe gives me a headache."

"It's the weather. And what you smell is some disinfectant I scattered around."

"I don't think that's all. Pardon me for saying so, but I suspect it has more to do with your personality, Captain. Overly defensive. Frankly, with a captain who's so determined to shut people out, I must say the prospect of a long voyage doesn't offer much excitement."

"Look—if you were dealing in pots and pans or medicine bottles, you'd have an obligation to make them watertight, wouldn't you? With a ship, it's even more vital. Your whole life depends on it."

"I'm not taking the shill's part, mind you," he said. "Don't get me wrong. But a ship's captain has got to be a trifle more broad-minded, it seems to me. . . ."

"*You* were the one who kept insisting they were people to keep an eye on."

"You've got to keep an open mind. If they managed to get inside despite all the obstacles in their way, they'd deserve a prize, wouldn't they?"

"That's right; it would be too much for that girl, anyway."

"But then, anything *you* could handle—" he said, and quickly caught himself. "Oops, sorry, I shouldn't have said that. Remember now, a ship's captain has to be tolerant. . . . That just shows how much I really trust you. Anyway, don't forget we live in an age when women climb the Himalayas. Although between these dogs and this garbage dump, it might be too much for her at that."

I was starting to feel the same way. Maybe I was only jumping at shadows. It seemed impossible that the padlock on the entrance—or the gangway, properly speaking—would be missing. Was it merely fear of shadows that had led me to acquire a weapon in the person of the insect dealer—a weapon for which I would have no use?

"Okay. If the dogs go after you, I'll distract them," I said. I turned off the engine, and together we stepped out of the jeep. I handed him a penlight, and lit the way for him with a large flashlight. "The door on the driver's side of that car opens directly into the tunnel, so watch your head. It's about thirty feet to the entrance. I'll be right behind you."

The insect dealer grabbed the rope and hauled himself up, his feet knocking down large clumps of dirt and sand at each step. This did not signify that he was any less sure-footed than I; the slope was steep, and on it lay junk of all sizes and shapes, precariously piled together, each item supporting and supported by the rest. A monkey could have done no better without knowing where the footholds were.

A thin, runty black dog with long ears came sidling over to my feet. Was this a newcomer, paying his respects? Thanks to my talented howling, the pack of dogs had quickly accepted me as their leader. With humans it wouldn't be so easy.

I put on my rubber boots and heavy-duty gloves. The insect dealer disappeared inside the abandoned car with a wave of his penlight. After the rope stopped swinging, I grabbed it and followed him. As I went up, I placed my feet safely and securely in the footholds, enjoying a mild sense of superiority. The rusted metal plate of the car door came before my eyes—beyond it gaped the mouth of the tunnel, exactly 4.83 feet square. I could see the insect dealer's light flickering up ahead. Why they had chosen that exact measurement I did not know. The entranceway itself had a steel frame, but from there on the walls were bare rock, still showing the marks of the power saw with which they had been carved out. At my feet were rusted rails, their width adjusted to that of the handcars used for hauling stone. The tunnel cut directly under the town road, and continued another sixteen feet. Directly above the inmost part was where my biological mother had run her tobacco store— the place, incidentally, where I was born.

The farther in you went, the more pronounced the acoustical alteration: high-pitched sounds created mutual interference and were absorbed into the stone walls, leaving only the deep roar of low-pitched sounds. The howl of wind, the boom of waves, the singing of tires on the highway, all had a common denominator: the sound of a great wet canvas flapping in the wind.

"Oh, no—the lock's gone. Come have a look." His voice was muffled, as if he were speaking over the telephone.

"It's over on the far left, as you stand facing the latch."

He was right. The padlock was gone. It was stainless steel, a fairly big one several inches across, so there was no way we could have missed it. Someone had opened the door. It could only be them. Since it was a padlock, just turning the key wasn't enough; you had to remove the whole thing from its fastening. They certainly weren't going to stop there and just take the thing home as a souvenir. I'd been invaded. Bitterly, I regretted the lack of a keyhole that would have let me peer inside. I sat cross-legged before the steel door and listened attentively. Such a mélange of sounds came to my ears that I could hear nothing.

7

THE TRAPS AND THE TOILET

"L O O K S like they're here, after all. I'm glad we didn't make that bet." The insect dealer spoke in an undertone, wiping the sweat from under his chin with the tail of his shirt. In the process, his pale abdomen was exposed, revealing next to his navel a dark red birthmark the size of my palm.

"I *told* you I wasn't being an alarmist," I said.

"But is it really them?" he asked. "Couldn't it be somebody else?"

"Forget it. Who else has a key?"

"But we didn't see any cars parked along the way—and that shortcut would be impossible to figure out from a map."

"Maybe they took the train."

"Eh? You never said anything about a train."

"If you can get right on the express without waiting, it's faster. Put out that light."

The door was heavy steel, nearly half an inch thick, so the burden on its hinges was great. There was a certain trick to opening it. You had to pull it toward you, then push it up diagonally to adjust the hingepin before it would swing open silently and smoothly. I listened, and heard only the rumble

of the sea, murmurings of conches, drops of water falling—
whether near or far was impossible to say.

It was too quiet. I pushed the door open still farther, went
inside, and stood on the cedarwood deck. The insect dealer
followed behind, gripping my belt. If what we had just come
through were the gangway, this would be the hatch, not the
deck. We were on the top landing of the stairs leading down
into the hold. There was a damp green smell, and perfect
silence. Nothing more. What had happened to the invaders?
I felt an uneasy premonition.

I had not yet told the insect dealer, but the entire ship
was booby-trapped to guard against trespassers. This very
staircase leading down into the hold was a dangerous trap.
It appeared to be the only way down, but the boards from
the fourth step to the seventh held a nasty surprise: on one
side they were fastened down with a spring hinge, while the
other side was left free so that anyone putting his weight
on them was bound to slip and fall. It was twenty-three feet
to the bottom. An unlucky fall could easily prove fatal. The
only safe way to go up and down was to use the ladder
propped inconspicuously alongside the stairs.

Assuming you managed to pass this first hurdle, you still
had to get by the stairs leading up to the bridge, a sort of
terrace off the first hold. (I always refer to it as the bridge,
although technically it's my own cabin—the captain's quarters.) Set foot on those stairs without first pushing the cancel
button, and a fusillade of skyrockets will instantly fire. Put a
hand on the drawer of my desk, and a spray can of insecti-
cide will go off in your face. Nor would it be wise to show
any interest in the bookmark stuck invitingly in my diary:
Merely reaching for it would trigger an ultraviolet warning
device, sending out a shower of crushed glass I made by
grinding up old light bulbs. Individual fragments are as thin

as mica and as sharp as razors; once they get in your hair
you can't brush them out, and if you tried to shampoo them
out, your scalp would be cut to ribbons.

I had never expected any of this to be put to use. I had
thought of it lightly as a sort of protective seal on the ship
until the crew officially came on board. What got me started
was a small Austrian utility machine that I bought to make
duplicate keys. One day I used it to make a tiny screw to
fasten on the sidepiece of my glasses. Next I repaired a
fountain pen, and then added some parts to a used camera.
Gradually it became a consuming passion, and I went around
fixing, adding to, and remodeling everything I could lay
hands on.

My masterpiece was an automatic air gun. It was no
ordinary air gun; apart from a slight thickness of the shaft,
it looked exactly like an umbrella. Unfortunately, there was
no way to attach a sight, so I was forced to omit that feature.
As a result, it could be used only at extremely close range,
and never did achieve as much as I hoped in my war on
rats—the original purpose for which I'd designed it. As an
umbrella, however, it functions admirably. If I ever put it
up for sale in that department store rooftop bazaar, it would
certainly do better than the water cannon, anyway.

But what if I did inflict injury on a trespasser, I now wondered—would I be legally responsible?

After an interval that might have been two seconds, or
twenty, the steel door clanged shut of its own accord, the
reverberations conveying a vague sense of immense weight.
The insect dealer switched his penlight on, but the shaft of
light illuminated nothing; it only tapered off and disappeared,
emphasizing the depth of the darkness (the room was 225′ ×
100′ × 60′). He cast his voice into the blackness.

"Anybody here?"

"Yes." The response came bundled in reverberations, and the beam of a flashlight bounced back. "You kept us waiting long enough. Hurry and turn on the lights, please."

It was the shill, no doubt about it. His voice was cheerily off key, but it had a defiant, cutting edge. Next came the voice of the girl.

"Ooh! It hurts," she said, but as she was not moaning, I assumed her injuries were minor. It was a relief to know they hadn't been killed.

Drawn by their voices, the insect dealer took several steps forward, lost his balance and landed heavily on his rear. The beam from his penlight, which had been aimed at the floor, was swallowed up in the darkness.

"Why haven't you got a banister here, for crying out loud? A person could get killed." His voice was shrill. He coughed, cleared his throat, and said in a different key, "So it *is* you two. How'd you sneak in here?"

"Hey, it's Komono!" The girl's voice was bright. The shill must have said something to her, for she immediately started complaining again about the pain.

"You two are worse than a pair of cockroaches," said the insect dealer. "How'd you get past the dogs?"

From the swaying shadows beyond the flashlight, the shill shot back, "That's a fine hello. Let me ask *you*, then—who invited you to come poking your ugly face in here?"

Plainly the three of them were well acquainted. The insect dealer hadn't leveled with me.

"You're a fine one to talk," countered the insect dealer. "I happen to know how you got your ticket—swiped it, didn't you?"

"Now, now—don't talk that way. One thing just led to another. We looked all over for you, you know."

"Oh, you did, huh? Came all the way here to look for me, did you? That was big of you. Come off it."

"As long as we pay the admission fee it's okay, isn't it?"

"There are certain qualifications."

"Who's asking you, Komono? Butt out."

"Sorry, but I've been officially hired on by the captain here."

I was pleased to hear myself introduced as the captain right from the start. Was the insect dealer genuinely taking my part?

"Captain?" said the shill. "Oh, right. He's selling boat tickets, so he's a captain."

"Correct. I *am* the captain." Better take a firm stand here. "And since this is a rather special ship, crew members *do* need some rather special qualifications."

"What are Komono's qualifications, may I ask?" The girl's voice was tinged with sarcasm. "Ooh, it hurts. . . ."

"He's sort of a combined adviser and bodyguard, you could say. Are you in a lot of pain?"

"My ankle is killing me."

The shill's high-pitched, high-speed voice cut in: "Well, imagine that. With Komono your bodyguard, we'll all have to stay on our toes, won't we? But you know, Captain, if it's a bodyguard you want, then you ought to take a look at my qualifications too. Whatever I may lack in strength I can make up for in combat experience, I assure you."

The girl spoke again. "Save the fighting till after the lights are on, please. What's the matter with you, leaving me to suffer in the dark like this?"

"The young lady does have a point; it would be nice to get the lights on," the shill conceded. "And she does seem to have sprained her ankle."

The young lady, he had called her. A curious yet altogether old-fashioned and charming sort of appellation. It could have been simply a nickname, yet it bore a certain air of formality that rekindled my flickering hopes. Although for all I knew, that might be exactly how he intended for me to react. Perhaps this was more of his "fishing" gambit—a mere professional habit.

"There's no feeling at all in the toes," she said. "I think I may have broken the bone."

"That stairway has a couple of rotten boards in it," said the shill. "I wrenched my back too. You two had better watch out. Fall the wrong way and you'll be lucky to get off with a fracture."

Very well. There was no turning back now, anyway; I might as well accede to their request and switch on the lights. The switch was on an infrared remote-control device hanging from my belt. I traced along the vertical row of five buttons with my finger, tapped the top one lightly, and slid it to the right. Instantly the lights came on—fifty-six fluorescent lights, all blinking into action at once. However often I witness it, the drama of that moment never fails. Darkness itself has no spatial dimensions: the black expanse of a starless sky and the confinement of covers pulled over one's head are equally dark. Perhaps that explains why images we conjure in the dark seem constricted and miniature: people become dwarfs; landscapes, potted plants. All the more reason why seeing the full aspect of the quarry interior come springing into view is as great a shock as if a mighty range of mountains had jumped full-blown out of an egg. In some ways it's like gazing at a three-dimensional aerial photograph, but the scale is far greater.

Towering blue space. Massive stone walls intersecting sharply, as if sliced with a knife. Numberless horizontal lines, like marks left by the teeth of a comb—the signature of the power stonecutter blade. The walls do not appear to be even parallelograms but seem rather to undergo a certain curvature, as if falling in toward the center, probably an effect of the uneven light cast by the wall light fixtures.

When you focus on particulars, things shrink and miniaturize again: the thirty-two storage drums to my right in the corner of the hold were like scales on a carp; the shill, staring open-mouthed at the ceiling, was no bigger than my thumb. Beside him, sitting at his feet with her arms around her knees, was the girl, the size of my pinkie. She too was sweeping her eyes across the ceiling, from end to end. They were both dressed exactly as I had last seen them on the store rooftop—only the girl's hair was again short. Her own hair became her far better than the wig.

"Incredible." The insect dealer was backed up flat against the wall, barely able to speak. He seemed afraid of heights. "I had no idea it was so huge," he said. "This place is like a sports stadium. You could fit five tennis courts in here."

"This is just one small part." Their stunned looks revived my spirits. "My preliminary surveys indicate there are at least eighteen other holds this size. In that wall over there to the right, past that row of storage drums, there's a narrow opening between the pillar and the wall—see it? That's the passageway to the next hold. And on the upper left over there, that area hollowed out like a terrace is my cabin. There's another hole in there that you crawl through to reach another hold, and you see the place is actually a vast honeycomb of—"

"What's that thing over there?" interrupted the shill, pointing his chin toward the left-hand wall. It scarcely needed pointing out; one's eyes traveled there automatically, drawn by the gleam of white.

"That? That's the toilet."

"The toilet? You mean that's the john? That's where you go?"

"The design's a little unusual, but the water pressure is terrific."

"Doesn't it feel a little strange taking a crap right out in the open like that?"

The girl clapped her hands. "Wow," she said. "Listen to that echo."

The insect dealer looked up, attentive to the reverberations. "If you tried singing in here, you'd sound like a pro," he said.

"We'll pay our passage, of course," said the shill. "This is worth a lot. Nobody's asking for a free ride. We'll talk it over with you and pay a fair price." He moistened three fingers and rubbed them on his forehead as if performing some magic rite, then added as an afterthought, "Before I forget it, Komono, you still owe me my fee for sales promotion."

Ignoring this, the insect dealer bent down to inspect the stairs. "There's nothing rotten here," he said. "It's all in perfect shape."

I grabbed his elbow and pulled him back. "Watch out! It's a trap. This way down, over here."

The ladder was propped up in such a way that it could easily be mistaken for part of the scaffolding. I started down first, and immediately regretted not having let the insect dealer take the lead. Too late. The shill came striding over, heels clicking on stone; he grabbed the ladder and began to shake it.

"So that's the way it was, eh? You knew about the danger all along and did nothing to warn us. It's *your* fault the young lady got hurt."

My position was highly disadvantageous. Was he planning to use violence? In any case, it wouldn't do to betray weakness.

"I had no obligation to warn you of anything. You, sir, are in the wrong for breaking and entering."

The insect dealer leaned down from above the ladder, showing rodentlike teeth. "All right, you two," he said. "Break it up. In any quarrel, both sides are at fault."

"This isn't a quarrel," said the shill. What was that supposed to mean? He went on shaking the ladder. "I'm just trying to help. Two injured people is enough. We certainly wouldn't want anything to happen to the captain."

The girl tossed in an irrelevant remark. "Is the stone in these walls really blue, or does it just look that way?" Sitting all alone in the center of the vast stone room, arms clasped around one knee, she was as conspicuous as a tin can in the center of a soccer field. I'd heard that the female sex took cold easily; would she be all right, sitting directly on the cold stone floor all this time? If her ankle was sprained, there wasn't much else she *could* do. I found her pose unbearably provocative.

"It really is blue," I told her. "That's why it's called waterstone. Maybe you've heard of it. When it's polished it shines like marble, but the shine doesn't last long. When it dries out, the surface turns powdery."

The shill let go of the ladder and stepped back, adopting a neutral stance. The insect dealer started down the ladder, calling out to the girl as he descended:

"How are you doing? Pain any better?"

"No," she shouted back.

His feet were almost to my head. There were still three rungs below me, but I jumped to the floor. The shock of landing was translated into bunches of needles hammered into my knee; I staggered, and the shill held me up. The insect dealer slipped past me with a smile and a pat on the shoulder, heading straight for the girl.

"How's that ankle?" he asked. "Are you okay? Do you want to see a doctor?"

"I can't walk."

"There's a jeep right outside."

The shill cut in impatiently, "Her *bone's* broken, you know. Just how do you think she's going to climb the ladder and hang on to the rope?"

"I'll carry her piggyback. Fractures need attention fast."

"Don't be an idiot." The shill made a noise in the back of his throat like a balloon popping. "You can't climb a rope with someone on your back."

"I used to be a member of the Self-Defense Forces. They trained us in that sort of maneuver. Besides, there won't be any climbing; on the way back it's all downhill."

"You mean uphill." The shill's voice was thick with saliva; his voice quivered at the end of the sentence for lack of breath. "The way here was downhill, so they way back is uphill."

"You mean to say you two climbed *down* to get here?" The insect dealer shot me an accusing look out of the corner of his eye. I grew flustered. "Where from?" he demanded.

"From the road overhead, of course."

"You mean the town road?"

"Whatever. The one overhead."

"There's no rope there."

"I brought my own." He bent down under the staircase and picked up a bag like a photographer's case. "See this?" he said. "I keep a set of essential tools in it."

"What for?"

"Just in case."

"I see." The insect dealer nodded, drawing an X with his large head. "That explains how you got past the dogs."

"But how did you find your way here?" I asked.

"I just showed that map to a taxi driver, and he brought us straight here."

"A *taxi* driver?" Hold on, mustn't get too excited. It would only amount to a display of weakness. "Well, that was a damn fool thing to do. That's why I didn't want to let you have a ticket in the first place. That's the sort of person you are, I could tell. You wreck everything—"

"Calm down, please. All I did was show him the map."

"That's *exactly* what you shouldn't have done."

"The captain does have a point." The insect dealer squatted down comfortably on the floor next to the girl. "The fewer people who know about this, the bigger each one's share, after all."

"It's unpardonable. Hand me that ticket and get out of here right now."

"But what about me? I'm hurt," the girl said forlornly, looking up at the insect dealer, beside her.

The shill added deliberately, in a hard voice, "If a taxi driver is dangerous, I'm more so. I know too much—more than any cabbie. You can't afford to throw me out."

The silence that followed, though short, seemed interminable.

"What's that smell?" murmured the girl.

There *was* a smell of some kind. I had already decided it was the scent of the girl's body—but she would hardly react to that herself.

"Maybe it's the bleaching power I use for disinfectant."

"No. I have a very good nose. This is more like . . . burned soy sauce."

Simultaneously we three men began to stick our noses up and swing our heads around as we sniffed the air.

"Do you know, you're right; I had squid with soy sauce for dinner yesterday."

"Not spear squid, was it? The ones around here are fit for a king." The insect dealer's voice was eager, and he spoke with that twitch of the soft palate that comes when one is fondly recalling a particular taste. "Good raw too."

"As a matter of fact, I fried up the leftovers of some I ate raw the night before."

"Look, will you hurry and call an ambulance, *please*," the girl begged, drawing out the vowel at the end of the sentence as if she were singing. It really seemed as much a test of the echo as a cry of exasperation. I was about to tell her that it was out of the question; the insect dealer opened his mouth too, apparently on the verge of some similar remark; but it was the shill who said it first:

"Forget it. We can't possibly do that."

"Oh, I know. Never mind." She gave in without a fight. "If you're trying to avoid contact with the outside world, then it doesn't make sense to call an ambulance, does it? But God, it's killing me. . . ."

"Oh, let me give this back to you before I forget," said the shill. He took my padlock out from a compartment in his bag and threw it at me all of a sudden, though we were barely an arm's length apart. I missed it, and it fell to the floor—but there was no clank when it hit the stone. It was still twirling around the shill's finger. More parlor tricks. This time he passed it slowly into my palm. "You can never be too careful with a lock, can you?" he said.

"How about the key, while you're at it?"

"Sure thing." He fumbled in his pocket. "Komono, you give back yours too."

"All right." Without the slightest hesitation, the insect dealer tossed over his passkey, which flew in a precise parabola, landing smack in the shill's hand before being transferred to mine. I was not impressed. Such virtuoso performances leave me cold. It's always the same: the ball goes back and forth, back and forth, in a quick, light rhythm . . . and then before I know it, somebody switches it for a hand grenade; I catch it, and that's the end of the game. I had recovered the padlock and keys, but in return I had been forced to acknowledge that the shill and the girl would stay.

"Just tell me when you want out. I'll open the door right up."

"No problem. I have no pressing commitments." He sucked in a bit of saliva at the corner of his mouth. "Besides, in here you don't have to worry about bill collectors chasing after you."

"That's right," the insect dealer chimed in. Everybody laughed but me. The girl began massaging her ankle as if she'd just remembered. I could see right through her little ruse, but there seemed no point in bringing it up.

"Doesn't anybody know a good doctor? Someone discreet, who makes house calls."

"Yes, we'll need a ship's doctor. Ships always have one, you know." The shill sought the insect dealer's concurrence; the insect dealer nodded. "Not only should he be exempted from paying a fare; he should be paid a salary. Does anybody know a good person?"

I did, but I didn't want to say so. "For now, why don't you let me have a look at that leg?" I offered. "I used to work for the fire department. I can at least tell a sprain from a fracture."

Again everybody laughed. I could only join in, estimating as I did so the distance between her and me. A good eighteen to twenty paces. The thing to do was to stroll over casually, timing it so that as I finished talking I was right by her side. If all went well, I might be able to touch her leg without anybody stopping me.

"They make you learn first-aid procedures even if you're not a member of the emergency squad," I said. "Things like splinting a fracture or administering artificial respiration—but this is a bit uncomfortable, so why don't we go to my cabin? It has a sofa and some cushions. Nothing too fancy, but comfortable."

Just as planned, I maneuvered myself into place directly opposite the insect dealer, with the girl between us. She nodded and raised her right arm high, signaling that she wanted to lean on my shoulder. Unbelievably, she had accepted my invitation. I knelt down by her side on the left, scarcely breathing, like someone slipping a windfall in change into his pocket. Such a chance would never come again. I could not afford to worry about what anyone else might think.

Her hand rested on my right shoulder. This was no fantasy, but a real woman's hand. The sensation was so novel that I can scarcely describe it; if anything, it felt as if someone had applied an icy flatiron to the surface of my brain. Under the circumstances, no one could have objected if I slipped an arm around her waist, but I forbore, content merely to imagine what it would be like. As I stood up, a hand reached in my crotch and tickled my balls. It had to be the insect dealer. I ignored it.

The shill had gone ahead toward the bridge—my cabin. He kicked at the toilet below the stairs and let out a nervous laugh. These people laughed a lot for no good reason.

"Sure looks like a toilet," he said.

"It *is* one," I said.

The insect dealer caught up with the shill and peered over his shoulder. "This is a special-order size. Are you sure it isn't for horses? Does it work?"

"Of course it does."

"You must be some kind of exhibitionist." The shill leaned against a stick beside the toilet. "How you could drop your drawers here, in such an open place, is beyond me."

What he had leaned against was a steel rod sticking up out of the floor like a railway switch; it looked like something to grab for support, but actually it was the flush lever. Befor I could warn him, the lever moved, and he staggered back. An earthshaking tremor arose, as if a subway were roaring in. The noise was concentrated in the core of the toilet, as if it had been passed through a parabolic lens and magnified. An instant later, water came surging in with a cloud of spray, rose up just level with the bowl, formed a whirlpool, and vanished with another roar. There was a wet noise of rupture, then a hush.

"How awful." Shaking my shoulder, the woman emitted a soundless laugh. Judging from the way she carried herself, the ankle was certainly not broken. I doubted if it was even sprained. That was fine with me. I only wanted to stay forever the way we were.

"That water pressure is ridiculous!" The insect dealer looked back at me and said sharply, "Is this really a john? It's big enough to service ten elephants—all at the same time. The shape is funny too. I mean, it looks sort of like a john, but it's really not, is it?"

"Well, who says that all toilets have to look alike?" I countered. "There's no law, is there?" I wasn't dead sure myself. Maybe it *was* something else. It was bigger than your ordinary facility, and higher; its back was indistinguishable from its front, and it was unusually wide. The absence of a seat made it difficult to straddle and hard to keep your balance. It was also a peculiar shape: the heavy porcelain bowl rested like a giant tulip on stainless-steel pipes protruding from the floor.

My first encounter with this toilet went back to the time I was confined here under suspicion of rape, and my biological father, Inototsu, had chained me to those very pipes. Every prison cell needs some sort of facility for disposing of human waste. The men at work nearby (who regarded me with a mixture of disgust and awe for having supposedly committed rape so young) used to share their lunches with me and then relieve themselves right in front of me without batting an eyelash, while I was still eating. Also, they would dispose of cigarette butts, the paper bags they brought their lunches in, things like that. Sometimes they would drag over a cat carcass or a bug-infested cushion and flush it away. Kittens could fit in whole, and the mother cat could be managed either by hammering the body to bits or by severing it in two. It was doubtless constructed in such a way as to take advantage of different water levels underground— but why and how it generated such tremendous pressure I never understood. Despite its mystery, it was in fact all-powerful, capable of washing anything away.

"If you say so. But I wish you'd put a screen around it, anyway," said the shill. Moving on ahead, he laid a hand on the banister of the steps leading up to the bridge.

"Watch out!" I yelled, pulling away from the woman's arm. I grabbed the shill's shirt and hauled him back. "Please don't go anywhere or touch anything without first checking with me. I *told* you there are booby traps everyplace."

As I spoke, skyrockets went off at the top of the stairs, exploding as they hit the floor, and sending out a cloud of orange smoke.

"What in hell was *that*?" The shill's voice was shrill and unnerved. The woman made a sound like a whistling tea-kettle.

"I'd say you've gone a little overboard." The insect dealer spoke slowly and decisively. "That's going too far. Sheer paranoia." He signaled me with his eyes all the while he spoke. I couldn't get what he had in mind, but he was apparently seeking some sort of carte blanche.

"Relax. Registered crew members will be informed of all

booby traps aboard the ship. If necessary, I can turn off the power as a safety precaution."

I turned around, intending to offer the woman my shoulder again—only to find that the insect dealer had swiftly stepped forward and wrapped his arm around her. She was compliant, showing no signs of resisting. The shill looked away with a faint smile. That was a dirty trick. But *I* was the only one who had the right to put a compress on her ankle.

THE WATERY TASTE OF DISAPPOINTMENT

GROWS AS FAMILIAR

AS A PAIR OF OLD SHOES

I T W A S a steep stone staircase, six and a half feet wide, with twenty-three steps in all. The banister was a square-cut log of cryptomeria. At the top, on the right, was a stone pillar some thirty inches square, and in the back a parapet twenty inches high. The bridge (also known as the forward observation deck—my quarters) formed an elongated diamond some 235 square feet in area. The walls were open, balcony style. Living here alone with my imaginary crew, I had taken pleasure in the uninterrupted view, and in the sense of spaciousness (besides, I had foolproof measures in place to guard against surprise attack). But community life, it now struck me, would necessitate the acquisition of heavy curtains.

I led the way, followed by the girl on the insect dealer's arm, with the shill bringing up the rear.

"What a mess!" exclaimed the insect dealer, his voice an unconvincing shriek of dismay. "A junkman's backyard has nothing on this."

He needn't have said anything; I was quite aware of the room's shocking state. I had not planned on bringing anyone here for some time yet, and so everything was in the same topsy-turvy order as my own brain cells, scarcely fit to withstand the cold scrutiny of outsiders. I gnashed my teeth to think that if only I had known they were coming, I could have straightened things up and made the place more presentable. Both the TV and the stereo were fairly new models, but the effect this might have had was lost.

"Considering how messy things are, though," I said defensively, "you'll notice there's very little dust. The square box at the head of the stairs is a dust-collecting machine that I invented. It works pretty well."

"That *you* invented, you say?" the shill said mockingly, looking from me to the box and back again. It was a plastic box approximately twenty by twenty by eight inches; a fluffy covering of dust made it appear to be wrapped in old felt.

"Instead of an ordinary filter system, I used the adsorption power of static electricity."

"Oh, yeah?" The shill's voice picked up with interest. Perhaps he was a more reasonable fellow than I had given him credit for being. "A dust remover using static electricity? That's a new one on me."

"It *is* new; I thought it up."

"It makes good sense, theoretically." He squatted down in front of the machine, while I ran over to the chaise longue shoved against the wall and swept off a motley pile of old newspapers and magazines to make room for the girl.

"Never mind that. Get a load of this room, will you?" The insect dealer groaned, his teeth clenched, as he kicked three bananas and a bag of peanuts under the table. "Looks like a cross between a pawnshop and a den of thieves."

Supported by the insect dealer, the girl sat down on the chaise longue, holding one leg straight out before her. Still with his arm around her, the insect dealer sat down too, snuggling close against her. He bounced playfully on the old springs, then gave his own face a slap and muttered, "Shame on you. Behave yourself."

The shill, still squatting in front of the dust collector, paid no attention. "Is all this stuff on top dust?" he asked. "Pretty clever. You know something? You're a lot brainier than you look."

I took no offense. "Well, after all, it's not as if your brain gets fat."

"It's making a noise. Is something rotating inside?"

"To ensure uniform contact with the air, I have it set to rotate five times a minute, while the wool and nylon brushes inside turn in the opposite direction at ten times that speed. The friction creates static electricity. I set it right at the point where air currents intersect. Seems to work all right, as far as I can tell."

"I suppose you've already applied for a patent."

"Why would I want to do that?"

"No ambition?" He wiped the corner of his mouth dry with the palm of his hand. "Don't throw away your talents. Remember that sale at the department store today? An item like this could have gone over big. Right, Komono?"

"Yes, sir—the captain here is a great man, all right."

His answer came too readily. His glasses had fogged over, obscuring his expression, but he obviously had no real interest in the dust collector. Was this some sort of dodge, to put the shill off guard? People lacking in curiosity are said to be unfeeling. Had his original air of introspection been a deliberate act, just a way of getting himself aboard the ship? It wouldn't do to expect a lot of him as my bodyguard, and wind up paying for it in the end. Meanwhile, a few amendments seemed in order on my impressions of the shill. Generally, it's money and material goods that win society's respect, while intangible assets like inventiveness and resourcefulness get short shrift. After all the interest I'd shown in his eupcaccia, the insect dealer went on treating me like some kind of kook.

Come to think of it, the rest of the eupcaccias were still out in the jeep. I'd have to remember to bring them in later.

The girl began swaying, probably from the effort of holding her leg up in midair. The insect dealer made a move to get up, planning evidently to go over and support her leg himself. He was mistaken if he thought I was going to let such a prize go to him. I planted myself in front of him, blocking his way at close range. One or the other of us would have to step aside.

"Relax, relax—I wouldn't do anything to offend you." He gave my shoulder a light pat and moved aside. Then, heading toward the back of the room, he walked by the five steel lockers next to the chaise longue, snapping a finger against each one in turn. He stopped in front of two bookcases that intersected at an angle of 120 degrees and looked back at me. Avoiding his eyes, I knelt in front of the girl, a little to one side.

"Does it still hurt?"

"Naturally."

She clasped her hands under her knee and pulled her arms back, lifting her leg so that her artificial leather skirt peeled back to the top of the thigh. Fine soft hair covered flesh even rounder and richer than I had imagined. I pulled out a first-aid kit from underneath the chaise longue. The room might look chaotic, but it had a certain orderliness of its own: things were strewn in concentric circles around the chaise longue in order of usefulness, distance being in inverse proportion to necessity or frequency of use.

"Hold out your leg straight, and relax," I said, and brought my two palms up to the calf of her leg. She let out an exaggerated scream.

"Stop it! That tickles!"

"Don't scare me like that. I'm just trying to examine you."

The shill glanced our way. "Examine, huh. That's a good one." Slowly he stood up in front of the dust collector and swallowed, Adam's apple bobbing. Setting both hands on the end of the desk-table that took up half the available space, he leaned forward slightly in a pose of unmistakable menace. "If you're going to give first aid, just keep it cold. Make a cold compress out of a wet towel, and wrap a bandage around it. That's all."

"Wrong." Rubbing the cover of a large book he had taken from the bookcase, the insect dealer shook his big head. "Not cold. You've got to use a *hot* compress."

"Are you crazy? Everybody knows you pack a sprain in ice." The shill was adamant.

"No, it's heat you want. Hot compresses are the best." The insect dealer was not about to give ground, either.

Let them fight it out. In the meantime I had a clear field. It was a golden chance—one I had no intention of wasting. Without the least hesitation, I slid my hands confidently along the curve of her calf, and this time she made no sound. I had to act as if I knew what I was doing; a gingerly approach would only backfire.

"Leave it to me," I said, hands now firmly in place, as I savored the sensation of her flesh against mine. "I learned all about it when I was a firefighter. You chill a fracture, but you apply heat to a sprain."

The girl's finger touched the back of my hand. I thought she was going to push me away, but that didn't seem to be her aim. Never leaving my hand, her finger began to crawl along it like a wingless insect. Now it was *my* turn to feel ticklish. But it was a ticklishness I could happily endure.

"Why do they take X-rays at a hospital?" she asked.

"What do you mean?"

"It's because otherwise they can't be sure if the bone's broken or not, right?"

"I guess so."

"Then isn't this just a waste of time?"

The question was a heavy blow. The shill laughed, spraying saliva from between his teeth like an atomizer. The insect dealer shut his book with a bang.

"Tell me," he said, "what made you become a firefighter, of all things?"

"Nothing special. You know, when you're a kid you dream about what you want to be when you grow up. I wanted to be a fireman, that's all."

All three of them burst out laughing. "All right, what were *you* doing in the Self-Defense Forces, of all things?" I countered.

Instead of answering, he took off his glasses and wiped them on his shirttail. "My glasses are fogged up all the time. It must really be humid in here."

I stayed serene. The reason was that casually, secretly, the girl's fingers were rubbing the back of my hand in rhythmic circles.

"It's humid, but it feels comfortable, doesn't it?" she said. "As if a cooler were on."

Fortunately, her hands were shadowed by my body, so that neither the shill nor the insect dealer seemed aware of what she was doing. I hadn't known that secret pleasures could be so exciting. Warm air blew into my ear, and emerged from my nostril. My blood pressure must be zooming. What I could not comprehend was the meaning of the signal coming through her fingers. Was she uncommonly sympathetic, or had the shill merely conditioned her to flirt with whoever was at hand?

"Now that you mention it, it *is* cool. I'm dry as a bone." The shill put a hand under his shirt and rapped his chest several times.

"But if it's humid all year round, the air gets full of air mites. Terrible for your respiratory organs." The insect dealer threw in a cavil in his know-it-all tone of voice.

"Air mites? That's a good one. Typical," said the shill.

"I'm not making it up. Don't you read the paper?" He held out a book horizontally, making it swim like a fish. "They're one-hundredth of an inch across, like microscopic jellyfish; look in any encyclopedia. They float in the air and feed on dust particles. They'll reproduce in your lungs and bring on a nasty inflammation."

Paying no attention to this exchange, the shill skirted the table and peered down into the hold over the parapet opposite the chaise longue.

"What's inside those storage drums down there?" he asked. "I've been meaning to ask ever since I got here."

"Five are full of drinking water." My voice was thick, as if spread with glue. The girl's continued massaging of the back of my hand had swollen the mucous membranes of my throat. "In an emergency, there's got to be plenty of water, right?"

"This place is swimming in water. Look at this book—you could practically wring it out." The insect dealer held the spine of the book at either end and twisted it; the cover came off and the contents fell to the floor. "Oops, sorry. Looks like an interesting book—*A Manual for Self-Sufficiency*, it's called. Whoever wrote it must be a real nut, to worry about self-sufficiency in this day and age. Say, this is a library book, isn't it? Aren't you going to take it back?"

I had no obligation to answer. I was on the verge of remembering something far more important. Uses for bundles

of printed paper, old newspapers, old magazines . . . That
was it—a cast. Until a plaster cast was available, you could
use them as temporary substitutes, to immobilize an injured
joint.

"You know, I like it here," announced the shill, leaning
slightly forward to seat himself on the parapet. He continued
in a loud and enthusiastic voice. "To be honest, at first I just
wanted a look at the place, out of sheer curiosity. But this is
great! Absolutely fascinating. Who cares about a little
humidity? High humidity is typical of underground space;
all you have to do is think of some way to put it to use.
Having the winters warm and the summers cool, with a fixed
temperature year round, could be extremely useful, it seems
to me. Just to take an obvious example, it's perfect for
storing vegetables or grain. Or maybe unhulled rice and
seeds would be better. The price is high, and there's a stable
demand. . . ."

Too pedestrian. It was like seeing a diamond in a king's
crown and associating it with mere glass-cutting. This sort of
man could become a great nuisance. It struck me now that
the noncommittal insect dealer was the safer of the two.

"Nobody tells *me* what to do." Numbness in my leg blunted
my tone. I raised my eyebrows, tightened my grip on the
girl's calf, and said, "For now, anyway, let's make a cast.
Whether it's a fracture or a sprain, the most important thing
is to keep the injured area immobile."

"That's all right for now, but what happens after that?"
he said.

The girl's calf twitched slightly. Without hesitation, the
insect dealer came butting in.

"It's all settled, isn't it? I'll climb down with her on my
back." He put a cigarette in his mouth, then returned it to
the pack unlit. "You two came down here from the highway,

but the real way in is along the shore. There's a jeep waiting outside, so relax and let me take care of things. I'll just have a cup of coffee before we go."

"Takes you a while to catch on, doesn't it? You're a bit slow—like an old fluorescent light." The shill dragged out his words for greater effect. "This place is so top-secret we can't even call an ambulance, right? If I were the captain, I can tell you *I* wouldn't want to grant any shore leaves, either, not unless it was to a trusty who had really proved himself."

"You stay here as hostage, then," the insect dealer said easily, with a wink at me, seeking my approval.

Taken by surprise, I was unable to decide quickly whether his suggestion would work to my advantage or not. If *she* were the hostage, it would be a different matter; but was there any conceivable advantage in being left alone with the shill? She might disappear, stuck fast to the insect dealer's back, and never return.

"You'd like that, wouldn't you?" The shill sucked in his saliva with an offensive sound. "Just look at the captain's face. Talk about black looks . . ."

"Shall we be off?" Unperturbed, the insect dealer addressed the girl across my shoulder. It might have been the angle, but all of him—not just the dome of his head—looked a size bigger than normal. "Captain, will you see us out to the jeep? I can't handle those dogs alone."

"Dogs? What dogs?" The girl gave my hand a light pinch.

"A pack of hungry strays. We took our lives in our hands getting in here. There must be five or six really ferocious ones. But there's nothing to worry about: the captain here does a great imitation of a dog's howl, and the moment they hear that they calm right down."

My hand, covered with sweat, felt as obscene as if it had been coated with lubricant. The insect dealer was standing now where he could see our hands, but he said nothing. Was he intentionally overlooking it? In that case, his request that I see them out to the jeep took on a deeper significance: I would be one of those to leave rather than stay, and my wish to see the shill excluded would be brilliantly fulfilled. It was an ingenious idea. Once the padlock was locked from the outside, the shill would never again set foot aboveground. How long he could stay alive would depend on when, and whether, he found the provisions. If he never did, then he would certainly die in a matter of weeks. Even if he did find provisions, he would probably fall in one of the anti-invader traps and be fatally injured. I could dispose of the body single-handed. Chopped in pieces and flushed down that high-pressure toilet, it would be gone without a trace in a matter of minutes.

Perhaps I should trust the insect dealer, after all. It was like facing a broken traffic signal that blinked red, then green, then red, then green, over and over. I hesitated, unable to decide whether to step on the brake or the accelerator.

"First let me get that cast on," I said, and reached out for the pages of the *Manual for Self-Sufficiency*, which lay strewn across the floor. The floor spun and I toppled over. My leg had fallen asleep from spending such a long time in an unaccustomed position. The girl, despite her supposed injury, dodged and sprang to her feet. The shill exploded into laughter with the suddenness of a cork popping off a bottle of champagne. The water cannon on the department store rooftop, which hadn't attracted a single buyer, would probably fire its projectile with a similar noise, I thought.

"All right, miss, you can quit acting now." The shill snapped his fingers and jumped nimbly from the parapet to the floor. "That's enough. Time to take a break."

"You mean she was faking?" Slowly the insect dealer planted his feet wide apart, exuding menace. I remained surprisingly calm. Things never go the way you plan them, except in fantasies. The watery taste of disappointment was as familiar as a pair of old shoes.

"You knew it all along. Stop bullshitting," replied the shill, wiping the corner of his mouth with a fingertip.

Feeling began returning to my leg, with such discomfort that I could not have borne the touch of a fly's wing.

"Now this is going too far." Looking grim, the insect dealer removed his glasses, slumped forward, and rubbed the area between his brows. "We have an agreement with the captain here. You can't get away with this."

Not to be outdone, the shill pressed his elbows tightly against his sides, crouched over, and lowered his head. Except for their tense breathing, it was as if each had withdrawn inside his own shell, ignoring the other. Wild animals feign the same indifference as they sharpen their claws, waiting for a chance to pounce.

"You're going to have to throw me out, you know."

"I know."

"Pretty sure of yourself."

The insect dealer folded his glasses and dropped them in his pocket. The shill stuck the fingers of his right hand in his pants pocket. Did he have a concealed knife? They stood twelve feet apart, with the corner of the table between them.

The girl stepped on my foot and whispered, "Do you suppose it's still raining outside?"

In that taut atmosphere, her whisper stood out like a piece of dirt in the eye. The men's excitement ended abruptly. The insect dealer put a fist to his mouth and coughed, while the shill went on clicking his tongue.

"The walls are thick and there are no windows, so for both weather and time we have to rely on instruments." I switched on the monitor sitting on the middle shelf of the bookcase between the couch and the locker. Electric signals from the outdoor sensor were translated by computer into symbols that flashed on the screen. "Looks like the rain is over. Wind velocity is thirteen point eight feet per hour, coming out of the southwest."

"You're really something, Captain." The shill's gaze swept me boldly up and down.

"Humidity index is eighty-two. Air pressure's still low and falling."

"*That's* why my head feels so heavy," the girl said, sweeping the hair off her forehead. "Anyone else want a cup of coffee?"

"Not a bad idea. Take the bad taste out of our mouths." The insect dealer relaxed a bit.

"Everything you do, Komono, is so phony it leaves a bad taste in the mouth," said the shill. To the girl he said, "To celebrate your recovery, miss, how about fixing us all a cup of coffee?" His motive was transparent: by having her help out, he meant to settle the issue of whether they stayed or went, by means of a fait accompli. "Captain, would you mind showing her where the coffee and everything is?"

"Never mind, I'll get it myself," I said.

The girl glanced at the shill to ascertain what he wanted her to do. He urged her on with brisk waves of his hand, as if chasing a fly.

"Let me do it," she said, her voice suddenly animated as if in amends for malingering. "I make a mean cup of coffee."

"Yes, but it's an electric coffeemaker, so it comes out the same no matter who does it," I said. I too had an ulterior motive: this was it, my chance to be alone with her. "Why don't you help me wash up some cups instead? All that sort of thing I do downstairs, by the toilet. Cooking and laundry too. I don't use the toilet water, you understand—there's a sink built into the wall, with its own faucet. The coffee-maker only makes three cups. We'll just have to brew it a little stronger, and then add hot water."

She smoothed her skirt and led the way, motioning for me to follow.

"I don't like violence." The insect dealer stood aside, taking a *kamaboko* stick from a pouch on his belt and offering it to me as I went by. "Want one? In the confusion, I forgot all about them. Coffee on an empty stomach is bad for the system, you know. Upsets the nerves, and it can make you constipated too."

I took four and dashed after the girl, dragging the leg that was still partially numb. Three steps down, we entered the shadow of a pillar, out of sight of the bridge. The shill's voice sounded.

"What a crazy machine. What the heck is this for, sharpening rats' teeth?"

"It's a small precision machine tool," replied the insect dealer, his mouth stuffed with *kamaboko*. "You know, I've always wanted to play with one of these."

9

BACK TO THE POT

"**R E A L L Y** , the more you look at this toilet, the stranger it is. . . ." The girl spoke in a nasal whisper that sounded almost deliberately provocative.

I had to agree with her about the toilet, all right. Squatting over it, you were totally unprotected, longing desperately for a cover behind, or just for some way to tell front from back. In a place as vast as this old quarry, the anus developed rejection symptoms even *with* a wall behind you. When I first started living here, constipation was my bane. I tried all kinds of laxatives, to no avail. After a week my ears were ringing; by the tenth day my vision was clouding over.

I tried enemas, but that only made it worse: they gave me the urge to go, and that's all. My sphincter remained stubbornly corked. To feel an intense urge to evacuate—a violent one, I should say, as in intestinal catarrh—and to be incapable of doing anything about it is an excruciating form of suffering that must be experienced to be believed.

At the hospital they brushed it off lightly: "If you feel like moving your bowels, that only proves you have a light case, so don't rush yourself. Just keep sitting on the toilet." They needn't have told me *that*; the moment I got off I would feel the summons of nature, and tear straight back again. For two whole days I sat there leafing through the *Family Medical Book*, convinced that death was imminent.

The *Family Medical Book* was written for laymen, as the title suggests, but in the end it provided the solution. At least it gave better advice than the doctors. Mention constipation and generally they'll ascribe it to one of two causes: desiccation and hardening of the stool, or poor muscle tone. Intestinal malfunction, in short. But in the *Family Medical Book*, as an example of intestinal hyperfunction the authors mention difficulty in evacuation due to a spastic rectum—a type of constipation not even listed in the constipation section. I felt a flash of light.

Despite my large bulk, I am of surprisingly nervous temperament, and two or three times a year (when I must meet with someone unpleasant, such as my biological father, Inototsu, or when I'm called to traffic court for a violation), I come down with diarrhea. When the symptoms worsen I am attacked by severe pain, as if my bowels were being twisted and wrung. If this constipation had resulted from an especially acute case of diarrhea, I reasoned, then it might pay to try my regular medicine. (In fact, it's a drug to relieve menstrual cramps, but I find it wonderfully effective for an irritable colon.) The results were dramatic: in minutes, an enormous movement erupted, leaving only a delightful sense of hollowness. Thinking he might be interested, I did mention this to the doctor, but his only reaction was a look of faint annoyance.

That time of suffering did, however, enable me to grow accustomed to the vastness of the quarry. Besides losing my fear of constipation, I became able to straddle the toilet forward, backward, or sideways, from any angle. I even became relaxed enough to contemplate other uses for the thing. More and more frequently, I used it for garbage disposal.

Soon I was using the sink and counter to prepare food. Waiting for the contents of a pan to heat, I could seat myself on the toilet in comfort. Even while eating my meals and drinking my coffee, I had no need to go elsewhere. I could do my aerial-photography traveling, or go over the results of the day's surveying, right while drinking coffee on the pot. And so the toilet came gradually to occupy a central place in my life. Metaphorically speaking, I was beginning to change into a eupcaccia.

The galley was a hollow in the wall, about a meter off the floor; inside, it had been polished to a blue, enamel-like finish that deserved to be set off by a loving cup, if I'd had such a thing. Once, on the ceiling there, I found some bumps that had been puttied over. Prying with a knife, I uncovered a lead pipe whose end was capped. When I unscrewed the cap, water came gushing out. I installed a faucet, electric wiring and a socket. Then I added a small refrigerator and a fluorescent light, a large electric stove, a kitchen cabinet, and a foldout counter. When I wasn't using it, I kept the area hidden behind accordion curtains. Finally I added a high enclosed shelf you reached by standing on the toilet; rubber sealing made it airtight. Up there is where I keep my camera equipment and travel necessities (i.e., the aerial photos), surveying equipment and so on, protected by drying agents. My safety precautions are airtight too: I set it up so that if you touch the door handle without first flicking a hidden switch, an electric shock will burn your fingers, and tear gas will go off in your face. The spot right next to the camera equipment would be a good place to keep the eupcaccias.

I opened the curtain, which made the lights go on.

"How pretty!" she exclaimed. "It's like marble."

"Actually it's something called hydrous shale; as long as it stays moist, it has a nice shine. It's probably an underwater stone. The only trouble with it is that when it dries out, it gets covered with fine powder. After four or five years, buildings decorated with it look as if they've been dusted with confectioner's sugar. In fact, that probably explains why the quarry closed down."

"Hmm," she said. "It certainly lacks a woman's touch." She looked at five days' worth of dirty dishes piled in the sink and laughed.

"Of course it does. What else did you expect?"

"Want me to wash these up for you?"

"That's all right, I always do it once a week, without fail." I stuck one of the *kamaboko* from the insect dealer in my mouth, and gave another to her. "They're not chilled, but we just bought them a little while ago, so I'm sure they're all right."

"Thank you." Like thin rubber, the girl's lips expanded and contracted, following the shape of the *kamaboko*. "These are high in protein and low in fat, so they're very good for you," she said.

"Oh, I'm incorrigible. I've given up." Talking openly about my weaknesses, I figured, would make me come across as a frank and likable type. "But this is mostly monosodium gluta-mate held together with starch. Glutamic acid soda is sodium chloride, so it could be bad for your blood pressure."

"Can you hear something? Like dogs barking?" the girl said.

"You can hear anything here if you try hard enough," I answered. "This place is so full of tunnels and caves, it's like being in the middle of a gigantic trumpet."

"It's like one of those foreign movies on TV. There's al-ways a house—a big stone building with an iron fence, right? —and a big yard and a watchdog. If this *were* a movie, the story would just be getting under way. All we need is some music."

"You're different," I told her.

"How?"

"I mean different in a nice way. Interesting."

"Don't tease me. *He's* forever groaning about me—says I have holes in my head."

"He's disgusting."

"Maybe that's why he is the way he is—because he knows people don't like him."

"What do you mean, 'the way he is'?"

"How many cups' worth of grounds shall I put in?"

"Five, if you like it strong." Perhaps because of the peculiar nature of where we were, sandwiched between the kitchen sink and the toilet, I began to feel an excitement attended by visual stricture, like that of a child playing in closets. "I'll tell you what I don't like about him. It's his attitude toward you—he's so damned overbearing."

"I know, but he's sick, so what can I do?"

"Sick? What's the matter with him?"

"Cancer."

Mentally I reviewed my impressions of the shill, as if starting again at page one of a book I'd read partway. "What kind of cancer?"

"Bone marrow. Maybe I shouldn't have said anything. It's evidently a kind of leukemia. Don't tell anyone, okay? He doesn't even know about it yet himself."

"Is it serious?"

"Isn't cancer always? They give him six months to live."

"Tell me the truth. What's your relationship to him?"

"It's hard to say exactly."

"Why does he call you 'young lady'? Isn't that a bit formal?"

"Probably he does it to excite people's imaginations."

"More fishing?"

"I don't know; maybe."

"But the only ones to be told the truth about a cancer patient's condition are the next of kin. Isn't that so?" I felt a rising irritation that was totally at odds with the thrill of being alone with her like two children snuggled in a closet.

Instead of answering, she looked up and waved. The shill and the insect dealer were standing side by side, elbows on the bridge parapet, munching on *kamaboko* and looking down at us.

"You want your coffee up there?" she asked.

"Nah, we'll come on down." The insect dealer placed his hands on the small of his back and stretched. "Less trouble that way, and easier to clean up."

"No, let's have it up here." Waving both hands, the shill disappeared in the recesses of the bridge, then rounded the pillar and came down the stairs. "But first I've got to use the john."

"You can't—me first!" the girl exclaimed, thrusting at him a tray piled with four clean cups, no two alike. "I'll bring the coffee up as soon as the water boils."

What could we say? Wordlessly the shill took the tray and withdrew, and I followed. Together we laid the cups out near one corner of the table. The insect dealer called down to her over the parapet:

"Got anything to eat down there?"

Her voice came echoing back, colored by the reverberation. "Hey! No peeking." I detected a note of playfulness that I found distasteful. A half-smile lingering on the corner of his mouth, the insect dealer turned away with visible regret.

"Let's eat, Captain," he said. "I can't talk on an empty stomach."

I was hungry too. The problem as I saw it was to decide what *kind* of meal we should have; it might well have a profound impact on our future relationships. Broadly speak-

ing, there were three possibilities: the four of us could share
a simple meal of instant noodles; we could sit down to a
slightly more substantial meal, in a spirit of welcome to the
new crew (in that case, we would need more booze); or I
could take them all to the food storehouse, where they could
each pick out what they wanted, at their own expense. In
that case, everybody would be on their own. Personally, I
favored the last option, but seeing that living quarters had
not yet been formally assigned, it might set some unfortunate
precedents. An enjoyable welcome party might serve as an
effective social lubricant for all the various relationships
among us. If there was some guarantee I could talk to the
girl without worrying constantly about the shill, I certainly
had no objection to opening a bottle or two of sake. Right
now, in order to settle my mind, I needed time for another
cup of coffee.

"Is this where you sleep, Captain?" asked the shill, tapping
an armrest of the chaise longue.

"Yes—why?"

"What about us? Where do we sack out?"

"For now, anyplace. I have sleeping bags for everybody."

"Well, in that case, you'll have to excuse me for a while.
Sorry," said the shill.

With people switching back and forth all the time this
way, how could I formulate any plan? I decided to stop
worrying about the dinner menu.

"Nothing to be sorry about. Do as you please," I said.

"I can't help it," the shill said, explaining, "I can't get to
sleep without my own pillow. Always carry it with me on
trips."

"That's ridiculous."

"No, it isn't." The insect dealer was stuck to the edge of
the chaise longue like a half-dried squid. "It doesn't have to

be a particularly soft one, or anything. But there *are* people with attachments to a certain pillow. It must be the smell of their own hair oils, absorbed into the pillow."

"Pillows pick up smells, all right, that's for sure," agreed the shill. "Ever stay in a cheap hotel somewhere in the sticks? It's enough to make you gag."

"Of all the senses, they say the sense of smell is the most primitive," said the insect dealer.

"Other people's smells may be unbearable, but your own never are," said the shill. "Everyone has a certain affection for their own body odors."

"That's true," said the insect dealer. "Ever see somebody scratch his dandruff, and then sniff the dirt under his nails?"

"Please, would you both just be quiet?" I was fed up. I certainly had never expected life with a crew to be so bothersome. "I went a long time without hearing any human voices here," I went on. "Now it's a strain on my nerves."

Would the old quiet never return? This arrangement was scarcely worth the trouble. Did any of them have the slightest idea of the enormous price I was paying?

We heard a sudden gush of water. The girl had begun to urinate. I hadn't expected the noise to carry so well. It took little effort to imagine the precise amount and pressure of liquid released. It sounded as close as a cricket would have sounded, chirping under the chaise longue. Too late, I regretted having asked them to be silent. All three of us pulled at our ears, sucked air through our molars, and pretended not to hear. The sound continued unendingly, until I could no longer endure it.

"Anytime people begin living together, there have got to be some rules." My words serving as a substitute for ear-plugs, I jabbered on at a speed even I found offensive to the ear. "And rules aren't rules unless they're kept. And in order for them to be kept, they must be based on the premise of a shared set of fundamental values. What I mean to say is that only people who fully appreciate the utility value of this old quarry can comprehend its true worth. I'm not being overly fussy, I can assure you."

The insect dealer followed up my words swiftly in a gravelly voice. "That's right. Just having this much space at your disposal is worth an incredible sum. After all, Japan is a tiny country suffering from absolute space deficiency."

Was that big skull of his stuffed with bean curd instead of brains, or did he talk like an asshole on purpose?

"Don't get me wrong," said the shill. "It's not only the pillow I'm worried about." There must have been something catching about the insect dealer's rapid-fire, hoarse way of talking, for now the shill rattled on in the same way. "There are some pills I've been taking, and a book I'm halfway through—after all, we've got to get our things and move in, don't we? But I won't come back empty-handed, Captain. Will you let me sell some of those passkeys for you? I'll bring you back some absolutely first-rate people. The kind that think fast and are flexible. This cave has all sorts of possibilities, after all. Right off the top of my head I can think of farm-produce storage, lacquerware factories (they need plenty of moisture), mushroom cultivation, the brewing industry . . . you name it."

"Haven't you got the message yet?" I said. "I don't *want* people finding out about this place."

"I know. What you're really after is a way to work without paying taxes, am I right? Leave it to me, I'm an expert. For instance, you could form a film studio to make porn videos. They say that *really* rakes it in. Or you might consider running an underground hotel as a hideout for escaped criminals. You wouldn't have to spend much on facilities, and you could charge as much as you liked. Even better would be intensive-care rooms for mental hospitals. A mental hospital is really a kind of prison for lifers, so what with local citizens' protests and one thing and another, finding somewhere to build can be a problem. But once you have that, you've got the goose that lays the golden egg. Patients in lifetime isolation wards."

The man was totally uncomprehending. But how could I explain the need for an ark to a cancer victim with only six months to live? Even if he had no inkling of his condition, persuading him would be a vain effort, one I could not bring myself to make. Yet I couldn't very well let him do as he pleased, either. I was saddled with one heck of a nuisance.

Finally the trickle of water stopped, and the roar of the flushing toilet echoed in the air.

"No need to make a special trip," I said. "The weather's bad. . . . Go ahead and let me know if there's anything you need, and I'll do my best to get it or approximate it."

"Right, you can always make do for a pillow." As if to say he had everything figured out, the insect dealer began drumming his fingers on the edge of the cup he had chosen, a look of sangfroid on his face. "Even if it's borrowed, if you wrap it in a dirty undershirt of your own it comes to the same thing, doesn't it?"

10

P E R H A P S because of having had to wait to go to the toilet, the shill descended the stairs in a sort of fox-trot, his knees pressed together.

"I'm hungry," murmured the insect dealer, eyes turned vaguely on the spot just vacated by the shill. "By the way, Captain," he went on, "how do you manage to support yourself here?"

I could well understand the motive of his question. His was an entirely natural curiosity: the world over, a man's source of income is the measure of his worth. Even so, I had no obligation to reply, and no intention of doing so, either. As a matter of fact, the electricity was all stolen, as were most of the fittings, which came from the city hall. There was no law that said I had to let him know my weakest points. I pretended not to hear.

Light footsteps approached, as those of the shill faded away; there remained less than ten seconds, I calculated, before she set foot on the top stair.

"Maybe I shouldn't have forced him to stay."

"Don't worry about it. You're the captain. Just follow your instincts."

"I heard he's got cancer."

"No!"

"She told me. Keep it quiet—he doesn't know."

"Kind of ironic—the guy's so much like a cancer himself."

We laughed loudly and freely in a burst of mutual understanding. Then the girl appeared, coffeepot in hand. I was
unable to look her square in the face. The echo of that gush,
still fresh in my ears, made me picture not her face but the
outlet for urine.

She joined easily in our laughter, then announced gaily,
"Guess what I found out! The refrigerator's stuffed full of
canned beer!"

"For shame," scolded the insect dealer, pulling on the
armrests of the chaise longue to bring his body forward.
"You're forgetting yourself, miss. You can't let yourself come
that far under the president's influence."

Intuitively I sensed he was referring to the shill.

"President?" I queried. "Of what? Who?"

"You needn't sound so impressed," said the insect dealer.
"These days everybody and his brother is a company president. The neighborhood junkman walks around with a
namecard that says 'President of Eastern Reclamation, Inc.' "

"Still, what kind of a company is it?"

The girl smiled, lips open and teeth closed. "It's called
Saisai."

"What does that mean?"

"It's written with the characters for 'hold'—as in a function
or event—and 'festival.' "

"Peculiar sort of name."

"He represents festival stall owners." The insect dealer
waved his right hand as if flicking away imaginary dust, and
adjusted his glasses with his left. To the woman he said,
"Anyway, don't forget that without the captain's permission
you're not entitled to a glass of water, let alone a can of beer.

First you go and put on some phony act about a fractured ankle, now this. Try to show a little more sense."

His preachy tone of voice was far phonier than her act had been. She nodded, and for no reason I found myself feeling abashed.

"Don't exaggerate," I said. "All I've been saying is there's a need for caution about boarding procedures. The beer doesn't worry me."

A fat lot it didn't. I like to drink my beer all alone. I'm a beer hog—a beeraholic, in fact, who breaks into a sweat at just the sound of the word. What's more, I like my beer with a little chocolate on the side. Every day, once a day, I sip a leisurely can of beer and munch on chocolates. It is a time of supreme piggish delight, a time I could share with no one.

"You don't mind, really?" Behind their thick concave lenses, the insect dealer's questioning eyes widened in happy excitement. "Coffee before a meal is bad for the stomach, anyway. Shall we presume on the captain's generosity this once? Let's celebrate our embarkation—that's as good an excuse as any."

It was a sensation I'd often experienced in dreams—losing my footing on a hill of garbage. In trying to recover lost ground, I made yet another concession.

"Very well, let's drink to that," I said. "But maybe beer alone isn't enough." I could hardly suggest chocolate as an accompaniment—although when you try it with an open mind, the hops and cacao blend together in a bitter harmony that I find irresistible. "How about some canned sardines?"

"Excellent," said the insect dealer. "They're very good for you. Sardines have lots of a nutrient called prostaglandin, which makes them effective against all kinds of diseases. Hardening of the arteries, even cancer."

The idiot. What did he have to go and say that for? But then, I was the one who had spilled the beans to him, so what could I say? Luckily, her expression didn't flicker. Turning toward the hold, she called down:

"When you're finished down there, we're having beer and sardines up here."

Not to be outdone, I too called down. "The sardines are in a basket on top of the refrigerator."

No answer. I felt an unpleasant presentiment.

She set the coffeepot on the table and smiled. "So the coffee turned out to be a waste."

"No—I'll have some," I said. "Westerners drink coffee and alcohol together and think nothing of it, I've heard. Somehow it protects the liver."

She poured out a cupful. Still not a sound from the hold. It was time we heard something; since the point of emission is higher in the male than the female, the noise ought to be correspondingly louder.

"Where's the sugar?"

"Let me think." I take both tea and coffee without sugar, so I couldn't recall immediately where I did keep it. I had a feeling it might be in a jar in the back of the refrigerator, where ants wouldn't get into it. It would probably be better to have the shill look for it while I gave instructions. I went around the table, into the interstice where the bookcase and the parapet came together at a sharp angle, and looked down into the hold. The shill was nowhere to be seen.

The meaning of the scene before my eyes temporarily eluded me. It was a clean-cut oblong room, solid stone, with nowhere to hide and nowhere to search. I felt the frustration of someone looking through the viewfinder of a broken stereoscope. I was used to seeing no one there, but how could I get used to not seeing someone who *should* be there?

"Now where did he roam off to?" I muttered.

The girl came around from the other side of the table

and joined me at the parapet. "Is he gone?" she asked. She didn't seem particularly concerned; in fact, she sounded rather intrigued. Not knowing the lack of places to hide would doubtless take away the peculiarity of the situation. Coffee cup in hand, the insect dealer joined us.

"Over there behind the storage drums, in the shadows," he said, slurping his coffee, and called, "All right, let's not be cute. We all know you're not so squeamish you can't go right out in the open there. Come on out."

"They're lined up smack against the wall," I said. "There's no way anybody could squeeze in there."

I realized what had happened. I didn't want to think about it, but I knew where the shill must have gone. From the bridge it was hard to see, but he must have crawled through the passageway cut into the far side of that same wall. Unless he had chopped himself up and flushed himself down the toilet, there was simply no other exit.

The girl called out, her voice trailing off in a long sinuous echo like the rise and fall of waves on a large, shallow strand. "If you want to play hide-and-seek, wait till we decide who's it."

I strained my ears, listening for a scream. He could not possibly get through that passageway on his own. I had set up a trap on the principle of the bow. It was triggered by a line of fishing gut stretched half an inch off the ground, which when touched would release a steel leaf spring. The basic purpose was to keep rats out, but it could easily shatter a person's ankle.

"The bastard—he got away." The insect dealer followed my line of vision and instantly grasped what had happened. He leaned over the parapet, trying to peer down the passageway. "What's down there, at the end of that tunnel?"

Had these been the crew members I'd anticipated for so

long, there would've been no need to ask. That would have
been the first place I'd have shown them: the heart of the
ark, where tunnels branch off three ways, one to each of the
other two holds, and one back here. If each hold were a
residential area, the "heart" was in the best location for communal use, so mentally I always referred to it as the "central
hold" or "work hold." It was my firm intention to interfere
as little as possible in the crew's personal lives, but some
tasks, like the operation of air-purifying equipment or electric generators, required a joint effort. The success or failure
of life aboard the ark hinged on how well people cooperated.
If everyone lived like the eupcaccia, there would be no
problem, since if no one had any urge to expand his or her
territory, there would be no fear of mutual territorial viola-
tions. Letting the shill aboard might have been as fatal a
lapse as if I had overlooked shipworms.

"Machinery." My voice sounded too belligerent. More
graciously, I added, "I'll take you there one of these times."

"What kind of machinery?"

"Machinery for survival, of course."

"Survival of what?" asked the girl, at last seeming to grasp
the situation. Bending her body at a right angle, she rested
her weight on the parapet and leaned forward as far as she
could. Her skirt of artificial leather was stretched to the limit,
revealing her round contours like a second skin. The reality
of those two soft globes right there beside my own hips
seemed more fanciful than my wildest fancies. My brain began to turn red and raw, as if peeling.

"Survival of what?" she repeated. What indeed, I wondered. If only she had asked not "of what," but "why." For if
it was possible for me to go on living near a skirt stretched
this tightly, over this round a pair of hips, then I had no
doubts whatever concerning the meaning of survival. Even

the eupcaccia emerged from its chrysalis in preparation for mating. Emergence is a preparation for rebirth—regeneration—as well as for death. Looking sideways at her round, tight skirt, I thought that perhaps I too was starting to emerge from my cocoon.

"Of course survival for its own sake is meaningless. It's pointless to live a life not worth living." My answer was no answer. The insect dealer then spoke up in my place.

"Don't you ever think about nuclear war or things like that?" he asked her.

"It doesn't interest me. Even on TV, if it's anything about war I change the channel."

"That's a woman for you," said the insect dealer, turning his back to the hold and settling against the parapet until he was at the optimal distance for viewing her hips (about ten inches away). "Women are born without any imagination."

Hardly a sensitive remark. Instinctively I came to her defense. "Look who's talking. You can't stand barking dogs, can you?"

"No, but so what?"

The girl purposely made light of it. "The reason women don't think ahead is because they have to go to the supermarket every day. This coffee is too bitter for me. I don't like it without sugar."

"No?" I said. "But it's better this way if we're going to have beer next, isn't it?"

The insect dealer gulped the remainder of his coffee with a noise like the pump of a dry well, never ceasing his close observation of her rump. Seemingly conscious of his eyes, she waved her hand now and then as if to chase off a pesky fly. But her right-angled posture remained the same, needlessly provocative.

"Let's go downstairs and see what we can see," I said, motioning to her, my real aim being to get her away from the insect dealer. "If he's injured, it'll mean trouble."

"I wouldn't worry," she said. "That man is as sharp as they come. He can catch flies in his bare hands."

"So can I."

"While they're flying."

"I wouldn't be too sure about him," said the insect dealer. He laughed sharply and gave the woman's bottom a slap, making a startlingly loud noise. In monkey colonies, what did they call it? Oh, yes—mounting: the losing monkey sticks out its rear end. Subjugation begins with control of the other's hindquarters. "I wouldn't be surprised if he's already dead. I don't know what sort of trap it was, but if he'd only hurt himself a little, he'd be screaming for help by now."

Despite the liberty the insect dealer took with her bottom, the girl reacted only by twisting away and jerking her head. Had she fallen so easily under his sway? Or was she used to this sort of thing? Perhaps it was not as serious as I'd assumed. I wanted to follow his example, but something held me back.

"I doubt if his life could be in danger," I said, "but it *is* pitch dark in there."

"He took a light," said the insect dealer. "Remember that one hanging from the locker handle—the kind coal miners wear on their heads."

His statements lacked consistency. First he exaggerated the danger the shill was in, then in the next breath he emphasized how safe he was. He was just out to find fault with whatever I said. She sided with him.

"That's right, it's a waste of time worrying about him— he's sharp as a tack," she said, and casually shifted her weight from the left leg to the right; in the process the two globes, still pressed close together, subtly changed shape. The skirt stuck to her bottom, becoming progressively more transparent.

I wasn't seriously concerned about the shill's well-being myself; I only wanted to put a fast stop to this unpleasant collusion between the insect dealer and her. Besides, it was barely possible that he had gotten safely past the trap and entered the work hold. I was unwilling to credit him with as much cunning and dexterity as she, but perhaps something—a rat, say—had tripped the mechanism beforehand.

I could not have people roaming all over the ship, in any case. The air-conditioning system and electrical generator were as yet unfinished, and I couldn't permit anyone to lay hands on them in my absence. I especially did not want him, or anyone, getting into the magazine, where locked in a safe I had five crossbows, seven model guns, and one rifle rebuilt with steel-reinforced barrel and hammer. I had test-fired each one five successive times with no difficulty. I was damned if I'd let the shill get his hands on those.

With the ark in danger of springing a leak, this was no time to loiter. It was essential to go straight below and take defensive steps. But the other two seemed content to stay where they were. After the insect dealer's ritual assertion of supremacy just now, I could not bring myself to go off and entrust the girl to his keeping. The situation called for deportment worthy of a captain, to make them recognize my leadership. What if I went ahead and gave her bottom a resounding slap myself?

"Anyway, let's get going," I said. Taking advantage of the opportunity my words provided, I gave the girl's bottom a slap that was bold in spirit, if less so in reality. The sound effect was poor, but the tactile impression was richly rewarding—the moist, clingy feel of artificial leather, and a heavy warmth that sank deep into my flesh.

The girl straightened up and turned red. She opened

her eyes wide and looked straight at me, whether in fear or embarrassment I could not tell.

"I didn't know you had it in you," said the insect dealer, licking his lips, and reaching past the girl to slap my shoulder. He flashed me a secretive, friendly grin in which I could detect no trace of irony or ridicule. Had it been a success? The insect dealer walked ahead, leading the way. Reality returned. It was as if at last the ship's rudder had begun to work. The day's events had not been a total waste.

AT FIRST GLANCE THE PASSAGEWAY

APPEARS TO BE A MERE CRACK

OR SLIT IN THE SEAM BETWEEN WALLS

A T first glance the passageway appears to be a mere crack or slit rising high in the seam between walls. This is because of its enormous height, over fifty feet in all; actually it is wide enough for a small truck to pass through easily. We were dwarfed as we drew near.

About fifteen feet in, it turned to the right, thus blocking off our light source from the first hold. As we moved on in darkness, the floor began rising. Calling a warning to the others, I halted and stared ahead into the blackness. If the shill was there, the light from his lamp should be visible. Those shadows, light and dark, that moved with my eye-balls—were they mere afterimages, within the eye? I could see nothing else. Had he switched off his lantern, hearing our footsteps? Why? I pushed the second button on the switch control panel hanging from my belt, and fluorescent lights spaced evenly along the walls came sputtering to life. The right-hand wall of the passageway continued on to become the south wall of the work hold. The first hold and the central work hold were linked directly by this passage. The cluster of white pipes along the west wall, like a scale-model factory, was a manually operated air-conditioning system.

"Looks like he found the switch," the insect dealer whispered in my ear. He hadn't caught on that I was operating a remote-control switch. I saw no reason to relieve him of his misapprehension.

The girl took a step forward and called, cupping her hands, "Come on out. Hide-and-seek's over."

"Watch out." I grabbed her arm and pulled her back. Why, I wondered, was her skin so soft? For a while I let my fingers stay as they were, pressed into her flesh. It was the first such change in mental state I had undergone since the bottom-slapping incident. He who controls the woman controls the group. Leering in my imagination like a movie villain, I strained my eyes to see the stone floor a few steps ahead.

The worst situation possible met my gaze. The flat steel spring lay blocking our way like a railway crossing gate. By rights it should have been fastened to the wall, set so that the moment anything or anyone touched the silkworm gut, suspended in a zigzag just off the floor, the latch would release and the spring would mow down its prey. Someone (possibly the shill) had either seen through the device and dismantled it safely, or else fallen into the trap.

"Is that a trap?" She clung to my arm. A most favorable sign. The sound of urinating . . . bottom slapping . . . and now direct contact. At the same time, I found myself still more apprehensive: a sprung trap, and no sign of prey. . . .

"Yes," I responded, "but the spring's been released. Look, the strings on the floor have all gone slack."

"I'll be damned. You're right." The insect dealer crouched over the steel spring and removed his glasses. "These lenses aren't right for my eyes—but wait a minute, where's the victim? If this came down on your leg, you'd sure as hell know it."

"That's right; we didn't hear a scream," said the girl.

"It didn't have to be a person, you know. A rat could have set it off easily," I said.

"Yes, but a rat would get killed, wouldn't it?" said the insect dealer. "Not only is there no dead rat here; the spring is perfectly clean. There's not even any hair on it, let alone bloodstains."

"Then it *was* a person. Somebody stood back at a safe distance and poked it with the end of a stick, or threw a stone at the string. But to do that you'd have to know beforehand that the trap existed. So it's impossible."

"It's possible," the girl said flatly. "He's a master at anticipating people's moves. Cards, mah-jongg . . . you name it."

"Yes, and he's already been hurt, twice." The insect dealer put his hands on the small of his back and stretched. "First the staircase, then the fireworks. But, Captain, it doesn't necessarily have to be the president, does it? Couldn't it be somebody else, like a spy who sneaked aboard when you weren't looking?"

There was no point in discussing hypothetical possibilities. The important thing now was to ascertain the shill's whereabouts.

"Whoever it was, he couldn't have just melted away. He's no snowman," I said, stepping over the steel spring and moving forward.

"He's terrible, running off like this without a word to anyone," the girl responded fretfully. The genuine irritation in her voice seemed to rule out any possibility of collusion.

We entered the work hold. It was the same size as the first hold but seemed smaller, as the length and breadth were equal. The ceiling, however, was high, so glancing up, one had an impression of spaciousness. The pillar thrusting upward directly ahead, near the back wall—or in other words along what was an extension of the right wall of this passageway—was exactly twenty-three feet around. The number of pillars, and their girth, were apparently fixed according to ceiling height. Behind the pillar was a tunnel over three feet across and six and a half feet high, easily overlooked because of the old bicycles piled up nearby as camouflage. There were twenty-eight of them, which I planned someday to turn into a foot-powered electric generator. Catty-corner from the pillar—or from where we were, at the far end of the near left-hand wall—gaped the opening of a second passageway. Rusted rails indicated that this had been a main tunnel when the quarry was still in operation. A third opening was near the ceiling, straight ahead on the left, below which a lift—a sort of vertical conveyor belt—was attached. Excavation work customarily proceeds from high to low, so probably in the beginning this was used to transport excavated stone to the surface. When it became apparent that the layer of high-quality rock extended deeper than was anticipated, they must have dug out the main passageway, to raise efficiency.

"What a mountain of rock! Whoever made off with all this must have earned themselves a pile of dough." As he said this, the insect dealer swung his big head around as if his neck had no vertebrae. "So where do you think our friend went? Where would you look, Captain?"

The lift was over forty feet high—a bit much even for a former Self-Defense Forces member. The secret passage in the shadow of the pillar looked like nothing more than a scrap heap. Our eyes turned as if by agreement to the large tunnel entrance on the left, where the end of the rails could be seen.

"Come on out, will you!" shouted the girl, the echo extending her voice. "You've made enough trouble. Just when we were going to eat, too."

"Remember, he polished off eight of those *kamaboko*

sticks all by himself." The insect dealer lifted his undershirt and began rubbing dirt off the skin on his side.

"Anyway, let's have a look." I led the way down the tunnel. Their footsteps behind me rang out with appalling loudness.

"What's this jiggledy-joggledy thing?" asked the girl, regarding a seesaw-style pump fastened to the wall along the way.

"It's a pump hooked up to the ventilation system. It's set up so that two people working it by hand for four hours a day can purify the air of three holds."

"You've got it all worked out, haven't you?" The insect dealer wiped his finger on his trousers, and laid a hand on the seat of the upper arm of the seesaw. The pump functioned smoothly, operating on the resistance of air inside six-inch-diameter stainless-steel pipes. "Not bad," he said admiringly. "Pretty darned clever, in fact."

"Why doesn't it run on electricity?" the girl cut in with a dissatisfied air.

"When the time comes to use the system, there'll *be* no electricity," I told her.

"Don't waste your time explaining," said the insect dealer. "You can't talk logic to a woman." He raised his right arm, bent at the elbow, and hauled back, aiming for the girl's rear end. She dodged nimbly aside. Kicking the pedal of one of three wheelless bicycles lined up beside the pump, she said boastfully:

"I know what these are. They look like exercise machines, but really they're generators. Right?"

"Yes. They're hooked up to car generators. Of course they function as exercise equipment too; lack of exercise is a perennial problem. . . ."

"One of these would supply about enough electricity for one twelve-watt bulb, and that's it," said the insect dealer, and launched a second attack on her backside. There was the sound of a wet towel falling on the floor. He'd scored a direct hit, in the area of the crease in her buttocks. She emitted a scream that was half wail.

"Eventually I intend to convert all those old bikes in that pile over there. With twenty-eight bikes operating at the same time, charging up the car batteries, there would be enough energy to supply an average day's needs."

Pretending I was going to activate one to show them, I drew closer to the woman and laid a hand on her myself, not to be outdone. It was not so much a slap as a caress: that prolonged the contact by a good five times. Using her hand on the handlebars as a fulcrum, she swung herself around to the other side, bent forward, and giggled. On the other side, the insect dealer was waiting, palm outstretched. It was a game of handball, her bottom the ball.

"In that case, you have to have a fairly large crew." He served.

"Not all *men*, I sincerely hope," she said, reentering my court.

"Of course not; there'll be lots and lots of women too. . . ." Bold now, I took my turn, giving her bottom a good pinch into the bargain.

"That's enough." She squatted down, hands covering her posterior. "If the captain and I got on the same seesaw, it would stop moving, wouldn't it? Please don't get me wrong. . . ."

I couldn't completely fathom what she meant. And yet suddenly my excitement ebbed. She had referred to what bothered me most—the difference in our weights. The insect dealer too seemed to return to himself. Licking the palm of his serving hand with his long tongue, he sighed and glanced up at the ceiling.

"Say," he said, "isn't this a terrible waste, all this electricity?"

How like him—a totally practical view. This hold alone had ninety-six fluorescent lights, plus five halogen lights of five hundred watts each. Not only were the ceilings high, but the blue stone walls were dulled by nicks and scratches from the electric saws, reflecting the available light so poorly that in order for the hold to function as a center of operations, extra intensities of illumination were necessary. If an electric bill came, I could never hope to pay it. But it was too soon to show my hand.

There was a sound of water dripping. The girl started up and exclaimed, "What was that?"

Allowing for some variation according to the weather and the time of day, at intervals of once every thirty minutes to three hours a barrage of water drops fell from the ceiling in the first hold onto the row of storage drums. They made a dry, unwatery noise that sounded as if a chair had overturned, or the bottom had burst in a bag of beans. Since it's impossible to tell what direction the sound is coming from, the imagination swells limitlessly. Without explaining, I turned and headed straight down the second tunnel entrance.

The lights of the operation hold illuminated the rusty rails for another twenty-five feet or so. The lights all shone straight down, so the sheer walls at either side vanished halfway up into darkness, as if stretching all the way to heaven.

"Got some kind of a trap in here too?" asked the insect dealer in an undertone.

"Of course."

"I'm telling you, he really is very agile." She too spoke in an undertone.

"This next one is different." Holding my arms out at shoulder level, I took three steps forward into the dark, guided by the rails, and then slowly I lowered my arms. An alarm bell rang out. The shadow of the insect dealer, which had been following close behind me, suddenly disappeared; he'd tripped on a tie and fallen, crashing into the girl, who let out a scream.

"Quick, turn that damn thing off—it's bad for my heart." Seated where he had fallen, the insect dealer covered both ears with his hands.

The left side of the seventh tie from the front. I groped for the switch under the rail, found it, and gave it a flip. The ringing stopped, leaving only a buzz in the ears.

"See what I mean? This one is foolproof."

"Says who? That's the same kind of thing they install in banks, right? A burglar alarm using infrared lights. If you look carefully, you can see a red beam in the air, and all you have to do is duck under it."

"Wouldn't work. There are three different beams, which get lower as you go. The lowest one is only a foot off the ground. How the hell could anyone duck under *that*?"

"Where does this lead to?" The girl was crouched down, with a hand cupped behind one ear. "I hear something."

"It's a dead end. It used to connect over to the western side of the mountain, just under where the city hall is now, but there was a cave-in, and it became a blind alley. But there are lots of little rooms along the way. It might make a good place to live."

"There's a town on top of this mountain, isn't there?"

"Yes, a big residential district."

"I hear noises. . . ."

"It's not what you think. Inaudible sounds become audible here, amplified as they bounce off the ceilings and walls: winds of different velocities passing by each other, bugs crawling around, drops of water falling, stone cracking. . . ."

"I don't care, I'm not going up there." The insect dealer looked up at the tunnel at the ceiling edge, brushing stone powder off the seat of his pants. "Granted the guy's reckless and athletic—but doesn't it seem funny that these lights came on just twenty or thirty seconds before we came in here? In fact, all we did was check out the trap, so maybe it wasn't even that long. That contraption would be hard to climb, and it must be a good twenty-five feet high."

"Forty-two, to be exact."

"No way."

"Then where do you think he is? There's nowhere to hide." The girl thrust out her chin, tilted her head back like radar, and turned around in a full circle. "What's that smell? It's stronger than it was before. And it's definitely *not* fried squid."

"I smell it too." The insect dealer likewise tilted his head back and sniffed the air. "I've smelled it somewhere before."

"It's the smell of the wind," I said. "It blows down through that hole in the ceiling."

"That doesn't lead to a Chinese restaurant, does it?" she asked.

"Don't be ridiculous." I had my own explanation for the odor. But I was not duty-bound to tell them, nor did I think it was at all necessary. "Even fifteen seconds is longer than you think. A woman can do the hundred-yard dash in that length of time."

The girl started walking straight toward the lift. From around her feet, shadows stretched out in all directions, light and dark, like the spokes of a fan. She put both hands on the bottom of the scaffolding and hung from it, suspending her full weight. "It's perfectly strong," she said. "Somebody climb up."

"Forty-two feet in the air?"

"Well, you had training for a rescue squad, didn't you?"

"After I left them, I got acrophobia." The insect dealer spoke glumly, lifting his shirt and scratching his belly. "Captain, how about leveling with us? Is there some reason you don't want him wandering around in here? Something you don't want him to find out?"

"No, nothing in particular. It's just that it turns into a real maze; I haven't finished surveying it yet. Once I made it all the way to the tangerine grove on the other side of the mountain. I carried a lunch, and it took nearly all day. The inside of the mountain's full of other, smaller mountains, and valleys, and rivers."

"Yeah? Any fish?" asked the insect dealer, his forehead wrinkling—a sign of serious interest.

"Not a chance. The only living creatures in there are snakes and beetles and centipedes."

"Then he won't make it," said the girl. "He's terrified of snakes." She looked at me and the insect dealer in turn. Was she worried about the shill's safety after all?

"A bigger problem would be finding the way back," I said. "I had a heck of a time, believe me. It took me all morning just to get over to the other side, and then coming back I tried to follow the same route and got lost. A compass isn't worth a damn underground. The going was dangerous and I was hungry, and so tired my knees were knocking. Before I knew it, it was the middle of the night. Frankly, I thought I was done for. You know, like those stories you hear about people who wandered in the wind holes under Mount Fuji and died there without ever finding their way out. . . ."

"So what happened?"

"So there I was, camping out with nothing but a bar of chocolate and what little water came seeping out of the rocks, no sleeping bag—not even a flashlight, since the batteries had given out. I never felt so forlorn in my whole life. But when the sun came up—"

"How could you tell the sun came up?"

"That's it, you wouldn't believe it. I'd retraced my steps back to the other side of the mountain—the north entrance, I call it, or the tangerine grove entrance—and spent the whole night there. When I woke up, the morning light was pouring in."

"That *is* unbelievable." The girl's tone was stinging, but her eyes emanated sympathy. "People's instincts don't amount to much, do they?"

"In the dark, your senses are numbed."

"So," said the insect dealer, stretching and narrowing his eyes. "You're saying *he's* the only one who'll suffer; you have nothing in particular to lose if he's in there. Right? Then who cares—let him go. Let it teach him a lesson."

"You have a point there," said the girl, falling in easily with his opinion. For some reason, this sudden switchover seemed entirely natural. "It's just silly to waste time worrying about him. Last December, when we were at a fair near a ski slope, a truck came sliding down a steep hill. It must have been doing at least forty miles an hour. Right then he was crossing the street, and he slipped and fell in the truck's path. What do you think happened? After the truck rolled on by, he got up and walked away, not a scratch on him. He's invulnerable."

"He is, huh?" I said, thinking, Another six months and he'll be a goner. I started to say the words but caught myself in time. She didn't react. Didn't it seem ironic to her that a man with only six months to live should have such great reflexes that he was "invulnerable"? I was the only one who felt abashed. Inwardly I tendered an apology to the shill. Heroes fated to die untimely deaths have an inescapable air of privilege. I began to think it was high time to drop my unwarranted hostility toward the guy and issue him a special complimentary boarding pass.

The insect dealer gave his belly a couple of resounding slaps. "Let's eat."

The girl glanced up at the top of the lift. It still seemed to weigh on her. Never mind if it was a stunt worthy of an acrobat—there did remain the small possibility that he had somehow clambered up to the ceiling. I, however, was more concerned about the shadow behind that far right pillar. Before we ate, I wanted to make sure he wasn't lurking in there.

"This is a long shot, but I just want to be sure. . . . Behind those old bikes over there, there's a small storage space with a trapdoor. This'll only take a minute."

The twenty-eight old bicycles piled in a triangular heap between the stone pillar and the wall were a tangled mass of handlebars and wheels that formed an ingenious barrier: not only did they make entry difficult; they kept one from suspecting anything was there. It looked as if nothing but wall was behind them. Light was particularly dim, as if the overseer (me) set no great store by the area. But it was all a trick. Of all the shipboard traps, this one was the most elaborately camouflaged: the entire triangle formed by these tangled old bikes was in fact a door. The "key" was the front wheel on the far right bike. All you had to do was twist the handlebars sharply and pull out the pedal that was embedded in the spokes of the neighboring bike.

"Now it's unlocked. Mind aligning the wheels of the bikes in the front row?"

A slight pull, and the triangle of all twenty-eight bikes swung around to reveal, alongside the pillar, a gaping wedge-shaped passageway. At the far end lay a section of dirty canvas, roughly six feet by three. In the dim light it looked like something to throw over the bikes, but it was in fact camouflage for a trapdoor, backed with plywood and fastened with hinges.

"Isn't there some kind of bug that makes a nest like this, covering it over with leaves?" asked the girl.

"I think you mean a fish."

"No, a bug."

The construction inside was worthy of the camouflage outside. Just beyond the door was a small room with a low ceiling, just over six and a half feet high. Tunnels had been dug out in three levels—top, middle, and bottom—each leading to yet another small room, all interconnected by irregular narrow stone steps. It was rather as if several playground monsters, the kind whose labyrinthine innards children love to climb around in, had been lined up and joined together.

"This is just a guess," I said, "but I suspect these were all trial borings. They tried digging in different directions, but the quality of the stone here fell short of their expectations, and so they gave up. All these tunnels are small, and the excavation is rough. But they're handy for storing materials according to type."

A largish, high-ceilinged room at the top of the right-hand stairs was where I kept food supplies, sorted by kind. Thirty dozen cans of hardtack. Seventeen cartons packed with eleven-pound vacuum-packed bags of uncooked rice. Two hundred meals' worth of dried noodles. Assorted dried vegetables. Miso, soy sauce, salt, sugar. Five big cartons of canned foods, including stewed beef, tuna, sardines, and so on. There was also a complete kit for cultivating vegetables by hydroponics, and an assortment of seeds.

On the middle level was a cubbyhole with a complex jumble of irregular undulations, less like a room than a model for a fallen castle. I kept all sorts of supplies there, from hardware to everyday items like razors, soap, toothpaste, as well as medicine, bandages, and other first-aid supplies. There were also rechargeable batteries, light bulbs, solid alcohol for fuel, film, a whetstone, solder and soldering iron, adhesive, assorted fishing line, fire extinguishers . . . If I didn't get busy and make a list of everything, I was in danger of losing track of it all myself.

The lowest level was the most comfortable. This was not mere storage space but a real room, with seven chairs, a table, a slide projector, and a screen. The front wall, moreover, was hung with a large rough sketch of the quarry, which I had made two weeks before—too soon to include the results of my latest survey. Still, as a three-color ground plan, it wasn't too bad.

On the adjacent wall were twenty-eight gas-and-smoke masks; wrench, hammer, crowbar, and other tools that could double as weapons; thirty-five twelve-volt batteries. Along the opposite wall were seven small automatic guns—remodeled toys—along with empty cartridges and boxes of ammunition, raw materials for gunpowder, five crossbows and one hundred and two arrows. In addition, there was a box of sand marked, in large letters, SAND FOR FIRE EXTINGUISHING. Inside the sand there were forty-three leftover sticks of dynamite, which I intended to leave hidden right there for the time being. All I had to do was plant a flag next to the map, and the room would look exactly like one of those underground strategic command headquarters you see in the movies. What sort of flag would look best— the Rising Sun? I have a feeling that's not it. I've never given the matter deep thought, but somehow I have a feeling *no* flag would look quite right.

"He doesn't seem to be anywhere in here." The girl stood in front of the map, studying it with her head tilted sharply sideways, as if she couldn't tell which way was up. "Although it's not surprising, with that entrance."

"You're well prepared, I'll grant you that." The insect

dealer ran a finger over the tabletop, then rubbed the accumulated dust on his trousers, twisting his lower lip as he
spoke. "Still, isn't there something a little childish about
your taste in furnishings?" Evidently a reference to the
model guns. Did he really think they were there just for
decoration? Then let him go on thinking so.

"Supposing he went down the ceiling tunnel," said the
girl, her head still sideways as she traced the surface of the
map with a finger. "That's this black line, right?"

"All the parts I explored myself are in black. The red lines
are hypothetical, based on a map done by the quarry
companies, on file in the city hall. Strange, don't you think?
—they overlap, but there are no actual points of con-
gruence. Probably because everybody ignored the agreement, and went off digging on their own. Small wonder the
roof caved in."

"And the blue lines?"

"The solid ones are canals and waterways, the dotted
ones are underground veins of water."

"By the time you need firearms, it's always too late." The
insect dealer picked up a crossbow and aimed it at the map.
"Those black lines go off the bounds of the map."

"I'll add on the rest as the need arises."

"I'll bet *he's* left the bounds of the map too," said the
insect dealer.

The girl turned around and shrieked, "Stop that! It's
dangerous!"

"No, it isn't—it's not loaded." As he spoke, the insect
dealer pointed the weapon directly at her face. "But it feels
awful, doesn't it? Even when you know it's a joke, it still
does. There's just something about firearms I don't like.
They never settle anything, anyway."

"Quit preaching; it doesn't suit you," I said, adding, "Look, they're only model guns. And the crossbows are for rodent control."

The girl came around the table, reached out an arm, and flicked the bowstring. "Can you really shoot rats with one of these?" she asked.

"Sure. If you hit one square, you could knock it dead." The insect dealer held the bow down with his foot, and slipped the bowstring in place. Deftly he fitted in an aluminum arrow and set up the sight, adjusting for distance before handing it to her. "Go ahead and try it," he said. "When you look through the hole, the target should be sitting on top of the sight."

"I don't know why, but it scares me a little."

"There's nothing to it, because it has no kick, unlike gunpowder." He set an empty cigarette carton lengthwise on the back of a chair some thirteen feet off. "Here's your target. Don't make any conscious effort to keep your arm steady. Just relax, take a breath, and hold it."

There was the snap of the string being released, and— beginner's luck, of course—a bull's-eye. The cigarette carton was in pieces, and the arrow, having shot clean through it, ricocheted back off a wall. She twisted and whooped in triumph.

"Wow, I hit it! Is it okay if I borrow this for a while?"

"Sure," I said. "Those are legal." My feelings were mixed. In line with the insect dealer's opinion, my prize stockpile of weapons was beginning to seem terribly juvenile. "Hunting is forbidden, but you can use them for fishing."

"Where can you fish?" She was holding up the crossbow and aiming through the sight this way and that. "Feels a little heavy. But it seems to have a lot more power than an airgun."

"The only trouble is, it's not suited for live combat," said the insect dealer; unhesitatingly he selected an Uzi submachine gun from the gun rack, and gave its barrel a few meaningful pats. "Loading it takes too much time. If you're conducting a preemptive strike, with plenty of time to aim so your first shot scores, well and good; but in combat, you'd probably be better off with a slingshot. A crossbow is capable of inflicting a mortal wound only if fired at a range of one hundred feet or less, so if your first shot misses you have to fall back on your fists. This Uzi, now, is another story."

"You seem to know enough about it. Where did you learn all that?" I asked.

"I wasn't in the Self-Defense Forces for nothing. But, Captain, aren't *you* the one who knows a hell of a lot? Your average person wouldn't think of an Uzi. That's not used by regulars so much as it is by commandos."

"Come on, it's only a toy. While I was watching the news about the Reagan assassination attempt, I noticed the Secret Service men were all using them. I liked the small size and the design, that's all."

"Sorry, I don't buy it. This has been converted into a real gun." He scraped the rust off the cocking bolt, sniffed the muzzle, and peered at the breechblock, then stuck in a finger and explored the interior. "And I'll be damned if it hasn't been test-fired. Some guts. No cracks or other damage, so it must have been a success, too. What is it? Single-loading? Semiauto? Don't tell me it's an automatic."

"Pull out the magazine and have a look. Toy bullets."

"Give up," he said. "So you stuck in a couple of blanks for camouflage, and for warning shots. Very smart. But I have news for you—back in your cabin, around that machine, there were metal shavings on the floor. Right? As I said, I didn't sign up for the SDF for nothing. I always liked guns. I knew right away what you'd been up to."

Further protest seemed futile. The third shot, and all the

rest, were in fact real cartridges, albeit homemade. "You know your way around guns, all right," I commented.

"Want me to check them out for you?"

I was tempted to take him up on the offer. I had test-fired each one five times with no problems, but I was still uncertain as to how they might hold up in a shoot-out.

"You don't think much of my arsenal, though, do you?"

"I'm only saying it won't serve the purpose. It's certainly interesting. This looks like some special steel, though; about all you can do is reinforce it and make up the difference by adjusting the amount of gunpowder."

"I can't do it!" the girl cried. She was sitting on a forty-four-pound keg of active carbon, both feet braced on the crossbow, unable to fit the bowstring into place. "Not enough strength in my back, I guess."

"I don't think you can do it bare-handed," I said. "Afterwards I'll lend you my leather driving gloves." I fixed it for her, and grabbing five arrows, she ran up the tunnel stairs.

"Look at her go. You can't stop her."

"She's charming. Makes me feel like getting out my camera for the first time in a long while."

"Weapons have a way of changing people."

The insect dealer pulled the trigger on the Uzi, replaced the cocking lever, and held the weapon in his arms. "Captain," he said, "are you sure you aren't a misanthrope at heart? You're too exclusivist."

Suddenly there was a shout from the work hold. It was the girl.

"Come on out or I'll shoot!" Perhaps because the high tones were absorbed by the moist, uneven surface of the stone walls, her voice sounded lower than usual; that in turn might have explained the note of urgency in her voice, which seemed to preclude the possibility of a joke. There was a muffled response.

The insect dealer and I raced neck and neck up the stairs. We arrived on the scene just as she was relaxing and lowering the crossbow from her shoulder. The shill was climbing down from the hole in the ceiling. He appeared nimble and surefooted. He turned his head and looked at us with a provocative smile.

EVERYBODY'S GOT A FEW

SCARS ON THE SHIN

W E all knew this was not a propitious moment for sounding one another out. Round one, a time of mutual sizing up, was over, and now we were about to enter on the decisive round two. The important thing now was to control your breathing, and try to anticipate the others' moves. Everyone seemed to feel the same way; and so until the beer was opened we observed a careful truce, keeping the sensitive matter of the shill's expedition firmly off limits.

Supper was instant Chinese noodles topped with chopped green onion, a couple of ham slices, and an egg. To go with the beer, I opened, as promised, a can of sardines. I could have come up with a fancier menu if I'd wanted, but it didn't seem necessary.

Besides the noodles, we lugged five cans of beer per person up to the bridge. I sat in the chair by the stairs, the insect dealer sat on the parapet, and the shill and the girl sat at either end of the chaise longue; this had the drawback of being so low that their chins barely reached the tabletop, but it had the compensating advantage of greater comfort.

The insect dealer downed his first beer in one gulp. The

shill, having taken charge of the crate of beer, promptly tossed him another, over the table, and then picked up the loaded crossbow from the girl's feet.

"Komono," he said, "mind setting your empty can over there? I want to try a little target practice. Let's see, now, where's the safety catch on this?"

The girl put her chin on the shill's shoulder and removed the pin at the base of the trigger for him. Even assuming there was something between them, her manner was far too intimate for so public a setting. Was she a born flirt, or just an innocent? Dogs that fawn on everyone appeal only to children.

"Knock it off, you two." Even as he set up the can on one end of the parapet in compliance with the shill's request, the insect dealer spoke in a disgusted tone of voice. "Hurry up and eat, or your noodles will get cold."

The shill pulled the trigger. The can appeared to sway slightly, but he had missed. In the distance we heard the arrow ricochet.

"Some marksman!" The girl laughed and stole a glance at me. "Why, I could hit a pack of cigarettes straight on, bang."

The shill buried his face in the large bowl of noodles, slurped up a mouthful, and then muttered, mouth full, "Rats! If only I'd had something like this before, I'd never have let that little bastard get away."

"What was it, a rat?" asked the girl innocently.

"We've made our toasts," said the shill, "so shall we move on to the business at hand?" He wiped his mouth and stared straight at me. End of truce. "Let's have it, Captain—who the hell was that guy?"

In my stomach, the beer and noodles formed a lump of sticky tar. What had he seen? What was he trying to say?

"What do you mean, who? There *isn't* anybody else. How could there be?"

"Don't try to play games with me."

"You must have imagined it."

"Hold on a minute, please," said the insect dealer, and washed down a mouthful of sardines with a swig of beer. "As the captain's adviser, naturally I'm on his side—but in any case, I think we'd better get the facts straight." He turned to the shill and said, "Now, Mr. President, tell me the truth. You had on that miner's light before you even left here; are you sure you weren't planning on doing a little exploring all along? If people think you're bullshitting them about having seen some suspicious character, how can you blame them?"

"Very observant, Komono—I've got to hand it to you." The shill opened a second can of beer and flashed a friendly smile. "All right, it's true that I thought I'd take a little walk after I finished using the john. But that doesn't make me crazy enough to go so far for no reason."

"I'm still suspicious." The girl raised her head from the bowl, a noodle trailing down from her mouth; she sucked it in with almost invisible speed and went on: "Then why didn't you call for help? If you trusted the captain, that's what you should have done."

"You keep out of it. And I *don't* trust the captain." He thrust out his arm in my direction and snapped his fingers with conviction. The thought crossed my mind that his story might possibly be true.

"What kind of a guy was he, then?" I asked. "When you first laid eyes on him, where was he and what was he doing?"

"Then you admit he exists," he said arrogantly, kicking the floor. "Who is he? Why are you hiding him?"

"I'm not hiding anyone!"

"You asked me what he was like, didn't you? That shows you know something."

"Don't get so excited." The insect dealer reached across the table and took his third beer from the girl. Purple spots

were starting to show on his forehead and cheeks; he probably had low resistance to alcohol. "What we need now is a
lie detector. But think about it; even if you have an obligation to tell the truth, the captain here doesn't. You two were
never invited on board, after all—you're a couple of crashers."

"The hell you say." He sprayed us with saliva. "I thought
I made it clear—I can't sleep without my pillow. *He's* the
one who's forcing *me* to stay against my will."

"That's a bit strong. Don't forget, legally he's not a
certified ship's captain." The insect dealer tapped the area
above his stomach and emitted a loud belch. "In other
words, he can call himself captain all he likes, but without
the consent of the crew, it doesn't mean a thing."

"In that case, we settle it by force—"

"Or by an election. I don't approve of violence."

"I know!" The girl's voice was bright, as if she'd made a
great discovery. "All he has to do is pay us a salary. People
always follow the orders of whoever's paying their wages."

"You may be onto something there," said the insect dealer
slowly, staring at her as if appraising collateral. "The captain may be well off, at that. He's poured a lot of money into
fixing up this place. But his photography business doesn't
amount to anything, and he doesn't seem to have any other
means of employment . . . so who knows, maybe he's a man
of independent means, who made his fortune by selling off
some piece of land or other. Maybe that fishermen's inn outside under the highway was really registered in *his* name."

"Aha. If that's true, that changes everything." The shill
sank back in the chaise longue, setting down the crossbow
and lowering his eyes. "Then we naturally have certain obligations to fulfill, and the captain has certain rights. Maybe
I misunderstood the whole situation. How could I help it?
Back at the department store rooftop you made it seem as if
the ticket and key were for sale."

"That's right," the girl said, nodding.

"But you two didn't pay!" The insect dealer shook his big round head slowly, with a triumphant smile.

"Did *he*?" Suspicious, the girl turned to me.

He answered her question himself. "I'll say I did—to the tune of six hundred thousand yen."

Swept along by his tone of conviction, I could hardly demur. It was true enough that with eupcaccias going at twenty thousand yen a head, and thirty of them in the suitcase, his figure had some basis in reality.

"Something's funny." The shill was not to be put off. "You've been letting on that you're a paid crew member, but this means you're no such thing. You're a paying passenger."

"What, for a paltry six hundred thousand yen? Even for a screening test to permit me to come aboard it'd be a real bargain. I'm really grateful, let me tell you. You should be too—especially considering that neither of you has paid for your ticket yet. When you figure it all out, it's as if you'd each been paid a handsome sum already. Let's have no more complaints."

The shill and the girl seemed completely taken in. You had to give the man credit for being a smooth talker. I began to understand why he had asked for carte blanche in dealing with the shill.

After a pause while he drained his third beer, he continued: "Well, as far as I can see, everybody's had their say, and nobody's come out the winner. There don't seem to be any real victims among us, either. All we need now is some guarantee of mutual trust. Mere verbal agreements aren't enough, and real intimacy—the kind where you look right up each other's behinds—takes too long. In the old days, people exchanged hostages as a kind of mutual check. So I have an idea. What if we all show each other a few old scars? Everybody's got something he'd just as soon people never got wind of—a tail he doesn't want grabbed. Why don't we all bring ours into the open, right now? Then nobody would feel tempted to do anything nasty like running to the police."

"How do we know the other guy isn't making it up?" asked the shill. "How about you, Komono—can a guy like you bring yourself to be that honest?"

"You don't understand. Anybody can invent a story that makes him look good, but it's next to impossible to invent weaknesses for yourself." He half shut his eyes and licked his lips, serenely confident. "If you think you can do it, try."

"You might be right," said the girl, opening her second beer.

"When I'm borrowing money, I can think of things, all right. . . ." Grudgingly, the shill opened his third beer.

The insect dealer gave a couple of dry coughs and went on. "Captain," he said, "would you mind setting up a tape recorder? It's a peculiar thing, but for some reason people can't lie when a microphone is staring them in the face. Besides, later the tape could serve as material evidence. You're excused, of course; this ship itself is *your* weak spot. Let's flip a coin to see who goes first, shall we?"

Nobody objected. First the girl won, then the shill.

"Okay, turn on the tape recorder." The insect dealer started his confession. "My basic reason for joining the SDF was that I liked uniforms and guns. I was disappointed right from the start. From the time I was a kid, I was no good at fitting into groups, see, so I hoped I could straighten myself out with that uniform—but it got to be too idiotic. I decided I'd have been better off becoming a priest. Finally I got so fed up with it all that I took to stealing pistols and selling them to *yakuza* on the black market. As to who my smuggling partner was, you'll probably be hearing soon enough from the horse's mouth. . . ." He glanced at the shill, who reached out and covered the mike with his hand.

"Hey, no fair." His speech was slurred; apparently he was the kind whose liquor didn't show in his face. "Everybody's got the right to decide for themselves what to tell about, right? Besides, the statute of limitations ran out on that ages ago."

"Okay, we'll write that one off. Take your hand away. Anyway, three times it went off without a hitch, but the fourth time I blew it. They had a room displaying small arms from around the world, including a Belgian gun called an M.W. Vaughn. Ever hear of it? It's one helluva gun—functions like a machine gun, and it's no bigger than a pistol. Its only flaw is the price tag. So what was I supposed to do, just stand there with my tongue hanging out? My grades were high, so I was able to get a special study pass. The room had nearly a thousand guns on display, and right in the doorway was a computer-controlled surveillance apparatus. The system was surprisingly lax. When you went in you inserted your pass in the apparatus, which recorded your name and weight, and then when you went out you put your pass in again. It was set up so if your weight showed a discrepancy of ten ounces or more, the door would lock and an alarm would sound. So how do you think I did it?"

"You must have taken it apart and carried it out piece by piece," said the girl, stating the obvious.

"Of course. Piece by piece, starting in the middle, till finally only the gun barrel was left. That alone weighed almost two pounds."

"I've got it." This was the sort of problem I liked. I thought I could give a better answer than she had, anyway. "All you'd have to do is carry in something that weighed a little over a pound, and leave it there."

"Too lacking in originality." He disposed of my idea like that. "They'd already anticipated that little tactic. When you got up to go, you pushed a switch to signal you were through, and if at that time the weight for the area around the desk in a three-foot radius wasn't zero, a red light flashed. Even the wastepaper basket sounded an alarm if you put in anything weighing more than two ounces."

"Hmm, that makes it tough." The shill was staring into space, tracing squares in his lap.

"Don't keep us guessing." The girl crossed her legs on the chaise longue, slipping off her low-heeled sandals and throwing them on the floor.

"There was one blind spot." Bobbing his head up and down, lips pursed in triumph, he went on: "What do you think it was? The drinking fountain. After setting everything up so carefully, they went and installed a drinking fountain. That set me thinking, and finally it hit me. Are you ready? I brought in three cups' worth of water in a plastic bag and dumped it down the drinking fountain."

Silence, as everyone absorbed this.

"And you failed anyway?" The girl's voice was hushed.

"Hell, no. I made clean off with it."

"But wasn't that why they threw you out?"

"Oh, my luck ran out. I had all the parts sewn up in my pillow, nice and cozy, and then those bastards go and conduct a metal-detector test right in the barracks, of all places. There was no way out. Hiding loot is always harder than lifting it."

"That may be a tail," said the shill, "but if you ask me, it's like a lizard's tail that's already broken off—not worth a damn." He sprawled back against the armrest of the chaise longue, and slurped the rest of his beer. "Once you were discharged, the charges were dropped, weren't they?"

"The hell they were. I'll have you know I'm on the wanted

list right now; I skipped out before they could make me stand trial. All right, now it's your turn. Let's have it straight, please."

The shill looked wordlessly from me to the insect dealer and back again. He sniffed, and looked at the girl. Then, as if resigned, he took a sheaf of cards out of his hip pocket and said, "Take a look. Why the dickens they do it I don't know, but they all issue these cards, like bank cash cards. Twenty-six of them I've got, and all from different loan companies."

"It's so they can exchange data among themselves, using computers."

"Counting the ones without cards, it comes to over thirty companies. I've borrowed a grand total of seventy million yen. I used to be a collector for loan sharks myself, so I know all the angles. I'm notorious. Almost every one of their offices has my picture on the wall, marked 'Wanted.'"

"So *that's* why you were in disguise." I felt relieved, as one of my unspoken questions about him was answered.

"I understand there are hit men out looking for me full time. I'll bet the reward is pretty high, too." He paused. "That's all. You can turn off the tape recorder."

"Hmm," said the insect dealer. "Not bad, not bad. Yes, I'd say that qualifies you to come on board." He pushed the pause button and said, "Captain, you'd better confiscate those cards as material evidence."

"Oh, no you don't." That familiar sleight of hand. The cards were gone before my outstretched hand could reach them. "The tape's enough, isn't it?"

"Well, all right, if that's the way you want it. Then shall we proceed?" The insect dealer made a circle with the fingers of one hand, and peered through it at the girl.

"No, I can't." Her face stiffened, as if coated with starch.

"Why not?"

"It's too embarrassing."

"Of course it's embarrassing. Otherwise it wouldn't be worth anything, would it? Come on now, don't hold back."

Suddenly the effects of all the beer I had drunk began to tell on me. Filled with a mixture of revulsion and anticipation, I could not look squarely at her. My pulse was pumping like a treadle under my ears.

"I don't mean that," she said. "I mean it's embarrassing because I haven't got anything to tell."

"Look, why don't you let her off the hook?" It was the shill, coming to her support for once. Was there some secret between them he didn't want her to divulge? "There's no way she could get out of here on her own, anyway."

"Why not?"

"Because one of the loan collectors who's after me wants *her* as security. Let's get back to where we were. We've all shown our tails now, and we're all on an equal footing. You can be honest with me, Captain, so tell me, what's going on? Who *is* that character I was chasing before?"

The insect dealer resettled himself on the parapet and began to rock backward and forward; apparently the beer had dulled his fear of heights. The girl, still sitting cross-legged, stretched out her arms, her clasped hands turned palm out. Her too-short skirt was like a rope around my neck. The gazes of all three of them seemed to grab me by the lapels and shake me without mercy.

"I truly do not know. Until I heard you tell about him, I had no idea—the whole idea was frightening. But the more I think about it, the more it explains. You see, I was blaming it all on rats. Would you mind telling me in detail what you saw?"

"You first. I'm not going to have you changing your story to fit mine."

"Relax, will you?" The insect dealer changed his forward-

and-back motion to a right-and-left sway. "Here's our chance to prove to the captain that he wasn't wrong to let us on board."

"Watch out, don't fall!" the girl cautioned. Abruptly he ceased moving, as if caught in a freeze-frame.

"My story is simple. Somebody poked his face in from a back tunnel, so I followed him. That's all."

"Are you sure it was a person?"

"What else could it have been? There sure as hell aren't any rats that big."

"To tell the truth, for some time now I've sensed the presence of an intruder. But it's too quick for a human. I'll see something move out of the corner of my eye, and by the time I look that way, it's gone. The center of your field of vision registers shapes, but the periphery is sensitive only to movement, you know. So a rat and a person *could* look the same."

"Does a rat wear sneakers and a jacket? I'll grant you he was fast. Seemed right at home in there, too. He followed a complicated course, and kept running ahead without ever slowing down or showing the least hesitation. Just when I'd think I had him cornered, he'd find a way out. He knew his way around, all right."

"How far did you go?"

"How do I know? I doubt if I could find my way back again, either. We went down a couple of flights of stairs, but it was uphill most of the way. Twice we came on running water, and once it was wide enough and deep enough to call it a sort of river."

"You went all the way *there*?"

"That's where I lost him. Just when I thought I had him, he vanished into the air. How on earth he got over that river I can't figure out. Aren't there any other ways in and out of this place? There must be."

"I don't know too much about that end."

"Well, I sure hope it doesn't turn out that somebody you didn't know about's been living over there, watching every damn thing you do."

"Did you notice a peculiar smell?" asked the girl.

"Yeah, maybe I did," he said.

"Just before the river there was a narrow bottleneck, wasn't there?" I asked. "That's the far boundary of the quarry. I've had it in mind to close that off—but still, it's unbelievable! It's a good four miles that far and back, as the crow flies, and you've got cliffs, valleys, and all kinds of hurdles in the way. I never thought those people would go so far as to cross over that boundary."

" '*Those people*'? Then you *do* know something you're not letting on."

"Oh, they're nothing to worry about. The Broom Brigade, they're called—an old people's club."

"The broom what?" The insect dealer, who'd been sitting stiffly, stuck out his paw. His glasses slipped askew. His right eye was watering.

"The Broom Brigade. They do volunteer work, sweeping and cleaning, as a public service. Their average age is seventy-five."

"And they live somewhere in this quarry?"

"No, they probably just use it for their garbage dump. In any case, they're over two miles from here. You remember, don't you, Komono?" I said, using his name for the first time. With some trepidation at this change in our relationship, I went on, "On the shortcut, that slight outcropping of rock—"

"That's it! It *was* the smell of garbage," interrupted the girl, her mind still on the same track.

"But why would a cleaning brigade come spying around here?" The shill too had a one-track mind. "And whoever was doing the running wasn't any seventy-five years old, either."

"It might have been someone from the supervisory squad. I gather they use younger people for supervisors."

"Is it a large battalion?"

"Thirty-five to forty men. They work only late at night, so hardly anybody's ever seen them. They go around in a straight line, swinging their brooms in time to martial songs."

"Sounds creepy."

"As far as I know, nobody's ever complained about the noise. They sing in hushed voices, so the sound must get mixed in with the sighing of the wind and the swish of their brooms."

Layer upon layer of heavy, relaxed inebriation settled over everyone but the girl.

THE BROOM BRIGADE WAS

WRITTEN UP IN THE PAPER

T H E Broom Brigade's been written up in the local paper; everybody from this area knows about them. It all began with a movement to collect empty beverage cans, organized by a few elderly citizens. They attracted a growing following, and the movement began earning a name for itself as a way of getting old people reinvolved in society and giving them new purpose in life. Gradually it became more structured, with uniforms and a badge showing two crossed bamboo brooms. Clad in dark blue uniforms like combat suits, the oldsters parade around in the middle of the night, when ordinary people are in bed, and sweep the streets till dawn. They work in the wee hours because generally old people are early risers anyway, and because they don't want to get in people's way. Imagine them marching abreast in a single row, softly intoning an old war song and swinging their brooms in rhythm, casting a shadow under the streetlights like some monster centipede creeping through the night.

There definitely *is* something creepy about them. The matter of the martial air was debated in the city council, but the issue was laid to rest when one councillor declared that the words, beginning "Here we bide, hundreds of miles from home . . ." expressed the universal grief of soldiers everywhere, and that to lump this with the "Man-of-war March" was a piece of left-wing radical hokum. The brigade members' practice of soliciting donations in areas they had swept, moreover, won acceptance with the reasonable argument that it's only wholesome good neighborliness to give a helping hand to senior citizens seeking to build their own retirement home. As a matter of fact, the city of Kitahama is exceptionally clean. You can walk the streets barefoot without dirtying your feet. Not only that: the city has become a leader in cutting the use of synthetic detergents. How could the authorities fail to be pleased?

"What a disgusting bunch of old men," snorted the insect dealer. "Must be something wrong with them. Doesn't sound normal to me." He slipped down from his perch on the parapet, came over by the table, and rested his cheek in one hand. In the depths of his glasses his gaze flickered. "Basically," he went on, "nobody who enjoys cleaning up can be worth much. I hate it, myself. 'A place for everything and everything in its place'—you can take that motto and stuff it."

"Besides," said the shill, "there's something disturbing about the whole thing. We don't know beans about them, and here they've been staring up our asses." As he spoke, he pulled the bowstring on the crossbow and fixed an arrow in place. "What I can't figure out is where in hell did that spy disappear to? It was like a subway platform out there, steep cliffs on right and left, up to the edge of the water. The only way to escape would be to dive in."

"Then he must have swum across," said the insect dealer, sinking to a sitting position on the floor. I did not at all like where he was: from there he could peer through the table legs at the girl, sitting cross-legged on the chaise longue, and see right between her legs.

"Impossible." The shill too seemed to take notice of the situation. All of a sudden he took aim with the crossbow and put his finger on the trigger. "The other side of the river was a sheer wall, straight up to the ceiling."

"Put that thing down," said the insect dealer. Instinctively he snatched up the Uzi that was leaning against the parapet, cocked it, and rose to a crouch. "Save it for when you're sober."

A thin smile on his lips, the shill ignored this and pulled the trigger. The arrow missed its target for the second time, skimming by the beer can and ricocheting with a dry scrape somewhere off in the distance.

"Look who's talking," he said mockingly to the insect dealer. "Aren't you a little old to be playing with toys? Or is a gun freak like you happy to get his hands on anything?"

The insect dealer lowered his gun without comment. But he made no move to go back under the table. The girl started to speak, then clamped her mouth shut.

Flicking the bowstring, the shill added, "Captain, what do you say? Shall we head back to that river for a look?"

"Too late now," I said. "Better wait till the sun comes up."

"Underground, what difference does it make?" he protested. "There's no day or night in a cave, is there?" He slurped up the rest of his noodles and started in on his fourth beer. "My mental faculties are sharpest when I'm drinking, believe it or not. Although noodles and sardines make a hell of a combination."

"No need to go searching them out, you know," said the insect dealer, picking up the last sardine by its tail and curling his tongue around it. "If they have something on their minds, they'll be back."

"No," said the shill, "we've got to take the initiative. Don't forget, that place where they're dumping their garbage is right next door. Who do they think they are, anyway, cleaning up the streets at *our* expense?"

"And it's not just ordinary garbage." The girl clung tenaciously to her theme. "That smell is from some harmful substance, I'm positive. You know they say you can make a lot of money cleaning up industrial wastes."

"That's right," agreed the shill. "Whoever heard of building an old people's home out of the proceeds from street sweeping? It would never be enough." The two of them seemed to be growing in rapport. "Some ticket for survival," he wound up sardonically. "Now it turns out we're being slowly poisoned by toxic fumes!"

A snail covered with wire netting full of gaping holes, imagining itself shielded by a giant shell of some superstrong alloy: how soft-headed can you get! There was a pop in the vicinity of my lower eyelids like that of a tiny balloon. My vision clouded, as tears sprang to my eyes. I remembered having had the same experience when Inototsu locked me up in this quarry, chained like a dog. I read somewhere that there are three kinds of tear glands, each used with a different degree of frequency. These tears probably came from a gland I rarely used; that would explain the popping noise, as if the tear ducts were clogged from lack of use.

"I'll bet you it was a spy who came to see if the captain was dead yet or not," said the girl. "Right about now they must be in a tizzy as they find out that (a) the captain is still alive, and (b) he's got three new people in with him." She stared in sudden surprise at my face. "What's the matter —are you crying?"

"Of course not." Ashamed to wipe them away, I let the tears trickle down the wings of my nose.

"The captain has no reason to cry," said the insect dealer, eyes tightly shut, leaning on the table with his elbows planted far apart.

"They could be tears of mortification," said the shill with emphasis, spraying a mist of saliva. "A ship's captain can't very well sit back and watch while his air supply is slowly poisoned, after all."

"I told you before—I'm going to close off that passageway just as soon as I can get to it."

"No, you've got to act now. Look, that guy came poking his nose in here only a little while ago. What's the Broom Brigade anyway? Just a bunch of decrepit old street cleaners. Let's go have it out with them!"

"Or we could simply assert our territorial rights, much as it might inconvenience them," said the insect dealer, crawling up on the table like a wounded sea slug. "*They* look on it as a garbage dump, but we can put the space to far more significant use. Remember, Japan is a very small country, suffering from acute space deficiency, getting worse all the time. . . ."

"What are you going to do, plant a flag?" The girl kept staring curiously at my tears.

"Why not?" said the shill. "That or something else." He spoke with great assurance, driving his words home. "The thing to do is to see that they give us service at a special rate, or pay us for the space they're using. Somehow we've got to draw a firm line."

Despite small individual differences, overall it appeared that everybody but me was in favor of some form of association with the Broom Brigade. I had a sense of double defeat: first the spy and then, as if that weren't humiliation enough, the fact that it was the shill, not me, who discovered him. The Broom Brigade, for its part, having had its spy exposed, would surely be devising some swift countermeasure. If a confrontation was inevitable, what better time than now, when I was flanked by two self-appointed bodyguards?

I decided to let the girl score a few points. "I give up—you're right," I said, addressing her. "They've been scattering around a chromic waste fluid. Highly poisonous. You know," I added, "*ninja* used to have keen noses too. Even in the dark they could distinguish people and objects by scent, like dogs." (This comparison was perhaps a touch inept.) "They say the whole body of *ninja* lore comes down to perfecting the sense of smell. Why, you're probably qualified to be a *ninja* right now."

As it happened, my association with the Broom Brigade was a good deal more intimate than any of them suspected. Our first contact dated from just about a year ago. As the girl had divined, we were engaged in the illegal disposal of industrial waste (although the instigator was not them, but me). Once a week they furnished five polyethylene containers full of a heavily chromic waste fluid, fifty-eight times the permitted level of concentration. It was a pretty awful job, and the pay was accordingly high. To dispose of one container was worth 80,000 yen. That's 400,000 yen a week; 1,600,000 yen a month. More money than I could ever hope to lay hands on again.

Of course it wasn't as if I'd drawn up a contract directly with the Broom Brigade. There was a middleman. Every Tuesday just before daybreak, he came by with the goods, hauling five containers along the town road in a pickup truck. The rest was up to me. First, using a pulley, I lowered them to the roof of the abandoned car I used for camouflage (a Subaru 360); then I shoved them in through the back-seat window, where the pane was missing, and loaded them aboard ship in a handcart. It's fairly hard labor, but when you want to raise money in a hurry, you can't pick and choose. Besides, I didn't want anybody finding out about my toilet.

Before setting up in this business, I did the necessary groundwork. I couldn't rest easy without having some idea of where things flushed down that toilet would end up. Common sense said it was somewhere out at sea. But where? The complex topography of the sea bottom made it impossible to predict. Since I knew I would be handling illegal wastes, it was imperative to investigate the matter thoroughly beforehand: if toxic substances and corpses of small animals started popping up along the shoreline, people would inevitably ask questions.

One windless day, choosing an hour when there was little current, I flushed twenty ounces of red food coloring down the toilet. I then kept a steady watch from atop the pedestrian bridge on Skylark Heights, which commands an excellent view, but saw no telltale red stain anywhere on the surface of the water. Nor at any time since then have I even heard rumors of dead fish floating nearby. The underground water vein from the toilet must empty very far out at sea. Or perhaps an especially swift current sweeps the outlet clean. As long as no one raises any fuss, there's no problem. The work goes along smoothly. In any case, the world is coming to an end soon, so what difference does it make?

Then, early this month, things suddenly changed. One day shortly after the rainy season was declared officially over, I was waiting in my jeep for a red light to change at the corner by the Plum Blossom Sushi Shop, when next to me there pulled up a black van like a paddy wagon or one of those paramilitary soundtrucks used by the neo-fascist right wing. On its side was an emblem of two crossed brooms, and on the corner of one bumper, a flag bearing the same emblem fluttered in the breeze. So *this* is the famous Broom Brigade patrol car, I thought, having heard about it from our middleman. I gazed at it not with any strong sense of identification but with genuine (quite neutral) interest; we were, after all, business partners. Then my eyes met those of the man sitting next to the driver. A big fellow, whose head brushed against the car ceiling, he was staring intently into my jeep. The shock was like sticking your hand into the chill vapor of dry ice, expecting hot steam. Large sunglasses and a goatee had altered his appearance, but there was no mistaking that green hunting cap. It was my biological father, Inototsu.

I had not seen him in five years. Just to find him in apparent good health was bad enough (a more fitting fate being pauperism or softening of the brain), but of all things, here he was seated in the patrol car of my best customer, the Broom Brigade, as snug as a yolk in its egg. Barely six feet away, the facings on the left sleeve of his dark blue uniform were plainly legible: three gold inverted V's. Gold for the rank of general, three for the highest grade within his rank. That made him their chief, or marshal, or supreme commander. Of course I couldn't have known—but still, I had picked one hell of a business partner. My head throbbed as if I'd come down with Raynaud's disease,* and after the light turned green I had trouble putting the car in gear.

The reaction from his side was swift: the following week, orders for work were abruptly terminated. Naturally, my first suspicions rested with the intermediary, Sengoku. Unless he had said something, I figured, not even Inototsu was crafty enough to connect me with the consignments of hexavalent chromium. Probably, carried away by some desire to boast of his own evildoing (since bullying his family was part of the sadism he secreted like poison), Inototsu had told his followers about meeting me in front of the sushi shop; Sengoku, who happened to be present, then boasted that he knew me as the final recipient of the illegal wastes. For Inototsu to order an immediate halt to all deliveries would

* A circulatory disorder affecting habitual chain-saw users.

be the logical next step. His goal would be to starve me out, cutting off my supplies and attempting to recover my territory. As the one who had chained me to the toilet, he was no doubt well aware of its power.

Not surprisingly, Sengoku firmly denied my allegations. For his services, he pointed out, I regularly paid him twenty percent of the intake, which made him no less a victim of the work stoppage than me. That too made sense. No matter how attractive the Broom Brigade's terms, he could do nothing without first finding another safe place for disposal of the chromium waste. Still vaguely suspicious, I resolved to leave the negotiations up to him, and meanwhile to prepare for a long siege.

"And now that I think of it," I concluded, "it was just about then that I first began detecting the presence on board ship of what I took to be a rat."

"You know, if it were me, I wouldn't trust that Sengoku person an inch." Tracing endless small circles on the armrest of the chaise longue, the girl recrossed her legs. She had sweet, unpretentious kneecaps.

"I agree," said the shill, licking flecks of saliva from the corners of his mouth. "Who knows—that guy who gave me the slip before might have been Sengoku himself."

"You have nothing but supposition to base that on."

"Here goes," said the insect dealer, carefully lighting a cigarette. "My last one for today."

"Actually I don't trust Sengoku one hundred percent myself," I added. "The name means 'a thousand *koku* of rice,' and it has a great air of nobility about it (and for all I know, his ancestors were aristocrats), but when you come down to it, he's nothing but the son of a confectioner who gave his creditors the slip and set up a little confectionery just off the town road."

He's three or four years younger than me. The store—

you know the kind of place—has a lattice front backed by glass instead of paper, with a faded sign; he lives there with his mother, who's involved in some religious sect or other, and often goes out. They sell things like cheap sweets and snack breads, milk and fried donuts made from unsold leftovers from other stores. The one exception is their homemade sweet-potato cakes. Made from real sweet potatoes with plenty of butter, they would be any baker's pride; they fill the store with a wonderful fragrance, and were even marketed wholesale to coffee shops and restaurants near the station, with great success. Sengoku's father was formerly a baker in a confectionery factory, specializing in sweet-potato cakes. I'm fond of them, and they're easy to pop in your mouth, so I got in the habit of dropping by every morning to buy them fresh-baked. Besides, if you time it right, you can get all the way there and back without encountering anyone.

One morning about six months after I'd started doing this, Sengoku's mother was out, and he was manning the counter himself. I'd seen him working in the back before that, but this was the first time we'd ever spoken.

"Ah, Mr. Inokuchi," he says. "That *is* your name, isn't it?"

"No. You're thinking of the old fishing inn that used to be down under the cliff. You can just call me Mole. Back when I worked as a photographer, that's what everyone called me. I look like one, don't I?"

"Not really. Moles have long whiskers. Are you sure it isn't bad for you to eat so many of those?"

"Oh, no—sweet potatoes are an excellent source of vitamin C and fiber. An ideal food, in fact. Their only drawback is the price."

"Goes up all the time. They used to be the poor man's staple. No more."

"Where's your mother?" I asked.

"Busy, lately, with church duties. She just got promoted to junior executive. It's a little hard on me—I've got to do everything here myself now, from laying in stock and mashing and straining potatoes to timing the ovens and minding the stove."

"Church? You mean she's a member of some religious outfit?"

"You mean she's never invited you to join? She must have you figured for a hopeless degenerate."

We both burst out laughing. It felt pleasantly intimate, like sharing a secret. I had no great need for friendship, you understand, but I did feel a bond of sorts with the man. As he lined up the cakes on thin strips of paper, arranged them in boxes, and rang up the bill, he went on talking in a quiet, unobtrusive way. He asked no questions, veiled or otherwise, about my life-style (of which he must have had some inkling). It seems now almost as if he was actively cultivating my friendship.

"My father ran off and disappeared," he said, "and no one knows what became of him. Making sweet-potato cakes is damned boring. Not only that, it takes up all your time. There's a big difference between just bored, you see, and *busy* bored. Too much of that can take away your manhood. I can remember my mother pulling down my father's pants and blowing on his thing—which would be all shrunken up like dog crap—or winding her prayer beads around it and chanting an invocation. You try baking one hundred of these a day, and it'll happen to you too, he said; I swore it wouldn't —in fact, I wished it would. So maybe that's it: both my father and I lack strength of character. When by some fluke guys like him and me get lucky, it's about as fitting as a fur coat in July.

"One time about three years ago, a friend of my father's who worked as a tipster for the bicycle races got sick, and

Dad was hired to fill in for him. Racing tips don't usually amount to much anyway, so you didn't need any special knowledge or inside information to do the job. Racing tips always turn out wrong, and if his did too, so what? But for better or worse, three days in a row he picked a long shot that came home. That kind of news spreads faster than an epidemic, so all of a sudden there was a rush of business. Anybody with sense would have hightailed it, but after the monotony of sweet potatoes, Dad was having the time of his life. Finally he fell in his own trap. He took all the proceeds from those three days and bet the whole thing on the next race. I don't have to tell you what happened. The tipster got after him to produce the money, and when it wasn't there he beat him up. He had to go into hiding, bleeding heavily. It made me think: maybe our family name really *is* an old one. It must have taken a long time to produce someone as foggy-brained as my father. Of course, from his point of view it must have been a dream come true. No more sweet potatoes. He's probably cured of his impotence by now."

"What about you?" I asked. "Is it your turn?"

"There are signs."

"Shall I see what I can do for you, before your old lady starts chanting invocations over you?"

"It won't work."

"How do you know?" I said. "Don't give up so fast. I tell you what—give me a hand in my business. It may not be as exciting as a tipster, but it's a great opportunity for you to make use of any sixth sense you may have inherited."

"Forget it," he said flatly. "Remember what I said—sweet-potato-cake bakers are bored to death *and* busied to death. I haven't got the time, and my mother would never let me, anyway."

"As a junior executive, she must have a lot of financial obligations. What if you made enough money to cover them all?"

"No, no. I can see it now. I jump at some story that's too good to be true and there I am, a replay of my father."

"Whether you go for it or not is up to you, but let me at least explain the deal. Here's a hint: suppose there was a secret manhole somewhere where you could get rid of anything. Nothing barred. What would you use it for?"

The answer wasn't three days in coming. Like a thirteen-year-old wrapped up in a computer game, Sengoku became completely engrossed in looking for ways to use such a manhole. From the outside he and I may look as different as a pig and a mouse, I thought, but we are kindred spirits. Not only because we share the fate of having been born to a no-good louse of a father, but because we are both addicted to outlandish ideas.

He soon arrived at a Grand Manhole Theory. One summer years ago, he had tried to run a beachhouse. From this he learned that the issue is not whether to use real tatami mats or plastic covering; nor is it how many showers you install, how many gallons of hot water per minute you allow, how many blocks of ice or watermelons you lay in—none of that makes a particle of difference. Customers are smart. They let their noses lead them. The thing to do, in other words, is to pour as much money as you can into the rest rooms. Sanitation comes first *and* second. For that reason, flushing toilets are a must. In the end, you stand or fall by the size of your sewage tank. If you fail to appreciate that fact, then before you know it the smell of ammonia will permeate the place, business will fall off, and that will be that.

Japanese history books tell about "moving the capital," a ritual that took place at fixed intervals in ancient Japan. The reason for this was the same, I think—people's sensitivity to smell. With a dense population, waste disposal eventually becomes a problem. Sewage, trash . . . and dead bodies.

Once, when I was a boy on a school excursion to Kyoto, somebody explained that one particular ancient classical poem from that era (when, exactly, I don't recall) meant roughly that whenever the wind blew a certain way, it stunk to high heaven. I remember how shocked I was. But back then, of course, they didn't bury their dead. They piled them up on the ground, say in a bamboo grove on the outskirts of town. (Maybe that explains why Kyoto is famous for its bamboo shoots to this day; I don't know.) Anyway, it's obvious why they would have had to move the capital periodically. People can't win out over waste matter; at some point it takes over and gets the better of them. In foreign countries, you often come across the ruins of abandoned cities and towns. Buildings made of stone couldn't easily be moved, so raw sewage and dead bodies accumulated, epidemics were rampant, and the cities were left to fall into ruins. Wooden structures disappear without a trace, but they might have been that much more sanitary. The only way to avoid having to move, or leave empty ruins, is to build your city around a large manhole. The ideal sewage system, in other words, is like a giant umbilical cord: the lifeline of the city of the future.

Sengoku's first practical application of his manhole theory was to take over the disposal of aborted fetuses from local obstetricians. The plan was successful as well as clever. Previously, the only recourse had been the makeshift device of mixing the fetuses in furtively with raw waste from the fish market. This system had never appealed to those involved, and they were only too glad to wash their hands of it.

Sengoku and I quickly set up a company that we called SWAMDI, or Special Waste Matter Disposal, Inc. "What title do you want?" I asked him. "You can be president, or executive director, or secretary-general. Take your pick."

"What will you be?" he answered. "Chairman?"

"Just plain manhole manager is good enough for me."

"Then I'll be secretary-general. No president or vice-president. More democratic that way, don't you think?" he said, adding, "Are there any other members?"

"For now it's just you and me," I said.

"Even better," he said. "The more people, the less each one's share of the take."

"The fewer faucets," I said, "the less leaking."

"Exactly."

"So for the time being," I continued, "I want there to be just *one*. Not that I don't trust you—I do, but I think you're better off not knowing too much about the manhole. Then there's no way you could tell anybody anything. I know it seems unfriendly . . ."

"No, I don't mind," he said cheerfully. "If anything ever happened, I'd get off lighter not knowing."

The very unconventionality and flamboyance of this first project of ours made it difficult to attract orders. And unless you're dealing in dead bodies or industrial waste, the disposal business pays next to nothing. Finally, in our third month, we began handling hexavalent chromium. Soon we were doing so at regular intervals, and this became our chief source of revenue. Sengoku gave spending money to his mother, who was still busy proselytizing, and talked her into letting him virtually close up the store. Sometimes, when he was in the mood, he would bake some of his prize sweet-potato cakes just for me.

That was all about a year ago. Since then everything had been going smoothly, until I ran into Inototsu in front of the Plum Blossom Sushi Shop. Sengoku and I worked together well, in a spirit of genuine friendship. Besides meeting once a week at 4 p.m. for the delivery of hexavalent chromium, we met often in a back room of his store (now closed), to drink coffee, chat, exchange last month's magazines, and play an occasional game of chess. Sometimes we would drink a toast to the manhole. Sengoku used to declare that he had never known such a sense of fulfillment in all his life. The vague anxiety he felt was probably due to his recovery from impotence, but that, he said, smiling, was like the sense of exhilaration you get after washing your face with fine soap. Time seemed to weigh on his hands, so sometimes I had him help me with other things besides the SWAMDI work. Things like purchasing and transporting supplies for the ark: parts for air conditioners, materials for gunpowder, and so on. I realized now that I should have explained everything to him then. It wasn't that I doubted him at all. I fully intended to give him a ticket to survival too, but I kept putting it off. My failure to include him owed solely to my own lack of decisiveness. He must have suspected something, but he never once asked anything approaching a question—either because he knew his place or because he had suffered a lot for a man his age. He had a habit of saying, "Peace is wonderful."

"So we beat out your friend Sengoku, eh?" said the shill, upending his fourth can of beer and sucking up the last remaining froth. "He'd be mad as hell if he knew."

"That's why I feel guilty. I'll have to tell him about you three, who've contributed nothing, and get his approval after the fact."

"I wouldn't trust that person Sengoku," said the girl, leaning back and tugging at the hem of her skirt. Man-made leather hardly stretches at all, so the only effect was to accentuate the gap between her knees.

"Try to remember, Captain," said the shill, stifling a yawn.

"Was it before or after you ran into Inototsu that you began to sense the presence of an intruder?"

"How do I know?"

"But that's the crux of it all: that'll tell you if you can trust your secretary-general or not."

"Why?"

"It only makes sense," said the girl. "That man Sengoku sounds too reserved." She covered the end of her sentence with a smile, to keep me from opening my mouth. "Are you sure he wasn't in league with the Broom Brigade from the start?"

The question was not lacking in merit. I myself wondered at what point Sengoku had learned of Inototsu's connection with the Broom Brigade. He certainly knew both that the hexavalent chromium came from there and that Inototsu was my biological father. If he had remained silent while knowing Inototsu to be the head of the Broom Brigade, that suggested not mere reserve but a deliberate lack of candor. Had he wanted to keep his trump card hidden until I was more open about my life in the quarry?

The insect dealer slumped from the table down onto the floor. He landed in a sitting position, eyes half open, but the angle of his neck showed he was fast asleep. Too bad— he was back in position to look up her skirt but unable to do anything about it. Now if only the shill would go to sleep too. I threw him his fifth beer.

"Shall we get ready to turn in?" I said.

"Are you serious?" The shill opened his can, peering under the table.

"That's right—don't you know what time it is? It's still only five after eight." The girl too looked under the table, pressing her cheek against the chaise longue.

Everyone but me disappeared below the surface of the

table. As I kept my gaze level, I was assaulted by a wave of loneliness. Along with quiet came unrest.

"The evening is young. Shall we be setting off?" said the shill.

"Where to?" I asked.

"Cave exploring, of course. Spelunking." He was still under the table. "What's this in the bag next to the Styrofoam box—a sleeping bag?"

"Could be, if it's got dark blue and red stripes."

"It's covered with dust."

"That's a top-quality brand, I'll have you know. It's in a different class from the chintzy stuff they palm off on you in sporting goods stores."

"What's the difference?" asked the girl.

"Enough so that a little dust doesn't matter. The bottom is triple-layered, with nylon, carbon fibers, and a spring, so that whether you're lying on rocks, gravel, or whatever, you can sleep as comfortably as in a hotel bed."

The shill tucked the crossbow under his arm, inserted the remaining aluminum arrows in his belt, and stood up. Going around the table, he pulled out a sleeping bag and threw it down from the parapet. Then he grabbed the shoulders of the insect dealer, who was asleep, leaning against the table leg, and began to shake him roughly.

"Okay, Komono—time to go downstairs and go beddy-bye. Wake up, will you!"

"There's no point in moving too fast," I counseled. "At least let's wait till Komono is sober. The more help we have, the better."

"It's worse to let the enemy get an edge on you. Don't forget, the best defense is a good offense. When politicians want to sound tough, they start talking about their indomitable resolve. In a fight, the trick is to let fly a stiff punch that will put a damper on your opponent. You can't let guys like that Sengoku have it all their own way. Corrupts discipline."

"But there's no hard evidence that he *did* turn traitor. It's all circumstantial, isn't it?"

"The best way to check it out is to go back there for a look."

"Why are you so eager for a fight?"

"Drink sharpens my faculties, remember? What is there to be afraid of?"

"All right, then, let me *contact* Sengoku. His radio is set up in the store. If he's there, that'll give him an alibi, and disprove your idea that he's in league with the Broom Brigade."

"I haven't got anything personal against the guy, mind you," said the shill. "He's just one possible suspect. But go ahead and try to contact him, if that'll make you feel better. If he's there, he may have some new information for you, and if he isn't, the cloud of suspicion will deepen and you can throw away your doubts."

"I'll give it a try—but somehow I just cannot believe that he's that rotten."

My radio set was in locker number three. The lock combination was easy to remember: 3-3-3. I set the dial and switched it on.

—Channel check. Channel check. Is anyone using this channel?

No answer.

—I repeat. Hello, this is Mole. Mole here. Come in, please.

No answer.

Twice more I repeated the call; still there was no answer.

"That settles it." The shill clapped his hands. "You'd better give up, Captain. You want to take your camera along when we go? I hear you're a professional. A photograph of the evidence could be worth a fortune. And, Komono, you wake up. We've got to get moving. Come on, I'll take you downstairs."

He gave the insect dealer's shoulder another hard shake, until at last Komono stood up, his whole body emanating sleepiness. Even so, he never loosened his grip on the converted toy Uzi.

"I've got to pee," he mumbled.

The insect dealer leaned on the shill, whose knees buckled. There was a good four-inch difference in their heights, and their weights must have differed to a corresponding degree. Using my head as a prop as he went by, he passed in back of me, nearly knocking over a chair in the process. He had terrible body odor. The odor itself was menacing, and even apart from that there's something about big men I don't like—probably from association with Inototsu. As he wavered, unable to negotiate the turnabout, the shill grabbed his belt and held him up. Their unsteady footsteps receded down the staircase.

"What shall I do?" The girl, still lying curled on the chaise longue, looked up at me with a troubled expression.

"Can you swim? I think probably we'll be diving underwater."

"No, I can't. And I can't hold my beer very well, either—unlike him."

"Then you shouldn't come. You'd just end up an encumbrance." As I went by, I gave her bottom a light slap. Without a flicker of expression, she sighed and said:

"You know, you've got to hide your feelings better than that."

"Was it so obvious?"

"Just like a dog looking for a pat on the head."

"You've got to be kidding."

"I think he wants to start a new life. But don't forget, he has only six months to live."

From down below, mixed with the sound of someone passing water, came the noise of voices quarreling. Then a queer voice, with laughter in it. A pause, and then the roar of the toilet being flushed, like a subway train thundering by in the middle of the night.

"He seems nicer than he looks."

"He's a fairly complicated person," she answered thoughtfully. "That may be the very reason why he acts so simpleminded."

"Has he ever used violence on you?"

She put a hand on her hip where I had slapped her, and said nothing. From below, the shill's voice boomed out, echoing through the hold.

"C'mon, Captain, let's go!"

14

T H E shill went first, clutching the loaded crossbow in his arms, and I followed, holding a trigger-
operated tear gas cylinder. Kicking aside the sprung trap,
we cut across the work hold, our footsteps resounding. From
habit I tried to muffle mine, but the shill strode boldly ahead,
apparently eager to cover ground. Each step we took created
its own echo. The sum effect was a loud pattering like the
noise of falling raindrops.

"If we make this much noise they'll hear us coming," I
said. "You know, whoever it was that got away before might
have doubled back, and be waiting in ambush up ahead."

"That's okay," he said. "As long as the enemy isn't planning
an all-out attack, it's safer to make a lot of noise as you
approach, whether it's a bear you're up against, or anything
else."

By the time we reached the top of the lift, I was panting.
I stopped to lean against the wall and catch my breath, but
the shill signaled me to hurry, indicating his watch. After a
few more yards we reached a room of medium size (still
easily as big as a school auditorium), with a split-level
floor. Light from the work hold provided soft, indirect il-

lumination, covering the walls with a thick velvety sheen. I planned to set up a periscope here someday for outdoor observation. For the present, taking advantage of the room's soundproof structure, I used it to test-fire converted guns and mock bullets.

"We're up so high now, the ground must be just overhead," said the shill, switching on his cap light. His breathing remained unaffected by his exertion. He must have a liver the size of a cow's, I thought, able to convert beer directly into water. It was hard to believe the man had only six months to live.

"Even so, there's a good thirteen feet of solid rock up there, at the minimum," I answered. "So the law says."

"This is where the smell starts to get worse, notice?" he said.

Besides the passageway through which we had come, two other ceiling-high openings extended on right and left, separated by a wall of rock. The shill headed for the one on the right.

"You got through there with no difficulty before, did you?" I asked.

"Yes—why?"

"There's another booby trap planted in there."

This was one route I had figured an invader would be sure to take, and so, without begrudging the effort required to replace the laminated batteries once a month, I had installed a rather nasty device: a cylinder of cockroach spray, activated by an infrared sensor.

"Oh, yeah? I didn't see anything." He paused just before entering the passageway. "There was a trap where we just came through, I know, but that's all. I swear I never saw anything else."

He was telling the truth. The safety mechanism was intact—and that wasn't all: the working part of the cylinder had been hardened with spray coagulant, so skillfully that the eye could scarcely detect anything amiss. This was the work of someone who knew all my secrets, I feared. How long had I been under surveillance? There was no denying that Sengoku was in a position to know or surmise a great deal about my traps, having had access to the list of goods I ordered.

"I wonder if all my traps have been tampered with," I said.

"Looks that way," said the shill as we pushed forward, our only source of light the beams emanating from our helmets. "If there *were* any traps in working order, they'd have caught the intruders, and there'd be nothing to fear. It all goes to show our coming on board wasn't such a bad idea, after all. Am I right?"

Several yards ahead, the ceiling suddenly rose. On the left was a gentle flight of stairs, and straight ahead, an array of small, irregular cubicles like ancient cave dwellers' homes. The results of numerous test bores here had apparently been uniformly disappointing, each soon abandoned.

"If the rubble were cleared away," I said, "I thought this would make a good living area. All private rooms."

"Great idea." He turned around and grinned. "Put up steel bars and it would make a good isolation ward for violent patients."

"You know, I'm sorry," I apologized.

"What for?" We started down the stone staircase.

"I should have leveled with you from the start. There was never any question of how I planned to use this quarry. It's got to do with the tickets to survival. You see, this will be a bomb shelter in case of nuclear war."

"You're weird, you know that?" He turned to look back at me without slowing his pace. For a moment the light on his helmet blinded me.

"The danger is real—and imminent, let me tell you," I said. "Even if everybody goes around looking as if nothing were the matter."

"You're not telling me anything I don't already know," he said. "I mean, really—tickets for survival, qualifications to board a ship, man-powered generators, air filters . . . what could it be *but* a bomb shelter?"

"So you knew."

"Naturally. You *are* weird."

"Then what made you suggest dumb ideas like vegetable storage, or a hotel for escaped criminals?"

"Well, you've already managed some pretty good businesses on the side, haven't you, Captain? Disposing of fetuses, illegal dumping of toxic wastes . . ."

"That's different," I protested. "I can call it quits anytime I want, without repercussions. But fugitives and loony birds are *human*. Once I let them on the ship, I couldn't just toss them overboard whenever I felt like it."

"Like you will us." The shill swallowed noisily, a sign of nerves. "Let me ask you one question. As captain, what sort of people have you got in mind for your crew? So far I get the idea you're after people with more respectable backgrounds than us—but you know, respectability isn't everything. It could be boring as hell. Besides, we don't know beans about who you really are, either, do we? There's no point in putting on airs."

"I'm not putting on airs. But when the time comes, this ship's crew will form the gene pool for future generations, don't forget. That leaves me with a heavy responsibility."

"Let me make one thing clear," he said firmly. "As long as she stays, I'm not setting foot out of here, either."

We came upon a third large room. This one was no simple rectangular shape but fairly convoluted, rooms within rooms extending along diagonal lines, high and low, each one supported by pillars. The effect was one of haunting solemnity, as in some ancient cathedral. Or perhaps it would be truer to say that ancient cathedrals are a practical application of that effect.

The shill lowered his voice. "Just between the two of us, she's a very sick woman."

"She is? What's wrong with her?"

"Cancer. The bone marrow has lost its blood-making function. The doctors give her six months to live."

I started to smile, and couldn't breathe. The air had turned hard as glass. One of them was lying, or both. They hadn't checked their stories out with each other, and ended by dropping separate fishlines. There was also the (admittedly small) possibility that both were telling the truth. Perhaps they had met by chance in some hospital waiting room. It wasn't inconceivable. But I hadn't the courage to ask. Two cancer patients, each ignorant of the truth about himself/herself, each protecting the other: to take away their tickets to survival would be too cruel.

In the wall facing us, at roughly three-foot intervals, were three tunnel entrances. The one on the right had tracks and headed downhill; the center one was a dead end; and the one on the left was a gentle ascent, up stone steps. The shill cocked his head.

"That's funny. Which one was it?"

"If you went to the river, it's got to be the one on the left."

"I'm damned if I remember this—three passageways lined up side by side. I guess it's because we were running so fast. I almost caught up with him here, too."

"The one on the right is another dead end. It leads to a cave-in."

"You know your way around, don't you?"

"It's part of my daily routine: morning exercises, and then two hours surveying or more. I've never missed a day yet."

The way leveled off, then went sharply downhill. We took the stairs by the wall. A wind blew up at us, caused by the difference in temperatures. Mixed with the smell of water and seaweed was the sharp odor of metallic ions.

"Does that river empty into the sea?" he asked.

"I think in part it leads into a spring at a Shinto shrine. There are a couple of noodle stands that serve rainbow trout."

"No effects as yet from the chromium?"

"None that I know of."

"Later on, let me have a look at your surveyor's map," he said. "You've got one, haven't you?"

"There's a rough sketch hanging on the wall of the conference room," I said, unable to bring myself to say "operational headquarters."

"But you did do some surveying, didn't you?" he said. "You must have some record of your work."

So I did. In fact, I had kept detailed records: sixteen ichnographic projection drawings that had taken a full six months to complete. But for some reason, when I tried to convert them to orthographic projections I ran into trouble. When I forced myself to visualize a perspective drawing of the quarry interior, landslides and cave-ins took place in my head. Doubtless there were flaws in my surveying techniques and drawing ability. But a bigger source of the problem, I believed, lay in the slipshod, hit-or-miss operations of the stone-quarrying authorities themselves, or their workmen. No straight line was in fact straight, no right angle was in fact ninety degrees. Errors accumulated little by little until finally southwest was skewed around to southeast, and the floor that should have been below a flight of stairs came out on top.

Yet the degree of complexity involved could not be attributed solely to haphazard, trial-and-error procedures. Four companies had leapfrogged through the mountain in fierce competition, ignoring all agreements. If Company A crawled under the belly of Company B and tied up its legs, Company B swung ahead of Company C and pinned down its head; Company C poked holes in Company D's arse, while Company D slammed Company A in the ribs. Unreported cave-ins—even bloodshed—had apparently been everyday affairs.

"Right now I'm working on a new system of surveying," I said. "By correlating temperature, humidity, and wind velocity, it seems to me you should be able to make a contour map, or a map of air pressure distribution, the kind they use in weather forecasts."

"Have you got something against it?"

"Against what?"

"Showing me your surveying maps. Why are you holding back? Is there some reason you can't show them to me?"

"They wouldn't do you any good."

"I'm the one to decide that."

I did not like the way he was talking. It was like hitting someone and then complaining that he'd hurt your fist.

"Listen—there's the sound of running water."

"Yeah. It's not far now."

At the bottom of the slope the footing was suddenly precarious. The walls were rougher too. The floor was littered with fragments of scaled-off stone. Casually I turned and shone my flashlight on the point where the terrain changed. Along with the terrain, the color of the rock changed as well: the shift from dark green to a paler hue, the color of dried mugwort leaves, was clearly delineated in a slanting line. That line was dotted with a number of holes, hollows in the wall where rock had scaled off. Second hollow from the top . . . Outwardly it appeared no different from the others, but to me it bore a special significance: here was where I had set a charge of dynamite. When the time came, one flick of the switch would blow it up. This very spot would mark the division between the interior and exterior of the ship. The area from this point on would, in effect, cease to exist. All I had to do was take a few steps back, pull the switch, and the shill too would be trapped in that nonexistent space, unable to move either forward or backward.

If he thought he could hijack my ship with the aid of a simple map, he was dead wrong. He underestimated me. This wasn't the only place where I had set dynamite: in all there were nine hidden charges. Wires connecting the detonators led to a single spot where I could set off all the explosives at one stroke. (For safety's sake, I had used two separate systems of wiring.) The trigger switch also set off the infrared sensors for lighting in the captain's cabin. The manipulation of the switches on the board I carried with me was barely more complex than turning on the lights. This was simultaneously the signal for the ark to set sail. Vibrating from the blasts, the ship would be cut off from the outside world in an instant, and a siren would sound the alarm, calling all hands to their posts. And then, for however long, this would be all that remained of the world.

At first I hesitated over where to set the explosives. I thought the bigger the ship's tonnage, the better. Eight years before, when the stone-quarrying companies ceased operations, they had sealed off all mine shafts and tunnels, according to regulations. The city council and government offices alike were of the official view that no aperture remained. True, apart from this passage to the tangerine grove, and the one leading to the boiler room of the city hall, there were no apertures large enough for a person to squeeze through. But a nuclear bomb is a different matter. No opening, however small, can be safely overlooked. Unfortunately, my investigations showed that the entire quarry was riddled with holes—apertures for wiring, plumbing, water supply, ventilation, and so on. The more I checked, the more I found. The only thing to do was to alter my approach. If I couldn't cut off the mountain from an outer world contaminated by radiation or radioactive substances, the only recourse was to abandon the bulk of the mountain that was vulnerable. I decided to set dynamite in those places that seemed most likely to cave in. Pulverized rock would make an excellent filter.

Of course, being neither a geologist nor a civil engineer, I can't say exactly what will happen in the blasts. All I know is what area I *think* will withstand them safely. Starting with the work hold in the middle, it should be safe as far as the second hold out from there. I can't offer a professional guarantee, but I *am* sure it's more than wishful thinking. Waterstone, as its name implies, is highly compatible with water; as its moisture content increases, its characteristic green grows deeper and it becomes harder, stronger, and so fine-grained that it polishes to a high luster. I settled on the present work hold as the heart of the ark by taking into account the distribution of that hue. For the rest of it, people will just have to take my word. Should the explosions set off a chain reaction that ultimately destroys the ark, so be it. The important thing, after all, is not really survival per se, but the ability to go on hoping, even in one's final moments. And we would certainly be guaranteed a gigantic tomb, at least the size of the pyramids!

"The going gets tricky here."

Piles of stones blocked the way—pieces of rubble great and small, less hewn than smashed. Some were heaped up like cairns built to guide the souls of dead children to paradise. The tunnel ended there. Beyond was a steep cliff, thirty-five feet down or more. In my mind this was the boundary.

"Shall we take a leak?" he asked.

"Might as well."

He seemed fairly tense, now that we were about to plunge into enemy territory. After all that beer, it was hardly surprising that he should want to relieve himself. Side by side, we urinated across the heaps of stones, into empty space. The sound echoed from so far away that I grew uneasy, leaned backward instinctively, and ended up wetting my trousers. The light from my helmet did not reach the bottom. Heavy fog at the base of the cliff also cut off visibility.

"That's funny. There wasn't any fog before." Setting foot on the top rung of a steel ladder in the left corner on the edge of the precipice, the shill peered fearfully down.

"It's probably caused by the difference in temperature and humidity between the subterranean water and the open air."

"After making sure which way he went, I grabbed the ladder and took off after him. But when I got down there, damned if he hadn't disappeared."

"I'm telling you, he dove underwater. There's probably a tunnel below the surface of the water."

"It couldn't have been more than ten or fifteen seconds. I still can't believe it. There wasn't any of this fog then, either."

"Well, let's go down."

"And just what do you intend to do when we get there? Be honest, Captain."

"Well, I think it's probably better not to come on too strong—no needless provocation. I know, I know, attack is the best defense, but still I'd prefer to try talking things over. We could try to reach some sort of compromise, with this river as a boundary between us. . . ."

The shill glanced at his watch, in the light from his miner's hat.

"Eighteen minutes."

"Pardon?"

"Since we left, I mean."

"It doesn't seem that long."

"What are you going to do, Captain? You suit yourself. I'm going back."

"Back where?" I couldn't grasp what he meant.

"Where we came from. That'll be just over half an hour, round trip. Perfect timing."

"But why? The river is right down there."

"That was just an excuse. I don't really give a shit about it."

"Well, *I* still think it's worth investigating. If we look around, we might even find some wet footprints."

"Nah, that ladder is too risky. It's not worth it."

"You're the one who started this."

"I told you—it was an excuse."

"For what?"

"Look, I'm not crazy enough to go picking a fight with some guy when I don't even know if he's an enemy or a friend." He glanced at his watch again, and kicked the dirt like someone getting ready for a foot race. "But I'll tell you this: whoever underestimates me is going to live to regret it."

He went even faster on the return trip. I tried to call out to him, but I was gasping for breath, and it was all I could do to keep up with him. I couldn't understand. Who was he accusing of underestimating him? The insect dealer was drunk and asleep, and I couldn't recall any particularly stormy exchanges between them. But there wasn't anybody else. I had the feeling that cancer wasn't the only shadow hanging over him.

He did not stop until he reached the firing range. I had no intention of asking questions, but even so he fitted an arrow into the crossbow, drew the bow full, spun around and took aim at my feet.

"From here on, don't utter a sound. Better take off your shoes too."

"Komono was drunk, you know. I can't believe he was only pretending to be asleep."

"I said shut up!"

His voice was so charged with electricity that it all but gave off sparks. I took off my shoes and stuck them in my belt. I wanted to hold him back, but he gained another big lead on me at the lift. By the time I had lowered myself back onto the floor of the work hold, he was way across the room.

I tiptoed into the last tunnel. I had no great mind to stick up for the insect dealer. In a sense, he had it coming. His overbearing ways—especially his overly familiar way with the girl—had riled me too. But the shill was not a terribly good shot. Whether the girl was on the top or the bottom, he might err and hit her instead. Even if he did hit his target, things would be sticky. Calling an ambulance would be bad enough; once the police were called in, the ship was doomed even before its launching. Perhaps a mortal wound would be better. Once the body was chopped up and flushed down the toilet, nothing would remain but a lingering un-pleasantness. And in six more months (following the worst-case scenario), burdened now with two cancer-ridden corpses, I would go back to being a lonely captain, probably never recovering sufficiently to seek other buyers for the tickets to survival.

The shill was standing stock-still in the tunnel entrance-way, weapon poised. The arrow was still fixed in place, with no sign that he had fired. Below the bridge, the blue-and-red-striped sleeping bag was rolled up like a potato bug, and from it emerged deep snores.

The shill put his weapon on safety and smiled awkwardly. "I have a feeling . . . I'll bet those old geezers in the Broom Brigade are planning an attack for right around tonight."

"What makes you say that?"

"Just a feeling I have. Anyway, Komono should be ashamed of himself—knocked out flat by a few beers!"

T H E girl too lay asleep, face down on the chaise longue, with a light blanket pulled up over her head (by which I do not mean to suggest that the lower half of her body was exposed), her snores rivaling those of the insect dealer. The shill sat down in the middle of the stairs and wiped the corner of his mouth with the back of his hand. He said:

"I wasn't really going to shoot. That's the honest truth. Even if the worst possible thing was happening right before my eyes, I wouldn't have pulled the trigger. I'm not as tough as I look and talk, really; it's all an act. . . . I'm just a failure. And I go into jealous fits over her. Even though in six months she'll never belong to anyone again. She's something, isn't she? I mean, don't you think so?"

"Yes, I do. I have from the first."

"Back when I was with the gangsters, I happened to read Darwin's theory of evolution. In comic book form—but still, it changed my whole view of life. *Yakuza* pride themselves on living dangerously, but you know, if their fights are real, so are everybody else's. If a gangster is somebody who lays his life on the line every day, then everybody's a gangster. But gangsters can see only their own little world. Life is reduced to a bunch of fights over territory. You wouldn't believe how spiteful they are."

"So the problem is who the 'fittest' are."

"Exactly. Basically, everyone who's alive is fit. Suppose Komono were to try to take her pants off and succeed—he'd be one of the fittest."

"Everything seems so clear to you."

"Not really. It's just evolutionary theory."

"Speaking of fights over territories—the eupcaccia has a very small territory, doesn't it? Barely the length of its own body."

His mind continued on its own track. "Religions aren't fair," he said, "with their heavens and hells."

I laughed. "I'm starting to see what you meant when you said a shipload of respectable people would be dull as hell."

"Absolutely. This is no Olympic village. No point in gathering a lot of clean-cut athletic types."

"Speaking of the Olympics—did you ever hear of something called the Olympic Prevention League?" He didn't answer, and I dropped the subject.

The coffee was ready. I placed two cups side by side on the edge of the toilet, and poured out coffee that looked like watery brown paint. The shill propped up the insect dealer and held a cup of scalding coffee to his mouth.

"All right, Komono, wake up. It's only nine-thirty. I've got to talk to you, so wake up."

Opening one bloodshot eye, the insect dealer slurped a mouthful of coffee, made sure he was holding the gun, shook his head, and went back to sleep without uttering a word.

The shill and I went back up the stairs, and sat drinking our coffee and waiting for something to happen. Yawning without opening his mouth, he said, "I wonder if they're really going to attack. What do you think, Captain?"

"Shall I try again to get hold of Sengoku?"

"Why?"

"Based on circumstantial evidence, he's a strong suspect, isn't he?"

"Why are they all old men in that outfit? Aren't there any old ladies?"

"Apparently not, although I don't know why. Maybe the old ladies are too in touch with reality."

Too much coffee upsets my stomach. Thinking I'd boil myself an egg, I headed for the galley, when out of the corner of my eye I glimpsed a human figure lurking around the tunnel entrance. I set down my coffee cup, snatched the converted Uzi out of the insect dealer's sleeping bag, and took off.

"What is it?"

"There's somebody over there."

The shill jumped down the stairs in a single bound, quickly overtaking me and running on ahead. As he planted himself in the entrance to the work hold, crossbow at the ready, he looked reassuringly strong and reliable.

"Nobody in sight. There wasn't enough time to climb the shaft; maybe he got out that way." He snapped his fingers in the direction of the tunnel leading to the second hold (the future residential area).

"Impossible. It's a dead end, and besides—" I caught myself. That's right, the shill still didn't know. I took a step forward, held out the barrel of the Uzi, and waved it up and down. A bell rang. I turned off the switch under the rails. "I tested it before too. The warning system is all in working order."

"That's funny."

"Maybe I only imagined it. The same thing's happened before, more than once. This place is so big and empty, and the light is so dim, that even a piece of dust in your eye can look like all sorts of things."

"Are you telling me I only imagined what I saw?"

"I didn't say that."

"It's not impossible, though. I've never lived anywhere as big as this."

"But if you caught sight of him repeatedly . . . I mean, if it was an optical illusion you'd have seen him once, period."

"I suppose so. You want to have a look in that pile of stuff over there?"

The shill aimed his crossbow at the palisade of old bikes concealing the entrance to the storerooms. The bike handles were turned at odd angles, with no sign that anyone had been through. Whoever knew about the camouflage would also know that inside was a dead end. If he meant to use the arsenal, however, that was different. In that case, there was even the possibility of counterattack. I cocked my Uzi and held it ready. Lining up the handlebars in the right and left corners so they faced the same way, I swung the palisade out and switched on the lights. While the shill guarded the entrance, I checked out the interior, step by step. Nobody was there.

"My nerves were getting to me, I guess," I apologized.

"You're not the only one. I made a damned fool out of myself." The shill ran his fingers lightly along the barrel of my Uzi. "Aha, so this was no toy after all. Now I see why it attracted Komono, with his eye for guns."

"It's converted. If you go easy on the gunpowder, you can use it as a semiautomatic."

"Put it on safety, please. Things like that have a way of causing more trouble than they're worth."

"Komono says a crossbow isn't much use against more than one enemy, since you can't fire in volleys."

"Have all the guns in here been converted?"

"Yes, more or less."

"I'll be damned. You've got yourself enough for a small army."

He sat back in the chair in the lowest armory and looked around excitedly. He'd spoken like a pacifist a moment before, but now that he found himself surrounded by weapons, it seemed to set his blood racing after all. It was certainly true that guns could be the source of much trouble. I kept them to use against rats, snakes, and stray dogs; to date, I had exterminated seven rats and one cat. For protection against human invaders, I had greater faith in dynamite. In the end, man-made cave-ins would protect us like the door to a safe.

"I'll go get the sleeping bags," I said.

"Wait a minute. This is where we are now, right?" The moment he set eyes on the wall map, he was absorbed. When I came back lugging two new sleeping bags, he was tearing off strips of red vinyl tape and sticking them on the map, like some big chief of staff.

"Here, and here—see, the enemy has to cross at least three barriers. Especially climbing down the shaft here, they've got to go single file with their backs turned toward us. It'd be a cinch to wipe 'em out."

"As long as they didn't attack while we were sleeping. This one with the yellow stripes is a medium. You can have it."

"Looks like we'd better have sentry duty tonight, anyway."

We went back under the bridge and laid out the sleeping bags, with the insect dealer at the far end, me by the stairs, and the shill in the middle. My brain felt suddenly exhausted, as if somebody had kneaded it in flour. Without asking, the shill helped himself to a beer from the refrigerator.

"If the free drinks go on forever, that only reduces their value," I said.

"Is that a nice thing to say? Of course I expect you to bill me for anything I eat or drink. That's a fundamental rule of community life, isn't it?—pay for what you consume."

"About the night watch—you and I are the only ones awake."

"I know. Funny, isn't it?" He opened the can and lowered his mouth to it as carefully as if it contained hot soup. "Get a load of Watermelon Head here, sleeping like a pig."

"Watch your language." My voice went shrill despite myself.

"I didn't mean anything by it." He smiled apologetically, then quickly straightened his face and said, "After all, if I really thought so I'd never say so, right?"

"You shouldn't look down on pigs." I took off my shoes, tore the label off the brand-new sleeping bag, unzipped it, and stretched out inside, propping myself up on my elbow. "Sure, they're stupid. At least as stupid as people. But what's *really* stupid is to go around thinking pigs are inferior to people. I've already told this to Komono too: I'm not having any muscle-worshipping types share this ship with me. It's going to be a long trip."

"All right."

"Do you know what mark the Olympic Prevention League chose as their symbol?"

"No—what?"

"A pig. A round green pig, like a ball with legs. Olympic Prevention League members wear the badges on their chests. You may have seen them—round green badges trimmed in silver. When they march in demonstrations, the members carry a flag with the same design. Just so no one will think it's an ad for pork cutlets, the mouth is slightly open, with tusks bared. OPL is still a tiny fringe movement, but I hear people with that badge are scattered all across the country, and all around the world. Most are obese, or at least fairly overweight. Which Olympics was it, now . . . remember, on the TV news? Members of the Olympic Prevention League marched boldly onto the playing field, waving their flags. I remember I felt a little bit sympathetic to their aims, but also a little put off, a little embarrassed, actually. The slogans began pouring in from hand mikes:

" 'Down with muscle-worship!'

" 'Down with vitamins!'

" 'Down with the national flag!' "

. . . They wanted to pull down all the national flags on display overhead. It certainly is true that that cluster of national flags in the Olympic stadium is presumptuous. People are all too ready to pick sides for no good reason. Showing the national flag only takes advantage of that inborn weakness. And why should any country get excited about a well-developed set of muscles? It's unnatural. There's got to be some plot. Besides, to raise the national flag and play the national anthem in honor of robust bodies constitutes a clear act of discrimination against the rest of the citizenry. There in that sports arena being used openly as a ceremonial hall to exalt national prestige, it was only natural for the pig group to launch an attack on the flags, and for the steering committee to take the defensive.

Grounds keepers ran around blowing police whistles. Angry at having the games interrupted, the spectators began throwing things:

hamburgers

boxed lunches   *tin cans*

spectacles   *strings*   *tissue paper*

false teeth

condoms   *chewing gum*

Next the players and guards together attacked the league members. The announcer issued earnest appeals, as if gargling in sand:

"Players, please return to your assigned positions   and stand by. The games will resume momentarily.
Spectators are requested to wait quietly.   The lavatories are presently all   occupied."

But by then it was impossible   to stanch the flow of waste articles that came   pouring down the bleachers like lava.   The conical   stadium was soon buried in trash, and   some of the judges announced they were   leaving. The players became more and more crazed.   Not   content merely with ripping the prevention league   pigs apart, they con- signed the officials to   oblivion and then advanced against the specta   tors. A sports commentator offered his analysis: "If   things go on this way it will be a darned shame for the   athletes."   Finally the whole stadium swelled up   like bowels with the anus sutured shut, in the shape   of a giant toilet.   It also bore some resemblance to   a dirigible with the back hollowed out.   At any moment   it would lift off tearing away from its anchor and go   scudding over the seas where a hundred tropical   low-pressure zones clustered.

Better split before they come checking tickets.

Everybody knows they were pork cutlet restaurant owners in disguise.

[And they all lived
happily ever after.]

"**H E Y**, Captain, isn't there any TV here?"

I awoke at the shill's voice. I had a feeling we had had some sort of run-in over hogs, but I could not tell exactly where that had left off and my dream had taken over.

"Forget it."

"Darn. It's almost time for my favorite show."

"Look, TV isn't going to be around forever."

"Don't you get bored?"

"I just take a trip somewhere if I do: with three-D aerial-photograph maps, I can fly anywhere I want. Want to take a look?"

"That's okay, I'm not in the mood."

The shill gave a huge yawn, fell on his sleeping bag, and wiped tears from his eyes. At last, for the first time in hours, it was back: silence. The walls of the underground quarry sighed as if they knew my feelings. *CCCCCCcccccccchhhhhh . . . . . .* a silent mutter as of grass seeds bursting open. Until now these walls had seemed a second skin to me. They had seemed the inner walls of my own bowels, turned inside out for my contemplation. Now that special intimacy was gone forever. Community life meant that they must appear the same to all. The walls were ordinary walls, the floors ordinary floors, the ceilings ordinary ceilings. I would have to refrain from talking out loud to no one but the stone; from singing crazily off key till I was covered in sweat; from dancing ecstatically in the nude. Yes, everything had changed. Even if I could somehow have chased away the shill and the insect dealer, the old tranquillity would never return. Someone was watching me. Even if what I saw had been an illusion, the figment the shill had spotted and chased had at least a ninety percent chance of being real. How else could I explain the way my traps had been tinkered with?

Even if the mysterious interloper was Sengoku, it would mean that he not only knew about the secret toilet and the alarm system but also had been listening in on my monologues and songs. The mere thought made every mucous membrane in my body feel soaked in tannin.

Until I could devise a definite counterplan, there seemed no choice but to keep watch, after all. As I was thinking this, the shill suddenly began to snore. He was fast asleep without any pillow at all, let alone one wrapped in an old undershirt. Now I was the only one awake. That saved the trouble of drawing lots to see who went first. I was angry, but I didn't feel like forcing either of them to wake up. Collecting the crossbow and the Uzi, I headed for the galley to do what I always did when I couldn't sleep: sit on the toilet and munch on chocolates, washing them down with beer. I might have a good look now at my eupcaccia too.

But the focus of my interest turned from there up the stone steps to the top of the bridge. Unreal images began to proliferate. The girl lay asleep now, her whole body pressed tightly against the chaise longue, which was permeated with the smells of my body. Her body nestled in the very curves hollowed out by mine. Perhaps in her dream she was even now smelling my smells. The chaise longue was embracing her bare flesh in my stead. She must be receiving some sort of signal in her dream; if she had normal reception capability, at any moment now she would arise. . . . And then in fact she *did* get up and cross over the bridge toward me. She peered down from the end of the parapet, leaned her chin on her hand, and waggled the fingers.

"Captain, something's making a funny noise in the lockers."

"Ssh."

From the waist up she was wrapped in terry cloth the color of a dried leaf; from the waist down she might very well be nude. A T-shirt had been her only upper garment, so it was entirely possible. Pointing to the two men fast asleep in their sleeping bags, I made an exaggerated show of discomfiture, acting as if she and I were accomplices. She waved back. Could she be thinking what I was thinking?

"I think it's locker number three. Can you hear?"

"It's probably someone trying to reach me on the wireless."

At any rate, I was lucky to be able to respond to this new development by myself. Holding the crossbow in my left hand, the Uzi in my right, I climbed the stairs with slow steps. Sniffing, I wondered what it would feel like to slap her bottom on the bare skin, without any skirt in between.

16

—**M O L E** here. Over.

—Sengoku here. This is an emergency. Can you talk now? Have you got time? Over.

—What do you mean, have I got time? I've been looking all over for you. Over.

—I've got to see you and talk to you in person. It's very important. Over.

—Relax, will you? Stop exaggerating. Over.

—It's about the Broom Brigade. But I can't risk having anyone listen in. Over.

—I've already checked to see if anyone's on this channel. Over.

—There's a body. They want me to get rid of it. I can't have anyone listening in. Over.

—A body, did you say? Whose? Anyone I know? Do they know who the murderer is? Over.

—Meet me somewhere and I'll tell you all about it. Over.

The girl whispered in my ear: "Don't let yourself become an accessory to crime. It could be a trap."

I was perched on the armrest of the chaise longue. She was seated with knees raised, shoulder against the same armrest.

If I so much as turned my head and looked down, our eyes would meet at close range. The voice kept calling.

—Hello, hello, manhole manager, please come in. Is there someone there with you? Over.

The girl smiled and stuck out her tongue.

—You know perfectly well there isn't. Over.

—Anyway, it's not such a bad idea, is it? Considering the nature of the item, I think we could probably charge a fairly exorbitant amount. Of course the Broom Brigade wants to open direct negotiations, but I knew you wouldn't like that. I explained that you're something of a recluse, and they finally accepted that. But if you don't cooperate, they're going to send their representative charging over there. Over.

—Who's that? Not my dear old dad, I hope.

—Just meet me. Although he isn't as bad as you make him out to be. Over.

—You keep your opinions to yourself. Now the son of a bitch has taken up murder, is that it? Over.

—Nobody said that. Over.

—I can't trust you if you're going to stand up for him, Sengoku. Over.

—All I'm doing is carrying on hardheaded diplomacy, as secretary-general of SWAMDI. I'm completely neutral. Stop being such a goddamn mole, will you? Over.

—You'd better have a barbecue or something before that body starts going bad on you. Over.

—That's not as safe as you might think. You'd better talk it over with Inototsu. He's got lots of ideas. Look, now's the time to forget the past and be reunited, father and son. It's been five years. Listen to the advice of a friend. Over.

—I'm disappointed in you, Sengoku. I was going to give you a key to this place. You probably don't know what that means—then again, maybe you do. A key so you could come and go freely. But now I'll have to think again. That rat who was running around getting into everything was probably you, anyway. Over.

"Don't." This time it was the girl's turn to slap *me* on the bottom. "You mustn't show your hand."

—There seems to be some misunderstanding. Having both you and Inototsu look on me with suspicion puts me in a very difficult position. Over.

—I have nothing to discuss with you. Over and out. QRT.

—Wait. He's not the type to let anything drop. I'm afraid of him myself. Besides, if this new deal works out, I think he'll reconsider about the shipments of hexavalent chromium too. Over.

—No comment. QRT.

—Just the other day he grabbed a pushy junior high school student and crushed his fingers in a pair of pliers. The guy figured Inototsu was just bluffing, so he paid no attention— and damned if Inototsu didn't go ahead and do it. Crush, crunch. You should have heard the poor guy scream. Over.

—QRT. QRT.

—Mole, you're stubborn. If you change your mind, get in touch with me again right away. I'll be waiting. QRT.

As I returned the apparatus to the locker, the girl asked curiously, "What does that mean, 'QRT'?"

"It's an expression used by ham radio operators. It means 'communication ended.'"

"Really? How funny."

"I feel terrible. Bad aftertaste."

"That was amazing," she said. "Crushing someone's fingers in pliers! There really *are* people like that."

"Sengoku's no angel, either."

"You were too open with him. I'll bet Komono would have handled him more shrewdly."

"I bought his sweet-potato cakes every day for over six months; I'm his best customer. Not only that, I paid him a straight twenty percent commission on the hexavalent chromium business. . . ."

"What are you going to do? If you don't do something, he said they'll come charging in here."

"They're trying to scare me with that talk about a dead body. Who could it be? Do they mean to drag me into it so they can implicate me in the murder?"

"There's no point in wasting time worrying. The best thing to do is tell the others about it and see what they say."

"It won't work."

"Decide that after you've talked it over with them."

"I just wasn't cut out to be the leader of a group like this."

"Now now, there's only four of us."

"Do you know the three basic conditions necessary for survival in a nuclear shelter? First is waste disposal, second is ventilation and temperature control, and third is management."

"Wait," she said. "Before you wake them up, let me go to the toilet. The noise of flushing it will probably wake them all up, anyway."

Was she seriously thinking of straddling that seat wearing nothing but a terry-cloth blanket? Impossible; too indecent. Surely she would put on some clothes first. Here, right in front of me, she would stand in her panties and step into the red artificial leather skirt; then, nude from the waist up, she would pass her arms through the sleeves of that T-shirt with the palm trees on the front. I could gaze at close range on her underarm stubble and the shape of her navel. Finally I too would be able to share a moment of casual intimacy with a woman. All because I had built the ark. Or was I only a pig to her—no one to be shy around?

The blanket arched through the air, landing on the chaise longue. Unfortunately, she was fully dressed, wearing both skirt and T-shirt. I'd half expected as much. Still, I couldn't

help feeling the wistful pang of a child deprived of a longed-
for treat. After she was gone, the terry-cloth blanket remained where it had fallen, folded in half and twisted in a
doughnut shape . . . the shape of eupcaccia dung. Falling
on my knees, I buried my face in it, breathing its odor of
moldy bread. That was the blanket's odor, not hers.

The sound of urination, like an unsteady arc drawn with
trembling hand. The sound of paper being torn. Then the
roar of flushing: water and air engaged in mutual attack,
plummeting simultaneously. I regretted my failure to ask her
name. And who, I wondered, was the real cancer patient—
him or her?

After a time, there came the sleepy, cheerful laughter of
the men, evidently teasing her about something. With me
not there, they seemed to feel liberated. I myself grew weary
of my gloomy personality; and yet when I was alone I'd often
managed to feel quite gay. Singing, laughing, acting out solo
dramas with only the stone walls for audience . . . dancing
with spidery nimbleness on wafers of stone . . . seldom
bored or lonely . . .

"Captain," called the voice of the insect dealer, still thick
with drowsiness. "So you heard from them, did you?"

"Come on down, I'll make some coffee." The girl's too-
innocent voice continued, and at last I raised my face from
the towel.

"Looks like we'd better be prepared to stay up all night,"
said the shill with a yawn.

Doing what one wants to do, and refusing what one doesn't
want to do, seem alike, but are in fact utterly different. I
didn't want to meet anyone's eyes. Holding the converted
gun, I sat on the third step. The girl was at the sink, measuring out ground coffee. The shill was seated on the john,
rubbing sleep out of his eyes. The insect dealer was sitting

up in his sleeping bag, waving a lighted cigarette over his head.

"This one puts me over my quota for the day," he said. "Somehow I feel as if I've been dreaming a long dream."

"I don't know—however great the water pressure may be, could you really flush a human body down this hole?" The shill stared down between his legs. "It *is* a human body, I assume."

"It must be." She switched on the coffeepot and wiped her hands on the shill's shirt.

"I did flush a dead cat down there once," I said, and purposely held my hands wide apart, exaggerating its size. "One this big, a tortoiseshell. It just popped right down."

"A human body isn't the same as a cat. The head alone is huge." The insect dealer inhaled deeply on his cigarette and blew the smoke out slowly through his nostrils, as if loath to part with it. "It can't get through anyplace narrower than the head. That's how they space the bars in animal cages, did you know that? By matching the spaces to the size of the animal's head."

"Stop it—how sickening!" The girl seemed genuinely angry. "Do you intend to go through with it?"

"Certainly not. That's the last sort of thing I'd want to get mixed up with."

"In that case, why didn't you come out and say so before? You sound so wishy-washy that you end by giving them an excuse."

"An excuse for what?" asked the shill.

"Well, Sengoku said that if the captain wouldn't enter into negotiations, they'd storm the place."

"Starting to talk tough, eh?" The insect dealer snuffed out his cigarette on the sole of his shoe.

"They'll come in here over *my* dead body," I declared.

"I don't even want to talk to Inototsu. Let me make one thing clear: as long as I'm captain of this ship, he will never, ever, have boarding privileges. Even if I could fit the entire population of the world in here, I'd still keep him out in the cold. For me, survival means one thing: having *him* die."

"I can appreciate how you feel . . ." The insect dealer opened his eyeglass case and took out a pair of glasses. ". . . but how are you going to turn him back if he does come on board? Maybe you could if he was alone, but he's apt to come with his entire entourage."

"In other words, the captain's stymied." The shill took off one shoe and began to massage the arch of his foot. "Which means it's our turn now. All we have to do is go to the bargaining table in his place."

"That's right." The girl poured coffee into the cups. "After all, Inototsu is using that Sengoku person as *his* representative. There's no reason why the captain should have to handle this in person. Come get your coffee."

"He's got his representative, you've got yours. What could be more fair?" The shill took his cup and without warning dealt the girl's left cheek a sudden hard slap.

"Ow!" she screamed, raising a hand to her cheek. Then she held out her hands like a magician, and smiled. "Didn't hurt a bit."

"A little trick I learned." The shill passed a cup to the insect dealer and nodded. "You fit the hollow of your hand perfectly against the curve of the cheek, and make the air explode. It makes a terrific noise, with practically no pain. Perfect for making it appear you've had a falling-out with your companion, and confusing the other side. Works like a charm. What do you say, isn't that quite a trick?"

"It is indeed. Thanks to you, I'm wide awake." The insect dealer finished polishing his glasses and put them on, reseating himself on top of his sleeping bag. "If you agree,

Captain, he and I will take over the negotiations. A charlatan and a shill—now there's a combination for you."

"One practices deception, and the other's taken in by it. Perfect." She held out a coffee cup and peered up at me through her lashes. Since I was above her, she could hardly do otherwise, but I deliberately chose to read a hidden meaning into her look. If the insect dealer and the shill went out together, she and I would be alone.

"Sure," I said, "go ahead if you want. It's okay with me." I descended the steps and accepted a cup of coffee. The touch of her fingertips was like cold bean curd.

"But he's no pushover," I warned. "Logic doesn't get through to him. Besides, you talk about 'negotiations,' but my position is non-negotiable."

The girl gave me a swift wink. I broke off. Blowing on her coffee to cool it, she said:

"Now that you're awake, Komono, there's something I've been meaning to ask you. That bug called the eupcaccia—it moves around in a circle with its head facing the sun, while feeding on its own eliminations, isn't that right? So when it's dark and it goes to sleep, it's facing west. Right?"

"I suppose so," answered the insect dealer without enthusiasm.

"Then that's strange. What happens when it wakes up the next morning?"

"You're asking me? Ask the captain. He bought one, he must know."

"Actually I never gave it any thought," I said, "but now that you mention it, it *is* strange."

"Not really." The insect dealer put his glasses in the steam rising from his cup, clouding them on purpose. "Just use your head. A clock doesn't have to have a twelve-hour dial. There *are* such things as clocks with twenty-four-hour dials. I saw one once."

"But doesn't its head always point to the sun?"

"All it has to do is push against its dung and turn a half-circle. It all fits."

"Brilliant." The girl laughed, and pressed against the coffee cup, rippling the surface of the coffee. "You could make anything sound plausible. And it all comes off the top of your head—I really have to hand it to you!"

"Well, I'm afraid I can't be much of an optimist," I said gloomily.

"Don't worry," said the shill, and slurped his coffee noisily.

"That's right. My guiding principle," said the insect dealer, "is to think first, last, and always of your viewpoint, Captain. You've asked for our assistance, and we won't let you down."

"But this request for negotiations could be just an excuse for a skirmish, couldn't it?" I said.

"As a former SDF man, what do you say, Komono?" One eye on my Uzi, the shill kept going through the motions of pulling the trigger. "Could we defend ourselves if we had to?"

"Well, the enemy is a bunch of old men, and amateurs to boot. Structurally this place would make a good stronghold . . . and besides, you've got five crossbows, and seven re-modeled guns, right? Pretty good fighting power."

There was an intermittent buzz—a call on the radio. All four of us stood up at once and raced to the stairs, the shill in the lead, with the insect dealer holding the girl's hand and me pushing her by the hips (there was no need to do so, but somehow it made me feel better).

The voice that came out of the radio receiver sounded like an elephant with a cold. This time it was not Sengoku, but Inototsu.

—H E L L O, son, how're you doing? It's been a long time. This is your dad. Over.

—You've got one hell of a nerve. I have nothing to say to you. Period. Over and out.

—Wait. Let's bury the past. We're both grown men. Over.

—Impossible. Over and out.

—Listen, this is a deal you can't afford to pass up. Over.

—Over and out, over and out.

—*Listen*, will you? They're onto me.

Suddenly the shill gripped my wrist. My fingers opened and the microphone dropped, to be passed to the insect dealer's waiting hand. He shouldered his way up, pushing against my chest and forcing me out of the front position. That loss was more than made up for by the fact that my buttocks now pressed squarely against the girl's abdomen.

—Hello, please continue. This is the captain's representative. Over.

—Who the hell are you? Over.

—The name's Komono. I'm the captain's liaison man. Please state your business. Over.

—Liaison, huh? That's a good one. Suppose you tell me what you *really* do. Over.

—I sell educational materials. Insect specimens, that sort of thing. Now let's get straight to the point—who is onto you, and why? Over.

—You're quite a character. I'm talking about the body, of course. Over.

—Yes, I understand you have some problem about a dead body. Exactly what kind of body would this be—homicide, or accidental death, or what? Over.

—How am I supposed to know? Ask my son. Over.

—Stop playing games. What's that supposed to mean? Over.

—Just what I said. This is a body you people abandoned, after all. . . .

"You're crazy!" I yelled. "I don't know a goddamn thing about any dead body!" The radio was one-way, not adapted for integrated conversation; as long as the other person didn't push the right button, your voice wouldn't get through. Knowing this, I still yelled out, in reflex. The insect dealer patted me quickly on the shoulder to shush me up, and the girl pressed harder against my buttocks. Inototsu's voice continued, oblivious.

—Of course I have no hard evidence to prove it, but there's circumstantial evidence galore. If this gets out, it's going to be rather awkward. You see, my garbage collection business is a responsible social service organization: any illegally discarded objects we come across, we have a legal obligation to turn in to the authorities. But I'm willing to be flexible. Why not settle this just between ourselves? My son is still there, isn't he? You tell him not to be so stubborn. Children never understand their parents' feelings. Son, can you hear me? I think you've got a very worthwhile enterprise there, and I want you to know I'm supporting you one hundred percent behind the scenes. I certainly don't want to put you in a compromising situation. I think we can work together, help each other out. Over.

The shill called loudly from beside the mike. "What do you mean by a 'worthwhile enterprise'? Garbage collection?"

—Save your breath. I know all about it. You've got a nuclear bomb shelter, right? A very promising venture. Shows great foresight. I can't go into all the details now—that'll have to wait till we can get together—but I'm already making some moves on my own. Signing up members. My roster has some pretty impressive names on it too. You see, I think I can help you. . . .

"It *is* a threat," whispered the girl, her breath brushing the back of my earlobe.

"That dead body is a trick of some kind too, you can bet on it," said the insect dealer.

The shill bit his lip. "Looks like he's one jump ahead of us."

Inototsu continued talking, aware of these interpolations.

—You'd really be surprised. Why, I've got city officials, the director of a credit union, two doctors at the city hospital—even the president of Hishitomi Storage has signed a contract. Very promising, this little venture—it could really go places. You're not going to let a little thing like a body or two cramp your style, are you? That's all I have to say. Over.

Leaving the radio switched to reception, the insect dealer stuck out his jaw, teeth clenched, and said, "Captain, are you positive you know nothing about that body?"

"Of course I am," I answered.

Without even waiting for me to finish, the shill grabbed the microphone out of the insect dealer's hands and pushed the switch to transmission.

—Would you mind telling us the victim's age and cause of death? Over.

—You're new. What's your department? Over.

—I'm the purser. In charge of passengers' quarters. Over.

—Cute. To answer your question, I'm no pathologist, so I haven't any idea. Aren't you the ones with that information? Over.

—That's a leading question. No fair.

The shill switched off the radio and looked hard at me. "Couldn't one of those old men have wandered in and got caught in a trap? Say he got temporarily blinded, and staggered off that cliff. . . ."

"But the traps were all tampered with. Knocked out. Remember?"

"Whoever it was might have started doing that *after* he had already met with some sort of accident."

"I doubt it. Spray plastic takes a long time to harden that way."

"As far as that goes, the body may not be fresh, either," put in the insect dealer.

The buzzer sounded, urging the resumption of communication.

"Maybe it's that guy I chased before." The shill snapped his fingers. "Maybe he fell in the water and drowned. Wait a minute—that's it. I bet it's that fellow Sengoku."

"No, it couldn't be him," said the girl, her breath again tickling my earlobe. "The captain talked to him on the radio while you were both asleep."

"In that case, this body could be very fresh indeed," said the insect dealer, and slowly took back the transmitter, with an air of grim determination. "The murder could have taken place after that conversation. Even now, by rights, it ought to be the sweet-potato man we were talking to. Inototsu must know the captain hates his guts."

The buzzer kept squawking impatiently.

"That's right," I said. "Now that you say so, it *is* odd—

because the other transmitter is in Sengoku's store. It's strange for Inototsu to be talking on it."

"That's peculiar," said the shill. He licked his lips and swallowed. "Then was the sweet-potato man given the job of disposing of his own corpse?"

The insect dealer flicked the transmitter on.

—Wait a minute, please. We're having a consultation.

He turned the switch back off and said, "Supposing the sweet-potato man was killed at his store. Circumstantial evidence could very well point to the captain as prime suspect. But what motive could there be?"

"None—seeing as how I didn't do it!" I retorted.

"I mean Inototsu's motive."

"There's no point in thinking about it," said the girl. "You don't even know for sure that the sweet-potato man was the victim." Her hand rested lightly on my shoulder.

Instantly her opinion struck me as unassailable truth. "Check it out," I commanded the insect dealer. "Ask to speak to Sengoku."

Nodding, he flicked the transmitter back on.

—Come in. Sorry to keep you waiting. Would you mind putting the sweet-potato man on the line? Thanks. Over.

—He's gone out, but I can leave him a message. Over.

—What do you mean? You're in his store, aren't you? Over.

—No, I'm in the office over by the tangerine grove. There's a radio transmitter here too. "Sweet-potato man," eh? That's a good one. Suits him, all right. [Sounds of whispering.] Ah— it seems he's gone out on his motorcycle to get some cigarettes. He should be right back. Over.

"Ask him where they found the body," prompted the shill.

—Where'd you find the body? Over.

—As if you didn't know. Over here, by the tangerine grove entrance, of course. If you won't get rid of it for me,

I'll have no choice but to go to the police. In which case, like it or not, the entire quarry will be the focus of a police investigation. I'd like to avoid that as much as you. Put my son back on the line, would you? I assume he's still there, listening. It's high time we had a reconciliation, son. You've got the wrong idea about me. If it's the way I punished you when you were a kid that bothers you, I want you to know that I did it solely out of fatherly love. If that incident had ended up in family court, the shame would have followed you for the rest of your life. Then and now, I have only your best interests at heart. . . . You're there, aren't you, son? Try to understand. And as for that business about trampling my wife to death, it's a damned lie. What do you say, shall we make a deal? We *are* father and son, after all. Let's team up and do something really big. Besides, I've changed. Mellowed. And I'm not getting any younger. Over.

Shoving my way between the insect dealer and the shill, I stuck my face up to the transmitter and yelled:

—Quit the father-son baloney. It gives me the willies!

—I can't help it, it's true. Half of your chromosomes came from my sperm. Over.

—Over and out.

—Wait. All I want is a little bit of happiness in my old age. The Broom Brigade has made a good reputation for itself, and I'd like to do more for society. I want to live a useful life. You see, I *have* changed. Over.

"Oh, why did that damn body have to butt in like this?" I muttered. I felt defeated. It had been a bad day. Every conceivable contingency had burst on me with the force of a tidal wave. It was enough to make a person believe in Friday the thirteenth, or unlucky days on the Buddhist calendar, or any such baleful influences.

The insect dealer drew the microphone close to his mouth

and said quietly, in a voice suggesting strong willingness to compromise:

—I'm sorry, but could you give us a little more time? Over.

—I hate to repeat myself, but I want to patch things up with my son. It's only human nature. I'm human too, after all. Over.

"What do you think?" The insect dealer switched the set off and sighed.

"There really isn't any choice, is there?" The shill turned toward me, speaking rapidly. "Isn't that right? If you don't want to get on the wrong side of the Broom Brigade, you've got no choice but to go ahead and dispose of that body. If the real culprit would only turn up, there'd be nothing to fear. . . . That's it, we've got to come on strong there. Because if the captain didn't do it, then the murderer must be one of *them*."

"Not necessarily," said the insect dealer. "I believe the captain too. But that doesn't guarantee they haven't tampered with the evidence. Even supposing it's all fake, if they did a good job we can't let down our guard."

"Are there really only two entrances to this cave?" asked the girl. She rested her knee on the chaise longue, thereby shifting her weight so that our bodies were no longer pressed together. "Couldn't some other outfit be camped out somewhere *else* in here?"

"It's awfully hard to imagine," I said. I had no proof to justify ruling it out. With the rapidity of a high-speed printer, I flipped mentally through the surveying maps stored in my memory. Certainly there were large areas of the cave that I had not yet attempted to map or explore—I had in mind especially those old excavations midway down the eastern cliff, like settings for rock-carved Buddhas. But no tunnel connected them to the interior. The ground there was dry, and the quality of the rock poor; presumably they were trial borings that had been summarily abandoned. To the best of my knowledge, there had been no indications of human comings and goings anywhere, except at the tangerine grove entrance. I added, "And there's been absolutely no sign of anything. . . ."

"Once you start letting your suspicions grow, there's no drawing a line," said the shill. "Based purely on circumstantial evidence, I'm a prime suspect myself." Covering his mouth, he giggled in a way I found unbecoming and unsavory. "You have only my word that I let some suspicious character get away; there's no proof. Maybe I killed him, and I've just been putting on an act all this time. Seeing is believing, isn't it? I think we should go on over and see for ourselves."

"We've got to draw the line somewhere. We're just groping around in circles." The insect dealer put the radio back on the shelf, clasped his hands, and cracked his knuckles. "In a case like this, all the conjecture and speculation in the world won't get you anywhere. We've got to analyze the situation according to the facts at hand, and map out our strategy. Right? At the moment there are two issues facing us. One is the handling of the body, if it *is* a body. The other is the proposal from the Broom Brigade, or from their leader, Inototsu, concerning management participation."

"Hold on," I interrupted. "Quit taking the discussion in your own hands, will you?" By the barest fraction of an inch, taking care not to be observed, I nudged closer to the girl. The difference was so slight that I could not tell for sure whether or not our bodies were again touching.

"Don't worry," he said. Perspiration made his glasses slide down his nose. "As captain, your word is final; that goes without saying. I was only trying to clarify our situation. In other words, those two issues—the body's disposal and

Inototsu's proposal—have to be dealt with separately. Otherwise you play into his hands. He's trying to use the body as bait for his deal, and you mustn't fall for it. Isn't that so?"

The buzzer sounded again.

"That makes sense." The girl nodded briskly; the vibrations conveyed themselves to my buttocks. "They are separate issues. But supposing we turned down his offer of a merger—isn't it possible that he'd refuse to hand over the body?"

"That's right," I said. "Somehow we've got to find his weak spot." Boldly I edged over another tiny fraction of an inch.

"Nothing could be easier," said the insect dealer, wiping his glasses on the tail of his shirt. "Leave the bargaining to me. My tongue has gotten me through many a tight spot before. It'd be a cinch."

Somehow it had become established that either the insect dealer or the shill, or both, would represent me in the negotiations. I did not fully trust either one of them, and yet it was a welcome development. For one thing, I doubted my ability to confront Inototsu on an equal basis; for another, if the two of them went away, I'd be alone with the girl.

"But it's so disgusting." Disgust rolled around on her tongue like a taffy. "The toilet won't be fit to use anymore once we stuff a body down it, will it?"

"Don't worry," I said, "there's no blood." It was a lie. Even when I had flushed away the cat's body, let alone the aborted fetuses, it had been a while before I could bring myself to come near the toilet again. Once I forced myself to urinate there, and ended up vomiting. It was four or five days before I could begin fixing meals near there again. The only reason I was so calm now was that I still didn't take seriously the existence of this "body."

The buzzer went on screaming at us.

"Okay?" The insect dealer looked at each of us in turn. The shill and the girl gazed at me.

"Okay," I said, "but I must insist you stick to the matter of the corpse. Whatever happens, I'm not letting Inototsu on board."

The insect dealer flicked the radio back on.

—Hello. Sorry to keep you waiting. This is Komono, the liaison man. Do you read me? Over.

—Come in, come in. What took so long? Over.

—We've decided to consider your overture. But we can't settle on a fee until we've had a look at the body in question, and hear a detailed report about its place of discovery, condition at the time, and so on. Where would you like to meet? Over.

—Wait just a minute. You've got it all wrong. I'm doing you a favor by not reporting to the authorities. Over.

—Call off your bluff, Inototsu. We've got this whole conversation on tape from the very beginning. And as the first person to come upon the dead body, you not only failed to report it to the police but plotted to dispose of it illegally. Wouldn't that be a little tough to explain? Over.

The shill tilted his head and wet his lips. "Did you hear that? He *is* good, the son of a gun. I'll be damned."

Apparently it worked; for no reason, Inototsu began to laugh.

—All right, all right—this is no time to quibble. I'll meet you anywhere. I'll go there, if you want. It's fine with me. I've got a pickup at my disposal right now. Over.

"No! Don't let him near here!" I said.

"Why not?" The insect dealer covered the microphone with his hand. "Aren't you being a little paranoid? Of course it's up to you. . . ."

"He's got us outnumbered, and the Broom Brigade is a paramilitary force," I said. "What if they should attack?"

"If being outnumbered is the problem, it's more dangerous

for *us* to go *there*," said the shill, adding in a thin wheedle, "If they take us hostage, will you come rescue us, Captain?"

The insect dealer spoke into the microphone. —Well, that's the picture. . . . You heard, didn't you? Nobody trusts you. Over.

—Great. Well, then, how about someplace more neutral? I know . . . Laughter Hill. Nobody'll see us there. Ask my son, he'll tell you. Over.

"What's that? Laughter what?" Leaving the radio switched to reception, the insect dealer turned to ask me.

"Hill. Laughter Hill. It's an out-of-the-way place along the coast," I told him.

"Funny name."

"You go south from the station until you come to the Fishermen's Union warehouse, and then turn. There's a sea cave nearby, and depending on which way the wind blows, sometimes it makes a peculiar noise. Doesn't sound like laughter so much as it does a sniveling child with a bad cold. Quite unpleasant. But some people find it amusing, and laugh themselves silly when they hear it. Geriatric patients fighting off depression take bag lunches to the foot of the hill, and sit there just waiting for the wind to blow."

"How funny! It makes me laugh just hearing about it." The girl giggled, and twisted her body in such a way that her abdomen pressed like a softball into my buttocks. I in turn moved so as to expand our shared space (the area where her flesh melted into mine). No adverse reaction. I felt myself about to forget that I was a pig. As long as Inototsu stayed away, I didn't give a damn where the talks were held.

"Count me out," said the shill, flicking the radio off with a fingernail. "Once you get there you'll find nothing in sight but a dead body, and then all of a sudden the cops—no, thanks."

"You've got a point." The insect dealer switched the radio back on.

—Sorry, no go. None of us has enough nerve. The last thing we want is to get there and find nothing in sight but a dead body, and then suddenly have cops crawling all over us. Over.

—What? Would I play a dirty trick like that? Don't be preposterous. Remember, I'm the one who's devoted to cleaning up this town. Not just trash and empty cans, either—my real aim is a cleansing of the spirit. Nowadays it's essential—purifying the people themselves. I'm serious. I share your concerns from the bottom of my heart, and I want to join hands with you. What can I do to make you believe me? Over.

—Tell me this. You've already made a fair amount of money from advance ticket sales. Isn't that so?

—I told you I was recruiting people, in some very influential circles, too. You're welcome to supervise the whole operation, from members' roster to accounts. Over.

"He's crazy," I said. "When it comes time for the ark to set off, all the status and assets in the world won't be worth jack shit. And anyway, nobody accepts applications for boarding this ark but me."

—Hello. For now we'll limit the discussion to the question of the body. Still, you've got yourself a definite problem: how are you going to win our trust? Is that the best you can do? Over.

—Why am I so unpopular, anyway? I just don't get it. Over.

"It's because you never take a bath!" I yelled from next to the mike.

—What do you mean? For anybody engaged in sanitation work, taking baths is a duty—and plain common sense besides. The only times I don't take a bath are when I'm stone drunk. Bad for the heart. Over.

The girl began to laugh, her body chafing against mine with a hypnotic rhythm. I've never undergone hypnosis, but that must be what it's like: the flow of time disappears and "now" takes off alone, flitting capriciously here and there.

—For someone so generally disliked, you have an honest way about you. Shall I tell you what you could have said to allay our fears? There *is* something. Do you want to hear it? Over.

—Yes. Over.

—You should have said, "Try to think more like a real baddie. A real baddie wouldn't go to all these ridiculous lengths. He'd just haul the body over without a second thought, and dump it down from the overpass onto that pile of trash. Then you'd *have* to get rid of it, like it or not." Right? Over.

—You're right. My son is lucky to have a shrewd thinker like you for a friend. Is he listening? See, son, I'm not such a bad guy, after all. I can't help the way I look. All right, then, is Laughter Hill all right? Over.

—No, let's make it your office. That's near where the body was found, isn't it? Over.

—You tell me. Anyway, you're more than welcome. I've got drinks here, and all kinds of stuff to eat. If you want, I'll send somebody over to the beach entrance to pick you up. Now just don't spoil it by saying this will be a one-time visit. Over.

—Sorry, but that's just what it will be. When the body's out of the way, we'll have no more business with each other, right? What time shall we make it? Over.

—Who's coming? How many in all? Over.

—Two. Me, that's the liaison man, and the purser. You remember him. He said hello awhile back. Over.

—Isn't my son coming? Over.

—The captain? No. Out of the question. Over.

—Why? Over.

—Why else has he got a liaison man? This is my job. Over.

—Listen, I'm all alone here. That really has nothing to do with it, but—won't you please let me talk to him? You see if you can get through to him, will you? Just two or three minutes would be enough. Please. Over.

"Well, what do you say?"

"Never mind that. What's happened to Sengoku?"

—He wants to know where the sweet-potato man is. Over.

—That's funny; I guess he's still not back.

I spoke up.

—If that body turns out to be his, I'll never forgive you, you know that? He was one decent guy. He was one person I really thought I could work with.

—Don't get carried away. The man's in perfect health. I'm fond of him myself. You know what he's always saying? "Time to start over, time to wipe the slate clean. Serves 'em right, the bastards. . . ." I know just how he feels, too. It *is* time to wipe the slate clean and start afresh, sort out the ones who deserve to survive from all the ones who don't. There—isn't that it? Over.

—Isn't what what? Over.

—Isn't that the way you figure it too? We think alike, I'm telling you. Over.

The insect dealer interrupted. —What time shall we meet? Over.

—Just listen for a minute. When the apocalypse comes, deciding who ought to live and who might as well die will be no easy matter. Isn't that so? What sort of yardstick are you planning on using?

"What a joke," I snorted. "Who does he think he is, preaching to people?"

—I'm not preaching. This happened just awhile back, at the spring athletic meet of the local junior high school. They had a strange event called Survival Game. A contest to pick out the real survivors. Seems to have been the brainchild of some wise men who got together to decide how to use the underground air-raid shelter in the new city hall building. Shall I go on? Over.

The insect dealer looked my way to check my reaction. I refrained from issuing any objections. It weighed heavily on me to learn Inototsu had connections in that part of town.

—Keep it short, please. Over.

—Okay, I'll just cover the main points. As part of the fortieth-anniversary celebrations for the local junior high school, they had a contest to judge who was qualified to survive. From the day before, there was a front stalled just off the coast, and that morning it was drizzling; but the weather reports were encouraging, and they didn't want to waste all the money and effort that had gone into the preparations for the event—you know, preparing the athletic fields and the decorations and all—and this survival game was a major attraction from the start. How'm I doing? Shall I keep going? Over.

—Fine. Yes. Over.

—It was just a game, but at first everyone was a bit confused. The rules, you see, were unusual. There were winners and losers, but no direct competition. Which is maybe the way it goes with survival. First the playing field was divided lengthwise into three tracks, red, white, and blue, each with a starting line and a goal. Picture it. Then at the starting signal, all the participants headed for the flag of their choice. There was no need to hurry, and you didn't have to decide on a color till the last moment if you wanted, so it was all nice and relaxed. Everyone—teachers and students, families, special guests—they all set off casually, as if going on a hike. It could have had something to do with the prize, but for a junior high school athletic event it was a lavish production. Are you still with me? Over.

The four of us exchanged glances. For my part, as long as I didn't have to participate in the coming discussions, I was prepared to put up with a little inconvenience. As usually happens, silence was taken for reluctant consent.

—Yeah, I guess so. Over.

—So that's how the participants all started off. When everybody had chosen their color and lined up accordingly, the head judge rolled a die painted in the three colors. When the winning color came up, drums rolled and the flag of that color was unfurled. At that signal the losing teams were supposed to fall flat on the ground. Get it? Only the survivors were allowed to go back to the starting line. Then the starting signal would be given again. It went on like that, over and over, and the last one left would be the winner. Any questions? Over.

—If the winners were determined by a roll of the die, it wasn't so much a sporting event as a kind of gambling, was it? Over.

—Well, luck is a crucial factor in any battle, isn't it? So what if it was gambling? That only added to the excitement. After all, the first prize was a new little red Honda motor scooter, donated by the Association of Local Shopkeepers. I was in the event too, but with someone else throwing the die, there's really no point in wearing yourself out, is there? Over.

—Stay on the track, please. Just stick to the main story. Over.

—If you don't want to hear any more, that's okay with me. Over.

—You're off the track again. Over.

—Did I mention the weather? It got worse and worse—
just the opposite of the forecast—until rain was falling in
solid sheets. As if somebody was slathering it with a paint-
brush. . . .

The girl laughed. I didn't really think it was amusing, but
I joined in with an appreciative snort. Our hips were still
pressed firmly together. I knew I'd be called to account for
this eventually. Both the insect dealer and the shill had their
eyes tightly closed; the shill was licking his lips, the insect
dealer was swaying his head from side to side.

—The students' caps were plastered flat on their heads,
as if they'd been soaked in oil, and the sand in the playing
field was all mucked up with little pools of water here and
there. The school physician kept whispering in the principal's
ear, and each time the principal seemed on the point of calling it off. He'd sneak a timid look at the visitors' tent, but
there was nothing doing. That brand-new Honda scooter was
there just waiting for someone to claim it. If he'd called the
event off just because of a little rain, there would have been
violence. A promise is a promise. And so the game went on,
one way or another . . . and what do you think happened?
Over.

—What? Over.

—It turned into a circus. You see, the principal believed
that everyone's chances for survival ought to be equal, so
he imposed no limits on who could participate. And so the
athletic field was jammed with people. They had to shift
the starting line up fifteen feet to accommodate them all.
Starting time was delayed eight minutes, too. It was really
something; you should have seen it. That great mass of people, soaking wet, sending up spray in the air and wearing
down the ground under their feet. Mothers running past,
dragging bawling kids by the hand; old men waving canes;

an invalid, unsteady on his feet, leaning on a nurse's shoulder; members of the Fishermen's Union Youth League, charging forward in scrimmage formation. It took an unbelievably long time, but finally everyone poured into the goal area of their choice. The die was cast, the flag unfurled, the drums rolled. A few people got beat up for trying to switch places after it was all over, but for the first round, generally everyone was distributed evenly across the three goals. The only hitch was that at first the losing teams wouldn't hit the dirt like fallen soldiers, the way they were supposed to. To have to roll around in the mud and rain, on top of losing, is nobody's idea of fun, after all. The P.E. coach's voice came screaming from all the loudspeakers: "Losing teams, please fall down. You're dead. All losers, hit the dirt." People got sore and started to leave. I was one of them. Then a fusillade rang out: a volley of shots from an automatic rifle. Taped, of course, but it had a dramatic effect. Everybody recognizes the sound from TV and movies, even if they've never heard it live. The losing teams started falling down, right according to plan. They must have decided they owed the organizers that much, after all. Actually it didn't look like a battle so much as a mass execution. Are you still with me? Over.

The part of me pressed against the girl became a separate living creature, in growing control of me. It was wriggling, seeking to take me over completely. And there was another reason for the sense of unreality I felt: as the words came over the radio, each building on the rest like pieces of a puzzle, I sensed the shaping of another Inototsu, totally unlike the Inototsu I knew. I could hardly believe this was the same person. The Inototsu I knew would never talk this way, as if each separate word were just back from the cleaners, freshly laundered and pressed. I felt as if I were witnessing a cicada shedding its skin.

—Get to the point, will you? Over.

—So that's the way it went. Then the losing participants quit the field, and round two began, at a signal from the referee. The invalid hanging on to his nurse's shoulder—I think he must have had palsy—well, he was in the winning team, so he made a great nuisance of himself, getting in everyone's way. Even so, up to round four everything went swimmingly, the group decreasing by two-thirds every time. The end was in sight, and a lot of people started packing up to go. Then at round five, events took a strange turn. Shall I go on? Over.

—We're all ears. Carry on. Over.

—Thanks, glad to hear it. So they got down to about eleven people, I think it was. Everybody but the paralytic left the starting line together. So far so good. Then for some reason, right in front of the goals they all stopped. Guess what happened? Everybody just stood there, waiting for the paralytic to hobble down and catch up. Seeing him enter the blue zone, they all went in after him. Strange psychology, don't you think—call it superstition or mob psychology— the we're-all-in-this-together mentality. And the funny thing was that the die turned up blue. All eleven survived, but this way the prize stayed beyond their grasp. It wasn't a violation of the rules, though, so not even the judges could complain. At round six, exactly the same thing happened. Incredibly, round seven was the same. It began to seem uncanny. The rain was coming down harder and harder, and the lights came on, although it was really still too early. Even the students, who were usually a source of noise and confusion, stood lined up at the edge of the playing field like so many wet sandbags. Midway through round eight, the committee in charge went into deliberations, and just then the assault began, a sudden fusillade of automatic rifle fire. The sound effects director must have flipped out. All at

once the paralytic's knees buckled and he went down head-
first into the mud. Some people misunderstood, and laughed.
The school physician came running over, medicine bag in
hand, but it was too late. The game was called off. What do
you think? I think maybe that's what survival is all about.
Over.

—What happened to the scooter? Over.

—Ah, the prize. They had a raffle among the ten survivors. Then the family of the old invalid put up a squawk:
the others had all been waiting for him, they pointed out,
in order to do whatever he did, and since he had died *they*
should all be regarded as technically dead too. The argument does have a certain logic. Anyway, the issue remains
unresolved, and the scooter is kept locked up at the school.
Isn't that a strange story? Over.

—What does it all boil down to? Over.

—I don't know. Haven't any idea. That's exactly why I
want to get together with you and talk things over. Maybe
you can tell *me*. Over.

We all began smiling weakly. From the other end of the
wireless there came a noise like a blast of air escaping from
a heavy rubber balloon. That was Inototsu, laughing his
old, familiar laugh.

B A C K at the supply room in the work hold, we chose our weapons, the selections varying according to each person's perception of the situation. The insect dealer took a small converted revolver; had his goal been mere intimidation, something larger and more conspicuous would have served the purpose better. He and Inototsu had seemed to achieve a certain rapport in their exchanges over the radio, but perhaps inwardly he had been preparing for the worst. Or was this only a sign of his natural predilection for firearms?

After considerable hesitation, the shill settled on a tear gas pistol designed for self-protection. Actually it was a spray canister; I call it a pistol only because it was equipped with a trigger, and its range had been greatly increased. This too was for actual use, not mere show—although it served only to render the enemy powerless, and had no lethal effect. It was less potent than a converted gun, and yet it suggested he sought a sure means of self-defense; the knives and crossbows he never gave a passing glance.

The girl and I each took a crossbow. Just as our suppositions regarding the combat determined our choice of weapon, so those choices in turn would ordain the nature of the combat.

To appease the stray dogs out by the garbage dump, I picked out some pieces of dried sardines made from tainted fish (I got them at the fish market once a week, for dog food) and lifted the hatch. As if a curtain had gone up, warm air came sweeping down, and the singing of tires on concrete pavement filled my ears. I scattered the fish from the door of the scrapped car that camouflaged the entrance.

My way of imitating a dog's howl when I wanted to feed them differed from the howl I used to demonstrate my authority as boss. The effect, however, was similar. I signaled to the insect dealer and the shill to let them know the danger was gone. As long as that pack of wild dogs obeyed me, this was *one* way in and out, anyway, that was firmly in my control.

"When you get back, honk the horn, and I'll come out to meet you."

"We'll do our best not to come back with any unpleasant souvenirs."

Waving, they jumped hastily into the jeep. The dogs, as if sensing something unusual in the air, fought viciously over the food. I stood watching them off until the taillights disappeared in the shadow of the highway overpass. The high-level road cut off my view like a visor, so I could not see the sky. The rain appeared to have let up, but I couldn't make out the horizon, so probably there was still a heavy cloud cover. Only the lights of the fishing port on my far right gave any indication of where the sea lay. Traffic was fairly heavy. This was the hour when long-distance trucks passed by, aiming to be in Kyushu, far to the southwest, by morning. Out at sea, a gravel-carrier ship headed east.

On my way back inside the ark, I contemplated what might happen should the two men fail to return from their errand. Day after day alone with the girl, wrapped together in a world the consistency of banana juice—she in her red artificial leather skirt, with those red lips, and drooping eyes, and that straight nose, shiny at the tip; and beside her me, forever gazing at her like a mute gorilla. In fact, if I wished, there was no need to wait for some accident to befall my negotiating team. I could take unilateral steps to bring about the banana-juice conditions anytime I wanted.

All I had to do was set off the dynamite. Then all connection between the ark and the rest of the world would be severed. However many times they might circle the mountain, my two emissaries would never find their way back inside. Not only them—I had power to shut out and nullify the entire world. I knew the magic formula for escape from the world. Given that nuclear war was inevitable anyway, it would only be hastening its onset by a little bit. Then would begin the halcyon days of a eupcaccia (and eventually, no doubt, regret so searing that I would long to chop myself in a thousand pieces and flush myself down the toilet).

She was at the sink, washing coffee cups. Below her short skirt, her slim legs were like blown glass. Now that we were alone, she was somehow harder to approach.

"Never mind that," I said. "I'll do it afterwards."

She froze for a few seconds, then looked at me without a flicker and asked, "What were you planning on doing first?"

"I beg your pardon?"

"The dishes will come after something else, right?"

"I didn't mean that."

"Mean what?"

She turned off the faucet, went slowly up the stairs, and sat down on about the fifth step from the top, knees together, elbows in lap, chin in hands. Whether she was offended or being deliberately provocative, I couldn't tell. Remembering when the insect dealer got such positive results by slapping her on the bottom, I thought that on the whole it was probably better to assume the latter, even if wrong. But the right words wouldn't come. That's the way it always goes. I let my best chances slip away.

"I must say I don't like your attitude very much." Her voice was flat and colorless.

"What attitude?"

"It's like we're playing parrot. . . ." She managed a smile the size of a gumdrop. "Oh, I hate it. Really I do."

"Hate what? You can tell me."

"Being a woman. It's a terrible disadvantage."

"Not always, is it? You don't seem to be at a disadvantage."

"I look completely harmless, don't I?"

"Yes. I can't imagine you hurting anybody."

"That's why I'm so well suited for this line of work. I make people trust me and let down their guard."

"That's right, you're the shill's partner. . . . So you're dangerous, are you?"

"Yes. Twice I've swindled men by pretending to want to marry them."

After a short pause, I said, "But men do that sort of thing too."

"It's not the same. When a man does it, he's a doctor, or the heir of a wealthy landowner, or a company executive, or *something*—he dangles his position or his property in front of his victim's eyes as bait. But a woman's only bait is herself. It's a terrible disadvantage. A man can't very well say he's a man for a living, but no one thinks anything about it if a woman says, 'Oh, I'm just an ordinary woman.' "

"Look, I haven't got a job I can be proud of, either."

"Why not? You used to be a firefighter, and then a photographer, and now you're a ship's captain."

"Still, I could never carry off a marriage swindle on the strength of any of that. It would be a disaster."

At last she laughed. "If a policeman asks you your occupation, all you have to do is speak up and tell him. They don't even *ask* women. A woman is a woman, and that's that."

"It's discriminatory, no doubt about it." After another pause, I asked, "Shall I make some carrot juice?"

"Never mind that; let's fix some rice for dinner."

"I can do it," I said. "I know my way around a kitchen, you know."

"Lots of unmarried men say that. Those are the easiest ones to trap into a proposal."

"But I haven't had even a whiff of your bait."

"Is that what you want?"

The conversation had again taken a dangerous turn. I measured out four cups of rice, put it in a pan and left the tap running while I washed it off. No matter how thoroughly I wash it, rice I make always has a peculiar taste. Probably because the rice is old.

"So are women always on the lookout for someone to deceive?"

"Sure. Most women are chronic offenders, aren't they?"

"Nobody's ever tried it on me . . . but that's all right. It won't be long now before the apocalypse, when everything's wiped out and we start all over. . . ."

"When that happens, are you really sure you'll be able to survive?"

"Of course. My life began with an apocalypse. My mother was raped by Inototsu, you see, and that's how I came into the world."

Perhaps I shouldn't have said so much. But I wanted to impress it on her that I, for one, was not the sort of man who could go around brandishing the traditional male prerogatives. I was a mole, someone who might never fall into a marriage trap, but whose prospects for succeeding in any such scheme of his own were nil. Yet I was the captain of this ark, steaming on toward the ultimate apocalypse, with the engine key right in my hand. This very moment, if I so chose, I could push the switch to weigh anchor. What would she say then? Would she call me a swindler? Or would she lift her skirt and hold out her rump for me to slap?

"When I was a little girl," she said, "our house had sliding shutters, and some birds made a nest in the shutter box outside my window. They were like crows, only smaller, and kind of brown. I don't like birds. They're noisy in the morning, and they carry ticks and mites, and if you look closely they have spiteful looks on their faces. I couldn't sleep in the morning, so it got me mad, and I started to keep one shutter in the box all the time, narrowing the space so that they wouldn't be able to get in. I forgot all about them until the summer was gone—and then one day I saw it: there in the space between the shutter and the box was the shriveled corpse of a baby bird, with only its head sticking outside. It must have put its head out to be fed until it got so big that it couldn't get in or out. Isn't that horrible? And I've always thought that that's what a mother's love is like."

I finished washing the rice and put it on to boil.

"About once a year I have a nightmare," I said. "It's about rape. The rapist is me, but the victim is me too."

"That's fascinating. What sort of a child would be born of such a union, I wonder. . . . I bet it would be wet and sticky, all tears and saliva and sweat, and nothing else."

"That doesn't sound like you. It doesn't suit you very well, either, that kind of talk."

"Frankly, I don't care if it does or not."

There was an awkward silence. How did we get started on this?

"What if the nuclear bomb went off right now, and you and I were the only survivors? What would become of us, do you think?" I asked.

"We'd end up like that baby bird in the shutter box."

"Then there must be a mother bird somewhere. But where?"

"How do I know? Anyway, to the baby bird, the mother is nothing but a beak bringing food."

A mole's conversation: digging my way in further and further, with only my whiskers to guide me. Or else it was a heart-in-mouth dance on wafer-thin ice. But a *dance*, for all that. I was strangely buoyant. I wanted to grab this chance to come to an agreement with her about our life together here after the apocalypse, so that I could push the dynamite switch anytime.

"But we're not like the baby bird," I said. "We've got each other, and besides, rice is bubbling in the pot."

"Anybody who's leading a rotten life now isn't going to do any better just because the slate's wiped clean."

"Shall I show you my maps? They're three-D color aerial photos taken by the Land Board. Snapped every ten seconds from a plane, for surveying purposes. Since they're taken from just the right angle, with three-quarters duplication, if you line them up and look at them with a stereoscope they leap out at you in perfect three D. You can make out all the houses, and people going by, cars, even the condition of the pavement. You'd be amazed. It's as if you were actually there—TV towers and power cable poles stick right up off the page as if they might poke you in the eye."

"Three-dimensional maps, eupcaccias . . . I see you have a definite taste for fakes."

"Just take my word for it and give it a try. You can complain after that," I said.

The maps and stereoscope were on the shelf over the

toilet, along with my cameras and other valuables. The shelf was fitted with sliding glass doors on rollers, but they were insulated with rubber to protect against humidity, which made them a little tricky to open and close. I removed my shoes. The edge of the toilet was slippery, and besides, I was fond of the feel of stone against the soles of my feet; I usually went around barefoot. The knee I had injured on the department store rooftop still wasn't completely back to normal, either.

"If you had to choose between a real diamond one hundredth of an inch in diameter, and a glass stone three feet across, which would you take?" she asked.

Might as well let myself in for it, I thought. As long as I'd invited her on a map trip, why not get out my camera too, for the first time in a long while?

"Let's see. After the apocalypse, it would be the glass stone, of course. I like to work with my hands, and there's a line I always say to myself while I'm working: 'People aren't monkeys, people aren't monkeys. . . .' For some strange reason it makes me happy. Fulfillment doesn't mean filling your life up with external things, you know, but realizing your own self-sufficiency. People aren't monkeys, people aren't monkeys. . . . The movements of the human fingertips are unbelievably precise."

She answered, "Once, I forget when, I saw a contest on TV between a chimpanzee and a person, to see which was better at threading needles. Which do you think won?"

"The person, of course. Why . . ."

"It was the chimp, hands down."

"You've got to be kidding. I don't believe it."

"He was over twice as fast."

I lost my balance. My left foot slipped all the way into the toilet and stuck fast, from the toes. That was the leg bearing scars from the time Inototsu had chained me up.

Trying to prop myself up, I grabbed the flushing lever without thinking. There was an overwhelming roar as a cylinder
of water shot down through the long pipe. Suction clamped
on my foot like a powerful vise, so that my leg, acting as a
stopper, was dragged down deeper and deeper. The more
I struggled, the stronger the attraction became, until the
leg was caught all the way to the calf.

The girl sprang up and stood stiff with alarm. "What's
the matter?" she cried.

"How ridiculous! Nothing like this ever happened before."

Only my toes could still move, ever so slightly. A slimy
sensation ran up and down my spine. The pipes were certain
to be crawling with germs.

F O R a while the girl held her breath. She moistened her lower lip as if to laugh, but the frown wrinkles in her forehead were too deep; she was caught between fear and laughter. That wasn't surprising: even I, though my insides were knotted with panic, felt a certain desire to giggle.

"Well, this is some fix," I said.

"Can't you get out?"

"Won't budge."

"You've got to relax," she said. "Try a different position."

"You're right. Let's see, I guess I'd better get my weight off that leg."

In a case like this, getting hysterical only makes matters worse. The essential thing was to stay calm, keep up my courage, take my time, and avoid wasting energy. First, in order to distribute my weight more evenly, I tried shifting my body so that the edge of the toilet came just between my knees. Now it felt as if one foot had on a toilet shoe. My weight was equally distributed, but I knew I couldn't maintain that position for long. The leg bowed out at the knee. Was there nothing else I could do? Perhaps it would be

better to bend my knees ninety degrees as if I were sitting
in a chair. But there *was* no chair, no seat at all. I'd have to
have someone make me a stool of the proper height. But
fitting it to the curve of the toilet would take time and skill.
It was beyond the powers of the girl. Perhaps I'd better
negotiate with that chimpanzee—the one on TV that was
faster at threading needles than a human.

Like someone fingering a puzzle ring, mentally I traced
the connections among my joints and muscles. She was still
keeping a dubious eye on me, wary perhaps lest I catch her
off guard.

"In cases like these, don't people usually dial the police
or the fire station?" she asked.

"Yes—say, if someone gets stuck in an elevator, that sort
of thing, they do."

"Well, when you were working in the fire station, didn't
you get any calls like that?"

"I remember listening in while someone gave advice to
someone whose ring wouldn't come off."

"What was the advice?"

"Elevate the finger above the heart, and rub it with saliva
or soap—just common sense. But I can hardly elevate my
leg, and putting soap on it would have the opposite effect."

"I've heard of sawing rings off, too."

"Yes, they do that sometimes."

"That machine on the table upstairs—isn't it an electric
saw?"

"Forget it," I said. "Those are hard to use. Nothing for
amateurs to mess with. One slip and it's goodbye leg."

"I hope you get loose before you have to go," she said.

"*You* just went, didn't you?"

"Yes," she said, and added, "Don't worry about me. I can
go anywhere."

I felt a leaden weight around my ankle. My thoughts

began to lose coherency. It was as if a ball of string wound too tight had suddenly started to come apart in my hands.

"Would you mind lending me a shoulder? Let's see if we can't pull my leg out. The longer it's in there, the tougher it's going to be getting it out, once it starts swelling."

She stood in front of the toilet with her back to me. Without the least hesitation, I put my arms around her shoulders and pressed up close against her, leaning my full weight on her. Her hair smelled like toasted seaweed. If not for my laughable predicament, this dramatic event might well have turned my whole life around. There was still hope, I thought. That foot might pop right out without causing any relative change in our positions. Bending my elbows, I hauled myself up vertically. The only thing to change was *her* position. Her shoulders tilted, she slumped forward, and my knee curved forward too, defying its construction. The pain stopped just short of unbearable. I had achieved nothing. Only the sensation of physical contact with her saved me from blind panic.

"It's no use," I said. "The inside of the pipe is a vacuum."

"How long does it take to get from here to the Broom Brigade headquarters and back?" she asked.

"No more than ten minutes one way."

"Then if they finished quickly they *could* be on their way back now."

"It won't be that easy," I said. "They're talking about a human corpse, after all. Man, I sure would like to be out of here before they get back."

"They might at least call us on the radio. If they stop off somewhere for a drink, they'll be forever. Glued to their chairs."

"With a body stashed in the jeep?"

"That's true; I suppose it would be too risky. . . ."

She went back to the stairs and seated herself on the

second step from the bottom. That short move put her totally beyond my reach. So this was the cozy time alone with her that I had waited for so eagerly. I felt sick.

"When the cork in a wine bottle gets stuck, there's the devil of a time getting it out, you know," I said.

"Let me know if you want anything."

"I'm okay for now."

"Does it hurt?"

"It itches as much as it hurts. The blood must be congesting."

After a pause, she looked up. "The inside of the pipe is a vacuum, right? Isn't there a valve somewhere below? If you open the valve, the pressure ought to go back to normal."

"Maybe. I've never actually checked it out, but I imagine it's built to take advantage of the different levels of underground water. So the actual valve creating this suction is the water itself, and beyond that, somewhere, there must be something geared to a lever that cuts off the flow of water. Something on the order of a hydraulic turbine."

"I'll go take a look," she volunteered, bounding up like a spring. Anybody can move that way when they're light of weight. "Tell me the way."

"That's just it. I don't know. As far as I can tell, there *is* no way to get there."

"That doesn't make any sense. Somebody must have gone in to do the installation work. There's got to be a way in."

"I used to think so too, but I've gone over the area pretty thoroughly."

"Maybe it's blocked off."

"There's no sign of it. This is a guess, but I have an idea some other outfit tunneled underneath without permission. The competition was fierce, and the various explorations were like spiders' webs. One cave-in after another. You want to take a look at the maps? When I lost my balance I knocked down a scrap album along with those photos—over there. Mind getting it and bringing it here?"

Reluctantly she came down the stairs. "It *is* funny," she said. "It doesn't figure. After all, the plumbing was installed below so that it could be used up here. Don't tell me it just *happened* to connect up."

Gingerly she handed me the scrapbook, as if determined to come only so close and no closer, then she hurriedly withdrew her hand. I must have been a sorry sight. She was right; a stupid bungle like this deserved not sympathy but scorn.

"Look," I said, "here's a map of the work hold."

"Don't bother. I'm not a map person. You don't look very good. Shall I get you some medicine?"

"I guess a couple of aspirin wouldn't hurt. You don't mind? Remember that medicine box before—under the chaise longue? The aspirin are in a green holder."

While she was off getting the aspirin, I flipped through the scrapbook, scanning the areas that had not yet been closely surveyed. Mine shafts lacking either ladders or lifts, and waterways very far underground, were still virtually unexplored. There was danger in exploring them, and anyway they lay on the other side of the line that would be formed when my dynamite blasts cut us off from the rest of the world. But if I ever made up my mind to go back and investigate, it was just possible that I might come on a passage leading in under the toilet. My powers of concentration were dimming. My knee began to buzz, and suddenly a spectrum of pain exploded through me, branching all the way to my armpit.

"Is one enough?" she asked.

"Make it three. People usually fix the dosage by age, but it ought to be by weight."

"Want me to take your picture?"

"What for?"

"You look just like a human potted plant. It's so unusual—and then you'd have something to remember it all by. If the slate really does get wiped clean, and I get a chance to start over, I'm going to give up being a woman for a living, and take up photography."

"By then it'll be too late. This is the age of advertising—you can make a go of it as a photographer as long as you have a knack for business; that's all the talent you really need."

"Don't be mean. Say, how long do you think you can last that way?"

"Damn it, my knee is killing me. And the calf feels like it's about to pull right off. If lack of circulation brings on gangrene, it'll have to be amputated—same as frostbite. Even supposing I could tide along with sedatives and antibiotics, I suppose I'm good for only four or five days at the most."

"You've got to be able to relieve yourself. . . ."

"A worse problem is sleep. I don't know how long I can stay sane."

"It must be torture."

"Even though I have nothing to confess. It's not fair."

"Freedom to walk around really is important, isn't it?" she reflected.

"Of course it is. People aren't plants."

"And yet you're happy taking trips on paper."

"That's different. You talk about walking around, but you can't *fly*, can you? Well, on my aerial-photograph trips, I can. So could you."

"Looking at you is depressing," she sighed. "With survival like this, you might as well be dead."

"Oh, no. There's a world of difference between being able

to take a few steps and not being able to walk at all. Not being able to go to the bathroom on your own might be sad, but who cares if he can't make it to the South Pole?"

"You can't even take one step."

"I'll be okay. Nothing this idiotic can go on forever."

"Maybe you're right. Even a balloon starts to shrink in time. . . ."

"Freedom is something you have to discover for yourself. There's freedom even here."

"Are you a college graduate?"

"No. High school dropout."

"Sometimes you talk like somebody with a real education. And you've got all those books. . . ."

"I like to read. I take them out of the public library. But I'm really better at working with my hands. I can fix a handbag clasp in no time."

"If there's anything you want to read, I could go get it for you," she said, a half-smile playing at the corners of her mouth as if blown there by a passing breeze. She was teasing me.

"Even cancer patients who know they're dying go on trying to live, right up to the end. All of life is just that, in fact—carrying on until you die."

"Pardon me for saying this," she said, "but you don't really seem all that happy. This ark seems seaworthy enough, but even so . . ."

"Staying alive comes first, doesn't it?"

"You're peculiar. It's as if you couldn't wait for the bomb to fall."

"Have you ever heard about mass suicide among whales?"

"A little. Not much."

"Well, as you may know, whales are very intelligent creatures. But all of a sudden they'll go berserk, swim straight for the nearest shore, and beach themselves. The entire herd.

They won't go back in the water no matter how you coax them. They drown in the air."

"Could something be after them?"

"The only thing that could scare a whale is a killer whale or a shark. But this phenomenon occurs even in waters where there are no sharks—and the killer whales commit mass suicide too. So the scientists racked their brains and came up with a very interesting theory: they say the whales try to get out of the water for fear of drowning."

"How could that be? They're aquatic animals."

"But they're not fish. They evolved from land mammals breathing air with lungs."

"Then they're throwbacks?"

"That's funny—my foot's starting to prickle. Feels like ants are nesting in it. Anyway, it's true that if whales are unable to surface, they'll suffocate. There could be some sort of communicable disease that would drive them to suicide by making them fear the water, like hydrophobia."

"That may be scary for whales. . . ." She spoke in a low voice, rubbing the back of her neck. "If you want to know the truth, I'm more afraid of cancer. That's a lot scarier to me than some bomb you don't know when to expect either."

"You're coming down with whale disease," I retorted— but I felt as insecure as an earthworm burrowing in the dirt. Without her support, I doubted my ability to cheer when the ark set sail.

"I have to see the sky," she said.

"What do you mean?"

"I've got a magic spell I say. One time, I forget when it was, as I was looking up at the sky, the air looked like some great living thing. Tree branches look just like veins and arteries, don't they? Not only their shape; the way they change carbon dioxide into oxygen and absorb nitrogen. Always changing, metabolizing. . . . Changes in wind and air pressure are the flexing of the air's muscles, and grass and tree roots are its arms and legs and fingers and toes. Animals living in them are the corpuscles and viruses and intestinal bacteria. . . ."

"What does that make people?"

"Parasitic worms, maybe."

"Or maybe cancer."

"Yes, that could be. Lately the air just hasn't seemed itself. . . ."

"So what's your magic spell?"

" 'Hello, air—you're alive, aren't you?' "

"Sorry, but when the bomb falls, the air will be done for too. The earth is going to be put on ice for months and months on end, wrapped in a heavy layer of dust and debris."

"But I *have* to see the sky."

I had to stop her from going. Somehow, anyhow, I had to free myself. As long as you could take even one step, life here really wasn't so bad, I thought. The humiliation and anger of that time years ago when Inototsu had chained me to this very spot came bursting out from my tear glands like air out of a punctured tire. I ached to be free by the time the insect dealer and the shill returned. There was no need to invite them to take seats in the gallery for a hilarious sideshow.

"I wonder if you could do it," I said. "I mean break the concrete around the pipe."

"How?"

"With a drill. There's one in with the hammer in my toolbox under the table. There are five or six inches from the pipe mouth to the floor, and my foot is stuck about twelve inches in. The difference is six or seven inches. So if you dug down eight inches in the floor and opened a hole in the pipe, you could let air in without risk of hurting my leg. The same principle as opening the valve below."

"Well, not exactly."

"Why not?"

"For one thing, the toilet would then be useless."

"There's some waterproof putty in the toolkit."

"Putty's no good. It couldn't stand up to the pressure. We've got to dispose of a dead body down here, you know."

"Well, we can't, unless my leg comes out first."

"If it came to a choice between your leg and the toilet, it would be better to amputate your leg."

"Are you mad? I'm the captain here. This toilet belongs to *me*."

She stretched her lips out in a line, and balanced a smile on them like a dot. She'd meant it as a joke.

"But while we sit around waiting for your leg to come out naturally, the body will start to smell. I won't be able to bear it. I have a very sensitive nose."

"Well, as soon as they get back, there will be all sorts of alternatives. Like setting up a scaffold for a pulley, and pulling me out with a winch."

"How do you know the leg won't just tear apart at the knee?"

Would the insect dealer and the shill also object to opening a hole in the pipe? I wondered. If putty was out, there was always welding. No, that wouldn't work, either, on second thought. Once the plug of my leg was removed and the water in the pipe fell, it would refill all the way to the top, on the principle of the siphon. Water would pour out from the hole nonstop. There was a special technique for welding underwater, but I didn't have the equipment. There had to be some other, more practical idea.

My water-bloated nerves seemed to burst through the skin and touch the pipe directly, with a savage pain like that caused by biting on an ice cube with a decayed tooth. My entire body was riddled with holes, releasing fumes of pain.

"It's no good. My foot feels awful. I can't stand it any-more. . . . I've got to yell."

"Is it asleep?"

"No. Would you mind holding my hand? I have a chill. Just let me touch you somewhere, anywhere. Your tits, your ass . . . I don't care."

She sat motionless on the bottom step, her look frozen. Screams squeezed up through my body like toothpaste through a tube, and came pouring out my throat. I beat my thighs with both hands like a bird beating its wings, and went on screeching like a monkey. She covered her ears. While I howled, a thought crossed my mind: Of all the stupid things—I still haven't found out her name!

2 0

THE BODY WAS WRAPPED
IN A BLUE PLASTIC SHEET

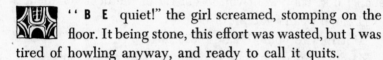 ''**B E** quiet!" the girl screamed, stomping on the floor. It being stone, this effort was wasted, but I was tired of howling anyway, and ready to call it quits.

"Listen," she commanded. "Isn't that a car horn? Maybe it's them."

I had to admit she could be right. "Go check it out, will you?" I said. My throat burned. The reverberations of my howls lingered deep in my ears, so that my ordinary speaking voice sounded no louder than a murmur.

Crossbow in hand, the girl circled around the toilet, keeping her distance, and headed for the hatch. The vertical ladder was impossible to negotiate holding the crossbow. She stood the weapon upright at the foot of the ladder and started climbing insecurely. With every step her red artificial leather skirt peeled higher, exposing bare flesh. Her every movement injected high-pressure gas into my veins. That I could still react this way, even though my trapped foot felt now as if it weighed more than all the rest of me, seemed nothing short of incredible. Fresh anger flooded me at my clumsiness in failing to capitalize on our time alone.

She unbarred the steel door and opened it. The sound of

the horn was now unmistakable. The dogs were barking for all they were worth. Their sensitive ears had probably picked up my howls through the wall, which would make them all the more excited. Signaling reassurance, she disappeared into the tunnel. Only a few minutes now and the two men would be here to rescue me. Some loss of dignity was inevitable. But now there was a good chance I could be freed at last, by whatever means. Perhaps because I had relaxed, my leg became several dozen times itchier than before. The itch was more maddening than the pain.

She came back and poked her head in the doorway. "What shall I do? They want you to get rid of the dogs for them."

"I can't. I can't get out of here."

"But they're going crazy, those dogs. . . ."

"Hmm. Well . . . maybe I could try using a hand mike." As she came down the ladder, I grew impatient at her excessive caution even as I savored the sight of her skirt rolling up.

"Look over on the side of the table by the bookcase," I said. "You'll find one in with the electrical parts, the soldering iron, and so on. Red, shaped like a trumpet . . . The microphone and speaker are detachable."

I got her to hand me the mike and carry the speaker down to the far end of the tunnel. When she gave me the mike, I deliberately saw to it that our fingertips touched; she did not seem to mind. Was it because the shill was back —or was it all my imagination?

"What do I do?" she asked. "Just turn it on?"

"Pull the antenna all the way out and turn the volume all the way up." I turned on the mike and pulled out its antenna. "Testing, testing, one, two, three . . ."

I whispered the words, but they came booming back at me in a voice as loud and bold as a foghorn. I quieted my breathing, positioned the back of my tongue up against my soft palate, and took a deep breath. There was a noise in the toilet like the sound of wet noodles hitting the floor. I felt myself slide in a fraction of an inch deeper. Or had I imagined it?

With all the emotion I could muster, using every skill at my disposal, I burst into a long, sorrowful threnody. The sheer volume of my voice surprised even me. It must have throbbed into the night sky over town with such force that even now, I thought, some well-meaning soul must be phoning the police. The girl reappeared and signaled "Okay" with her fingers. I worried that perhaps now the dogs would no longer be satisfied with my old way of howling.

The dogs were quiet, but there was still no sign of my two emissaries. I turned down the mike and tried calling them:

"Hey—what's the holdup?"

"They say they've got something with them," the girl called back.

"Tell them to save it for later."

She conferred with them a few minutes before reporting: "They say it's really important."

"What could be more important than my leg?"

"They're here," she said, and started down the ladder, recoiling. She, at any rate, could come down as slowly as she liked, as far as I was concerned. After an interval the shill appeared, his back to me. He was dragging something wrapped in a heavy blue plastic sheet of the sort used on construction sites. It was about the size of a human body rolled up in a ball, and it appeared to be fairly heavy. Oh, no, I thought. Was this the body, after all?

Next to appear was the one pushing the bundle: not the insect dealer, as I'd expected, but Sengoku, his shoulders rising and falling as he panted from the exertion. Dressed in the unlikely combination of a well-ironed open-collared white shirt and khaki work pants torn at the knee, he first bowed deeply to the girl, then caught sight of me. Seemingly unable to make sense of what he saw, he just kept staring.

The shill then turned around, stood on tiptoe, and let go of the plastic-wrapped bundle in apparent incredulity. Surprised myself by all this, I could not immediately think of anything to say. The girl spoke up on my behalf.

"He fell in and got stuck. Got any ideas?"

There was a long, preternatural silence. The first to break it would be the loser.

"Sorry, but I've got to take a leak," announced the shill in a flat, rapid voice, and retreated back down the tunnel.

"You can't get out of there? But why . . . ?" Sengoku spoke anxiously, his voice husky.

"I'm stuck. Where's Komono?" My voice too was hoarse. But it seemed wiser not to take in any liquid for the time being.

"In conference with the Broom Brigade. A lot's been happening."

"What's in that thing?" I asked. "Not sweet potatoes, I hope."

"Don't be ridiculous. You know very well it's a body." He controlled his irritation, and added more quietly, "That was the deal all along, wasn't it?"

"But I thought if there was a body it was going to be yours."

"Thanks a lot."

"How awful . . ." The girl retrieved her crossbow and came back toward me, measuring the distance between us as she did so, and halting about thirty feet away.

"Whose body is it?" I demanded.

"Whose do you think?" answered Sengoku.

"Somebody I know?"

"I think you'll be surprised."

"Well, if it's not *you*, then . . . you're kidding me. It's not Komono, is it?"

"It couldn't be," the girl broke in. "There was talk about a body even before he left here."

"Then who the hell is it?" Pain in my leg kept me from being able to organize my thoughts. Who else was there whose death might surprise me? When my own mother died, I'd felt less emotion than if I'd dropped a camera and damaged the lens. Of course, at the time I'd been living with Inototsu (I hadn't had any choice), and the death notice had come two weeks after the fact.

"This is a rather, uh, difficult body. It's going to be a bit ticklish to handle, I'm afraid." Sengoku's gaze swept rapidly back and forth from one end of the hold to the other, his eyes greedy with curiosity. This was his first look at the place where waste materials were illegally disposed of, and where that unknown quantity the manhole manager—his associate—lived. "Say, Mole," he started, and then corrected himself. "That john where you're soaking your foot— is that the famous manhole?"

The girl objected sharply. "He's not 'soaking his foot.' Does it look like he's enjoying himself? Haven't you got eyes?" Her no-nonsense manner made her seem older; she was in fact no child, I reflected. This might well be her real self.

"Now remember, I wasn't hiding it from you, or anything," I blabbered nervously, acutely self-conscious. "I was going to let you in on it when the time came. In my mind, you've been one of us all along. I knew I could make a go of it with you. I really mean it. I've got your ticket all laid aside. Now's the perfect chance, so—"

He interrupted me. "Are you sure you aren't talking that way for spite?"

"Certainly not. What makes you say that?"

"You sure you aren't putting on some kind of act just to keep us from getting rid of the body?"

"Of course not. I've been waiting for help. Come on over and give me a hand, will you?"

"An act, you say?" The shill came back through the tunnel, hunched forward, still zipping his trousers. When he saw me he froze, hand on his zipper, like a clumsy paper cutout. "What the devil are you waiting for? Aren't you out of there yet?"

"We tried everything," said the girl, and shook her head firmly, having at last regained her buoyancy. The presence of her old partner apparently bolstered her spirits. "The pressure is unbelievable. It's a vacuum inside, and he can't move his leg at all, either by pulling it or twisting it. I gave him some aspirin before and that may have helped, but until just before you came back it was awful. He was screaming his head off."

"Looking for sympathy, if you ask me." The shill closed the steel door and shot the bolt.

"Fall in yourself, and you'll see," I said caustically. "It's like having someone do a job on the sole of your foot with a wire brush."

"A vacuum, huh?" said Sengoku. "How much pressure is being exerted? That's what we've got to find out." He spoke with a cool detachment. "When the decompression ratio passes a certain limit, first blood oozes out, then the skin ruptures and the muscles split apart. Judging from the fact that the pipe and his leg are in contact, without losing equilibrium, the pressure may not be so high after all."

"Never mind the fancy explanation. Just get me out of here."

"First we'll haul the body over." The shill signaled to Sengoku, and together they started to drag the plastic-wrapped bundle. The shill headed for the ladder, while Sengoku, unaware of the danger, headed unsuspecting for the stairs. The rope slipped off and a corner of the vinyl sheet came askew. Under it there appeared no blood or flesh but only a glimpse of shiny black—a trash bag, it looked like— which in its own way intensified my impression of the corpse's physical reality.

"Careful, don't go that way!" the girl called out to Sengoku, her voice as bright and animated as an ocean breeze after a calm. Did she use that tone instinctively with strange men? "There's a trap on the stairs. It's not safe."

"This place is booby-trapped from one end to the other. You know that much, don't you?" Without seeming to expect an answer, the shill looked down from the landing and added, "Why don't we just throw it down from here? It weighs a ton."

"We can't do that," protested Sengoku. "This is a human being. Was, I mean."

"That's the whole point: it's dead, not alive. If it gets a little knocked up now, so much the easier to flush it away later."

The girl made some kind of motion, but as she had her back to me, I couldn't interpret it very well. Smiling sourly, the shill turned to the plastic sheet and brought his hands together in a gesture of respect. Sengoku put one foot awkwardly on the bundle and started to tuck the stray corner back under the rope.

"I *really* wish you'd leave that, and come give me a hand *now*." I tried to stay calm, but my voice was growing strangely shrill—first from the acute discomfort I was in (by now it felt as if my heart had slipped down inside my trapped knee) and second at my growing fear that no way of escape might ever be found. "Without this toilet, how do you plan on getting rid of that body, anyway?"

"Look, don't be in such a hurry, will you?" said the shill. He signaled to Sengoku and together the two men started to push the bundle off the landing.

"If you knew whose body this was, Captain, you wouldn't be so coldhearted," he added.

"Who's coldhearted?" I said. "*You're* the one who's dropping it on the floor."

As the girl let out a scream, the blue plastic bundle did a one-and-a-half twist in midair, then hit the floor with the unmistakable squish of flesh and blood. (Clay, of course, would make approximately the same noise.)

"Who is it?" I demanded again.

"We ought to pay our respects before we flush him away," said the shill as he came down the ladder, followed by Sengoku. The girl was staring at the bundle, her crossbow pressed against her chest.

"Who *is* it?" I insisted, refusing to be put off.

"Well, properly speaking, Captain," said the shill, "this is you." He wiped his mouth and turned around. His nostrils looked pinched, and the whites of his eyes had a bluish tinge. Evidently he was not as collected as he had seemed. No matter how he wiped the corners of his mouth, pale flecks of saliva kept reappearing.

"Come again?"

"Well, uh . . . actually, it's, uh . . ." Sengoku fumbled for words, his voice dry and scratchy.

"What in God's name are you talking about? I'm in no mood for practical jokes, let me tell you."

"In other words . . . it's you," said the shill, rubbing his mouth, and then wiping that hand on the tail of his shirt. "Your substitute, anyway. He was killed in your place. The killer, who made the first move, apparently mistook him for you. So if it hadn't been for this guy, *you'd* be wrapped up in this sheet right now."

"Who's the killer?" I asked. Simultaneously the girl asked,
"Who's the substitute?"

"Try asking the guy who was supposed to get bumped off;
he must know," said Sengoku with a false air of toughness.

"I haven't any idea," I said. "Someone who looked like
me?"

"Not really." Sengoku tilted his head in seeming discomfort, and looked to the shill for help.

"It must be Komono." Teeth clenched, the girl retreated
yet farther from the plastic-wrapped bundle.

"What about him?" I asked her.

"He died in your place," she said.

"Then who did him in—Inototsu?" I asked, the pain in
my leg forgotten.

"No." The shill indicated the motionless bundle with a
jerk of his head, and added with apparent effort, "If you
really want to know, it was the other way around."

"Komono killed Inototsu, you say?" My voice shook with
tension, as if needles were jabbing my eardrums. "Then the
thing under that plastic sheet is . . ."

"Well, let's get the ceremony over with, shall we?" said
the shill.

"You stay out of this," I snapped.

My eyes remained glued to the blue plastic sheet. Could
this really be Inototsu? That animal who wore a green hunting cap and went around smelling like fermented beans
wrapped in a dirty old rag? That monster who trampled his
own wife to death, raped my mother, chained me to the toilet,
and bulldozed concrete buildings on behalf of the waterstone
interests? That friendless bastard who sold a thriving fishermen's inn and two twenty-five-ton fishing vessels to run for
city council over and over—but never to win—and who first
pinned a badge on his chest only when he became leader
of the Broom Brigade? I felt liberated. I must have feared

him more than I realized—more than I hated him, even. There was no other emotion. Perhaps getting my leg caught in the jaws of the toilet had numbed my feelings. Had I witnessed the actual killing, no doubt it would have been different. I could not help being amazed at his enormous bulk, even folded up as he was. Had they merely bent him over, or had they dismembered him and rearranged the parts? I recalled having heard once that no evidence is so hard to dispose of as the human body; the full meaning of that statement hit me now with fresh force.

"It doesn't figure," muttered the girl, her jaw set. "Why would Komono mistake *him* for the captain? How could he?"

"He didn't. It's more complicated than that. I can't sum it up as well as Komono could, but basically it's not a simple case of right and wrong. Originally there was another suspect, who was after the captain, and that's who Inototsu mistook Komono for."

"That's right," echoed Sengoku, waving both his fists as he sought to explain. "The 'body' Inototsu was talking about referred to that suspect. Whether he actually intended to do him in or was just bluffing, I couldn't say. Right now Komono is gathering facts from the Broom Brigade, so we ought to know more soon. . . . Also, in my opinion, Komono was overly suspicious of Inototsu. He got too much of an indoctrination from the captain here."

The shill looked at the bundle and rubbed his hands on his pants. "It does seem as if he didn't give him enough of a chance. That revolver he had was bad. Mind you, I'm not finding fault; it was legitimate self-defense. The only problem is that he left bullets in the body. If an autopsy is done, a bullet could be found, and traced, which would make things rough for the captain. Komono told me to tell you, though, that he'd see to it that everybody in the Broom Brigade kept his mouth shut, so not to worry."

"That man is meant for better things than liaison work," said Sengoku, nodding seriously. "He's a born leader. Why, he's already taken over the leadership of the Broom Brigade. Inototsu hadn't been dead ten minutes before he'd reorganized the brigade on new lines, and was issuing commands right and left. . . ."

The ants nesting in my foot now changed to flies, whose maggots attacked my nerves voraciously. I hadn't meant to scream, yet here I was screaming. Wishing desperately that the scrapbook in my hands were a hammer, in rage I kicked blindly with my free leg. What bore the brunt of this frenzied attack was not the toilet but the knee of my entrapped leg.

2 1

I F the shill and Sengoku had not supported me on either side as I thrashed around, I might easily have broken my leg. The pain served to clear my head. In the interim I had wet my pants slightly, but that didn't matter. The benefit of it all was that now, taken aback by my outburst, the two men began to think seriously about my rescue.

First I had them get me two more aspirin and a triple-strength antihistamine. Then I had them wrap a chilled compress around the thigh of the entrapped leg. Finally I had them each hold up one end of a section of steel pipe left over from the plumbing installation, which I clung to, while the girl massaged my knee with both hands. I mustered all my strength; the insect dealer and the shill cheered me on, straining their voices to the limit. The steel pipe bent, Sengoku's shoulder made a popping noise as if on the point of dislocating—and again I wet my pants. More this time—about a full cup's worth. There was no sign whatever that the leg had moved.

Mindful of the liquid trickling from my pants down the inside of my leg toward the knee, I decided that holding back any longer could lead only to uremia. I had somebody bring me the steamer from the galley. The bottom was scorched black, so I had no scruples about using it. They all turned their backs while I relieved myself into it.

"Whoever heard of using a potty from inside a toilet? Nobody'd believe it," said the shill. Plainly he was trying to joke away his confusion and dismay. The seriousness of the situation had begun to impress itself on him.

"Well, once I saw a butterfly flying around inside an airplane, but it didn't seem particularly strange." The girl's voice was too bright; was she perhaps attempting to cover up the sound of my urinating?

Once the sound broke off and Sengoku, mistakenly assuming I was through, turned around. "Oops, sorry," he said. "Thought you'd finished. Say, you've got a whopper there, don't you?"

At this the shill turned around too. "It's just because he'd been holding his water so long," he opined. "Anybody would get that big."

The girl, of course, kept her eyes ahead of her. As I put the lid on the steamer and tried to ease it to the floor, a stabbing pain shot through my knee, erasing the retort I had prepared. Sengoku took the steamer from me. Perhaps he wasn't such a bad sort after all. Slowly the pain in my belly eased. Evidently the tension in my bladder had been aggravating the pain in my leg. Then my eyes fell on the badge on the collar of Sengoku's open-necked shirt, and though I knew I should thank him, instead I blurted out a sarcastic remark.

"Well, well—gold brooms, is it? Very fancy. And how long have we been wearing this?"

"It's just gold-plated." Sengoku rubbed his Broom Brigade badge with the ball of his thumb and added, "Ordinary members are silver. If you joined, Captain, of course yours would be gold-plated, probably with horizontal stripes to boot. Upper echelons have those."

The shill stepped back and gazed fixedly at me up and down, taking in my exact relationship to the toilet. "I get it," he said. "You're in the same trouble as a bottle of wine with a cork stopper, after it's stayed too long in the fridge. What's the procedure in a case like that?"

"You can either warm it to expand the air or open a hole in the cork with a nail to let air in," I said. "One or the other." I shot the girl a warning look, meaning for her to keep quiet, and went on. "In this case, there's no way to heat it, so the only thing to do is open a hole."

"I agree." Sengoku rubbed his injured shoulder, pursed his lips, and smiled. Something in his manner struck me as servile, though perhaps I only imagined it. "Logically you've got to achieve a balance with the external air pressure."

"Let's see—where'd be the best place to drive in a nail?" The shill studied the area between the toilet bowl and the floor.

"If you drilled seven or eight inches down in the concrete, you'd come out below my foot."

"Well, of course we can't do that," he said unceremoniously. He was smiling—rare for him—but the smile was cruel. "Your leg will heal with proper medicine and care, Captain, but what happens if you wreck this toilet? The ship is nothing without it. How would you ever explain it to Komono? Disposing of the body has got to be our number-one priority."

"How about inserting a rubber hose between his leg and the toilet wall?" The girl's voice was animated, but she didn't sound very confident.

"There's not enough room. I may be fat, but I'm no water cushion." Once again my pulse beat a threatening drumbeat in the calf of my leg. The mere thought of some foreign object being stuck between my skin and the pipe made my lungs start to expand with a budding scream.

"Wait—that's not a bad idea. A narrow pipe of copper or steel just might work," said Sengoku. He came over and made as if to poke a finger between my leg and the toilet wall. In his enthusiasm he had failed to reckon with the ferocity of a wounded boar. I grabbed his finger and twisted it sharply up. I have no illusions about my strength—but even so I'm close to average compared to Sengoku, whose muscles are like dried fish.

"Cut it out—you'll break it!" he screamed.

"Apologize," I said.

"What for?"

"Never mind; just apologize."

"I'm sorry. Stop hurting me!"

"I'm in a lot more pain than you are."

"I'm *sorry*."

"If you're really sorry, give it to me straight. However it happened, Inototsu here ended up dead, I can see that—but what ground have you got for saying he died in my place? Tell it to me in plain language. Who's to say you're not just making up the whole thing?"

"There were graffiti sprayed all over the walls down at the garbage dump by the tangerine grove—'Attention sausage stuffers: Dead hogs delivered free of charge.'" His voice was so feeble that I let go of his hand. After retreating a safe distance, he rubbed the joint with a sullen look. Once again my clumsiness had earned me an enemy.

"What proof is that?" I sniffed.

"It's obvious who would do a thing like that, isn't it?" he said.

"In other words, it had to be somebody who lumped you in with the Broom Brigade, Captain." In an apparent effort to sort out his thoughts, the shill pressed his forehead against his clasped hands, so that he appeared to be gazing through them. "Or maybe they had the idea you were the Brigade's real leader. So they took out their grudge against *them* on *you*."

"What was that about sausage—say it again, the graffiti," I said.

" 'Attention sausage stuffers: Dead hogs delivered free of charge.' You could take it as a kind of death threat, couldn't you?" said Sengoku, smiling slightly.

Still staring at his clasped hands, the shill went on: "Yes, now that I think of it, Komono and I should have marched right in, in plain view. Komono wouldn't hear of it. Thanks to his line of work, which involves pulling the wool over people's eyes, he was beside himself with suspicion, determined nobody was going to pull anything over on *him*. He hardly looks the part, but it turns out his favorite strategy is—what's it called?—a commando operation. Penetrating deep into enemy territory with a handful of men. It probably comes from an overdose of TV, more than any influence from his SDF days. So there we were—just like some hostage rescue squad. Well, I'm a shill by trade. What could I do but jump in with both feet?

"We stopped the jeep a fair distance away and then walked. After carefully looking the place over, we synchronized our watches and split up. Three minutes later I knocked on the front door. While the enemy's attention was diverted—I realize thinking of them as the 'enemy' was strange, but anyway—Komono sneaked through a back window into enemy headquarters. Assuming everything went according to plan, that is. What really happened I have no way of knowing. Since my knocking on the door was intended to form a diversion, I guess I overdid it a little; in fact, I broke the glass. The next thing I knew, the lights went out—

whether because someone turned them off on purpose, scenting danger, or because the power just happened to fail, I don't know. I do know that at almost the same moment I heard a pistol shot." He was silent a moment before continuing.

"What do you make of it, Captain?" he said. "I see it as a case of internal strife. On the personal level it's murder, of course, but if it were two countries involved, it seems to me they'd both be victims, caught in a trap. And the intended victim, after all, was you."

"Bravo," said Sengoku. "I could never have summed it up half so well." The remark was apparently sincere, meant as neither flattery nor sarcasm. That uncomplicated sincerity of his was what I found most amiable about Sengoku. It was something I, who postured like a hedgehog even with the odds all against me, could never imitate.

I said, "But who's responsible for the graffiti? I haven't got any idea. Besides, there's no motive."

"Cleaning up graffiti could have been part of the Broom Brigade's work. . . . Still, that's a weak motive for murder." Sengoku swung his injured arm around in big circles, taking deep breaths. "Komono should be back anytime now with the whole story. . . ."

"Mind if I borrow that steamer?" asked the girl in a low voice. No need to ask what for. No need even to reply. Cradling the steamer, still warm from the heat of my body, she headed for the work hold. My chest burned with a mixture of shame and something akin to happiness. The fever in my leg shot up to the limit. But it appeared the aspirin was working, for the pain was now minimal, and the high dosage of antihistamines had effectively soothed my nerves. Seeing Sengoku strain his ears, I was even able secretly to enjoy an ironic sense of victory.

Then the situation began to change rapidly. From the

work hold there emerged a buzzing sound that matched no-body's anticipation: a sound that no physiological function of hers could possibly produce, however one wrenched the imagination. Had the insect dealer returned through the maze of tunnels? For someone so terrified of dogs, it was certainly possible. Now that he was leader of the Broom Brigade (which I still tended to doubt—it seemed unreal), he would have access to reliable guides.

The girl came rushing back in. In her confusion and agitation, the movements of her legs were totally out of sync with the swaying of her body. She seemed to be trying to tell us something, but she was gasping too hard for the words to come out. Like a signboard torn off in a sharp gust of wind, she flew over to the bottom of the stairs and snatched up the crossbow. Shoulders heaving, she adjusted her panties through her skirt.

"What's the matter?" We all three said the same thing at once, our words overlapping.

The answer was not long in coming. Restless footsteps strode toward us down the corridor. The steps were quick, light, and squishy; my guess was rubber-soled sneakers. The girl loaded an arrow into her crossbow.

Two young men the shape and complexion of withered sticks bounded into the room and planted themselves side by side in front of the row of storage drums. They looked to be in their late teens. Their forelocks were teased till the hair stood on end; they wore leather jackets, one red and one purple, and baggy pants tied at the ankles. Evidently some sort of hoodlums.

"Keep out of our way!" yelled one of them, in a hoarse voice that still hadn't changed. He drew a chain off his belt. Not to be outdone, I screamed back at him and lunged for my Uzi, forgetting about my trapped leg. Apparently mis-taking my outburst for a signal to attack, simultaneously they raised their chains, swung them round, and charged. It was a clever plan, calculated to leave the enemy no time to think. In reflex, the girl pulled the trigger of her crossbow. The aluminum arrow scored a direct hit on the ear of the youth in the red jacket, struck the floor, and rebounded with a light, brief reverberation that sounded ominous, in view of the damage just done. The shill quickly loaded the other crossbow, while Red Jacket put a hand to his ear and stared at the moist red blood on his palm. Without another word, the pair turned and sprang up toward the hatch like a couple of jumping rats.

Had it been them all along? I asked myself. All those times I sensed the presence of something, only for it to disappear so fast that I would conclude it had been my imagination, or rats. . . . Even the shill, just hours ago, had been lured on in chase for the better part of a mile. These hoodlums were certainly capable of spray-painting graffiti on walls. Nor was it hard to imagine them plotting to eliminate me, in order to take over the quarry for themselves. They must have lumped me and Inototsu together in their minds. The shill's and Sengoku's statements took on more and more plausibility.

The request Inototsu had made for disposal of a corpse, before he turned into one himself, needed rethinking. My first reaction had been one of simple dismay at the imposition, but perhaps I'd been blind to what was going on. Those teenagers might belong to an army—an army of termites eating holes in the ark. Perhaps unknown to me, the ark was already spongy with holes, end to end. Then, they were no less my enemies than Inototsu had been. Was one of them dead? Or had the request been meant as a reservation for disposal of a *future* corpse? Sengoku had indicated it might have been either way. In any case, the bellicose attitude of those two young hoodlums indicated that the situation was extremely tense.

They ran along the row of storage drums and up the stairs toward the hatch. The next thing we knew, they stepped on the hidden trap and fell, exactly according to plan. The shill and the girl howled with laughter, clutching their sides—especially her. But with the agility of youth, the hoodlums grabbed the landing railing on the rebound and swung themselves nimbly to the head of the stairs. They lifted the latch and dived down the tunnel. The dogs began to bark. The door swung heavily shut, with a long, loud reverberation.

The girl at last stopped laughing, wiped her eyes, and said, "Didn't you leave the key in the jeep?"

"You expect me to go out and get it?" said the shill. "Didn't you hear those dogs?" He cleared his nose and spat.

"I've heard those dogs are savage," said Sengoku, frowning. "Please, let's have no more deaths."

"What do you mean?" said the shill. "You people are the ones who wanted to play war games for keeps, aren't you?" He nodded his head at the blue bundle, adding, "You had great plans for this toilet."

Sengoku replied in a spiritless voice, "It wasn't going to be that kind of war."

"War? What war?" asked the girl. Curiosity made her voice rise and fall like a kitten arching its back.

"The war against those hoodlums," said the shill smugly, and then looked at Sengoku for confirmation. "Isn't that right?"

"Who—them?" she said blankly, losing interest. "But there were only two of them, and they took off like jackrabbits. . . ." She came over and circled halfway around the toilet, her eyes on my trapped leg. "Look, we've got to do something about the captain's leg," she announced. "Let's all think harder."

"You're wrong," retorted Sengoku. "It's *not* only those two."

He was undoubtedly right. There had to be more of them than that. And as for my leg—in the end the only thing to do was to open a hole in the pipe, which I intended to have done; even so, tracking down the youths' headquarters might still be the quickest way to a solution. They were stowaways, living undetected in some unexplored section of the ark. Which made it quite possible that they knew all about the passageway to the toilet's lower mechanisms. Very possible indeed. I had had zero success in locating a passageway to the eastern entrance, by Kabuto Bridge—yet from the outside, one was plainly visible. The opening was midway up a cliff facing the Kabuto River, so it had been left unsealed. What better place for them to settle in?

In the old days there had been a road there, used for hauling rock, but during a huge landslip several months before the closing of the quarry, it had been sliced cleanly away, as if by knife. Compressed air had blasted through the maze of tunnels until the entire mountain howled like a wild beast, jerking half the local citizens from sleep. Over the following two weeks, a waterfall appeared and became a major tourist attraction. Removing fallen rocks from the river took over four months. The cause of it all—whether deliberate or the result of a miscalculation—was apparently the irresponsible actions of the quarrying company at the tangerine grove entrance. Ignoring their allotted boundaries, they had tunneled into the neighboring territory, destroying essential walls and pillars on the way. Seen from Kabuto City on the opposite bank, a portion of the tunnel is recognizable under a canopy of ferns and ivy, but the waterstone, which weathers quickly, has faded into an inconspicuous dirt-black. Through a pair of powerful binoculars you can see rubble lying scattered all around like the aftermath of a bombing raid—and mixed in with it, clear signs of human habitation: tin cans, empty cigarette packs, tissue paper stuck to the ground like jellyfish, comic books, and what look like dried, used condoms. . . .

"There's definitely more than two," repeated Sengoku. "And the skirmishing has gone on three full days now. It's time for a decisive battle—right around tonight."

"But your leader is dead," said the girl, holding her nose and shrinking back as if suddenly remembering the body. "Who's fighting whom? Who were those two guys running away from in such a hurry?"

"The leadership may change, but not the strategy. The old men are very keen on their strategy." Something in Sengoku's way of speaking was terribly disturbing. It made me think of a fishing barb wrapped skillfully in bait.

"How ridiculous," sighed the shill. "Who gives a damn?" He looked from me to the sheeted bundle and back again. "Maybe we should go ahead and call a doctor," he said.

Sengoku burst into loud, jeering guffaws.

"What's so funny?" demanded the shill.

"I was just thinking you wouldn't talk that way if you knew what the war was all about."

"I'm talking about a doctor."

"No doctors make house calls at this hour, and you know it."

"All right, I give up. What *is* the war about?"

"Oh, you'd be interested, I guarantee. I'd even bet on it."

"Of course he would," snapped the girl. Then, reverting to her professional smile, she added more graciously, "After all, that's his job. His and mine. It has nothing to do with our real feelings. Don't forget, we're *sakura*. Decoys. Shills. Our job is showing interest to attract customers. Anytime we can be of service, just give us a call."

"I must say I don't think you have the proper attitude," said Sengoku, puffing himself up self-importantly. "When

some problem arises, you've got to try to understand the
other fellow's point of view—isn't that the basis of communal
living? Before I express any doubts to the captain, I always
think back on all the sweet-potato cakes of mine he's bought
and try to figure out what went wrong."

"Bully for you." The shill sucked in his saliva and clucked
his tongue. "Sorry if our line of work offends you."

"I—I didn't mean it like that." Sengoku stumbled over his
words as if he'd lost his bearings. "I mean—I've worked in
election campaigns, and that's pretty much the same thing,
isn't it?"

"What are you trying to say?"

"That cleaning up humanity is part of the Broom Brigade's
business. Also that the kids in the Wild Boar Stew gang are
real punks, the lowest of the low."

"The what, did you say? Wild Boar Stew gang?"

"That's right. Clever, don't you think? It's apparently
deliberate provocation. Because the men in the Broom
Brigade go around puncturing the tires of their cars."

"Komono isn't going to go for any war like that," I argued,
rubbing the back of my knee. "No way." Even if he was a
former SDF man, in love with firearms, at heart Komono
was a selfish cynic who believed in nothing but quick, sure
profits. Nobody in search of everlasting hope could possibly
succeed as a showman like him. "Still, you know, if he ever
did catch one of them . . ."

"Don't forget, Komono's got a gold-plated badge with
three stripes," said Sengoku.

"Yes," said the shill, "and he issues commands like the
real thing. He's probably humoring the old men."

"No, he's serious, I think," I said.

"Don't be silly," said the shill. "What is there to worry
about?"

"I can't help it."

"Even granting the Wild Boar Stew gang is the dregs of humanity—absolute scum—there still isn't much to choose between them and the old men in the Broom Brigade. Anyway, basically I don't believe in dividing people into trash and nontrash. Evolution taught me that much." He gave a quick self-deprecating smile, and added, "Garbage is the fertilizer that makes the trees grow."

Again my leg began to throb painfully in time to the beat of my pulse. I had a presentiment of terrible pain, as if my skin were to be slashed with a knife. A dangerous sign. Even a person who normally can't stand dentists will head straight for one as soon as his toothache gets bad enough. You get so you wouldn't care if he used pliers to take it out. At this rate, I feared I might soon start begging them to cut my leg off. I addressed the shill.

"If anything should happen to me, I guess you'd make the best successor as captain," I said.

"Me? Captain?" The shill's face froze in the beginnings of a laugh. "You sure you haven't got me mixed up with somebody else? If I were the captain, this would be the S.S. *Sakura*—a shill ship. What a laugh! No compass, no charts. Just a ship that pretends to be going somewhere, when all along it has no intention of moving an inch."

"I never had a compass, either, you know." My leg continued to swell. "If you could catch one of those hoodlums, though, I sure would like to question him about a tunnel leading up under here."

"I'll bet they're still around, those two—maybe just outside." The girl supported the crossbow with her knee, and laid her fingers on the bow.

"It's probably hopeless," said Sengoku. "They couldn't know very much about the quarry layout. It's only the last

two or three days they came in this far, running away from
their pursuers. . . . Funny thing is, the Broom Brigade was
really after junior high school girls the whole time."

"I beg your pardon?" I asked.

"You heard me. Junior high school girls."

2 2

W E stared at the steel door over the landing. The girl was standing three paces in front of the toilet, crossbow at the ready; the shill was at the foot of the staircase, hand on the pillar, frozen halfway to a sitting position; Sengoku was leaning against the wall that connected with the galley. Each of us pondered separately the possible meaning of that striking remark about junior high school girls. We all sensed the importance of understanding it, in order to catch the youths cowering behind the door.

That was why when a figure appeared in the tunnel to the operation hold, nobody noticed until he spoke up.

"Excuse me," he said. His manner of speaking and his attitude were different from those of the other two, yet he was unmistakably one of them. Half of his teased hair was dyed yellow, and he looked like a dead branch soaked in oil. Swiftly the girl repositioned her crossbow, as Dead Branch gave the interior of the hold a nervous once-over.

"Excuse me," he repeated, this time with a bow and a salute in the direction of Sengoku, whom he clearly recognized. Sengoku acknowledged the greeting with an annoyed wave of the hand and said, "What are you doing here?"

"Excuse me," Dead Branch said again. What set him apart from the Wild Boar Stew gang was the small bamboo broom in his right hand, and the silver badge on his chest. He drew out the antenna on a large walkie-talkie slung around his left shoulder, and called: "Headquarters, come in. . . . This is Scout A, reporting from room number one by the oceanside entrance. All's well. Over. . . . That's correct. No sign of any suspicious persons. Over. . . . That's correct. Four in all. Over. . . . Roger. Over and out."

"Calling Komono?" asked the girl. She lowered her crossbow and made a sucking sound, as if rolling a pill on her tongue.

"Commander Komono is on his way here now. He'll be here very shortly. He's going to set up mobile headquarters in this room. I'm to wait here for him. Excuse me."

His peculiar way of accenting every sentence was typical of his generation, yet his expression and demeanor were as flat as those of a tired old man. Not even my queer predicament elicited any sign of interest or surprise. Was he playing the part of a modern, callous youth, or had constant association with old men turned him into a fossil? Or perhaps he was a very model of allegiance—the sort who gave constant obedience, even in the absence of a command. There was no denying that he inspired a certain dread. Yet now he leaped nimbly up onto the first storage drum and seated himself, swinging his legs and beating out a rhythm with the handle of his broom. Surely he wasn't humming an old war song . . . ?

"Get a load of him," muttered the shill.

"He's a spy," said Sengoku, loud enough for the youth to hear. "He was a member of the Wild Boar Stew gang till just a few days ago. Inototsu paid him to keep us informed." He turned to the youth. "Isn't that so? Why don't you say something? You're the one who dragged junior high school girls into it, aren't you?"

The youth shot him a wordless glance, his face a mask.

The girl turned around and asked Sengoku, "What's all this about junior high school girls?"

"Ask Komono," he said.

"It's nothing for a woman to be concerned about," said the youth in a crisp and businesslike tone.

"Watch what you say, kid, or I'll let you have it," she warned, crouching with her finger on the trigger.

He was unfazed. "Very impressive. But your panties are showing."

"You idiot!" yelled the shill. "She means it!" He scooped up the surveying scrapbook from the floor by the toilet and hurled it at the girl. It grazed her shoulder and fell on the sight of the crossbow, knocking the arrow off course so that it glanced loudly against the drum and ricocheted up to the ceiling.

"What did you do that for!" cried the girl, jumping up.

The shill strode past her to the youth, and slapped him in the face. The youth leaped to the floor and raised his broom threateningly. "What's the big idea?" he snarled.

"I'll tell you the big idea, pal. You owe me a little gratitude. I just saved your life."

Slowly the youth relaxed; then he began to fidget in evident embarrassment. "Uh, excuse me."

"All right. That's more like it."

"Horrid little person," said the girl. She held out her crossbow and the shill took it, drawing the bow to the full.

Sengoku, in apparent shock, pulled away from the wall, stiff with amazement; I, however, could guess what was going on. It had to be some sort of a trick by these two con artists. They had carried it off magnificently; the tables were entirely turned. Now was my chance to ask my question.

"There's some kind of engine room under here, isn't there?"

I said. "You know about it, don't you? Tell me how to get there."

For the first time, the youth looked straight at me. His eyes dropped to the toilet, then rose again to my face. "What are you doing?" he asked.

"Never mind," said the girl, fitting another arrow to the taut bow. "Answer the captain."

"We've had nothing to go on but copies of the sketches."

"What sketches?"

With his broom handle the youth pointed to my scrapbook, lying on the floor where the shill had thrown it. The girl picked it up, smoothed the pages, and returned it to me.

"How do you know about this?"

"I borrowed it from that shelf and got it copied at a bookstore in town."

A double blow. First the humiliation of having been hoodwinked by a pup like him, all the while I went on foolishly believing the scrapbook was my private secret. As if that weren't enough, this destroyed my last hope of escaping by adjusting the mechanism in the pipes from below.

"But you people are holed up at the old tunnel site out by Kabuto Bridge, aren't you?" I said in desperation. "It's got to connect out there. Try to remember if there's a tunnel leading down in. There's got to be. That's the only explanation."

"Leading down under here, you mean?"

"Yes, exactly beneath here."

"Then maybe that's where . . ."

"Does it ring a bell?"

"Isn't there someplace you might have overlooked?" he said.

"Come on, tell me," I begged. "At least give me a hint."

"Down by the Kabuto Bridge entrance—the cave in the

cliff facing Kabuto River, that is, on the east . . . I suppose you know there was a big cave-in there once."

"Yes," I said.

"Well, that cave comes to a dead end barely ten yards in."

"That can't be," I protested. "Then how do you know there's a room under here?"

"You just told me there was."

"But you said I'd overlooked something."

"How the hell else do you explain it?"

The girl re-aimed her crossbow, planting her feet firmly. "Watch the way you talk."

"Excuse me." He went on, his face still devoid of expression. "Actually we'd like to know too."

Sengoku interrupted in seeming irritation. "That could be true. I know they're out looking. All fifteen or so of the girls have disappeared."

"Huh?" The shill swallowed noisily.

"You baited the tangerine grove entrance somehow, and lured them in from there, was that it?" Sengoku said casually.

"We gathered up runaways and brought them here," the youth declared, speaking for the first time with youthful enthusiasm. "We're not spying on you. We just wanted to do our own thing without any interference from adults. We were going to make our own village and settle down. So we negotiated with Mr. Inototsu, the head of the Broom Brigade, and paid some money and got a share of the rights to this place. We've got a perfect right to be here."

"I don't know what to make of this, do you?" said the shill, an eye on Sengoku's face.

"Quit making excuses," said Sengoku with a jumpy laugh. "You tricked those girls into coming here, and then you had the Broom Brigade attack—admit it."

"No. Somebody was waiting for us in ambush," said the youth.

"Who?"

"The pig here and his men."

The shill ambled forward. "Now you've gone too far. Look here, you—"

"Never mind. Let him finish," I said. At last I was beginning to see. The Wild Boar Stew gang, having been attacked, must have escaped through the dark maze of tunnels. In the process they had gotten separated and some—including all the junior high school girls—were lost. Their whereabouts were a matter of immediate consequence to me. This was nothing I could close my eyes to.

Addressing the youth, I said, "Until now the only one living here was me. The other three all just came on board today. You can ask Komono. I couldn't attack you all by myself, now could I?"

"But we were attacked."

"Yes. By the Broom Brigade."

"No, they were there to protect us."

"What an idiot!" shouted Sengoku, swinging his two arms before him, hands clasped. "I've never seen anything like it. I've known plenty of liars, but here's a guy who can't face the truth. If what you say is true," he went on, "why did everybody but you run away from them? Don't talk nonsense. You knew there was only one person here. You knew everything. That's because you're a spy. Can you get that into your head?"

Suddenly the youth burst into tears. He pressed his forehead against the broom handle and sobbed, his shoulders heaving.

"Fool." The girl lowered her crossbow and went back to the stairs.

"Try to remember," I urged. "Where did you lose sight of the girls?" The maggots in my calf were as large as earthworms. I doubted my ability to remain sane through the next attack, whenever it might come. As soon as the worms sprouted legs and changed into scorpions or centipedes, it would be all over. If it came to that, I'd rather have them cut the damn leg off.

There was the echo of footsteps, their approach heightened by perspective. This time it was the insect dealer, as I could tell from the shadow of a massive round head in the doorway. He halted just before coming into view, and said in a rich, commanding voice:

"Very good. Two men remain here, and the rest of you go join the search squad. That'll be all."

Was this really the insect dealer? Of course it was. I breathed easier when he stepped into sight.

"That took long enough," said the shill cheerfully, with undisguised relief. Was he relying on Komono, after all?

"Yes, I got held up—"

"Excuse me, sir!" The youth stopped crying, held his broom up at his side like a musket, and clicked his heels together.

"Who're you?" asked the insect dealer.

"That's Scout A, sir," said a deep, husky voice, and at the same time a shadowy figure, that of an old man, appeared behind the insect dealer. He seemed less a man than a man-shaped hole in space. He was still in his sixties, broad in the shoulder, with an erect posture. His dark blue uniform looked too short for him. The end of his bamboo broom, which he held tucked under his arm upside down, shone darkly, as if it had a steel core. It looked like a lethal weapon. Slung across his other shoulder was a large canvas bag.

"Ah, yes, that's right. I remember." The insect dealer nodded slightly, held out a hand indicating the shadowlike old man (whose dark complexion nearly matched the color of his uniform), and introduced him to us.

"My adjutant. He's had a long and distinguished career under my predecessor."

"How do you do," said the shadow, with a deep bow.

Leaving his scout and his adjutant there, the insect dealer slowly advanced. He seemed to be stalling for time in order to decide what questions to ask first. Mysteriously, neither he nor the shadow was the least bit wet. If they had come by way of the tangerine grove entrance, they must have crossed that underground river somehow. Come to think of it, the young hoodlums were all dry too. Why? Was I the only one who didn't know my way around?

The insect dealer looked from me to the toilet and back again. Then he compared me with the plastic-wrapped body. Finally he looked around at the other three.

"The situation's gotten a bit out of hand," he said, indicating the body with a jerk of his head. "What do you think, Captain? From your point of view this is a calamity, isn't it? After all, you've lost a close family member. Or is it more in the nature of a minor inconvenience?"

"It's no calamity," I snorted. "As you know damn well. I'll admit it's sobering—*any* dead body is."

"The problem with the toilet *is* a calamity, though, isn't it?" he pursued. "Don't tell me you're just out to protest disposing of the body."

"Look at him!" said the girl. "Can't you see he's in trouble?"

"Well, yes."

"What are we going to do?" said Sengoku, fear in his voice. "He's in there as tight as a cork in a bottle."

"I'm getting sick of this," said the shill, rubbing his arms vigorously. "Too many damned complications."

"You can say that again," said the insect dealer, looking from me to the body and back again. He scratched the wing of his nose. "I thought the job was important for a lot of reasons, and I've worked it out with the members of the Broom Brigade . . . but I guess the captain's leg comes first."

"You know, I've been thinking, and it seems to me there

are two possibilities." The girl spoke quietly, looking around cautiously to check everybody's reactions. She was right—it needed to be said quietly. I could read her thoughts as clearly as if they were my own. She was also right about there being two alternatives. But how to choose between them?

"I think so too." Surprisingly, the shill quickly agreed.

"In principle, so do I." Even Sengoku was getting in the act. Had all four of us reached the same conclusion? Was it so clear and inescapable as that, like a straight road with no turnings?

The insect dealer rolled up his sleeping bag by the stairs and sat down on it. "Let's hear it, then. If this is unanimous, it must be brilliant."

Nobody wants to be the one to bell the cat. Finally the girl spoke up, smiling innocently. "Well, simply put, one way is to smash the toilet, and the other is to find the engine room below and adjust the valves to eliminate the pressure. Isn't that so?"

"Makes sense. . . ."

"But each plan has its flaw. If we break the toilet, we can't dispose of the body until it's repaired. And to find the engine room, we've got to track down the hiding place of those missing junior high school girls."

"How's that?"

"Well, the captain figures that since neither place has come to light in any survey to date, there must be some connection."

"I see."

The adjutant, standing by in the tunnel, called out his opinion. "I know how you can kill two birds with one stone— or serve two ends at the same time. . . . Excuse me, Captain, I ought to offer you my formal condolences, but allow me to defer that for the moment. First I should like to say that speaking in my official capacity, I recommend the latter course—tracking the missing persons. For years, under the leadership of Commander Inototsu, we in the Broom Brigade dreamed of the establishment of an independent self-governing old people's paradise. Only we never call it that. To us the word 'old' is discriminatory, so it's officially banned. Here, as in all things, Commander Inototsu was uncompromising. We use the word 'castoffs' instead. Strictly speaking, the concept of castoffs has no age limits; but since the aging process generally brings on a degree of physical decrepitude, with no hope of reversal, and since aging is the universal fate of mankind, in our dictionary people of advanced age are known as 'quintessential castoffs' and the facilities we are planning to build we call the Kingdom of Quintessential Castoffs. Fortunately, the day when our dream becomes reality is not far off. Hellfire of uranium and plutonium will rain from the sky, and that will be the start of the apocalypse—or what Sengoku over there calls the New Beginning."

"Listen to him!" marveled the girl, speaking softly.

"This guy's a real pro," muttered the shill.

". . . Listen, can't you hear?" the shadow adjutant went on. "The whole world is weeping with loud lamentation. The world weeps at the picture books of happy homes, and at TV commercials for wedding palaces, as it takes part in drunken medleys in bars and dives. We quintessential castoffs can hear every wail. Never let it be said that Commander Inototsu died in vain. Commander Komono, Captain—please lead us."

The shadow adjutant unzipped the canvas bag at his side and took out something resembling a half-rotten cabbage. Holding it up with reverence, he marched forward ceremoniously. Stepping directly in front of me, he held it out as if presenting me with a special award. It was the old green hunting cap that had been Inototsu's trademark. The shadow bowed his head and said unctuously:

"Please accept this remembrance of your esteemed father. We sincerely hope you will overcome your present sorrow, in order to carry on his great work and see it through to completion."

I could hardly bear to touch the thing. It symbolized the essence of all that I hated about Inototsu; it was the materialization of his stench. But I couldn't very well refuse it, either; that's a ceremony for you. This oily-smooth old man might possibly forgive me if I handled the cap with disrespect, but never if I ignored the ceremony. The insect dealer beside him was silent, without a trace of a smile on his lips. This was not only because they had just met, I felt sure, but because he too had sensed the core of madness lurking inside his adjutant. As he stepped back, the shadow peered inside the toilet.

"What an unfortunate disaster," he concurred. Then he turned to the insect dealer, leaning on his broom as on a cane, and addressed him with compelling politeness. "What do you say, sir, to calling back all the cleaning squads and having them join in a search for the lost little females? I daresay it would be good for morale. Not only could we be of service to the captain, but you see this is a question that bears directly on the fate of the Kingdom of Quintessential Castoffs as well. When the world is destroyed in hellfire, even if we survive, unless we leave descendants our survival is in vain. We would be letting society down. Besides, like bamboo, which flowers and bears fruit just before it withers and dies, most quintessential castoffs still have sexual prowess. And as has been scientifically proven, they are still fully capable of fathering children. In fact, they'd rather do that than eat."

"Hey, that goes against the agreement!" cried the youth in an unhappy voice, his body stiff. "You promised you wouldn't lay a finger on them!"

"And we won't. It'll be a different part of the anatomy altogether. Now what are you going to do about it?" The adjutant stood stiffly erect and banged the floor with his broom handle. There was a metallic clang. "If you expect us to share them with you, then I'd advise you to show respect for your elders. Respect, do you hear me? Or would you like to have this taken up in court? Speak up. You've been told how to answer when spoken to, haven't you?" His turn of speech reminded me of Inototsu. The insect dealer had dropped his eyes to the floor and was scratching himself behind the ear; he seemed to be struggling to maintain a disinterested expression.

"He's something, isn't he?" whispered the girl, and bit her lip.

"Isn't he, though. He'll be a cinch to work for," agreed the shill.

After some hesitation, the youth straightened himself and sang out, his face expressionless, "Excuse me, sir!"

"That's more like it."

"I see." The insect dealer nodded his large head and thrust his hands in his pants pockets. "But the final judgment will depend on the captain. And we've got to consider his limits of endurance."

"Yes, that's right," the girl responded at once, firmly. "We can't rely on that search; it's too chancy. The captain started going out of his mind just a little while ago."

"How would we break the toilet?"

"There's a vacuum inside, so all you have to do is open a hole in the pipe and let air in. Break the concrete about eight inches down. . . ."

"I see—it's a question of odds." The insect dealer plucked a gold-plated badge out of his pocket. "What do you say, folks? These carry a lot of weight around town in the entertainment districts, especially the gold-plated ones. . . ."

No one reached out a hand. The adjutant repeated, "Shall I send out an order to the cleaning squads outside, ordering them to return immediately and join the search squad?"

The shill, his voice like bubbles from a washcloth squeezed underwater, murmured, "So that's it . . . a dozen or so junior high school girls, and dozens and dozens of old men. . . ."

"I won't stand for it," fumed Sengoku. "No way. Even if the New Beginning comes, and we alone survive, those girls must be guaranteed the right to choose their own partners. I'll recommend that this be adopted as a central article in the bylaws. Who does he think he is? Little females indeed! If that's the way he's going to talk, I hereby withdraw all cooperation."

There were several seconds of silence. Then the youth whispered, "It goes against the agreement. It wasn't supposed to be like this, not at all. . . ."

"How about it, Captain—about how many more hours do you think you can hold out?" The insect dealer propped up both elbows on his sleeping bag and smiled at me, fondling his badge. It was the very expression he had worn when I stopped the jeep and he came back with the fish sticks.

"I have only one question," I said. "You and the others came by way of the tangerine grove, didn't you? So why aren't you wet? Your clothes, your hair, anything . . ."

"That's right," said the shill. "I've been thinking the same thing."

"We came by boat." The adjutant smiled faintly. "A rubber boat. Couldn't manage without it. . . . You mean you didn't know? It's stuck in below the ceiling on the eastern side near the floodgate, where the ceiling comes down nearly to water level. Help yourself anytime. You lie face up in the bottom and push against the ceiling with your hands and feet. Only fifteen feet or so from there, you come to a stairway. To pull the boat toward you, use the rope attached to a pulley under the ceiling there by the floodgate."

I could say nothing. His all-too-practical explanation shattered my frail hopes. There was no hidden passageway.

"A third alternative does exist," said the insect dealer, "but it probably wouldn't appeal to you." He rubbed a badge on his leg, and pinned it on his chest. "I mean amputating your leg. Logically speaking, it *is* another possibility, that's all. I just thought I'd mention it."

"We're wasting time, Commander," said the adjutant. "Inototsu would have issued orders long ago. *He* knew how to handle people. How do you expect to win the men over if you can't even stir them to action over the little females?"

He stepped up to the toilet. I braced myself, but he seemed to have no intention of hurting me. He picked up the green hunting cap of Inototsu's, which I had let fall unawares, brushed it off (though the cap itself was far dirtier than any dirt it might have picked up), walked across the hold, and laid it carefully on the blue plastic sheet. Bringing his palms together, he then clapped his hands solemnly—whether in Shinto style or Buddhist I couldn't tell, nor did it seem to matter. Even from behind he looked like a hole in space.

"All right, then—I'll give an order." The insect dealer got up. "Does anybody know a doctor? He needn't work exclusively for the Broom Brigade, but it ought to be someone we could rely on in an emergency."

"I know one, but he's an ob-gyn man," replied the shadow adjutant, in apparent discomfort.

"What are you going to do?" I asked. My mouth was dry, and yet I wanted to urinate again.

"The specialty doesn't matter." The insect dealer held up his hands, effectively shutting off further discussion. "If he can't make house calls, let him at least provide us with some drugs. A good strong sedative, not some over-the-counter kind. Something potent, like morphine. Can he do it?"

"I suppose so. If he doesn't have to do it very often."

"And we'll need sleeping pills, and antibiotics. Send out the order on the double."

"What about calling in the cleaning squads?" the shadow adjutant reminded him.

"I leave that to your judgment."

"I F only I could see the sky," sighed the girl forlornly.

"It's still the middle of the night," I said. The throb of pain in my leg was strange; it didn't match my heartbeat.

"Tomorrow, then."

"You want to get out of here?"

"Very much."

Casually, while pretending to wash the galley sink, she picked up my Uzi and stood it against the side of the toilet, where I could reach out and get it without twisting my knee. Was she concerned about my safety? It was true that the situation was growing tenser by the moment.

The adjutant returned from the work hold, apparently having finished relaying commands. He struck the floor with his broom handle and barked an order at the youth.

"Scout A!"

"Excuse me, sir."

"Bring down a table and chair from upstairs."

"Yes, sir. A table and chair from upstairs. Right away, sir."

"The hell you will," I yelled, turning to the insect dealer and the shill for support. The shill and the girl responded quickly: he planted himself at the foot of the stairs, blocking the way up, while she released the safety catch on the crossbow. The insect dealer only shook his head at the youth, restraining him passively. I still wasn't accustomed to the new distribution of power. Of them all, Sengoku, who only gave a deep sigh, may well have been most sympathetic to me.

"May I ask why not?" The adjutant seemed less disgruntled than surprised. "I should like to take this opportunity to explain several important daily procedures to our new commander. For him to be able to look through the necessary papers, we will need a table and chair."

"I don't care what the reason is," I said. "Nobody goes up there without my permission."

"Then you will please give us your permission."

"Oh, I don't think we need to get so touchy, do we?" said the insect dealer, mollifying the adjutant and me with a broad smile as he spread out his sleeping bag. "This'll do fine for now. I'll imagine I'm out on a picnic, enjoying the cherry blossoms at night."

The shill smiled—perhaps a professional reflex—as he watched the adjutant pull various articles from his canvas bag and arrange them across the sleeping bag. It was exactly like an outdoor stall, without the need for capital investment. Not even the insect dealer could suppress a small smile.

The girl sat on the bottom step of the staircase, and the shill settled himself three steps higher, leaning against the banister as he looked down. The insect dealer sat cross-legged by the wall on the bridge side; even Sengoku came around by the toilet for a peek. I, of course, had the best view of all from my vantage point atop the toilet. Only the youthful scout remained sulking beside the storage drums.

The state of my leg grew more and more disquieting. I had a violent chill, as if the symptoms were spreading throughout my body. Intellectually, my mind rejected the idea, yet somehow I seemed to be waiting for drugs from the doctor. Never mind antibiotics, I thought—get me morphine!

The adjutant spread out his items, conspicuous among them a telephone directory.

"What am I supposed to do with a phone book?" queried the insect dealer, a look of incomprehension on his face.

"We'll use it later, in the trial. I'll explain everything in due course. . . ."

"So the commander just listens to explanations, and has no final say?"

"Nothing of the kind. But I should advise against too-sudden changes. Customs that the entire brigade grows used to become almost physically a part of them. Casting doubt on established customs would be to no one's advantage. Pride in being part of the brigade is inseparable from a spirit of submission."

"Where'd you get all that?"

"Can't you guess?" The shadow man laughed for the first time. It was a colorless laugh, neither sarcastic nor amused. "I used to be active in politics."

"Politics *is* interesting, I'll grant you that."

"Nothing more so—as long as you're on the side in power. And as long as you're willing to live with the fear of losing that power, there's no greater pleasure in the world than to know the country is safely in your hands. Commander Inototsu was a fortunate man."

"The country?" repeated the insect dealer. "You're only talking about the Kingdom of Quintessential Castoffs."

"Don't talk foolishly about things you don't understand." The shadow launched into a speech. "The value of a country has nothing to do with its size or wealth: the only trick is getting other countries to recognize it in accordance with international law. As long as they do that, even a tiny country no bigger than the palm of your hand is a sovereign nation. Do you know what that means? There is no greater power on earth. Backed by that power, whatever you do—kill, steal, get rich and fat off confidence games—you can never be arrested or imprisoned. Criticized, yes; fined, no. This is the century of the sovereign nation, absolutely."

"He's funny, isn't he?" said the insect dealer, glancing around the room as if testing everyone's reactions. For a second his eyes grew thoughtful. Then he said, "But it's all a pipe dream. Whatever you say or do, nobody's going to recognize the Kingdom of Quintessential Castoffs as a sovereign nation."

"Ah, you don't understand. Or no, forgive me. You mustn't forget that we're entering the age of the apocalypse—the New Beginning. When that time comes, everyone can just grant himself recognition. It will be a brand-new era."

"So you're another one who thinks nuclear war is inevitable?"

"Absolutely."

"So do I." I couldn't help speaking up, despite a teeth-clenching chill.

"Do you? Why?" The adjutant did not seem especially pleased with the appearance of a fellow believer.

"Because once they discover a weapon so powerful that the first one to use it will automatically win—which is what everyone is racing to discover—I find it hard to believe they'd hesitate to put it into use."

"Very perceptive." For a moment I felt as if the shadow had opened his shadow eyes to reveal another set of eyes, deeper within. "But more important, even supposing a state succumbs to a virulent infectious disease, there is no way to force it to undergo a cure."

"Then there's no hope," wailed Sengoku.

"That only makes it more interesting, you might say,"

said the adjutant. "Imagine yourself a witness to Genesis, Chapter One. What greater thrill could there be? That's *real* nation-building."

"But kingdoms aren't for me," I said. "I told Komono that before—monarchies and dictatorships are not my style." The sense of swelling had spread up past my knee, until now the weight of my body on that leg was hardly bearable. I longed to sit down, even for a moment.

"It's all one and the same." The adjutant rearranged the telephone directories and sheafs of paper scattered on the sleeping bag, as if in accordance with some fundamental law. "You're talking about democratization, Captain, if I'm not mistaken. That, believe me, is a mere expedient the state was forced to adopt in order to increase individual production efficiency. It's no different from expanding the freedom of a terminal in order to increase computer efficiency. After all, every form of democracy places limits on the freedom to commit treason or acts of a similar nature."

"But there's the right to self-defense."

"Certainly. What guarantees it, however, is again the state. There are two kinds of national defense: external defense, to protect against meddling from without, and internal defense, to protect against treason or rebellion from within. Hence the two great pillars of any state are its army and its police. There can be no state in which the domination principle fails to function. Whoever is in control, issuance of passports goes right on. But what of it—all we're concerned with for the time being is the Kingdom of Quintessential Castoffs, after all. 'Kingdom' in this case is merely a manner of speaking, you understand, used to suggest an ideal realm isolated from the rest of the world. As far as concrete policy decisions are concerned, I personally intend to leave everything in your hands, Commander—or the captain's."

Instinctively the insect dealer and I exchanged glances.

The shadow had succeeded brilliantly in driving a wedge between us. The suggestive phrasing effectively underscored his own position as well. This guy was some humbug. I felt as if I'd once had a dream like this; it was the sort of scene that had probably been inevitable once I started selling tickets to survival in earnest. A haunted shrine in a forest holds no terrors if you run past it looking the other way, I had told myself, but such was not to be. This, undoubtedly, was the reality of survival.

"Who am I working for?" said the shill tiredly, shifting his position. After sitting on stone that long, his bottom probably hurt—though whatever exhaustion he felt could be nothing compared to mine. "I'm losing my grasp of things. Whose side am I supposed to be on? Who's hiring me?"

"I'll hire you," I offered. I needed every friend I could get. Besides, there was something I wanted him to do for me.

"And what are you trying to sell?" he asked.

"You know what it is, don't you?" I said. "My position. Anyway, never mind that. Would you please bring down the encyclopedia in the bookcase upstairs?"

"Just tell me what you want to know. I'll look it up for you."

"No—I want to pile it up and sit on it. My knee can't hold me up much longer."

"Five or six volumes enough? Seven would do it for sure, I guess," he said, and trotted up the stairs.

The adjutant opened a large notepad and drew a line with a felt pen. He marked it off at regular intervals, adding numbers. "Excuse me, sir. Allow me to explain briefly the daily routine. Work ends at 0430 hours. Then showers and baths, then chorus."

"Chorus means the martial songs," stuck in Sengoku.

"That's right. You know—'Here we bide, hundreds of miles from home, in far-off Manchuria . . .' "

"I don't like it. Too jaded," said the insect dealer, shaking his head.

"It's a good song for quintessential castoffs," said the shadow. "It expresses so well the heartfelt sadness of soldiers forced to die meaningless deaths."

"It's sad, all right—especially the part that goes: 'My friend lies 'neath a stone in yonder empty field.' "

"Ah, but that's not the line that gets to them the most. It's 'tears in my eyes.' That's the one place where they manage to sing in perfect unison."

"Same difference."

"At 0500 hours, everyone assembles in the mess hall."

"Where's that?"

"Starting today we'll be using room number two, next door to here."

"Oh, you think so, do you?" I expostulated. "Who the hell said you could do that? Who do you guys think you are, anyway?"

"But the construction squad has already started transporting food and materials."

"Look, Komono," I said. "Just because you're the new head of the Broom Brigade doesn't mean you can do things like that."

"Is it out of the question?" asked the adjutant, and went on swiftly in a well-rehearsed tone. "Oh, well, we could always switch to room number three, above the lift; about eighty percent of the items have been moved that far already. All the men are anxious to join the search squad in looking for the junior high school girls as quickly as possible. It has a direct bearing on morale."

"Captain, would you mind leaving this up to me?" said

the insect dealer. "It seems to me that in the middle of a confusing situation, changing everything around is only going to compound the confusion. I'm doing my best to work things out to everybody's satisfaction. . . ."

Having anticipated a more convincing argument in his old, flowing style, I felt vaguely disappointed. If this was how he stood up to the adjutant, I feared the worst. How had he managed to secure the position of commander in so short a time, anyway? If it was solely by virtue of having shot and killed Inototsu, then they were no better than a pack of monkeys. To push Komono any further might only be playing into the adjutant's hands.

Just then the shill came down the stairs, carrying the encyclopedia volumes piled on his shoulder.

"Besides," I said, "I'll have you know the room next door isn't room number two, anyway. It has a proper name—the work hold."

"I beg your pardon."

The girl and the shill together piled up the volumes catty-corner behind the toilet, adjusting them to the proper height. Sengoku held me under the arms, helping me to sit down without putting any additional strain on my knee. Once I had endured a pain rather like that of stretching a sprained muscle, I did feel more comfortable. A wreath of mist swirled lightly around inside my head, like drowsiness. In my knee and the arch of my foot, it was as if electrodes had been implanted, sending out electrical current in rhythmic pulses. Slowly, very slowly, the current was gaining in strength.

"It won't be long now," said the adjutant, crinkling his eyes; the wrinkles in the corners looked as if they'd been pasted on. His shadowy existence was gradually fleshing out, beginning steadily to fill its proper share of space.

"Drugs may ease the pain, but they won't solve the problem," I said.

"For now at least let's ease the pain," said the insect dealer, with a wave and a smile. "That encyclopedia was a clever idea. It must feel a little better anyway, with your weight off the leg."

"If he suggests knocking me out with drugs and then cutting off the leg," I said, looking first into the shill's eyes and then into the girl's, and finally resting my gaze on Sengoku, "I want you to protect me. Don't let them lay a finger on me, do you hear?"

The insect dealer turned till he was facing me directly and said, "Captain, watch your manners, if you don't mind. You're going too far. Please be more discreet."

"You're responsible. What do you mean, the SDF was a disappointment? You seem to be enjoying yourself, all right, the way you snap out those commands. . . ."

"You know, it surprises even me. I'm not lying, either. (I only do that for pay.) It's a fact: there's all the difference in the world between getting orders and giving them. It's like the difference between the steering wheel and the driver."

"I want to see the sky," said the girl, between sips of water over at the sink. Her voice was a monotone, like that of a child reading from a textbook.

"I still say that owning your own country is the greatest luxury there is. Excuse me, sir." The adjutant's pencil struck the third point on the line he had drawn on his notepad. "Breakfast begins with recitation of the Broom Brigade oath: 'I pledge to sweep away all trash blocking the way ahead.' This morning—at this time of year the sun must be about ready to come up; it must be morning by now—I'd like to include some time for silent prayer in memory of Commander Inototsu. Showing the proper courtesy toward the one you felled will go far in engaging the men's trust. If possible, a eulogy from the captain would be—"

"Don't make me laugh." I snorted.

"Very well, I won't insist. Excuse me." He continued with his litany. "At 0545 hours, breakfast is over. Then there's a fifteen-minute break. At 0600 hours, the trial begins. It's divided into two parts, the first being mutual arraignment, which involves having Broom Brigade members submit anonymous written indictments of each other. Yes, I know what you're going to say—but a certain amount of mutual distrust is like a shot in the arm, vital if the system is to operate smoothly. There is certainly no need to publicize all the reports; you and I can pigeonhole them if we want, Commander, or we can create our own—"

"You mean trump them up, don't you?" said the shill accusingly from the top of the stairs, shooting off the words like paper airplanes.

"As you wish."

"Depressing. These guys are all so depressing," lamented Sengoku.

"Nonsense," sniffed the adjutant. He sucked on a back tooth, stretching his jaws open as far as he could without opening his mouth. I suspected he had false teeth. "Let's have no high-sounding talk. This method is being used all over—corporations, schools, everywhere. It's called the 'self-supervision system.'"

"Well, shall we proceed to part two of the trial? This is by far the most important activity of the day . . . unless, of course, by this time the junior high school girls have been netted, in which case we may have to change plans. I'm afraid the brigade members are painting a rather lurid picture of what will follow in that case—something to the effect that they will divvy them up by lots on the spot. Extreme caution will be essential in handling the female brats, and in persuading the brigade members to exercise self-control. No one has to participate who doesn't want to—although I for one am looking forward to it, and the captain

might just find the information he's looking for. First we'll
line them up and introduce them to the brigade, and then
the four of us can conduct in-depth interviews in private.
How does that sound?"

"How can you sit still and listen to this?" said Sengoku,
his breath coming somewhat faster than seemed necessary.
"I can't stand it."

"Nobody's asking you to," remarked the adjutant, and
continued. "Leaving that aside, we now come to part two
of the trial, when *this* comes into play." He picked up the
telephone directory, which had a well-worn look, placed
his hand on top, and clamped his mouth shut as if weighing
the effect. The effect was all he could have hoped for.
Having some inkling of what this was all about, I became
still more depressed.

"Look—isn't he still crying?" whispered the girl over my
shoulder. The youth was standing motionless, his face buried
in his arms on the storage drum. It was hard to tell; he
might have been crying or he might just have dozed off.

"I think gangrene is setting in," I said.

"It won't be much longer now. Hang on. . . ."

"I suppose it wouldn't help if I just blasted a hole in the
pipe with my Uzi."

"You'd bleed all over the place, since your leg itself is
acting as the stopper," she said.

"To continue—we use this to search for the right people,"
said the adjutant, picking up the directory and flipping
through it. All sorts of symbols were inscribed on its pages
in different colors of ink: # * ♂ ♀ ☆ ★ ▼ ▲ ※ ¥ ♩ ○ ?
"This is what we use to screen people, to determine if they
are fit to survive. We go through the whole list in alpha-
betical order, proceeding at a rate of about thirty names a
day. Anyone who receives a strong majority of negative
votes will naturally be eliminated. What it comes down to,

really, is a death sentence. Where there is a division of opinion, we'll put a person on hold. There are various ranks among those on hold, and after reevaluation a person can be given a new rank, or have the sentence of death confirmed."

"What's the standard for that evaluation?" asked the shill. "How do you propose to gather the necessary data?" I noticed appreciatively that he said nothing about his evolution-based views that human trash would make the best crew, instead taking my side—as per our agreement—and voicing my own doubts.

"I can understand what deeply satisfying work it must be." The insect dealer nodded sympathetically. "You have absolute power of life and death. It's obviously very crucial work too—after all, you're assigning responsibility for the future of the entire human race."

"Naturally," said the adjutant, "we use all sorts of data for reference. Files in the city hall computer, giving fairly detailed information on family, occupation, income, and so forth, in addition to reports from private detectives, credit bureaus, and what have you. But there is precious little time, so we have to process an average of at least thirty people a day. No one person can be allotted more than five minutes. As a result, to expedite the process, we occasionally take into consideration gossip about the candidate, his general reputation—even the aura of his residence as seen from the outside—to help in forming a judgment. In the lack of relevant data other than the entry in the phone book, we go by our gut reaction to the candidate's name and phone number."

"Is it possible for someone who's innocent to receive the death sentence?" The insect dealer, sitting with his legs crossed, reversed their position.

"Everyone is innocent before standing trial."

"That's true. I guess it's better than throwing dice."

"Dice are no good. That way, not enough people receive the death penalty."

"That many have to die, do they? Well, I suppose it can't be helped. The number of people who can fit in here is limited."

"They're crazy." The girl's voice at my ear was hoarse.

"What's the ratio of death penalties to acquittals?" the shill mumbled, barely opening his mouth; his voice too sounded weak.

"There haven't yet been any complete acquittals." The adjutant's voice remained perfectly calm. Was he only putting on an act for his own amusement? "Most people get the death penalty, and the rest are on hold. There are various categories among the people on hold: retrial, pending, bail, temporary release, suspended sentence, appeal, and so forth. The case is reconsidered after new evidence or new testimony is brought in. Still, mainly it's the death penalty. If you've ever visited a courtroom, perhaps you'll understand—the greatest excitement among the quintessential castoffs in our company occurs the moment that the death penalty is announced. That seems to be when they feel the greatest pleasure and purpose in their status as quintessential castoffs. I do wish people would stop treating this as some sort of personality aberration." Laying a palm on the opened telephone directory, without moving his head he looked straight at the shill and the girl. "Sentencing people to death began as a painful means for choosing the few who would be able to survive—but at some point it became an end in itself, and a highly pleasurable one at that. Some might interpret this as the warped mentality of quintessential castoffs, I suppose. But there's far more to it than that. Out of all the stories I read when I was a boy, two scenes in particular stand out in my mind. I've forgotten the rest of the plots, but those scenes are vividly etched in my mind. One is the queen in *Alice in Wonderland* running around yelling, 'Off with their heads! Off with their heads!' at every little thing. The other is in one of Andersen's fairy tales—which one, I've forgotten—where a young prince hiding behind a tree hands out death sentences to passing travelers and cuts them down on the spot. That's the way it is even in the world of children—how much more so, then, among quintessential castoffs, who in a sense are condemned men (and women) granted a temporary stay of execution. Besides, the sentences we give out can only be executed by the condemned people themselves."

Leaning back against the flushing lever, which now did nothing but wobble ineffectually, I rubbed the sides of my knee, feeling rather as if I had wet the bed and gotten soaked. If Inototsu's ferocity and total disregard for others were dissolved, distilled, and crystallized, they would come out resembling this adjutant's logic. Could I have stopped there, and repudiated his words at face value, there would have been some hope. But the more I thought about it the less difference there was between what he was doing and what I, all unconsciously, had been doing too. How could I defend myself against the charge that my extreme reluctance to part with tickets to survival came to essentially the very same thing?

Both the insect dealer and the shill had repeatedly accused me of misanthropy. They were right. I too had been signing secret death sentences without benefit of trial, all along. Whose way was more cruel? It was hard to say. In any case, I had lost all grounds for criticism of the Broom Brigade. Instead I wanted to criticize myself, crush myself to death like a flea.

"I don't know," said the shill. "It sounds inefficient to me to concentrate only on whom you can eliminate." He snapped his fingers and banged the banister as if determined somehow to turn the tables on the adjutant. "Why not take the opposite approach, and compile lists of all the necessary trained personnel? Doctors, nurses, computer experts, car mechanics . . ."

"After the bomb, there won't be any need for computer experts," interrupted Sengoku with understated irony. "Electromagnetic waves will make computers useless."

"We've taken scrupulous pains to do just what you're saying," answered the adjutant. "Among the brigade members are accountants, cooks, even agricultural workers. We also have carpenters, plasterers, judo experts . . . butchers . . . plus a sweet-potato-cake baker, a cameraman, and our commanding officer here, who has a very special talent: mob pacification."

The last three were apparently offered in light jest, to show off the accuracy of his information. I was distracted, however, by the deliberate pauses before and after "butchers."

The shill spoke up defensively. "I happen to be a past master of legerdemain."

"We'll need you, then," said the adjutant, quietly closing the telephone book. "Because not only utility goods are necessary for survival. Any struggle requires a dream. Spiritual self-sufficiency is the greatest recompense of all; that's what the trial is all about."

"I used to sell dreams," said the insect dealer, gazing at me as if searching his way through darkness. "The rest of the eupcaccias are still out in the jeep, aren't they?"

"Dreams aren't enough, either," said the shill. "We need knives and guns . . . and toilets." Suddenly he sprang up, shaking with tension. Then he took a deep breath and sat back down. "In here it's as if there wasn't any need to sweat over money. I suppose even outside, after the apocalypse— the New Beginning—debtors and creditors will cease to exist. But right now, step one foot outside and they're crawling everywhere, playing hide-and-seek with each other. How can it ever be any different? How can there ever be a New Beginning?"

"We need air too," repeated the girl vacantly.

"That's why we carried out the hunt for junior high school girls," said the adjutant. "The younger the better—don't you agree, Commander? Like wet paper, in a way: the time you spend slowly warming them up, before they catch fire, is the most enjoyable. Say, that fellow's taking an awfully long time getting back, isn't he? Where's that medicine? Let's have the scouts check up on him, and on the progress of the search too. Commander, will you give the orders?"

Nodding, the insect dealer stood up. Lightly rubbing his gold badge with the ball of his thumb, he stared intently at the youth, whose face was still buried on the storage drum, and drew a deep asthmatic-sounding breath, filling his chest with air, about to speak.

Just then the steel hatch creaked open and a scream echoed. All the air the insect dealer had inhaled rushed out of him, before he could say a word.

"Help, help, they'll kill him!" It was Red Jacket, whose ear the girl had struck before. The bleeding had apparently not stopped; the earlobe was red, and swollen to twice its previous size. He tumbled in and fell to his hands and knees on the landing. "The other guy's being eaten alive by a pack of wild dogs! Help!"

"So *that's* where you were." The adjutant sprang up with remarkable agility, then crouched down again and moistened his forehead with spit. Probably a charm to get rid of pins and needles in the legs; I could remember my grandmother doing the same thing long ago. "Come on down; it's all right."

"Help him, for God's sake—the dogs are all over him!"

"Scout A, what was the meaning of that slipshod report

you filed?" barked the insect dealer suddenly, straightening himself up. "You said there were no suspicious characters around here. Isn't *he* suspicious? What have you to say?"

"Excuse me, sir," said Scout A, grinding his teeth. "No one told me he was there."

"You didn't ask," shot back Sengoku.

"I'm partly to blame," said the adjutant. "I should have warned you that these people might not cooperate." He walked ten paces toward the storage drums, eyes on the floor. "Look—bloodstains. I was careless to have missed them. Which one of you wounded him?"

"I did." The girl waved her crossbow aloft for him to see.

"I see. Then everyone here failed to cooperate, and the scout failed in his duty. I'll leave the question of discipline up to you, Commander."

"Please, you've gotta *do* something," begged Red Jacket. "He's being eaten alive! If he dies it'll be murder, don't you see? Please, hurry. . . ."

"Shut up!" The insect dealer's neck swelled until it was a match for his great round head. "At this point, do you think a dead body or two more is going to scare any of us? Scout, drag that young punk down here and make him tell you where he hid the girls."

"He doesn't know where they are." The scout's voice had reverted to a childish squeak. "Nobody knows but the ones who ran off with them."

Red Jacket chimed in. "If I had any idea where they were, I'd have gone along. Then this never would have happened."

"Commander, I advise against retracting an order once it's given," said the adjutant. He frowned, dropping his head on his chest as if he'd just realized he'd lost his wallet. He retraced his steps back over toward the toilet.

"I know," said the insect dealer, drawing a converted toy pistol from under his belt. He cocked it, aimed it, and planted both legs firmly. "Now you drag him down here, *fast*, and you make him talk."

Broom in hand, the young scout moved toward the landing with a resigned look. Red Jacket rose to his knees, unfastened the chain at his belt, and gave it a shake. Steel bit into the floorboards with a graphic sound that was somehow intensely physical: I flinched, imagining a butcher's knife carving into bone.

"Stay away," said Red Jacket.

"You get down here," said the scout. "Do me a favor."

"No, you do *me* a favor."

"I'm following orders."

"Lousy traitor."

"You don't understand."

A sharp report rang out, its echoes bouncing around the room like Ping-Pong balls. The insect dealer had fired at the ceiling. There was a smell of gunpowder, like scorched bitter herbs. Red Jacket, wounded once already, promptly collapsed in terror.

"Drag him down here. Make him confess if you have to stick your broom handle up his ass. If he doesn't, the captain will be in trouble. It doesn't matter if you kill him. Don't worry about disposing of the body."

"The captain will be in trouble. . . ." What did that mean? The insect dealer's own words—that firearms change people —came to me; he had fulfilled his own prophecy.

"You'd better get down here," said the scout. "Or you'll get killed."

"I don't know anything—and you know I don't know!"

As if his body were drained of strength, Red Jacket came sliding down the ladder, collapsing on top of the blue-sheeted bundle. "There's a body in there," warned the scout, at which Red Jacket leaped up, moved several feet off, and collapsed again.

"Get to work," said the adjutant in a businesslike way. "Just do as you've been taught." The young scout twisted the broom handle in Red Jacket's gut. There was a wail of pain.

"You're hurting me!"

"Confess, then."

"How can I confess what I don't know! Aagh!"

"That's enough," said the girl frostily, glaring at the adjutant with open hostility. A show of indifference would have been better, I thought; the more you let others know how you really feel, the worse off you are.

"I'm afraid an order, once given, can't be retracted that easily," said the adjutant. "Bad for discipline. As long as the men are following orders, they're forbidden to pass any sort of judgment on those orders. Where an order is concerned, there can be no second thoughts, period."

Red Jacket was weeping. Covered with sweat, the young scout kept on grinding the broom handle into the victim's belly.

"If he really doesn't know, then no amount of torture is going to get anything out of him." The shill had covered his face in dazed disbelief, and was peeking through his fingers at the scene.

"This could take time," admitted the adjutant, his peregrination around the toilet coming to a sudden stop; he studied the insect dealer's expression. The insect dealer gave the barest of nods, his face an expressionless mask. "In the meantime I'll go up to room three—ah, excuse me, I did it again. What should I call that room up over the lift?"

"Anything you want."

"All right, then—how about Main Mess Hall? It's easily four times as big as the one by the tangerine grove. Someone will have to keep a sharp eye on the cooking squad; otherwise it would be easy for irregularities to creep in, and any carelessness regarding sanitation can only lead to harm. Unfortunately, tomorrow's breakfast is fish again. It's a pity, when we have two former butchers among us, both skilled meat carvers. Excuse me for a moment."

The adjutant cut across the hold, walked past the storage drums, and disappeared down the tunnel leading into the work hold. It seemed to take ages—a half-hour or more—before he was gone.

"Hey, Komono," called the shill, to no response. "Make him quit that, will you? Komono, what's the matter? Are you out of your mind?"

"*I'll* make him stop," said the girl, releasing the safety on her crossbow, and fitting it with an arrow.

I was busy taking steps of my own. Sliding off the encyclopedia, I twisted back and reached out for the Uzi that the girl had left propped up against the toilet. Slowly the muzzle of the insect dealer's gun rose, aiming straight at me.

"Cut it out. . . ." He came around and wrested the Uzi away from me. "I *haven't* gone mad, much as it may seem I have. I'm all right, I think. Just wait a little longer. I'm thinking. . . . I know what—I'll have a smoke."

He withdrew to a safe place and crouched against the wall; there, with the Uzi across his knees, and his own gun still in his hand, he lit a cigarette. The young scout kept on raising and lowering his arms mechanically, as if pounding rice for rice cakes. He did seem to be letting up a little. Red Jacket went on moaning in time to the movements of the broom; he did not appear to be taking a decisive beating. Hundreds of barbed slugs, or some such creatures, were crawling around on the surface of my paralyzed leg.

"I'm going to go take a leak," said Sengoku, and headed for the hatch, with a sidelong look at the sheeted bundle. No one had any reason to stop him, and no one did: the pack of wild dogs would do that. The realization that Red Jacket's partner had gone outside was a bit troubling—but then, it was probably true that he'd been attacked by the dogs. That would take care of him. Puffing on his cigarette, the insect dealer went into a crouch and cocked his gun.

Mentally, in those few seconds I played up and down the keyboard of my brain cells, fast enough to compete in a contest, and made a decision. I whispered to the girl, "Will you do me a favor? Keep it secret." My voice was so low I could barely hear it myself, but her response was instantaneous.

"Yes."

"Locker number two upstairs has a switchboard inside. There's a red lever on the left end, just at eye level. I want you to push it up. Will you do that?"

"What's the combination?"

"Same as the locker number, two—two right, two left, two right. Just two-two-two."

"The red lever."

"Nothing will happen right away."

For safety's sake, I had set up the dynamite detonating device in two stages. The panel I had now at my fingertips could do nothing on its own. Contact with the switchboard relay would awaken the slumbering fuse and ready it for reception. My Uzi had been taken from me, but now—if only she managed her task successfully—I would gain a weapon many times more powerful.

The girl went casually up the stairs. Anticipation and nervous tension seemed to make the pain in my leg recede somewhat. When she was halfway up the stairs, the shill shot her an inquiring look, which she answered with a frantic signal.

Naturally, it would be hard for him to understand what she was up to, but at this point the only secret she and I could possibly share would have to concern a way out of the current impasse. He fell in with her. If all went as planned, I had no intention of leaving him in the cold. The insect dealer followed her movements briefly, then showed no further interest. Women are expected to have their own reasons for coming and going, beyond men's understanding; in fact, men have a duty to pretend *not* to see. She disappeared safely onto the bridge. I thought of tiny air creatures faced with death. Of schools of whales seeking survival that end up committing mass suicide instead. My vision of eupcaccia tranquillity—had it been only an illusion? Then why was there a merry-go-round in every amusement park worthy of the name? If it could be proved that children on holiday were all schizo, very well; then I would resign myself, and withdraw. . . .

A destructive pressure now bore on my calf. Had I not been wrapped in the protective bandage of the pipe, the flesh might well have ruptured. It felt like the time my gums were inflamed with toothache. I only wished I could lance it, and clean out the abscess within. Had a surgeon chosen that moment to menace me with his scalpel, I doubted my ability to fend him off. A butcher's cleaver I would resist to the death; a surgeon's scalpel could be the tool of my salvation. But this weakening was a sign of danger. The failure of the drugs to arrive probably meant the scout was haggling with a doctor reluctant to prescribe morphine; then again, it could have been that the doctor was taking a long time to dress, or even that the car engine wouldn't start. Would the doctor go along readily with an amputation? He could always justify it on grounds that it would relieve suffering. If he succeeded in stopping the bleeding, and if vascular suturing went well, and if effective measures to prevent suppuration could be taken, then medical ethics wouldn't seem to argue against it. Even if the doctor should witness my amputated leg vanishing down the hole with a pop like that from a popgun, followed by the dismembered parts of a corpse, one after another, his ethical propriety would remain unimpeachable.

The girl signaled to me from the parapet.

At last the time had come, just as I had known that one day it would; I had always known, too, that it was something I would have to decide myself, without orders from anyone else. I had put off that decision until now for the same reason that I had refrained from betting with the insect dealer as to whether or not the nuclear war would begin in five minutes. But in a nuclear war there could be no advance warning, which would give the enemy an irreversible advantage. The button could be pushed for only two conceivable reasons: either a sudden, unforeseen accident, or the development of technology which conferred automatic first-strike victory on the user, thus ending the balance of power. That moment could come at any time, without forewarning. By its very nature, nuclear war would begin all of a sudden, and as suddenly be over. The variables are far greater than for an earthquake, making prediction far more problematical. Warnings were unthinkable. Any attack that left room for the operation of a warning system would be subject to the restraining forces of both sides. The launching of the ark would inevitably take place one peaceful day, catching everyone unawares. There was not the slightest reason why that day should not be today. All decisions are arbitrary in the end.

Sengoku came back inside, having relieved himself.

I brought out the remote-control panel from my belt, slid off the safety device, and held my finger quietly on the red button. My conviction was low, but my expectations were high. There would be vast alterations in the flow of the underground vein of water. I might even be able to free myself from the toilet. It would be a lonely, quiet launching, with not a single toast in celebration. This, I thought, was the only way to enter upon nuclear war—*before* it began. Of those who were aware of the actual outbreak of war, the vast majority would be wiped out; only those whose ears were covered, who remained ignorant, would be able to survive.

◆◆◆ **A FLASH.** Innumerable whips lashed my skin where it was exposed. Then the hatch exploded, eradicating the oceanside entrance. There was no boom such as I had expected to hear, but my eardrums felt an excruciating pain. The light gave way instantly to black darkness. Power failure. The insect dealer switched on his cigarette lighter, its tiny flame emphasizing the vast darkness. His shadow swayed against the wall; the rest of us were totally invisible. Red Jacket's groaning stopped. Even if he was still groaning, with the ringing in my ears I could never have heard him.

Next there was a distant echo like a crack of thunder, and the whoosh of wind currents crossing and crisscrossing the ark. It had worked.

A warning buzzer went on and off, feeble in my ears after the roar of the blast. As the one who had installed it, I felt a responsibility to make a statement:

"Looks like a nuclear explosion. That signal is the emergency warning."

No one answered right away.

"It's an earthquake, isn't it?" said the girl in a scared voice. "It's got to be."

"For an earthquake, I don't notice many tremors," said someone—perhaps Sengoku.

"I hate to say it," I repeated, "but I do think it's a nuclear explosion." I wished I could have the insect dealer do the talking for me. "The system is designed to seal us off automatically in case of a nuclear explosion, by dynamiting all tunnels to the outside."

"I don't know what kind of sensors you may be using, but how can you be so certain?" The insect dealer's light came closer, leaving a wavering tail of flame in the air.

"I'm not; I'm just stating the most obvious possibility."

Darkness in a room or a cave is of varying dimensions. The darkness of, say, a clothes closet can actually be soothing, not frightening in the least. But the vaster the scale, the more menacing darkness becomes. The custom of burying the dead in coffins might have arisen from the desire to protect them from the uncertainty of large darkness by surrounding them with small darkness. Here there were only seven of us, but it sounded like hundreds of fish gasping in a water tank lacking sufficient oxygen.

"I want to know what makes you think so," said the insect dealer, thrusting the flame of his light toward me. "It could have been set off by a sudden squall, couldn't it? There's a front going by. Maybe your sensor is just too sensitive."

"It's far more sophisticated than that," I said, feeling less and less confident in my ability to outtalk this man whose tongue was his fortune. "It's computer-controlled. There are pressure anemometers at the northern and southern extremities of the mountain, and when the difference in their measurements is greater than one-third, the computer registers it as a local, small-scale disturbance without proceeding to the next stage. Other factors taken into consideration are duration of pressure, presence or absence of a heat wave, rate of temperature climb, and, of course, tests for radioactivity. . . . There's no way it could be set off by a mere squall."

Light fell on the tunnel entrance. It was from a large portable lantern hanging from the adjutant's shoulders, carefully positioned in such a way that his body was visible from the waist down only.

"Excuse me, sir." His tone hadn't changed a whit. Nerves of such steely resiliency demanded respect.

"An emergency situation has arisen," responded the insect dealer. "Possibly a nuclear explosion." He seemed inclined to affirm that possibility rather than deny it. Flakes of light appeared in the flame of his lighter—a sign he was running out of fuel. "Nuclear weapons are essentially designed to be used in a preemptive strike. It's common knowledge among military analysts that in all-out nuclear warfare there would be no declaration of war."

"I'll go get a lantern," said the shill, and groped his way upstairs.

"What's that smell—radioactivity?" It was the young scout.

"No, ding-dong—gunpowder," said the adjutant flatly. "Powder smoke, it's called. To a real man it smells sweet as roses."

"We'll be safe from radiation in here," said Sengoku, reassuring himself.

"Is there a radio?" asked the adjutant, and clapped his ear with the palm of his hand. He had apparently received a considerable physical shock.

"There won't be any broadcasting stations left," I said.

"A one-megaton blast wipes out everything in a three-mile radius. Within a six-mile radius, high winds full of glass fragments whip around."

"Yes—so if there *was* reception, that would be a good sign."

I had to be cautious. This man was not only deranged but fast-thinking. "The walls are so thick I don't think radio waves would have a chance of getting in. Even if we had a radio."

"You know, Captain," said the insect dealer, "you should have put everything you had on that bet. You were too fainthearted." He explained to the adjutant, "The captain and I had a bet going, you see, as to whether or not the bomb would fall in the next twenty-four hours."

"It was the next five minutes," I corrected.

"What's the difference?" said the insect dealer. "Money's worthless now, anyway. You couldn't lay wagers even if you wanted to."

"I know something just as good as money, or better," persisted the adjutant. "How about those junior high school girls? They'd make perfect stakes."

Lamplight flashed from the parapet on the bridge, crossing the ceiling in a straight line until it rested on the ruined hatch. The destruction was more complete than I had imagined. The center of the steel door was smashed, and stone rubble had poured through; the shape was that of an expensive Japanese-style confection. The dogs had doubtless been scared out of their wits. The light moved on, fastening on the blue-sheeted corpse, which was covered with several fist-sized chunks of stone. If he hadn't been a corpse already, he would have been screaming in pain. Maybe he would even have died from the injuries.

Suddenly Sengoku slammed a fist into his palm and hollered, "Then we did it, man! We survived!"

The light vanished, and the shill came down the stairs.

"You mean we're not dead. That's all," retorted the girl glumly.

"We're alive! We survived!" Sengoku repeated, in tears, and sniffed.

"Now comes the tough part: going on surviving," said the adjutant, stroking Sengoku with his light. "Commander, what are your instructions?"

"I don't care—we survived," said Sengoku again, kicking the floor. "Everybody else has croaked. Right, Mole?"

"Lower your voice, will you?" I said. "You're giving me a headache."

There was a percussive sound, clear and carrying, but not sharp; rather like a distant drumbeat. If this was the sound of falling water, then just as I'd hoped, there might have been an alteration in the flow of water underground. I detected a change in the wriggling of the worms in my calf. Was I imagining it? Surely it was too soon for the effects to reveal themselves.

Beaming his lantern ahead of him, the adjutant approached Red Jacket—who, had he stayed where he first was, would almost surely have been severely injured in a fusillade of stones.

"Excuse me, sir!" screamed the young scout.

"Is he dead?" asked the adjutant.

"No, sir."

"Did he confess?"

"No, sir."

"Scout A, have you forgotten your orders?"

Just as the adjutant raised his steel-centered broom, the insect dealer issued a brisk, professional command.

"Emergency directive. Divide the Broom Brigade into squads, and assign each squad a turn at the air-purifying equipment. A schedule of shifts will be issued later. All men

will be expected to participate in the work of charging batteries with the pedal-operated generators. Choose all those
men with mechanical experience, and start work on building a new generator, top speed. Register all men according
to their skills, make up a list of names arranged by specialty,
and appoint one man in charge of each division."

There was no mistake; it was definitely the sound of water
drops hitting the storage drum. Three in a row, a pause, then
two. A clear sign that the flow of water had altered.

"Repeat those orders," said the adjutant to the young
scout, jabbing him with the broom handle.

"I can't," the youth replied, his voice shaking.

"You have to be able to repeat an order," said the adjutant.
He might equally have been reproving the youth *or* the insect
dealer.

The flame of the cigarette lighter went out.

"Adjutant, let's be off," said the insect dealer, leading the
way toward the work hold. "Bring along the captive and
set him to work." He seemed desperate not to lose command. In the light from the shill's lamp, held up to see him
off, we could see that he was gripping the small of the
Uzi's butt. As if suddenly remembering, he swung around
and said, "Captain, how about the filters on the air purifica-
tion system? All in place?"

Knowing this to be sheer claptrap, I responded in kind.
"Absolutely. BG-system triple-layer cooling filters."

"Everyone who can spare the time, report to the work
hold," he declared. The adjutant followed, driving the youths
before him. After him went Sengoku, muttering to himself.
"We survived . . . we survived. . . ."

"'Spare the time'? Who could have more time to spare
than us?" said the shill in disbelief.

"Careful," warned the girl. "Don't let them out of your
sight, or who knows what they might do." She pushed the

reluctant shill along, lighting the way for him with the lantern. The beam traveled on, crawling along the wall and up to the ceiling, where it captured some sort of movement, like the swarming of bees. Of course it was no such thing: it was a curtain of water spilling out over quite a wide area. The noise of droplets hitting the drums came from a very small portion of the water on the ceiling. With change proceeding at this pace, I became hopeful that the inner workings of the toilet might soon be affected too.

"Water's leaking," said the girl, exploring the whole area with her lantern. "Is it always like this? Look, there's enough behind those drums to raise goldfish in."

The flood was building up swiftly. It was just after that that some sort of shock took place in the depths of the toilet. My ears couldn't hear it, but my leg did: it was like the sound of elevator doors echoing down in the base of a high-rise building. Had the control valve turned around at last?

"Would you mind gathering things up before they start to get wet?" I said. "The maps and tickets and eupcaccia box, for starters."

"You think the water will come this far?" she asked.

"Probably."

"Are these chocolates?"

"Liqueur-filled. I eat them with my beer. I'll bet you think that's weird, but it tastes surprisingly good."

"What shall we do?" the girl said anxiously, choosing a chocolate. "Now that this has happened, won't the toilet be more important than your leg, after all?"

She stepped up on the edge of the toilet with one leg and put the eupcaccia box on the upper shelf. The hem of her skirt was at my eye level, her bare kneecaps just in front of my lips.

"There's nothing to worry about," I said. Cautiously, as when mixing gunpowder, I held my breath, and then said in a rush—as if unwrapping a gift that had cost an entire year's salary—"It's all a lie. Now listen to me calmly, without getting excited. There was no nuclear explosion. I lied. Nothing of the kind happened."

The girl did not say anything right away. The liqueur-filled chocolate in her fingers was crushed without a sound.

"A lie? You mean what you said was a lie, or the explosion was a lie?"

"It was all a lie. That was only some dynamite before. You helped me, remember? By pushing that lever on the switchboard."

"But why . . . ?"

"Two reasons. First, I was scared. The nuclear war hadn't even started yet, and look what was happening already. I couldn't bear it. The other reason is selfish: I did it because of the toilet—because of my leg. I figured there was only a fifty-fifty chance it would work—or less; maybe one in three. Remember, you and I talked about it before—the valve below. It was my last hope. I wanted to change the flow of the water underground, and see if that wouldn't change things."

"Did it?"

"Yes. Look how the water is dripping from the ceiling."

"What about your leg?"

"Just as I'd hoped. It feels completely different."

"Better?"

"Well, I wouldn't say that. When your leg goes to sleep it feels worse when the circulation starts coming back, after all. Right now it hurts even to cough. But that sensation of being slowly sucked down is definitely gone. If someone gave me a hand, I bet I could manage to get out of here somehow."

"You'd better not tell anyone."

"I know. If they found out I'd wrecked the toilet, they'd murder me."

"Why did you tell me?"

"You're going to run away with me, aren't you? To where we can see the sky."

"How? The passageways are all blocked off."

"There's a way out. A secret passageway."

"Where?"

"Don't tell anyone. Nowadays all you hear is the public's right to know, but it seems to me that lying is often more practical. It's upstairs, locker number one. . . . I'll tell you everything. The combination is one-one-one. Take off the back panel and there's a tunnel there that leads down underneath the city hall."

"The outside world is safe, then. . . ."

"Yes. And the sky. Cloudy skies and sunsets, blue skies, smog. . . ."

The shill returned from the work hold, following the small circle of light emitted by his penlight; he was walking slowly and carefully to avoid splashing himself—as if making his way across a swamp.

"If you want someone to help you, it'll have to be him," she said.

"I suppose so," I agreed.

The shill hailed us cheerfully, his voice a sharp contrast with his dragging footsteps. He seemed already completely at home with the Broom Brigade. "Everybody's hard at work," he said, "taking turns pedaling the five bikes. But the strongest ones are all out in the search squad looking for the girls, and so far the pedalers have managed only to light up seven miniature light bulbs, the size of a candle flame. But you should hear the way they talk! Just like a bunch of cats in heat. Old men have the dirtiest minds."

"The captain says he thinks his leg might come out." I did not know what to make of her mentioning only this and not the hidden escape route.

"Why?" he asked, in exaggerated surprise. "Maybe his blood started flowing backward, and it's affected his mind. Do you suppose that could happen?"

"Why not tell him the truth?" I said.

"The truth?" he said. "What are you talking about?"

She ignored me. "How are things going over there?" she asked. "Do you think you can hit it off with Komono and the adjutant? Do you think you can make a go of it here?"

"Good question." He rubbed his face with his palms and said, "Oh, I'll probably manage one way or another. I'm used to playing up to people. Not like the sweet-potato man; he strikes me as a manic-depressive type. After being all that gloomy, now he's whooping it up hysterically. Just sitting still doing nothing, he says the joy of being alive comes in through his belly button and goes out the top of his head. Says it makes a noise like the beeper on a wristwatch. Can you believe it? I'm not that far gone, but I'll admit it will be a relief not to have to wear disguises and run away from loan sharks. The ones following me around are all old buddies of mine, which only makes it worse. Of course, I have to say being superintendent of the captain's weapons and supply room sounds a bit out of my line. That place is a real fortress."

"It's stocked with guns and medicine and food supplies—"

"No, foodstuffs all come under the jurisdiction of the sweet-potato man."

"There's a bazooka in there too, you know."

"That's Komono's little toy. What I really like is that gun chamber that doubles as a conference room. If only *our* office had been like that. A big round table surrounded by armchairs. . . ."

"Do you think relations between Komono and the adjutant are going to stay like that?" she asked.

"I'd like to hear what *you* think." The shill indicated me, waving one hand as if in supplication. "With your leg free, there'll be two separate lines of command. Things could get a bit sticky."

"Everyone must need to use the bathroom," I said. "How have you been managing?"

"Making do with the storage drums, and wondering vaguely what to do when they're all full. But that's all right, if your leg is coming out. . . . What are you waiting for? Come on out! If you can't manage it alone, I'll give you a hand. Shall I go get some more help?"

"No, just you is enough. I'm waiting for the prickles to go away."

"It's a terrible feeling, I know. But I certainly am glad it turned out this way. Now that the crisis is over, I don't mind telling you we had quite a confrontation over which to choose—the toilet or your leg. Remember the pirate in *Treasure Island*—what was his name? Long John Silver. He had a wooden leg, and he cut quite a figure with it. The others said if the ship was really important to you, you should take a tip from him."

"How'm I going to do this?"

"Grab on to my shoulders. I'll walk around in a circle, like the donkey at the millstone."

I hung on to his burly shoulders, looking no doubt like a fresh-pounded rice cake draped on a tree branch. The girl poured cooking oil from the shelf between my calf and the pipe, for lubrication. His penlight in his mouth, the shill started circling the toilet, while with another penlight the girl lit up his feet for him. The skin on my leg, especially around the shin, chafed against the pipe walls as if it would tear off. Even so, I began turning. Slowly I completed a quarter-turn, without the least sensation of being pulled down inside.

"Attaboy! Say, they'll be knocked over dead when they see this." Since he still had the penlight in his mouth, the words were muffled, but his voice was cheerful. I felt guilty. If possible, I had wanted to escape alone with the girl, but this was certainly no time to suggest such a thing. The shill had rights too. If I left him behind without telling him either that the toilet was now unusable (without, I guessed, extensive redesigning and reconstruction) or that I planned to escape through a secret passage, doubtless afterwards I would hate myself. Barring special circumstances—though, indeed, I could scarcely imagine what they might be—he deserved to come with us.

"Doesn't it hurt?" asked the girl. (Why didn't *she* tell the shill the truth?)

"A little pain makes it easier to bear—cancels out the pins and needles."

"You're coming up—a good inch!" she said encouragingly. "Keep it up!"

"Funny," said the shill in the same muffled voice as before, penlight still in his mouth. "Who would have thought I'd outlive the whole rest of the world? Me! I can't believe it."

"What if it's not true?" I couldn't keep still. Would the girl feel disappointed? She didn't look that way. She just looked from me to the shill and back and tilted her head to one side, her mouth drawn out in a line.

"Eh?"

"All that happened was that I set off some dynamite, to see if I could release the pressure inside the toilet."

"You sure do things in a big way." He didn't seem especially outraged. "So you mean the bit about the nuclear blast wasn't true?"

"That's right."

"Well, that's the way it goes. Shall we try turning the other way now? I bet you're feeling a lot lighter."

"He's come up almost an inch and a half," she said. "Just a little bit more now. Once the calf is out, you're home free."

"Aagh." I grimaced with pain.

"Shall I slow down?"

"No, I'm okay. It just gave my knee a twinge there for a minute."

"Well, well. So it was all a lie—the world is going on the same as ever, this very moment?"

"We aren't trapped in here, either; there's a secret way out. I didn't tell anyone."

"In other words, not one thing has changed. Go ahead, lean your full weight on me. It's okay."

He was acting too blasé. Had his extraordinary suspiciousness sealed off all his emotions? That couldn't be. He had been overreacting to every little stimulus. Even the insect dealer had said to watch out for him, that people with heavy secretions of saliva were violent. Could he possibly not be aware of the seriousness of the situation? Or was the situation possibly not as serious as I found it? Perhaps his self-respect was involved: Someone who prides himself on his own sleight of hand can't afford to fall all over himself with surprise every time someone else reveals the secret of a trick.

From the work hold flashed the highly condensed beam of a flashlight; footsteps drew near.

The girl whispered, "Should we turn off our lights?"

"That would only seem more suspicious. Just act natural."

A figure stood in the tunnel entrance. By now the floodwater was ankle-deep, so whoever it was made no attempt to come further. The beam swept around the floor in a circular motion, like a lighthouse light. Of the storage drums, the five in the back containing kerosene, the three filled with alcohol, and the two filled with drinking water (I changed it once a week) stayed put, but the dozen or so empty ones had already floated out of line and were starting to drift over to the seaward wall. Probably the floor tilted in that direction. The vinyl-sheeted bundle lay in the same place as before, soaked in water. He must be sorry he's dead now, hating baths as much as he did in his lifetime, I thought. Despite the flash of understanding, I couldn't help him, and wouldn't have, anyway; but slowly I was beginning to see that he had been a man of irremediable loneliness. The light swung around and found us.

"Terrible flood in here. What are you doing?" It was the insect dealer. But he pressed us no further. Probably he found it too troublesome to take responsibility for me and my present difficulty. "We called roll and found that fortunately seventy percent of the men were inside the blockade line. We're incredibly busy. There aren't many places left we haven't looked, so we'll have to change our search methods. Right now the men are hunting in every cranny, using condenser mikes. We're going to try some excavating too. Captain, can you hang on a bit longer? It won't be much more. Just say the word if you need anything to eat or drink. The body will keep awhile longer."

"What do you suppose is happening outside?" said the shill innocently, asking the expected questions to avoid arousing suspicion.

"By now it's raining glass shards and radiation. Well, Captain, don't hesitate to let me know." With this, he passed his light over the ceiling and withdrew. The shill hadn't betrayed me. Evidently the seriousness of the situation had *not* escaped him.

"I think my calf just pulled free."

The girl shone her penlight down inside the toilet, and stuck a finger between my leg and the pipe. I felt nothing.

"You're right—there's about a finger's width of space there now."

After that everything went unexpectedly easily. With one arm around each of their shoulders, I hauled myself up in midair, as simultaneously water came welling up. Probably the pressurization from below aided in my release—but now this toilet was no longer a toilet. I had thought my leg would be all bloody, but it wasn't as bad as I feared: the shin and the top of my foot were skinned, and there was no other external injury. The whole leg was swollen and purplish-red, however, as if smeared with ink from a souvenir stamp pad at a Shinto shrine. Looking carefully, I saw that the old scar where I'd been chained long ago was sprinkled with tiny bloodstains, like grains of rough-ground pepper. It would be some time before I could wear a shoe again. The joint seemed unaffected, so I anticipated no difficulty walking, as soon as sensation returned. It was the rest of me that was totally worn out. I decided to sit down on the encyclopedia and continue hiding my leg in the toilet, until sensation returned to the sole of my foot and the crick in my ankle went away.

"Thanks a million. I'd about given up hope."

"So nothing's changed," mused the shill. "I'm no different from before. We didn't really 'survive,' after all."

Clawing the sides of the toilet, I sought to endure the agony of returning sensation; it felt as if the raw nerves were at the mercy of a merciless wind. I forced myself to exercise the ankle.

"You're strange, you know that?" I scoffed. "You actually sound regretful. None of that crowd is worth a moment's regret, if you ask me."

"They *are* a bedraggled lot, those old men," he agreed. "Scraggly eyebrows, long hairs sticking out of their noses, wrinkled hippopotamuses under their chins . . . Well, you can't blame them for how they look, can you? What I *can't* forgive is that miserable, know-it-all thickheadedness of theirs."

"As soon as you're ready, let's go. The longer we hang around here, the greater the chance they'll be back."

"He's right," said the girl, and added, laughing, "After all, you're bound to have a lot to do after your new promotion." She bent over in leapfrog position.

Laying a hand on her shoulder, I stood on my right leg and set my freed left leg on the floor. There was no pain, and the knee and hip joints did everything I told them to. The leg might *look* like a rotten eggplant, but inside, anyway, it was sound. Cheered, I shifted my weight. My vision whirled, and before I could tell what was happening, pain was shooting through my shoulder and arm, and I lay face down in water, Evidently sensation had not yet returned to the left leg. The shill and the girl helped me up.

"I'll carry you piggyback," said the shill. "Come on— this is no time to stand on ceremony. With you out of the toilet, every second counts."

He was right. If they knew I'd gotten free, our chances for escaping here would dwindle. I put my arms around his neck, keeping my right foot on the ground to ease his burden. Reeling, he spluttered:

"How much do you weigh? You're just as heavy as you look, aren't you?"

The girl's voice followed us. "You want your camera, don't you? Shall I get it?"

"Yes, the one that's out, and the case next to it, if you don't mind. They're heavy. . . . While you're at it, I'd appreciate it if you could bring the eupcaccia."

There were dozens of others out in the jeep, I knew, but

somehow they weren't the same. I could only be satisfied with *my* eupcaccia, the one that I had checked with my own eyes.

"Something bothers me . . ." said the shill, his breath coming hard. "It's all this water. You don't suppose the entire cave is going to be flooded, do you?"

"My guess, from the general topography, is that it won't go higher than a foot or so off the ground. The work hold will be all right."

"What about places lower than this?"

"Some will become pools, filled to the ceiling."

"What if those girls are really hiding out somewhere? Then they could flee from the water right into a waiting net."

I hadn't thought of it before, but there *was* such a possibility. Was that my responsibility too? My brain could not forget the adjutant's comment likening young girls to wet paper. It seemed unlikely, but what if these people, thinking this was all that remained of the world, should go on living here in this spurious ark for a year, two years, three, four—maybe a decade or longer—spinning out their days. . . .

The girl caught up with us in front of the lockers. "These are heavy. I see photography isn't all just pushing buttons—it's hard work!"

"You'd better believe it," said the shill. "Even flea circus trainers end up with a sprained back, you know." He used the back of his hand to wipe sweat from his chin, then rubbed the hand on the side of his trousers.

I glanced with satisfaction at the label on locker number one: "Flammable Solvents; Lathe Blades, All Sizes; Rubber Work Aprons; Infrared Lamps; Waterproof Sandpaper; Insulation; Corking Materials; Aluminum; Heat-resistant Facial Cream." A plausible list of items that nobody would be likely to need or care about, and yet that aroused no suspicions. Even the most rapacious thief would surely decide it was not worth the trouble of breaking the lock.

Right 1—left 1—right 1.

The items actually stored inside were a close match for the label on the door, although in some cases the containers were barely filled, or empty. The idea was to lower the overall weight, but even so, I was careful not to make it suspiciously light. Rails were attached to the locker ceiling, and when a hook was removed, the shelves swung out opposite the door. In other words, they served as a hidden inner door.

From beyond the back of the locker, now opened, there swept up a moist breeze smelling rather like the warehouse in the fish market. The shill's penlight lit up the casing of the escape hatch, which measured two feet by two and a half. The shill whistled.

"You could fool anybody with this."

"Maybe I had a presentiment something like this would happen."

"Where does it lead?" he asked.

"He says it comes out underneath the city hall," answered the girl in my place. There was a lilt in her voice, as if she sensed light at the end of a very long tunnel.

"Is it safe?"

"Of course. The nuclear explosion's a fake, and I deliberately left the dynamite unconnected here. Let's go—there's no time to waste. Once they're on to us, that will be that."

"What will they do when they find out?" asked the girl, hunching her shoulders and stifling a giggle.

"I wouldn't worry. They'll be too busy looking for those junior high school girls for the time being." The shill passed a critical hand over the locker door.

"I'm a girl too, you know," she said.

"They wouldn't dare lay a hand on a crack shot like you," he answered.

"What do you mean?" I said. "You're both coming with me, aren't you?"

"I can't decide . . ." he said.

"What is there to decide? You've had it with those old men, haven't you?"

"Still, I don't know. . . ." He stepped out of the locker and bit his lower lip. A sound like uneven hand-clapping, apparently an echo from the work hold, rose and fell like the sound of rain pelting eaves.

"The world outside is exactly the same as before. All that about a nuclear war was a pack of lies. Don't tell me you're going to stay here *knowing* it was a lie."

"That depends. If you imagine it really happened, then it *seems* real. And you've been saying so all along, haven't you? That one of these days it really would happen. That a nuclear war starts before it starts. . . ." All three of us pricked up our ears in the darkness. It was either an unintelligible command from the insect dealer, or a howl of laughter from Sengoku, or a scream. The shill went on: "I wouldn't mind a bit—staying on here as we are awhile longer."

"You're out of your mind." I fixed my eyes on the girl, seeking her support. "I don't care how good a shot you are— you can't stay awake twenty-four hours a day."

"That's true—the air here is too stale," said the girl, her voice muffled and hesitant.

"It's not only the air. There's no sky, no day and night. You can't even take pictures."

"If you're going, you'd better get on with it," he said.

The girl drew her lips into a sharp line, tilted her head, and looked from me to the shill and back. What a peculiar fellow—why in the world was he hesitating? I couldn't understand it.

"Let's go; there's no more time for jokes," I said.

"No—I really think I'll hold off. Wherever and however I decide to go on living, it doesn't make a hell of a lot of difference. Besides, professionally speaking, that's what I'm for—responding to lies as if they were true, knowing full well they're not. . . ."

"All right, then, I'll call Komono." I thought it was a bit reckless, but I couldn't just abandon them. "I'll talk to him for you."

"I wouldn't if I were you. You're only going to make things worse. Thanks, but no thanks."

"You're right," murmured the girl. "Believing it was true might make us happier in the end. . . ."

"We're at home with lies, anyway. They're us. We're *sakura*, don't forget."

If that was the way they were going to be, let them. I had simply felt a duty to tell them of this chance to escape, in return for their help in getting me free. Still, it seemed unreasonable of him to keep the girl there too. All along I had dreamed of escaping with her, just the two of us; and if only the shill hadn't interfered, she would have come. *I* was the one who had told the shill about this escape route; she had never opened her mouth.

"Why don't you at least let her go free?"

"She *is* free. Stop talking that way." He turned to her. "Right? You're free, aren't you?" He prodded her along, and she nodded hesitantly.

"Never mind that," he said. "Do you know how the word *sakura*—cherry blossoms—came to be used for people like us? It comes from the expression 'Blossom-viewing is free.' In other words, it costs us nothing to do our shopping."

I noticed he had stopped calling me Captain. So be it. I handed him the control panel, said what I had to say, and thus carried out what I took to be my duty.

"The key to the jeep is in it, right?"

The shill nodded as he accepted the control panel.

"That's right."

"They'll have it in for you for letting me go."

"Them? Have it in for me? No."

"How are you going to explain? I don't know about Komono, but that adjutant means business."

"I'll tell them you got all soft and squishy, and the toilet just swallowed you right up."

"Who's going to believe that?"

"They will. All right, go, will you? I'll look after the ship. Not that I'm all that sure of myself. . . . But now that the anchor's up, it would be a shame to sink her so fast."

"Sorry about that encyclopedia," said the girl. "The last three volumes are soaking wet."

She set my camera case down on the floor of the locker, sliding it back in with the toe of her shoe. Meaning to follow her, I tripped over her leg and fell forward, taking advantage of the situation to push her deeper inside the locker, covering her with my body. I couldn't let this sudden intimacy daunt me; we had a long trip ahead of us, traveling together down this tunnel. We would warm each other as we waited for dawn, protecting each other from cold and darkness.

But my shoulders were hindered by the locker, and my torso hung tilted in the air. My shoulders measured seventeen inches across, and the locker a mere thirteen; there was no way I could get through facing straight ahead.

"Are you all right?" With a wry smile, the shill grasped my left shoulder and pulled, while pushing on my right shoulder, turning me ninety degrees.

My leg was still not what it should be. I felt myself go on crashing to the right, unable to retrieve my balance. The girl slipped out from beneath me. For some reason, the shill's penlight went out. As I fell, I grabbed hold of the hem of her skirt. There was the sound of my shirt ripping in back; a couple of buttons popped off. Partly it was the fault of the inner construction of the locker, but mostly it had to do with the accumulation of fat on my stomach. My ribs banged against the camera case with a noise like someone pounding rice cakes. Pain flashed not so much there as in my knee and neck. Somebody was grasping my ankle and pushing it. I could feel myself slide with the camera case across the stone floor. Something fell on my back—a shoe. Where was the girl? I could feel her skirt in my hand, yet strangely I could not tell where she was.

"Take care. . . ." The voice was too far away.

The sound of the locker shelves moving, then the metallic click of the door closing. I pulled hard with the arm that held her skirt, and she came down against me . . . or so I expected, but to my chagrin, all that remained in my hand was the skirt itself. Had it come off? I could hardly bear to give her up. A moment later, I realized that what I had taken for her skirt was in fact a rubber work apron. When had that misapprehension occurred? She was free, I told myself. Of her own free will she had shut herself up in there. Or was *I* the one who had been shut up in *here*? For a while I lay where I was and rested, clinging to the case. Somewhere only a few feet away she was staring wide-eyed into the dark with those eyes that forced you to trust her, like it or not. But there was no meaning anymore in the units of distance between us. I got up, and immediately fell over again. I took off my shoes and tied them together, slung them around my neck, and started crawling down the tunnel on both hands and one knee, dragging my camera case behind me.

2 5

THE TRANSPARENT TOWN

I T took a long time. I seem to have slept more than once along the way. The numbness in my leg subsided, and sensation returned to my knees; but by the time I reached the basement of the city hall, the sun was coming up. After waiting for people to start coming and going, I went outside.

Transparent rays of sun, the first I had seen in a long time, stained the streets and buildings red. The area was lively with the mingled flow of bicycles moving south along the riverside fish market, and commuters hurrying north to the station on foot. On a truck marked LIVE FISH, a small flag fluttered in the breeze, inscribed with the words FISH BEFORE PEOPLE. Another truck, waiting at a stoplight, proclaimed, WHEN I AM GONE AND THE CHERRIES BLOOM, LOVE WILL ALSO BLOOM.

Facing the black-glass walls of the city hall, I set up my camera, using the wide-angle lens, and focused. I meant to take a souvenir photograph of myself and the street, but everything was too transparent. Not only the light but the people as well: you could see right through them. Beyond the transparent people lay a transparent town. Was I transparent, then, too? I held a hand up to my face—and through it saw buildings. I turned around, and looked all about me; still everything was transparent. The whole town was dead, in an energetic, lifelike way. I decided not to think anymore about who could or would survive.

A NOTE ABOUT THE AUTHOR

Kobo Abe was born in Tokyo and grew up in
Mukden, Manchuria, during World War II. In 1948
he received a medical degree from Tokyo Imperial
University, but he has never practiced medicine. Abe
is considered his country's foremost living novelist.
His books have earned many literary awards and
prizes, and have all been best sellers in Japan. They
include *The Woman in the Dunes, The Face of
Another, The Box Man,* and *Secret Rendezvous.*
Abe is also widely known as a dramatist. He lives in
Tokyo with his wife, the artist Machi Abe.

A NOTE ABOUT THE TRANSLATOR

Juliet Winters Carpenter lives in Japan with her
family. Her translation of a previous novel by Abe,
Secret Rendezvous, won the Japan-U.S. Friendship
Commission Prize for the Translation of Japanese
Literature in 1980.

James Joyce, Marcel Proust, Thomas Mann,
E. M. Forster, Isak Dinesen, Albert Camus, Günter Grass,
V. S. Naipaul, Doris Lessing, Gabriel García Márquez,
Wole Soyinka, Salman Rushdie, Primo Levi, among many others:
VINTAGE INTERNATIONAL is a bold new line of trade paperback books
devoted to publishing the best writing of the twentieth century
from the world over. Offering both classic and contemporary
fiction and literary nonfiction, in stylishly elegant editions,
VINTAGE INTERNATIONAL aims to introduce to a new generation
of readers world-class writing that has stood the test of time
and essential works by the preeminent
international authors of today.